Fragment of Divinity

Jamey Sultan

Fragment of Divinity

SultanLitrpg.com

Copyright © 2020 Jamey Sultan

ISBN: 978-1-7354644-0-4 (Paperback)

ISBN: 978-1-7354644-1-1 (Hardback)

ASIN: B08H4YX7B6

Edited by Joshua Mason

Cover Art by Jonathan Elliott

<u>Dedication</u>

This book is dedicated to my parents who, bless their hearts, have no idea what a LitRPG is, but still read my book and told me they loved it.

Shout out to everyone who made this possible!

I want to take a second to thank all the LitRPG authors out there who inspired me to write my own books.

A few in particular stand out:

Tao Wong

Matt Dinniman

Aleron Kong

Dakota Krout

Andrew Rowe

Thank you. I never would have done this without you.

Thank you to my Patrons!

Shubham Chattopadhyay (Rogue)

Larry Baker (Rogue)

Thank you to my beta readers!

Sean Hall

Erin Balentine

Billy Jay House

Chapter 1

James woke in a small, unlit room.

This wasn't unusual for him. He'd just started his first job as a paramedic, and as the lowest employee on the totem pole, he'd been given the role of 'Rover'. This meant working in a different station almost every shift, depending on the schedule. So, waking to a blaring alarm and a sudden flash of light was nothing new to him. That being said, he'd never woken up in a room quite like this one.

As James looked around, his first thought was 'medieval holding cell'. He consulted his mental checklist.

Iron-barred door with comically large keyhole? Check.

Inexplicably damp walls? Check.

Unidentifiable green growth on aforementioned walls? Check.

Creepy man standing in the corner? Check.

Creepy man standing in the corner? Wait. What?

James paused. How hadn't he noticed the man standing in the corner? The dude had to be at least seven feet tall. James knew it was rude to stare, but it was also rude to lock someone in a cell, so who was the real asshole here?

The man had an almost sculpted angelic face, complimented by a well-fitting suit and tie. He looked like an actor on the way to the Golden Globes.

James would have laughed at how out of place the stranger looked in the dirty, dank cell, if he hadn't also been there.

The man returned James' stare with unreadable onyx eyes. The only noise in the room was a faint ticking sound coming from the man's watch. Finally, James broke the silence. "Umm... Hi?"

The man raised an eyebrow at James, sighed, and with tremendous effort, pushed himself off the wall. He walked over to James and held out his hand. "Baradiel."

James stared at the hand before hesitantly shaking it, wincing at the vice-like grip. Baradiel smiled thinly. "James, right? Welcome to Novis." He had an air of smug indifference that immediately irritated James. His tone said that James should be grateful to be in the room, listening to him speak. That James wasn't worth his time. That James should shut up and listen, if he knew what was good for him. Baradiel stared at James as if daring him to say something.

Fortunately, James was used to dealing with annoying pricks in positions of authority, so he kept his mouth shut.

Baradiel shrugged as if to say, 'Whatever, I didn't want you to say anything, anyway'. Then he spoke. His tone conveyed boredom, as if he'd given the same speech hundreds of times, but his eyes gave off a different vibe. They stayed focused on James' face, scrutinizing every slight change in his facial expression.

"I know you're probably confused about all this." He gestured at the surrounding cell. "Well, basically, we brought you here for a contest. We took you from your world because you showed a bit of the quality we seek." He looked at James as if expecting a reaction. When none came, he continued.

"Think of this as a job interview." He smiled. "A *deadly* job interview." His voice dripped with false cheeriness. "You'll have lots of time to figure that all out later. The only thing you need to know right now is that this world is like what you mortals call a video game. Observe." Baradiel waved his hands, and a screen appeared in front of James' eyes.

> *PLEASE CHOOSE YOUR NAME.*

James stared at the screen for a second. This certainly was a strange dream. "Uhhh... James?" Out of the corner of his eyes he saw Baradiel roll his eyes and place his head in his hands. His palms slid down his face with exaggerated slowness. James ignored the man... demon? No clue. He continued reading the prompts.

> *WOULD YOU LIKE TO CONFIRM UHHHHJAMES AS YOUR NAME?*

"No." James paused for a second. He still didn't really understand what was happening, and Baradiel wasn't helping. The... Entity? Entity sounded good. The entity stood in the corner, staring at James while tapping his foot in annoyance. "Just James." He said more confidently this time.

> *WOULD YOU LIKE TO CONFIRM JUSTJAMES AS YOUR NAME?*

Now James was getting annoyed. This may be a dream, but his inner psyche was kind of a dick. "No." He tried again. "James."

> *WOULD YOU LIKE TO CONFIRM JAMES AS YOUR NAME?*

"Yes." Another screen popped up.

> *WELCOME TO NOTIS, JAMES!*

There it was again. Novis. James turned to Baradiel. "What's Novis?" He asked.

Baradiel sighed. "Please save your questions until the end. And not what. Where." That statement left James even more confused than before. Baradiel sighed. "Just... read the prompts. You'll figure it out."

Another prompt appeared.

CHOOSE YOUR RACE:

HUMAN

Humans age much quicker than other races. Their shorter lifespan leads to a faster pace, allowing them to specialize into much broader categories than other races.

Bonuses:

+ *25% Experience gained in all skills*

+ *4 free attribute points per level*

DWARF

While short in stature, Dwarves are strong and sturdy. Their stature makes them the perfect size to live underground. Dwarves live in large cave systems dug into the mountains. The largest Dwarven settlement is deep within the Crimson Mountains, on the western border of the Forcyth empire.

Bonuses:

+ *2 Strength per level*

+ *1 Endurance per level*

+ *3 free attribute points per level*

WOOD-ELF

Elves are the longest-lived race in Novis with an average lifespan of five centuries. Wood Elves do not believe in large cities and live off the land in the Fertile Expanse.

Bonuses:

+ *10% Movement speed in wooded areas*

+ *1 Intelligence per level*

+ *2 Dexterity per level*

+ *2 free attribute points per level*

HIGH-ELF

Elves are the longest-lived race in Novis with an average lifespan of five centuries. High Elves are the most talented in the magical arts. Supposedly, there is an ancient High-Elf city tucked away deep within the Fertile Expanse, but if there is, no other race has ever seen it and lived to tell the tale.

Bonuses:

+ *10% Spellcasting speed*

+ *1 Dexterity per level*

+ *1 Intelligence per level*

+ *1 Wisdom per level*

> *+ 2 free attribute points per level*
>
> ### GNOME
>
> Gnomes are the most intelligent of the sentient races. Long ago, they fled the unceasing wars of the other races to pursue their obsession with advancing their understanding of the world. They combine magic and technology in new and exciting ways. Their Grand Library truly is a marvel to behold.
>
> Bonuses:
>
> *+ 10% to intelligence*
>
> *+ 2 Intelligence per level*
>
> *+ 1 Dexterity per level*
>
> *+ 2 free attribute points per level*

James was beginning to understand what was happening.

As an avid gamer, he loved role-playing games the most, and this was just like the race selection screen for an RPG. As James scrolled down the list with a thought, he saw that most of the races had been greyed out. He clicked on the gnome race, interested in the magic and technology, but a notification popped up, telling him he would have to choose another race.

He scrolled through hundreds of unique races. Some were too alien to him, like the Snake-Beastkin race, while others, like the Gnome race, were greyed out and inaccessible to him. Out of the corner of his eyes, James saw Baradiel tapping his foot in annoyance. But with so many races to choose from, James needed to make sure he was making the best choice.

Baradiel made a grand display of banging his head against the wall.

After an hour of reading through his options and ticking off this… entity, James decided. He would stick with Human. Out of the handful of races available to him, it was the only one he could see himself as.

But he wondered when this dream would end. Maybe it was one of the lucid dreams he had heard about. They were supposed to be super realistic. James tried pinching himself and yelped.

He turned to Baradiel. "This is a dream, right?"

Baradiel laughed bitterly, "I wish." He then went back to tapping his foot, waiting for James to finalize his choice, but James stood, frozen.

There is no way this was real. It's impossible. What about my friends and family at home? What about my life? I just got my first paramedic job.

James pushed those thoughts to the back of his mind and returned his attention to the menus. Once he chose Human for his race, a new menu opened up, giving him the option to customize his appearance.

He wondered how much he *could* change his appearance. He changed his skin color to pale, then dark, then he went through the hairstyle options. It was fun, changing his body on the menu and watching himself change in real time. But it felt strange, as if his body was made of a cold mist that reshaped itself at his command. Once he got bored with changing his appearance, he reset it to default. From there, he changed his hair color from brown to black and made himself slightly taller. *Perfect.*

A new menu popped up, asking him to confirm his selection. He turned to Baradiel. Now that he had time to process what Baradiel had said, he was angry. "What do you mean, 'you wish'?"

Baradiel sighed. "I mean, I wish it were a dream, and I wish I didn't have to put up with useless mortals like you. Now please get on with it. Some of us *important* beings have work to do."

James never took kindly to insults and didn't appreciate the implication that his kidnapping was unimportant. He glared at Baradiel, angrily curling his hands into fists. "You're a dick."

Baradiel shrugged, his nonchalant expression infuriating James even more. "Send me home." He pulled back a fist and punched Baradiel in the face. Or tried to.

Baradiel's hand blurred, and he caught James' fist in an icy grip. James could feel the cold spreading down his hand into his wrist and forearm. It hurt, and his skin was turning blue. Baradiel looked him dead in the eye, the anger clear in his gaze. His eyes changed from coal-black to a deep, bright blue, like two glowing splinters of ice lodged in his skull. "Never... speak... to me... like... that!" He hissed. "I am better than you. Remember that."

Baradiel released James' hand and smiled again, as if the incident never occurred. "I'll tell you what. When you wake up, you'll have a quest. If you can complete the quest, then I'll send you back to your family. Deal?"

James rubbed at his numb arm. "When I—"

Baradiel interrupted him. "Also, never try to punch me again." The message was punctuated by a fist to his face. Something about being punched in the face by a demon, or whatever Baradiel was, hurt. A lot. James clutched at his face, stars dancing in front of his eyes, and moaned. Baradiel smiled and snapped his fingers, and James sank into unconsciousness.

Baradiel whistled a little tune as he opened a portal and carried the Human through. He would enjoy watching this unfold. Shame that he would never follow through on his promise. If his plan worked out, all seven candidates would be dead, and Sytar would be none the wiser.

Chapter 2

J ames woke up with a splitting headache. He was lying on his back in a cave next to a pool, the water barely kissing his toes. He made a couple of quick observations—the cave floor was uncomfortably rough on his back, and he was naked. Well, he had a loincloth on, but other than that he was bare as the day he was born.

James glanced around the cave in confusion.

Where am I? Am I still dreaming?

Starlight filtered through the cave entrance. Clusters of crystal scattered throughout the cave let off a dim purple glow, just enough to see by. Boxes of text bombarded him as soon as he had gathered his bearings, appearing in the corner of his vision.

> WELCOME TO NOVIS, JAMES!

> YOU HAVE GAINED THE ABILITY: DEATH'S STARE.
>
> Death's Stare (1/7):

> The eyes of death pierce all. This ability allows you to see a character's name, level, and class floating above their heads. It also allows you to identify items. This ability is upgradeable if specific conditions are met.

Once James finished reading the box, another took its place, as if it could sense when he reached the last word.

> *YOU HAVE GAINED THE FOLLOWING ITEMS:*
>
> - Infinite Pouch
>
> - Iron Dagger
>
> - Leather Shirt
>
> - Leather Pants
>
> - Leather Shoes
>
> - Leather Bracers
>
> - Travelers Rations (x10)

> Infinite Pouch:
>
> Rank: Epic
>
> This pouch can hold an infinite number of items, reducing their weight by 99.9999%. To retrieve an item, simply place your hand near the pouch and think of the item name.

Iron Dagger:

Rank: Common

Forged from iron, one of the most common smithing
materials. There is nothing special about this dagger.

Leather Shirt:

Rank: Common

Crafted from hardened leather, this shirt will provide you
with some protection against damage.

Leather Pants:

Rank: Common

Crafted from hardened leather, these pants will provide you
with some protection against damage.

Leather Shoes:

Rank: Common

Crafted from hardened leather, these shoes will provide you
with some protection against damage.

Leather Bracers:

Rank: Common

Crafted from hardened leather, these bracers will provide you
with some protection against damage.

Travelers Rations (x10):

Rank: Common

An assortment of dried fruit, meat, and nuts. It's not a five-
star meal, but at least you won't starve.

James shifted uncomfortably. The longer he sat on the cavern floor, the more uncomfortable he was getting. *How did nudists do it?* He stood up and retrieved his armor from the pouch.

Stiff leather clothing fell onto the ground next to him and he stared at it, trying to make sense of all the clasps and buckles.

He'd never been a fan of leather clothing. It was too hot and sticky. Still, it was better than a loincloth. It took a while, because he had never worn armor before, but after a confusing few minutes, he stood, fully equipped and ready to take on the world.

To get his bearings, James peered out of the cave entrance. Moonlight sparkled off of water as a river rushed past the cave entrance. A heavy fog obscured his vision of the opposite bank but didn't cross the water, leaving James' side unobstructed.

Squinting through the darkness, James could just barely make out towering cliff faces rising on either side, He was on a patch of gravel that ended at the river. In short, he was trapped.

Another notification appeared.

> YOU HAVE GAINED THE SKILL NIGHT VISION.
>
> Night Vision (Skill Rank 1):
>
> +1% better vision in low light.

Immediately, his vision took on a slight green tinge, but he wasn't able to see anything clearer. He guessed that he would need to level up the skill more before he saw the benefits of a high Night Vision skill. The green tint brightened the starlight almost imperceptibly. The brightened starlight reflected off of James' hand.

That was when he noticed the ring nestled innocently on his right ring finger. When he tried to remove the ring to study it, it tightened painfully.

"Ouch! Fine." James cursed. "I won't try to take you off." He held up his hand and examined the ring. As its crystal band caught the light, it emitted a strange bluish glow and black script floated to the surface, crawling along the inside of the band like the crafter had trapped a wisp of smoke inside it.

James stared at the ring, trying to bring up its information. *How did I use this Death's Stare ability?* After a moment, with a small ding, a box of text appeared above the ring.

> Sytar's Gift:
>
> Rank: Epic
>
> - Greatly reduces experience required to level up.

> *- 3 charisma*
>
> Given to Sytar's chosen, this ring shows a connection to the god. Be warned, some people may look unfavorably on anyone who openly wears a gift from the god of the dead.

> *YOU HAVE UNLOCKED A HIDDEN STAT: CHARISMA.*
>
> Hidden stats are special because you can't put points into them. You can only adjust them through actions, items, or quest rewards. Charisma affects the rate of change in your reputation. A lower charisma score means that you will be more likely to lose reputation than gain it when you interact with people. To put it in simpler terms, the more people interact with you the more they'll realize what a greedy bastard you are and the less they'll like you. You can mitigate this by trying not to be an asshole, I guess...

The god of the dead? What was going on? James was having trouble processing his feelings, so he did what he always did when he couldn't figure something out. He pushed it deep down inside and ignored it. He focused on the positives. The ring gave him an insane boost to levelling speed. James tried to pull up his statistics page. In Role-Playing Games, statistics were numerical values assigned to different character traits. Players could get points that they could then assign to their statistics, or *stats*. These points could then be used to improve their character.

James' first attempts to access his stat page failed, but he finally figured out that he could pull up his stats by thinking the words "Statistics."

STATISTICS

STRENGTH: 10   DEXTERITY: 10

CONSTITUTION: 10

INTELLIGENCE: 10   WISDOM: 10   ENDURANCE:

10

CHARISMA: -3

James stared at his stats, glaring at his Charisma. It looked like each stat started at ten, and Charisma started at zero. That was probably something to do with hidden stats, so he ignored it. Instead, he read over a description for each stat.

Strength:

Increasing your Strength will strengthen you (obviously). This means you will be able to carry more and hit harder.

Dexterity:

Increasing your Dexterity will make you quicker and more agile. It will increase your ability to dodge attacks.

Constitution:

Increasing your Constitution will increase your resistances and health, making you harder to kill.

Intelligence:

Increasing your Intelligence will increase your ability to learn and retain knowledge. It will also boost your Mana capacity and spell damage.

Wisdom:

Increasing your Wisdom will increase your decision-making capabilities. It will also boost your Mana regeneration and spell damage.

Endurance:

Increasing your Endurance will make you heal faster and regenerate stamina quicker.

James sat back and leaned against a rock to finish reviewing his notifications. He was much more comfortable now that he was clothed. The leather was much softer and more pliable than he expected.

He took a deep breath to calm himself. He was reasonably convinced that he wasn't in a dream anymore, and was on the verge of freaking out, but he knew that pretending to be calm could trick his brain into actual calmness. It was the same tactic he'd learned in paramedic school: You walk to an emergency scene, don't run. If you run, then you're setting yourself up to freak out and kill someone by accident.

Taking controlled breaths, James read the rest of his notifications.

YOU HAVE BEEN GIVEN A QUEST: TEMPLE OF SYTAR.

Temple of Sytar: You have been chosen by the god Sytar. Travel to the Temple of Sytar in Fallmire and speak to the high priest.

Suggested level: 0-10

Reward: More information about your brand

Penalty for failure: Unknown

Brand? What brand?

As the thought ran through his mind, he was struck with a burning pain on his calf. Fumbling with the leather pants, James tried to pull them off to reach his calf and see what was happening. Instead, he tripped over the cuffs and landed face-first in the pool of water. Sputtering, he scrambled out of the pool and sat back down. As quickly as it had come though, the pain passed, leaving an ugly scar in the shape of a scythe seared into his flesh. Gingerly, he poked at it, but it had already fully healed.

YOU HAVE BEEN GIVEN A BRAND: MARK OF SYTAR.

Effect: Unknown

This brand shows a powerful connection with the god Sytar. Be careful who you show it to. Their reaction may not be positive.

Well, that was helpful. James had a ton of questions, but at least he had one thing going for him.

James was a gamer. His familiarity with video games helped him understand the prompts in a way he wasn't sure would be possible otherwise.

A skittering noise from above drew his attention from his notifications, and James looked up. An enormous spider, at least five feet wide, emerged out of the shadows of a stalactite and launched at him. He screamed in surprise and instinctively threw out his forearm.

The spider's fangs sank into his bracer, just barely short enough to miss penetrating his arm. There was a dull burning sensation as poison leaked inside the bracer and onto his arm, and James vowed never to insult leather again. With his free hand, he punched the spider in one of its dinner-plate sized eyes. It screeched in pain and yanked its pincers free; the motion sending James flying backwards.

It backed away cautiously, chittering angrily, one eye leaking a blueish ichor. James drew his dagger, suddenly remembering that he had one, and held it in front of him, not taking his eyes off the arachnid. Words appeared above its head in the same way they did for the ring.

CAVE SPIDER (LEVEL 2)

The spider lunged again. This time James blocked it with his left arm and stabbed it in the eye. Back on earth he had taken some MMA classes, but only a few, and never with a weapon. Still, any training was better than none.

The spider backed away again, its eyes glowing dark green.

James didn't like the looks of that. He backed away from the spider and bolted. A sticky thread hit the ground behind him with a *splat*. He sped up, dodging another bolt of webbing.

When its web attack didn't work, the spider launched itself after James, giving chase as he dodged through stalagmites and over small rock formations.

James stopped when he heard a crunching sound and turned to see the spider stumbling after him with a mangled leg. If James had to guess, it had clipped one of the rock formations and hurt itself. It fell down in pain, but still took a swipe at him.

Unlike James' legs, the spider's were tipped with a razor-sharp claw. James fell to the ground, a line of blood welling up from the back of his calf.

The spider wrapped another spindly leg around James' calf and pulled him towards it, slowly dragging him backwards. He tried to resist, furiously clawing at the ground, but it was futile.

He remembered he was holding a dagger and stabbed deep into the grasping appendage. His first couple strikes did nothing to penetrate its armor, but he kept stabbing until the ruined limb hung limply, attached by a thread. Then he kicked, snapping it in half.

He struggled to his feet and rounded on the spider. He took a few unsteady steps towards his enemy, close enough to slash at it, but it dodged his knife and countered with a venomous bite.

James braced himself with his dagger held defensively. Instead of trying to jump away from the spider's bite, he moved towards it, jamming his dagger into the unprotected flesh inside its mouth. Wrenching the dagger backwards, James sliced the creature's head in half, showering himself with ichor. His health bar—a red bar in the corner of his vision—flashed green as the spider's poison coursed through his body.

You have been poisoned:

- 3-5 health/second for 10 seconds.

James checked his health bar. He had 51 health left; just enough to survive the poison. He read through his notifications, breathing heavily.

YOU HAVE GAINED THE SKILL SMALL BLADES.

Small Blades (Skill Rank 1)

  + 1% to weapon damage and attack speed when using small blades

---

You have killed a Cave Spider (Level 2).

  + 5 experience points

LEVEL UP! YOU ARE NOW LEVEL 2.

CONGRATULATIONS!

You have gained your first level and been given 4 stat points to assign. Open your character screen for more information.

James pulled open his character screen and looked. Now that he had gained a level, he could see more information.

JAMES

HUMAN (N/A)

LEVEL: 2

HEALTH: 27/100   REGENERATES 1/HOUR

MANA: 100/100   REGENERATES 1/HOUR

STAMINA: 100/100   REGENERATES 1/HOUR

STATS

STRENGTH: 10   DEXTERITY: 10

CONSTITUTION: 18

INTELLIGENCE: 10   WISDOM: 10   ENDURANCE:

10   CHARISMA: -3

SPELLS

NONE

ABILITIES

DEATH'S STARE (1/7)

BRANDS

MARK OF SYTAR

ACHIEVEMENTS

NONE

Armed with this knowledge, James considered where to put his points. He wanted more Constitution, because he'd almost died in that fight, but he wasn't sure it was the best idea. Sure, being able to take hits would be nice, but being able to tank a few extra hits wouldn't be a game changer. He knew these choices would determine how he progressed in this world. With that in mind, he assigned half of his points into Dexterity and half into Constitution. It would help him avoid getting hit and help him take hits when he couldn't avoid them.

James yawned; overcome with a wave of exhaustion he couldn't avoid. He didn't have any sleeping gear, so he found a rock to use as a pillow and shifted his body until he was at least a little comfortable. He thought it would take more time to fall asleep, but after the excitement of the day, he sunk into the darkness without a fight.

Chapter 3

A spider launched at James, its mandibles open wide with venom dripping down its fangs. Staring into the monster's mouth, James was overwhelmed with the stench of fetid, rotting flesh. It was the smell of death.

He woke with a start, cold sweat dripping down his back. He shuddered, then adjusted his position before looking around, trying to get his bearings. He was snuggled into a rough, bristly pillow, like a beanbag with an overgrown beard.

A pillow? I don't remember falling asleep with a pillow.

The events of the previous night came flooding back, and with a rush of adrenaline, James shot up. He screamed, backpedaling away from the corpse of the spider he'd been inadvertently cuddling. In his attempt to escape, his foot caught on one of the spider's many legs, knocking him off balance. James fell, every movement trapping him further into the tangle of spider legs.

He was in his own personal hell. "Oh God, no. Please let this be a nightmare." He begged as he scrambled backwards, frantically trying to extricate himself from the mess of limbs.

I slept on that… that thing! Oh, God. Or Gods. Not sure who I should be cursing to in this world.

He still couldn't believe this was happening, but waking up spooning a dead spider convinced him he wasn't dreaming. There was no way his subconscious could be that cruel.

If I'm not dreaming, then what is this place? And why me?

Unsure of what else to do, James sat up to look around. His neck and back groaned in protest as the pain from his fight and stiffness from a night spent on a rock floor made itself known. He wanted nothing more than to curl up and lay back down, but he knew that the only way to combat the stiffness was to move, so he stood and tried to roll out his muscles.

First, he rolled his neck on its axis to work out some stiffness. Then he started swinging his arms in large concentric circles, working on his shoulders. He continued moving through a series of stretches for a few minutes before a gurgling sound interrupted him. He looked around nervously for the source of the noise, worried it was another spider, but couldn't see anything. When the noise came again, he realized that it was his stomach, and that he hadn't eaten before going to sleep the night before.

Sighing, he pulled a stick of jerky out of his bag, and a savory scent tickled his nostrils. When he took his first bite, a blast of flavor overwhelmed his senses. He smiled. at least this world had one good thing going for it. He followed

it with a sweet fruit that reminded him of a Devil's Fruit from his favorite manga.

After eating, James tended to his other needs. Maliciously, he relieved himself on the spider's corpse and washed his hands in the pool. Immediate needs met, he set out to explore the cave, but a notification blinked in the corner of his vision, just waiting for him to read it.

I have to remember I'm in a game.

ACHIEVEMENT UNLOCKED: DUMB LUCK.

Dumb luck

+ *1 Luck*

- *1 Intelligence*

Congratulations! You slept through the night in an unexplored cave where you had already been attacked by one monster. I can't imagine what was going through your mind when you thought of that genius idea.

YOU HAVE UNLOCKED A HIDDEN STAT: LUCK.

Luck can affect many things, or it can affect nothing. That doesn't sound right. I'll consult the book. Nope, that's the description they gave. That's stupid. Either way, it doesn't make a difference because you can't put points in luck, anyway.

What the hell was up with these notifications? They were weird, as if someone were writing them specifically for James as he progressed. They were also a little insulting. James chuckled. He had to admit; they *were* funny.

Luck sounded interesting, even if the description had made it seem lackluster. He was interested in what, exactly, Luck would do. If he were basing his guesses on a video game, then he would assume that Luck could affect loot rarity, or maybe increase the chance of a critical hit.

But he *wasn't* in a video game. This was a real universe with its own rules. There was no way to know how Luck affected anything in a real universe.

Is there?

While James was considering the implications of the different stats, his eyes landed on the spider corpse. Back on Earth, he identified as a pacifist. The thought of killing anything terrified him.

Except spiders. Fuck spiders.

But here, in this world, he knew he would have to resign himself to killing other creatures, because this wasn't a friendly place. If he hesitated, he would die.

He went over his options. The cave was well defended and would make a great base, but he hadn't finished exploring it yet. If he left the cave to explore outside, he'd be exposing himself to danger without a safe place to retreat to. He had no idea what was waiting for him outside of the cave but, based on his experiences so far, it wouldn't be pleasant. If he finished searching the cave and killed any other monsters he found, he would always have a refuge he could return to.

He crouched, creeping deeper in the cave, trying to watch where he placed his feet, so he didn't make any noise.

YOU HAVE GAINED THE SKILL STEALTH.

Stealth (Skill Rank 1):

+ *1% harder to notice when sneaking.*

Ironically, the notification distracted James from the task at hand. He stubbed his toe on a stalagmite, taking one damage. He cursed under his breath, vowing to focus more on his environment to avoid other obstacles.

> YOU HAVE GAINED A SKILL RANK IN NIGHT VISION.
>
> YOU ARE NOW SKILL RANK 2.
>
> Impressive. You only bumped into a few rocks. How's that toe feel?

As silently as he could, James continued his trek through the cavern on high alert. It wasn't until he made it to the back of the cave that he found another spider.

> CAVE SPIDER (LEVEL 2)

James tried to wrap his head around what he was seeing. The spider was about the size of a Human, with two crab-like claws accompanying the other eight legs. It was covered with a thick, bristly fur and, as he watched, it raised its beady eyes to look directly at him. His stealth was clearly not fooling it.

Whoever named this creature must have had a loose definition of what a spider was, because this spider was nothing like James had ever seen. He wished he had a flamethrower with him. Or fire magic. He could picture himself flinging a fireball at the spider, incinerating it and being welcomed as a hero spider vanquisher.

Trapped in daydreams of glory, James almost missed an obvious question. *Why didn't the spider attack me last night?*

He'd been defenseless and asleep, but it hadn't so much as scratched him. Also, why wasn't the spider attacking him now? The last one had been much more aggressive. This one wasn't moving.

James answered his own question when he saw that the spider was perched on a cluster of eggs. It wasn't leaving the nest because it was protecting its children. James felt a twinge of sympathy for the maternal creature. He'd probably killed her mate. But then he remembered that it was a giant flesh-eating spider and any sympathy he had felt for it vanished, replaced by musings on how to kill it.

He spent the next four hours doing reconnaissance as James watched the spider's every move, waiting to see if he could spot a weakness. For the first three and a half hours the spider stayed still as a statue in the center of its web, but in the middle of the fourth hour, a bug lazily floated past the spider. Reacting faster than James could see, the spider snatched the bug out of thin air with a lightning fast movement before spinning a web around the bug and draining it.

James had an idea. If the spider's mate wasn't around to bring it food, then it would probably get hungry, especially if it wouldn't leave the nest to look for food. If someone were to actively go around the cave hunting bugs, then the spider might get even hungrier. Once it was hungry enough, James had an idea on how to deal with it.

Before he put his plan into action, he would need to collect supplies. James retreated to the corpse of the first spider to plan his attack.

Back at the corpse of the previous spider, James pulled out his dagger and started cutting into the carcass. He was looking for the spider's poison gland, but wasn't exactly sure what it would look like. Hopefully, he'd know it when he saw it.

His first attempt to penetrate the spider's armor failed, and his dagger skittered across the spider's exoskeleton without leaving a scratch. When that didn't work, he smashed the pommel down repeatedly until it cracked the exoskeleton, revealing the soft flesh underneath.

Finagling his knife around, James worked it up against the spider's flesh and cut a deep hole inside. A rush of blue ichor flowed out of the spider's corpse, soaking his arms. He groaned, wrinkling his nose in disgust, before diving elbow deep into the spider corpse, fishing around for organs. His fingers found... *something*. Firm, yet squishy.

He gently tugged at it until it came loose, and he pulled it out of the spider. It was a black sac the size of his fist, dripping with blue blood. It felt delicate, but not fragile enough for him to destroy it by normal handling. Sort of like a rough beach ball. He placed it carefully on the ground next to him. A notification popped up.

YOU HAVE GAINED THE SKILL HARVEST

Harvest (Skill Rank 1):

+1% to harvested materials

Oh no. Oh no, no, no. You're butchering that poor spider, you monster.

YOU HAVE GAINED THE SKILL ANATOMY

Anatomy (Skill Rank 1):

This skill allows you to better understand the anatomy of monsters and sapients alike.

YOU HAVE GAINED 2 SKILL RANKS IN ANATOMY.

YOU ARE NOW SKILL RANK 3.

James wondered why he had gained so many skill ranks from one action. Maybe it was because he already knew a bit about anatomy from his prior life?

Not that spider anatomy was a big part of paramedic school, but still. Hopefully, his knowledge of medicine would translate into a boost for healing skills if he learned them. It would be cool to be a healer in this world, especially if he could use magic.

CAVE SPIDER POISON GLAND:

Rank: Unusual

- Causes 1-2 poison damage/second for 30 seconds if ingested.

The poison gland taken from a Cave Spider. Its durability has dropped a little from improper harvesting, but it's still usable. Just don't drop it.

With some quick math, James figured out that the poison gland would cause between 30 and 60 damage with an average of 45 damage. That meant… absolutely nothing to him. It would've been helpful if he knew his enemy's health, but he didn't, so it wasn't.

James spent the rest of the day busy hunting for bugs. When he caught one, he squished it into a ball around the poison gland. None of them gave him any experience, but they also didn't seem able to hurt him, which was nice.

That night he camped out near the spider, waiting for the right moment to attack. As far as he could tell, it didn't leave its web once, which meant that it wasn't getting much food, especially not with James hunting down most of the bugs in the cavern. It would get hungry soon.

Chapter 4

Finally, the morning came. Time to put his plan into action.

James had leveled his Stealth to four and Night Vision to six, due to his constant creeping around the dark cave.

Once he'd slathered the last bit of bug guts on the poison gland and made sure that he'd coated it completely, a notification popped up.

YOU HAVE GAINED THE SKILL: COOKING.

Cooking (Skill Rank 1):

+ 1% to flavor

Congratulations, you learned to cook. An essential skill, though maybe not the way you do it.

BUG BALL (POISONED):

Rank: Unusual

- Deals 1-2 damage per second for 30 seconds.

+ 1 strength for 5 minutes after consumption.

> A ball made from squishing bug parts together. Delicious and nutritious!

James stared at the notification, then back at the bug ball. It surprised him that the system counted the Bug Ball as food. *Not that I'd ever eat one.*

James crept back to the spider and prepared himself by drawing his dagger to finish it if the poison didn't take care of it. He crouched behind a stalagmite and observed the spider as it twitched in irritation. It was getting hungry.

A bead of sweat dripped down James' face as he concentrated. He wasn't a great pitcher. In fact, some people would say that, aside from gaming, he had no hand eye coordination at all, and they'd be right. But he needed this to work, so he took careful aim and tossed the meat in an easy underhanded lob. Bits of bug dripped off of it as it flew.

With a blur of motion, the spider's leg shot out and snatched the morsel out of the air and shoved it into its face, where the spider devoured the meat hungrily.

> YOU HAVE POISONED A CAVE SPIDER MATRIARCH (LEVEL 3) FOR 1-2 DAMAGE PER SECOND FOR 30 SECONDS

Not sticking around to see the aftermath of his stupid plan, James bolted.

He managed three steps before the Cave Spider Matriarch's razor-edged claw snagged his calf. Hot blood flowed freely down his leg as the spider dragged him back.

James kicked at it with his good leg, and his boot connected to the creature's face with a satisfying crunch. The spider screeched in pain and shook him from side to side until he couldn't tell up from down, then threw him into the wall of the cave.

James hit the wall. Hard. The wall knocked the wind from his lungs, and he collapsed, wheezing. He tried to stand but vomited everywhere instead. Dizzy, he crawled away from the spider as it advanced towards him.

Slowly, James pushed himself to one knee, groaning as pain shot through his leg. He tried to stand, but the wound was deep, and he couldn't put any weight on it. On top of that, his left arm refused to move, and his chest burned with every breath. Gingerly, he palpated his ribs. *Not broken. Just bruised.* His health bar flashed dangerously in the corner of his vision.

He finally got to his one good leg and raised his dagger, pointing it at the spider as it launched at him. He flopped to the side, barely dodging the attack. James realized the poison's duration had probably passed, so he slashed at the spider with his dagger. It skidded off of the spider's carapace, barely scratching it.

In a moment of inspiration, James reversed the dagger and smashed the pommel into the spider's abdomen as it turned towards him. A small chip crumbled off where he hit, but the monster didn't seem to notice. It slammed its clawed arm into James' chest, throwing him backwards again. This time he stayed on his feet, which was fortunate, as he didn't think he'd be able to get up if he were knocked down again. Wincing, James coughed up a spray of blood on to the rocks. Every breath he took was agony, and it felt as though he wasn't able to fill his lungs completely.

James prepared for another pass as he waited for the spider to come to him. James swayed, barely staying on his feet, but he was alive. The spider charged, swinging its clawed arm like a club. Ignoring the pain in his leg, James jumped into the air a half second before the arm hit him and grabbed on to the spider's appendage like it was a twisted carnival ride. When the arm recoiled, it brought James close enough to strike at the monster's face.

James buried his dagger in the spider's eye. It screeched, frantically swinging its arm around, trying to dislodge James, and the dagger by proxy. Unfortunately for the spider, James had let go of the dagger, leaving it lodged in the blood-red orb.

James landed on his back a few feet away. A bed of moss cushioned his fall, but his leg still screamed at him. He tried to get to his feet with no success. Giving up, James glanced at his notifications.

YOU HAVE GAINED THE SKILL POISONS

Poisons (Skill Rank 1):

+ *1% poison lifespan*

You have killed a Cave Spider Matriarch (Level 3)

+ *9 experience points*

You have gained 1 Skill Ranks in Small Blades.

YOU ARE NOW SKILL RANK 2.

It still seems like you're having trouble finding the pointy end.

YOU ARE AFFECTED BY THE FOLLOWING STATUS EFFECTS:

- *Bleeding (Moderate): - 5 health points per second until your wounds have healed*

> - *Broken bones: - 5% total health until fully healed*
>
> - *Unknown: Advance your anatomy skill to learn this effect*

Well, that's not good.

It was nearly impossible for James to breathe. His lungs felt like they were on fire. All that, and he hadn't even gotten enough experience to level up.

Slowly, he let the bliss of unconsciousness overwhelm him. The last thing he saw before collapsing senseless to the ground was a shadowy figure standing at the entrance of the cave, watching him.

***

Nana Rasner stepped out of the shadowed entrance to the cave. She approached his supine form, gave it a brief survey, then tutted. "Can't have that now, can we," she muttered to herself as she knelt next to him, tilted his head back and examined him.

Her eyes glowed yellow. Life Mana flowed through her body as she channeled a diagnostic spell, *Eyes of Aiana.* James' body glowed with a faint red light as her skill highlighted key clinical signs. A red glow on his neck drew her attention to his engorged jugular veins. She could also see a red light highlighting his ribs, suggesting that the spider had broken them. There were a few other highlights on his body for minor bleeding, but nothing else jumped out to her as urgent.

Quickly, she dropped her bag on the ground next to her. It was loaded with fresh herbs and it made a loud *thud* as it hit the ground. Hands expertly navigating through the clutter inside the bag, she retrieved a smaller bag that was stuffed haphazardly under some Sweetroot tendrils—her emergency kit. She pulled a slim, sharpened bamboo needle out of her bag and set it to the side, then placed her ear to his chest, listening. Normal breath sounds on the right side, but nothing on the left.

Just as she'd suspected. Cracked ribs and a punctured lung. With practiced hands, she felt his chest for his third rib and placed the bamboo needle against it. Slowly, she slid it in until it hit the rib, then angled the needle upwards, but not too far. She wanted to avoid the highly vascular area underneath the second rib. She slid the needle forwards and let it skate down the rib and into the pleural cavity. A whoosh of air whistled out of the bamboo, confirming that she'd placed the needle in the right place.

Now that the stranger wasn't in immediate danger, she pulled a large roll of gauze and a bundle of dried Roundleaf out of her bag. She placed the leaves in her mouth and chewed, careful not to swallow. She opened her pack back up and pulled out a few more bottles—liquids, powders, even one that contained a gas.

Nana Rasner talked to herself while she worked. "These poor kids. Go out on a grand adventure and get killed on their first outing. Why they think they can pick up a sword and tackle a dungeon..." Angrily, she spat the leaves, now chewed to a pulp, into a mortar and pestle. She then took a pinch of powdered Red Silkweed and sprinkled it over the Roundleaf, then three pinches of Flowered Whiteroot. It was important to add the Whiteroot after it had flowered because Whiteroot by itself was toxic. But the flowers not only canceled out the toxin, they reversed its effect and made healing potions more effective.

She pulled the stopper off of the Deadnettle gas bottle and, careful not to inhale, wafted the gas upwards out of the bottle and blew softly, coating the rest of the ingredients with Deadnettle gas, then stoppered the bottle before the gas could numb her mind and body. When the gas touched the Red Silkweed, the herb expanded, emitting a soft glow.

> YOU HAVE CRAFTED AN ITEM: BLOODLOCK PASTE

> BLOODLOCK PASTE:
>
> Rank: Rare
>
> + 10 health regenerated per hour.
>
> You can apply this paste to wounds to control bleeding
>
> Warning: External use only.

Tenderly she applied the paste to James' injuries before wrapping them with a bandage. She gasped when she saw the brand on his calf and quickly covered it up, shaking her head and muttering a short prayer. Once she'd finished applying the paste, his breathing audibly improved. She then pulled a softly glowing red liquid out of her pack.

> ROSEBUD HEALTH POTION:
>
> Rank: Rare
>
> - Instantly heals 130 health.
>
> - Will heal any broken bones.
>
> A health potion crafted from the Nightsand Rosebud.

The paste would do wonders for his external bleeding but wouldn't do much for his internal bleeding and the health he'd already lost. The Rosebud Health Potion would instantly set him back to full health. Combined with the paste that she had applied to his outer wounds, it should give him enough time to recover from his internal injuries without dying. Carefully, she lifted

James' head up and poured the glowing red potion down his throat. He coughed reflexively as some of it went down his trachea before his body reacted and guided the liquid down. Laying him back down, she dabbed at his forehead with a cool, wet cloth and settled down to wait. Over the next five seconds his body regenerated, pushing the bamboo rod out of his chest cavity as the hole closed.

Chapter 5

James woke from dreams inhabited by nightmare monsters with too many legs. He coughed violently, trying to clear his lungs, eventually hacking up what looked like a large clot. A hand rubbing his back caused him to flinch.

Where am I?

He looked around, relieved to see the familiar cave around him. Sure, it had been inhabited by spiders and he'd almost died there, but it was his, dammit. His eyes drifted towards the figure behind him, an older woman with graying hair. She sat on the stone next to him, rubbing his back tenderly. She looked at him with concern in her eyes, but smiled. "Hello, dearie. How are you feeling?"

James groaned, but when he sat up, he realized that, miraculously; he wasn't in pain. He checked out a box of text floating above her head.

NAME: LILIAN RASNER

RACE: HUMAN

LEVEL: ???

CLASS: LIFEFIGHTER

He rubbed the back of his head, an anxious habit, and spoke hesitantly. "Did... Did you save me?"

She smiled at him. "I was gathering herbs by the riverbank and heard you fighting that awful spider. I made it to the entrance of the cave just as you collapsed."

"Thank you," James said appreciatively. He felt amazing, but a bit woozy. "Did you give me something for pain?"

She nodded. "You looked like you could use a little something." Then her gaze grew stern. She slapped him over the head with a rolled-up leaf and started lecturing him. "Are you that stupid that you would go out adventuring and challenge a monster three times your size with *this*?" She held up the dagger. "This toothpick couldn't hurt a fly. Honestly. Sometimes it feels like you young people have a death wish."

James stared at the dagger. "But I—"

"No." She interrupted him. "No excuses."

Who is this woman? She saves my life, then she lectures me? He supposed he should be grateful, so he nodded and apologized.

She sat in silence for a moment, as if thinking. "I'll tell you what. Come to my house in Riverside and I'll help you get stronger the safe way. Follow the road to the east once you've left the cave and gone up the hill. Look for the sign after you cross the first bridge. If you pass the second bridge, you've gone too far." She turned and headed out of the cave.

Her sudden departure caught James off guard. "Wait! you—"

"And bring my bag with you when you come. It's too heavy for a frail old lady like me." With that, she disappeared, moving much faster than she had any right to.

James looked down at the pack. It looked heavy. He picked it up and hefted it in his hands, groaning at the weight. Putting it down, he spent the rest of the day exploring the cave. He wanted to make sure he hadn't missed anything important. Riverside could wait—he wanted to check out the spider's nest. But before he could go deeper into the cave, a notification awaited his attention.

> *YOU HAVE BEEN FULLY HEALED AND ALL STATUS EFFECTS HAVE BEEN CURED.*

> *YOU HAVE BEEN GIVEN A QUEST: HELPING THE ELDERLY I*
>
> Helping the Elderly I: Nana Rasner is a frail old lady, and she needs your help! Deliver her pack to her in Riverside by following the river to the east.
>
> Suggested level: 0-2
>
> Reward: Unknown
>
> Penalty for failure: A savage beating

James rubbed his head where Nana had hit him and sighed. He didn't want to get on that woman's bad side, whoever she was.

His first order of business would be to harvest the poison gland from the Cave Spider Matriarch corpse. He wouldn't have had a chance against the Cave Spider Matriarch if he hadn't used the other poison gland. Using his knowledge from the previous spider, he cracked the carapace closer to its poison gland. It only took him a few moments of rooting around to find his target.

CAVE SPIDER MATRIARCH POISON GLAND:

Rank: Unusual

1-3 poison damage/second for 30 seconds if ingested

The poison gland taken from a Cave Spider Matriarch.

YOU HAVE GAINED A SKILL RANK IN ANATOMY.

YOU ARE NOW SKILL RANK 4.

James looked at his prize with satisfaction. It did slightly more damage than the other gland, and his cuts looked neater. He *had* learned something from his previous harvesting.

A flash of lightning interrupted his musings and made him jump as, outside the cave, bucket-sized drops of rain fell from the sky. Briefly, James worried about Nana Rasner, but the woman could hustle. She was probably already back at the village.

Looking over the spider, James wondered if there was anything else he could harvest. With a flash of inspiration, he remembered how tough the spider's armor was. Whistling as he worked, he chipped five large sheets of carapace off of the spider.

Cave Spider Matriarch Carapace (x5):

Rank: Unusual

A tough exoskeleton from the body of a Cave Spider Matriarch. Can be used as a crafting ingredient for low to mid-tier armor or weapons.

James smiled. One of his favorite parts in any video games was collecting loot after a battle. Nothing could beat the feeling of vanquishing your foe and using their defeat to grow stronger. Sure, this wasn't a legendary sword or anything, but it was still a great feeling. Luckily, when he placed the carapace in his pouch, its mouth expanded to fit the larger item.

He turned his attention to the spider's web. It was dark grey and matched the cave wall closely. If the spider hadn't been sitting in the middle of the web when he first saw it, he probably would have missed it.

A cluster of four oval-shaped sacs lay in the center of the web. James picked them up gingerly and deposited them in his pouch, trying to touch them as little as physically possible.

Cave Spider Egg (x4):

Rank: Unusual

+ 5 dexterity for 60 minutes when eaten

Some cultures believe that by eating the eggs of a cave spider, you can cling to walls like a spider.

Absolutely not. No way in hell I'm eating one of those eggs. Ever.

Still shuddering at the thought, he checked out the spider web. First, he plucked the web with his finger. He expected it to vibrate like a string, but it moved with his finger but stayed fixed in its new position after he'd moved it. James felt the web between his fingers. It felt like he was holding the cold stone wall of the cave in his hands. He tried to pull on the silk, but it had no give. James even gave it a quick lick but learned nothing. He knew some people would judge him for licking a spider web in a magical cave he'd been teleported to by a strange demon hanging out in a medieval cell, but fuck 'em.

Twenty minutes of chipping later, he finally freed the last bit of web from the wall.

> Rocksilk:
>
> Rank: Unusual
>
> A 30-foot-long segment of Cave Spider silk, also known as Rocksilk, for obvious reasons.

As James happily filled his bag up with the silk, he noticed what the web had obscured. A… passage? It only extended a few feet into the cave wall, basically an indent and barely worth noting.

He was about to head back to his sleeping spot to catch a good night's sleep, when some scratches on the cave wall caught his eye. If he squinted, they loosely resembled a skull. He lay his hand on it, which in hindsight perhaps not a good idea when the wall had an ominous skull on it. For a second nothing happened, then the wall flashed red. A notification appeared.

> WOULD YOU LIKE TO ENTER THE DUNGEON OF THE LION-ANT?
>
> RECOMMENDED LEVEL: 5-9.

James quickly backpedaled. *No, thank you.* He'd almost died fighting a level 3 spider. But maybe in the future. He mentally marked the dungeon as an interesting location that he would come back to and returned to his pack, settling down for the night.

Tomorrow would be an adventure.

Chapter 6

James sat up, stretched his arms over his head and yawned. He felt much better than yesterday—whatever Nana Rasner had done really helped. James rolled out his surprisingly limber neck. Apparently, large bags of leaves made great pillows. He carefully peeled back his bandages to reveal unblemished skin coated in a sticky, sweet-smelling paste.

There was nothing James hated more than being sticky, except maybe spiders. He approached the small pool of water in the dimly lit cave and set to washing himself off. Days of sleeping on the cave floor had coated him in spider guts and cave dust, so he was due a nice bath. He dressed, gathered his belongings, and prepared to leave the cave that had protected him since his arrival.

He hefted the pack and groaned. It felt heavier than it had last night. *What did she put in here, rocks?* Once it was on his back, it was much more manageable, and he headed to the mouth of the cave. The silence gave way to birdsong and rustling leaves.

The morning was still young, but after a week in a cave, it was unbearably bright. Still, James relished the feeling of the warm wind against his skin. If Novis followed Earth conventions, then it was probably late spring or early summer. He squinted, waiting for his eyes to adjust before taking in the scene before him. Details that had escaped him during the night were much more apparent in the harsh sunlight. He was in a ravine, cut by a fast-flowing river with a forest on the far side. Even in the daylight, it was still difficult to make out anything other than dense foliage through the thick fog, but James heard the terrified cry of an animal as it dodged through the underbrush.

James' side of the river wasn't nearly as interesting. He was standing on a spit of loose gravel that extended about fifteen feet in either direction. The only point worth noting on his side of the river was the cave mouth at the base of the cliff. To get anywhere, he'd have to scale a twenty-foot rock face. James took a deep breath, trying to suppress his fear.

No time like the present.

His heart skipped a beat every time his foot sent another shower of scree plinking down the cliff wall into the river below. Eventually, he crested the top of the cliff and tossed the heavy pack onto the level ground. James collapsed next to it, alternating between gasping breaths and cursing Nana Rasner. "'Hill' she says. I'll show her a hill. I've said it before and I'll say it again, beating old ladies is not below me," he muttered. He staggered to his feet, hoisted his pack and trudged towards the road ahead of him.

James looked to the left. A path followed the ravine into the distance.

Same to the right, but there was an impressive red mountain range in the distance.

"Where the hell is east?" James muttered under his breath. Nana hadn't provided him with any direction except for east. *Does the sun rise in the east here?* James looked around for any landmarks that might point to a town, but he saw nothing useful.

He sighed. Luckily, he only had two directions to choose from. He could head towards the red mountains, but when he looked at them the hairs on the back of his neck stood up, as if something watched him. The other direction led through a much tamer forest than the one he'd seen across the river. The trees were widely spaced, and there was no trace of mysterious fog.

He gave up and headed for the trees, putting the unnerving mountains behind him.

After an hour of walking, he was startled by a rumbling behind him. He'd zoned out, staring into the trees to see how many animals he could see, completely tuned out to everything else. The answer: not many animals. Apparently, life in a major city did not prepare someone for the great outdoors. James could spot a crackhead with a knife from fifty paces, but he'd be damned if he could see a moth on a tree right in front of his face.

The rumbling intensified, and James turned. Behind him, a rickety cart filled with carrots trundled up the path, led by two horse-like creatures. A sizeable man sat at the front of the cart, working the reins.

> NAME: FERKO LASSEN
>
> RACE: ORC
>
> LEVEL: ???
>
> CLASS: AGRONOMIST

"Whoa, there," the Orc called out to his horses, slowing their gait. "Ho, traveler!" He waved to James cheerily.

James considered the Orc riding the cart. He'd never seen an orc before. Ferko was big and burly, with a pronounced belly, and deep smile lines around his eyes. Two short tusks poked out from beneath his lips. They were only a few inches long and looked dull at the end, as if he'd shaved off the tips. His skin was leathery, with a dark greenish color. A wide-brimmed straw hat perched on his head.

My lucky day! "Hey, there!" James waved. "You wouldn't know how to get to Riverside, would you?" Normally, James might have been more wary of an orc. They were always portrayed as the bad guys in books and video games, but Ferko had one of those faces with an infectious smile that made James want to trust him.

The farmer squinted at him suspiciously and scratched the side of his head. "You don't know where Riverside is?"

"I'm not from around here," James replied.

Ferko quirked an eyebrow and waited for James to elaborate. When he didn't, the farmer's eyebrow jumped higher. When he realized James wasn't going to talk, he pointed down the path he was already on. "Riverside's that way. Follow the road and you can't miss it."

"Thanks." James said, waving to the farmer.

"Well, hang on." The farmer called out, following James along the road. "Why are you heading to Riverside?"

James gestured at the bag of herbs on his back. "Delivering this."

Ferko's eyes lit up in recognition. "Is that Nana's bag?"

"Yea. How'd you know?"

Ferko grinned. "Everyone knows Nana." He patted the cart next to him. "Come on up. I'll give you a ride."

James thought about it for a second. Should he seriously consider taking a ride with some stranger? He knew nothing about this world or the people in it. What if Ferko tried to attack him? But the farmer seemed nice, and James considered himself a decent judge of character. "Sure. I'd be glad to get this off my back." James grinned and tossed the pack in the back of the cart before hopping up next to the farmer.

They sat in companionable silence for a bit as the cart rolled along, but James was getting bored with the scenery. "So, what brings you out here?" he asked.

Ferko gestured at the back of the cart. "I'm bringing my cinderstalks to Fallmire to sell." James turned and picked up one of the orange sticks piled in the back of the cart and examined it.

Cinderstalk:

Rank: Unusual

+ 1 to a random stat for five minutes when eaten.

Sought after for its renowned health benefits, the cinderstalk is a rare vegetable that can only be grown in the mana-rich soil of the Fertile Expanse.

James turned the cinderstalk over in his hands. It felt rough on the outside, like sandpaper, but was otherwise carrotlike. "It looks… crunchy?"

Ferko laughed, slapping him on the back. "Good one! Just for that, you can try one for free. But don't go telling people, I don't want them to think I'm getting soft."

James sniffed the cinderstalk cautiously. It smelled like cinnamon, but spicier.

"Go ahead." Ferko encouraged. "It's not every day you get a chance to eat nobles' food for free."

James nodded and bit into the cinderstalk. His teeth sank into the unexpectedly soft vegetable with ease. It flooded his mouth with a sweet, smoky flavor. "Mmm. That's good."

The two of them sat in comfortable silence for a bit longer until Ferko turned to James. "Truth be told, I'm glad for the company. Road's been dangerous lately."

The opening was perfect for James, who had been trying to think up some good questions to ask that would indirectly give him a little information about the surrounding area while at the same time not revealing that he wasn't from this world. "Oh? I haven't heard anything."

Ferko nodded vigorously. "Oh yes, people have been disappearing on the roads between Fallmire and the Crimson Mountains." He gestured at the reddish mountains behind them. "People have been disappearing from Riverside all the way to Fallmire." His voice dropped to a whisper. "Rumor has it the slavers have started to move again. The Red King and Vorgak the Vile finally came to an agreement."

That wasn't great. James hadn't planned on staying in Riverside very long. His primary goal was still to figure out why he'd been sent to this world, which meant he'd need to visit the temple of Sytar in Fallmire. Hopefully, he'd be able to hitch a ride with someone else—safety in numbers and all that. There was a brief pause in the conversation, but James wanted to keep it going, so he asked the first question that came to his mind. "So, why are you headed to Riverside anyways? Just selling the cinderstalks?"

Ferko grimaced. "Unfortunately, no. I was actually headed to see Nana Rasner for some help getting rid of a couple of pests. Normally I would deal with them myself, but this year they're acting—" A crossbow bolt interrupted him, hitting the wood about an inch from James' thigh.

Two figures stepped out from the tree line. The first was larger than any Human James had ever seen in his life. He was about seven feet tall, covered head to toe in heavy armor. His face was marked by a cruel scar that ran from the tip of his ear to the corner of his mouth, twisting his face into a permanent smirk. He held a heavy broadsword easily in one hand. James stared at the weapon—he wasn't sure that he could lift it, let alone wield the brutal weapon, even with two hands.

NAME: BATO ENKEL

RACE: HUMAN

LEVEL 27

CLASS: HIGHWAYMAN

Bato was imposing, but it was the woman pointing the crossbow at him. That held his undivided attention.

NAME: MIRABELL NUNN

RACE: HUMAN

LEVEL 17

CLASS: ARCHER

Slowly, James raised his hands into the air. He looked towards Ferko pleadingly. The farmer was such a high level that James couldn't even see the number, all he could see was three question marks. He hoped that meant that the farmer could take care of the bandits. It was a small hope, but still...

The farmer gave him a reassuring wink, then calmly addressed the two bandits. "Does the Red King know you're out alone?" His calm voice settled James' racing heart. Maybe he had a trick up his sleeve.

The two bandits exchanged surprised glances. " Of course. Why wouldn't he?" Mirabelle replied nervously, dropping her crossbow just a bit

"You know how the Red King punishes freelancers," Ferko said. "Walk away now and we can pretend this never happened. We both know you aren't working with him."

Mirabelle considered the offer. "Nah. If you're dead, there won't be any witnesses." She whipped up her crossbow to fire, but Ferko was faster. A dark green glow surrounded him, and the smell of forests, oceans, and fresh rain suffused the area. Tendrils of energy reached towards the cart.

The cart glowed, and the cinderstalks rose into the air in a swirling vortex of energy and vegetables. "Get them, you moron!" Mirabell screamed over the sound of the rushing wind.

Bato lumbered into action as a crossbow bolt flew past Ferko's head and slammed into a nearby tree. The cinderstalks swirled in the air for another moment, then disappeared into Ferko's chest with a bright flash.

The farmer vanished, and for a blessed second, all went quiet.

The sudden silence was broken by two snapping noises, followed by two *thud*s, one much louder than the other. Ferko reappeared in the seat next to James, panting slightly. Both Mirabell and Bato were on the ground, lifeless eyes wide in shock, their necks twisted at unnatural angles.

James stared at Ferko. "What... what was that?"

Ferko tried to speak, but his panting grew heavier, and he wasn't able to get the words out. Instead, he waved his hand at James, creating two notifications.

FARMER I

Glutton (7/30):

Consume all food around you in a 7-meter radius.

AGRONOMIST IX

Skilled Consumer (10 / 10):

Allows you to stack food-based bonuses that would normally not be stackable. Duration scales down the more food is consumed.

James gaped at the now-empty cart. Ferko had to have consumed a few thousand cinderstalks. The synergy of those skills was insane. He made a mental note to never mess with Ferko.

The display of power gave James a solid dose of respect for people with non-combat-based classes. He had thought that the two bandits would have the advantage in the fight, because they were geared for it, but clearly that wasn't always true. "What just happened. Who's the Red King?" James asked, overwhelmed by the experience.

Ferko caught his breath. "Those were probably some deserters. Sometimes, they abandon the war with the Goblins and flee south." He gave James a suspicious glance. "Hard to believe you don't know about the Red King. Everyone's heard of him."

James just shrugged.

"The Red King controls all crime from the Serpent Plains to the Endless Sands. He is one of the great powers of the land." Ferko hopped off of his cart. He gestured to James. "Come. Help me with this."

They loaded the corpses onto the wagon, while James considered what Ferko had told him. *Interesting.* All crime was organized in this part of the land. It didn't mean much to him now, but it was something to keep in mind. More importantly, James now had an overview of the surrounding geography.

Chapter 7

They arrived at Riverside later that day, the thick stone walls of the town coming into view as they crested a hill. When they approached the gate, two soldiers stepped out from their post and one held up a hand. The cart slowed to a halt.

The soldiers approached the cart nervously, hands on the handles of their weapons. They were both young, wearing identical leather armor dyed a coppery red.

The impenetrable walls and suspicious guards surprised James. He'd thought Riverside was supposed to be an insignificant border town, but apparently it was much more.

The guards split up as they approached, one turning to stand between them and the gate, while the other approached the car itself. James checked out their statuses.

NAME: LEW VICKER

RACE: HUMAN

LEVEL 15

CLASS: RECRUIT

> NAME: WILLEM BAI
>
> RACE: HUMAN
>
> LEVEL 15
>
> CLASS: RECRUIT

Lew was the closer guard. He had one hand on the hilt of his sword, and he looked nervous, mumbling as he approached. When he arrived at the cart, he stared at his feet and stammered, "Business your state... I mean, state your business."

Ferko smiled politely. "Turning in two bandits that held us up on our way to the city." He pulled back a sheet to reveal the two bodies stacked in the back of the cart. Upon seeing the bodies, the color drained from Lew's face, and he stumbled back a step. "Willem, get the captain." His voice shook as he called to his partner.

A woman wearing much nicer leather armor than her guards stepped out from the wall before Willem could react. She wore similar armor, but dyed blue. She held a leather helmet tucked under her arm. A heavy battle axe hung on her back, but she moved as if it weighed nothing.

> NAME: LAMIA PRICE
>
> RACE: HALF-HUMAN, HALF-SERPENT BEASTKIN
>
> LEVEL 25
>
> CLASS: LEGION

When she got close, she glanced briefly at James, her eyes bright yellow with slitted pupils. Through a gap in her armor, James could see a line of rust-colored scales running up her arms. He quickly glanced away, trying not to stare. She glared at the guards, and the teenagers withered under her gaze. "Remind me again, what job did I assign you two today?"

Willem was the first to meet her gaze. "Guard duty?"

"Right," She replied in a tone fit for toddlers. But as she continued, her voice got louder and faster, until she was practically shouting at them. "And tell me, how exactly are you guarding anything if every single time a traveler approaches the gate, you summon me? If I wanted to stand out here guarding the gate all day, I wouldn't need you morons!"

"B-B-But..." Willem stuttered, "they have bodies." He threw back the sheet in the bed of the cart.

Slowly, as if she couldn't believe how stupid the guards were, she replied. "Yes. They have bodies, and they explained *why* they had bodies. Let them in." She turned to James and Ferko, rolling her eyes. "Head on in. Don't cause any trouble."

Ferko nodded. "Of course." He turned to James. "I'm going to have to take care of this." He said, gesturing at the corpses. "Follow the road until you reach the blacksmith and make a left. That will lead you to Lillian's place. If you see the butcher's shop, turn back." He gave James a pat on the back. "Good luck out there. Hopefully, I'll see you again soon."

"Thanks, for everything," James said, hopping out of the cart.

Once inside the town, the road changed from packed earth to cobblestone as it wound around a large hill. James had expected a smaller village, with wooden buildings reminiscent of medieval Europe. Instead, he was getting ancient Roman vibes as he passed open air buildings of stone and marble. He passed a small fountain with three decorative fish, carved to look as though they were mid-jump, with their mouths open wide. The fountain was dry, except for a small trickle leaking out from one fish's mouth. He wondered why, considering everything else he'd seen pointed to this being a prosperous town.

The sound of hammer striking steel brought him back to the present as he came up on a large open stone building with a burly man standing in the center of the room, hammering on his anvil. James waved to the smith, who glanced up and waved back at him, wiping sweat off his brow. After the smithy, the road split. The right path continued to loop around the hill while the other, the path the farmer had instructed him to take, headed into a heavily wooded area.

As James followed the path, the surrounding plants grew more exotic. A vine in the center of the path grabbed his ankle and snapped taught, hoisting him into the air. He yelped, then started hacking at the vine with his dagger. A sharp voice cut through his panic. "What do you think you're doing?"

As Nana Rasner approached, the vine placed James on the ground and slunk away under her withering glare. "How many times do I have to tell you not to attack my guests?" she snapped, then turned to James. "Are you okay, dear?"

"Yea," he replied, a little shakily, sheathing his knife. *Is it me, or did that vine look ashamed?*

"Follow me." She turned and walked away, and James scrambled to follow as they strolled through the thickening foliage, which somehow always seemed to not be in the way, no matter how thick it got.

They reached a small wooden shack with a massive greenhouse set behind it. The inside of the shack was as bare as the outside, with a compact kitchen, a table, and a bed but not much else. A portrait of Nana hung above the bed, but she looked different. She was wearing pure white robes with green trim, standing next to a hulking figure in golden armor. "That's a nice portrait," James said, pointing at the painting. "Who's the warrior?"

Nana Rasner, who had been puttering around the kitchen, looked up and frowned. "My son." She turned away from him, opened a tinderbox, and started a small fire in the hearth, above which she hung a kettle full of water. She thanked James for bringing her herbs and took the bag from him as if it weren't twice her weight, then laid it in the corner.

> You have completed the quest: Helping the Elderly I
>
> + 2 experience

> LEVEL UP! YOU ARE NOW LEVEL 3.

James was disappointed with the experience, but at least it had been enough to level him up. "I leveled up!" James exclaimed. "Any advice as to where should I put my points?"

Nana tapped her chin with a finger. "You should put two into Strength and two into Dexterity. Focus on physical stats until we can see if you're able to learn magic."

Magic! Awesome.

He always played a spellcaster in video games. Conjuring fireballs or a lightning storm in real life would be a dream come true. Still, he took Nana's advice and put two points into Strength and Dexterity.

As he looked over his notifications, Nana poured them each a cup of tea and sat down across from him. Slightly bitter—not what he usually drank. He preferred tea that was more creamer than tea, but the notification he received made it worth it.

> YOU HAVE DRUNK TEA OF INSIGHT.

Duration: 5 hours

+ 5 to intelligence

+ 5 to wisdom

They sat in silence for a bit before Nana spoke. "I saw the brand on your calf," she said. "Can you explain what you were doing in that cave, and why the God of Death's mark is branded to your skin?" She stared at him intensely.

James had no reason not to trust the woman, she'd basically saved his life back in the cave, so he started from the beginning. He explained how he'd woken up in the cave, and how the spider had attacked him.

How he'd come from another world.

Nana thought carefully before replying. "You aren't the first youngster that I've found wandering, looking for adventure. Normally, I try to convince them to go back to their families. Most adventurers die early." She glanced sadly at the painting on the wall. "But, for you, that isn't an option. You've been given a mission from a god, and you must complete it. The gods don't take kindly to people who ignore their requests." She looked at him seriously. "I can teach you a little about this world before you embark on your quest, but your future will be dangerous, no bones about it."

James nodded in gratitude. "Thank you."

She gave him a kind smile. "Good. I'll make arrangements with the innkeeper to give you a place to stay while you're here. My house is too small. Go make friends with the locals. I think Kyrwin and Bartram could use some help."

YOU HAVE BEEN GIVEN A QUEST: HELPING THE ELDERLY

II

Helping the Elderly II: Nana Rasner has instructed you to

speak with Kyrwin the Smith and Bartram the Innkeeper to

see if they could use some help.

Suggested level: 2

Reward: Instruction from Nana Rasner

Penalty for failure or refusal: Nana Rasner will stop teaching

you

James was just about to leave when Nana Rasner pulled a sword out from under the table and handed it to him.

Steel Sword:

Rank: Common

Forged from steel, this sword is slightly stronger than the

same weapon made from iron.

"You don't want to spend the rest of your life fighting huge beasts with that tiny dagger. Tomorrow morning, go to the barracks and ask for Cairn. Tell him to train you, and that his favor is due."

YOU HAVE BEEN GIVEN A QUEST: HELP THE HELPLESS I

Help the Helpless I: You. You're the helpless. Talk to Cairn

at the Barracks and tell him Nana wants him to teach you

swordsmanship.

Suggested level: 1-5

Reward: Improved Swordsmanship

Penalty for failure or refusal: Probably a painful death

"Thank you. For everything," James said, turning to leave.

Nana spoke, her voice heavy with sadness. "I don't want to see any more young people die." She looked like she wanted to say something else, but then her expression steeled. "Come to me when you're done helping Kyrwin and Bartram and we can talk about your character progression."

James nodded. "Of course."

There was a knock on the door. She got up and opened the door to reveal Ferko. "Ferko!" She exclaimed, wrapping the farmer with a hug. "What brings you here? How's Ian?"

"Hi Nana," he said warmly, stepping inside. "Ian's good. He's 14 now. Just left for Fallmire to start his initiation."

Initiation? He filed away the question to ask Nana later, then wondered when she'd teach him magic. He wanted to cast lightning spells — they were his favorites.

James had zoned out and missed part of the conversation, but tuned back in when he heard his name. "—ready in about a month. I'll send James here over with them."

James looked at her. "Huh?"

She ignored his question and continued talking to Ferko. "Does that work?"

Ferko nodded and got up to leave. "Thank you for the tea. And the help." He turned to James. "See you in a month." He winked and left.

"What was that about?" James asked.

"Don't worry about it. Focus on your training now." She made a shooing motion. "It's getting late. Head to the inn and get settled in. Let Bartram know that I sent you."

As he turned to leave, she left him with a few words of parting advice. "A little advice. Don't tell anyone about that," she said, gesturing at his calf.

Fragment of Divinity

Chapter 8

James woke up in a superb mood. It was his first time sleeping on an actual bed in almost a week, and he'd had an amazing dinner last night. Initially, the innkeeper had been wary of James, but when he'd explained that Nana Rasner sent him, his attitude had changed completely, offering free dinner with a proclamation that any friend of Nana's was a friend of his. It was a good thing too, because he didn't have any money.

James came to realize that Nana's name carried a lot of weight in Riverside. It wasn't surprising—a high-level healer like her would be a godsend in an out-of-the-way area like this.

James stayed in bed for a few more minutes before the delicious smells seeping through the floorboards caused his stomach to rumble. He hopped out of bed and head down the stairs to the main room of the inn.

When he arrived downstairs, the innkeeper smiled and waved to him.

NAME: BARTRAM INOV

RACE: HUMAN

LEVEL: 51

CLASS: INNKEEPER

He gestured for James to sit down at a table, then disappeared into a side-room.

The inn was packed with mid-level adventurers sitting around in groups, joking in front of plates piled high with food.

A short while later, while James was lost in thought, the innkeeper returned with a heaping plate of eggs and meat. "Hey, Bartram?" James asked as the innkeeper turned to leave.

"How can I help you?"

"Nana sent me here to help you out. Can I do anything for you?" James asked him.

Bartram thought for a second before replying. "I could use some help making cider." He said, scratching the side of his face. "I go out and collect the fruit every year, but I'm not a spry young man anymore."

YOU HAVE BEEN GIVEN A QUEST: FRIENDSHIP FRUIT

Friendship Fruit: Collect 1,000 Bleufruit.

Suggested level: 0

Reward: 3 bottles of Bleufruit cider.

Penalty for failure or refusal: Decreased reputation with Bartram.

James promptly agreed and let the innkeeper know that he would come back after morning sword classes. Bartram smiled and bade him farewell, letting him get back to his food.

After a delicious breakfast and a few wrong turns, James found himself in the shadow of an enormous white-marble building that radiated power. A notification appeared as he stepped over the threshold.

DEBUFF ADDED: STRONGHOLD

- *15% to all stats for non-Legionnaires*

Carefully navigating through hallways crowded with soldiers, all going in different directions, James approached the first person who didn't seem to be in a hurry. The teenager sported a different uniform than the rest of the guards. His uniform was made from brown cloth and didn't seem to have any armor whatsoever. The kid looked almost as lost as James felt. If James had to guess, he'd say the kid was probably fourteen or fifteen years old.

NAME: VERYN ELSFORTH

RACE: HUMAN

LEVEL: N/A

CLASS: N/A

"Hey, Veryn?" James asked, startling the teen out of his reverie.

"Huh? Sir!" The guard snapped to attention, but after a second his eyes focused and he realized that James wasn't one of his superior officers. He dropped his arm and quirked an eyebrow at James in confusion, his mouth slightly ajar in a way that told James exactly why he was lost. "How... how do you know my name?" He stammered. "Did Lamia send you? Tell her I'm sorry. I'm trying to find it, I really am."

"Whoa, there." James raised his hands. "I have no idea what you're talking about. I'm looking for someone called Cairn. Do you know where I can find him?"

The look of confusion slid off of Veryn's face, as if he realized that he'd finally found the sole person in the barracks, possibly the entire town, that knew less than him. The corners of his mouth tightened in determination, and he stood up straighter. "I can take you to Commander Cairn."

Veryn spun on his heels and marched off, dodging through the crowd with practiced ease. James had no problem following—his high school had had over 3,800 kids in it. He knew how to traverse a crowd.

They nimbly wove through the barracks, miraculously not bumping into anyone as James struggled to match Veryn's pace. Eventually they came to an enormous set of double doors, made from a rich red wood and set with two enormous, gold lion-headed knockers.

"The Commander is in here." Veryn gestured, pointing at the door.

James tried to raise one of the knockers, but it barely budged. He had to use two hands to lift it, his muscles tense against the weight. When let go of the knocker, it hit the door with a heavy reverberation.

A deep voice boomed from behind the door. "What?"

"Sir," Veryn called out. "I brought someone to see you."

There was a pause, then the heavy doors swung open, revealing a wiry man in his fifties.

NAME: CAIRN ERIN

RACE: HUMAN

LEVEL: ???

CLASS: LEGION COMMANDER

The Commander was one of those people who didn't need bulk to have a presence, and could snap James in half without breaking a sweat. He made a note to stay on the Commander's good side. Cairn stared back at James, clearly confused as to who he was. "Thank you Veryn, you're dismissed," he said, beckoning for James to enter the room.

The Commander smiled as he shut the foot-thick door with a thud behind them. He gestured to an empty chair across from him at the desk. "How can I help you?"

James appreciated the Commander's to-the-point attitude, but for a reason he couldn't put his finger on, the Commander terrified him. "W... well, sir..." he choked out, sweat beading on his forehead.

"Are you okay?" the Commander asked James in concern. "You're sweating an awful lot."

James nodded, unable to speak under the Commander's crushing gaze.

A look of realization flashed across Cairn's face. His eyes glazed over as he checked a few notifications and then, suddenly, James was no longer sitting across from a monster. He now faced a kindly man with a salt-and-pepper beard framing a concerned smile. "Is that better?"

"Yea, thanks," James said, his voice coming out much stronger now that he wasn't in immediate danger of pissing his pants. "What was that?"

Cairn rubbed the back of his neck in embarrassment. "We raided a Goblin settlement last night and I may have forgotten to turn off my Conqueror's Aura," he admitted. "Sorry about that." He steepled his fingers and regarded James. "Now, then. How can I help you?"

"Nana wanted me to ask if you could help train me in swordsmanship," James said.

Upon hearing Nana's name, Cairn's face split into a wide grin. "Oh, Nana sent you! Why didn't you say so?" He stood up and clapped James on the back. "Of course I'll help. I just need to figure out who's going to train you."

You have completed the quest: Help the Helpless I

+ 1 experience

Cairn turned to look out a window, muttering to himself before he turned back to James with a gleam in his eye. "Come here." He gestured for James to look out the window and pointed to a group of soldiers training in the courtyard. "Go to Lamia. She's one of our Captains. Tell her I sent you."

> YOU HAVE BEEN GIVEN A QUEST: HELP THE HELPLESS II
>
> Help the Helpless II: Report to Lamia for swordsmanship lessons.
>
> Suggested level: 2 - 10
>
> Reward: Swordsmanship Skill training.
>
> Penalty for failure or refusal: No Swordsmanship lessons.

James nodded, then saluted. "Yes, Commander."

Cairn laughed. "No need for that, you aren't one of my soldiers," he said, walking over to the door and opening it for James.

***

Three hours later James lay in the dirt, spitting grass out of his mouth for the umpteenth time. His body was basically one giant bruise—he couldn't believe he hadn't broken anything yet.

Then the Words came. Oh, how he hated the Words.

"Get up."

Lamia's emotionless voice cut like ice through the fog surrounding James' brain as he slowly pushed himself to his feet, too tired to even groan. After what felt like hours, he stood once again on legs made of jelly, only to be immediately knocked down again as Lamia struck him with the flat of her blade.

Honestly, it wouldn't have been so bad if she'd show any emotion at all. After the original warm greeting, she'd tossed him a sword and asked him to show her his skills. Needless to say, she wasn't pleased.

She grabbed his shoulder and helped him stand. He focused on Lamia, who grinned at him as the terrified recruits looked on. "Anyone else want a go at me?" She asked. No one said anything, and Lamia laughed.

"Good job today," she said to James, then noted his skeptical look. "No, really. For someone who's never trained with swords before, you did an adequate job."

"Thanks, I guess," James wheezed.

"Go rest up. You said you had a month, right? I want you to report back to me here every morning at sunup for the next few weeks. I'll hammer the basics into you. Dismissed."

James thanked her and stumbled away to a nearby bench where he promptly collapsed. He needed to get back to Bartram's to help the innkeeper out, but first he needed a rest. He reviewed his notifications from the morning's training.

YOU HAVE GAINED THE SKILL: SWORDSMANSHIP

Swordsmanship (Skill Rank 1):

+1% Attack speed and damage with swords.

Careful. Flailing around like that can't be safe.

YOU HAVE GAINED 4 SKILL RANKS IN SWORDSMANSHIP.

YOU ARE NOW SKILL RANK 5.

Those bruises look like they hurt.

QUEST PROGRESS: HELP THE HELPLESS II (1/30 BEATI-
LESSONS)

James groaned, dismissing the prompts. In an attempt to put off standing for as long as possible, he pulled up his character sheet. He hadn't really gone over the full sheet since he'd appeared in Novis, and he thought that maybe looking at his improvements might make him feel a little better about the savage beating he'd just gone through.

JAMES

HUMAN (N/A)

LEVEL: 3

HEALTH: 121/121   REGENERATES 1.6/HOUR

MANA: 97/97   REGENERATES 1.2/HOUR

STAMINA: 130/130   REGENERATES 1.6/HOUR

STATS

STRENGTH: 12   DEXTERITY: 14

CONSTITUTION: 12

INTELLIGENCE: 9   WISDOM: 10   ENDURANCE:
10   CHARISMA: -3   LUCK: 1

SPELLS

NONE

ABILITIES

DEATH'S STARE (1/7)

BRANDS

MARK OF SYTAR

ACHIEVEMENTS

NONE

He dismissed his character screen and looked at the sky. It was almost noon; he needed to hurry and get back to Bartram in time to collect the fruit before dark.

He stumbled back to the inn, wanting nothing more than to sleep for a week. He greeted the irritated innkeeper, who took one look at him, told him he was scaring away all the customers and refused to let him help until he'd taken a bath.

After his bath, Bartram directed him to the back door. Fruit picking didn't seem like that bad of a task, until the innkeeper handed James a pair of boots with a long metal blade sticking out of the toe, a harness with a bucket attached, and two clawed gloves.

Strengthened Steel Climbing Boots:

Rank: Common

Used by climbers to get a better grip with their feet on vertical surfaces like trees. Enchanted with a low-grade Earth-core to bear up to 500 lbs.

Steel Climbing Gloves:

Rank: Common

These gloves are fitted with steel claws to aid in tree climbing.

If James weren't so worried about how high he'd have to climb, he might have been excited for his first enchanted item. He opened the rear door of the inn slowly, a knot of foreboding in his stomach. One look in the "garden" confirmed his fears. He wasn't just screwed.

He was royally fucked.

A little about James. He hated heights. Absolutely hated them. He stood speechless while Bartram showed him how to climb the enormous trees and harvest the fruit.

After Bartram left, James sighed and got to work. He pulled on the equipment, then approached the first tree. Swallowing his terror, he grabbed it with his clawed gloves, then stabbed a bladed foot into the wood.

YOU HAVE GAINED THE SKILL: CLIMBING

Climbing (Skill Rank 1):

+1% *Strength while climbing.*

+1% *Endurance while climbing.*

Don't look down.

Taking care not to look down, James used the bladed gear to climb the tree like a ladder until he reached the first set of branches, where he spotted an apple-like fruit hanging from a branch. He inched his way across the branch but ended up in a position where looking down was his only option. His stomach dropped, and he froze, hugging the branch with his eyes squeezed shut.

He steeled himself and pushed forward.

I have to do this. I need every advantage I can get in this world if I want to get home.

***

The next few weeks went the same way. Sword training with Lamia in the morning, fruit picking for Bartram in the afternoon.

After almost three weeks of this routine, James filled all the barrels, increasing his climbing to Skill Rank 9. He summoned the innkeeper to show off the spoils of his labor.

Bartram whistled appreciatively, then told him to get ready for the fun part. He donned an apron and handed one to James, then pulled a large mashing utensil out of a nearby shed.

They spent the rest of the day mashing the fruit in barrels and transferring the mashed fruit to bottles, where they would ferment. While they worked, Bartram talked to James about how he'd moved out to Riverside from Fallmire a few years ago to focus on his brewing and open up an inn. He explained that the proximity to the Fertile Expanse was beneficial to plant growth, so he could get the best ingredients here for next to nothing. It was also why he had built his inn next to a section of the forest overgrown with bleufruit.

Once they'd sealed the last bottle, Bartram approached James, handing him three bottles filled with an indigo pulp. "The final step of the brewing process takes place in these bottles." he said, giving James a wink. "Just leave them for a few months and they'll be perfect."

Unfermented Bleufruit Cider (x3):

Rank: Epic

- *Permanently increases a random attribute*

Rich in Mana and flavor, aged Bleufruit cider is one of the rarest and most sought-after beverages. The longer the cider is allowed to ferment, the stronger its bonuses.

James thanked Bartram profusely and slipped the bottles into his pouch before glancing at the quest completion notification.

You have completed the quest: Friendship Fruit

+ *1 experience*

+ *3 bottles Unfermented Bleufruit Cider.*

James smiled as he headed to bed that night. It had been a productive month. Training with Lamia had raised his swordsmanship to Skill Rank 13, and she'd even let him spar with her soldiers. Not that he'd won any fights yet. Hopefully, tomorrow would be his day.

Chapter 9

J ames stared at Lew, the level 15 recruit that had stopped him at the gate. James ignored the cheering crowd, his focus intent on the scowling 16-year-old noble's face.

Once she'd deemed him competent, Lamia let James practice with the rest of the recruits.

He'd gotten to know Lew.

He didn't like him.

James knew the kid was embarrassed at getting reprimanded at the gate when James had entered the city. Since then, he was certain Lew had made it his mission to get James to quit. Every interaction that he had with James was unpleasant. When they sparred, Lew would purposefully aim for James' face, throat, and groin. Even though they practiced with wooden swords, James usually ended up staggering home in pain.

But today was different. Lew had been trying to get the upper hand the entire fight, but James was holding his own. The other matches had long since ended, and the recruits cheered them on. If James hadn't been so hyper-focused on Lew, he would have seen the coins changing hands as the others placed bets on who would win.

James took a quick peek at his Stamina bar. It was hovering in the low teens and flashing in warning. He had maybe a few seconds of movement left before it bottomed out. *Game over.*

Lew's arms trembled as he struggled to hold up his sword. Sweat dripped down his face and into his eyes and he raised a hand to wipe it away.

There!

James took advantage of the opening and swung for Lew's unprotected left side. Lew failed to notice the obvious feint and wearily raised his sword to block, but James redirected. Quick as a whip, James spun, putting everything he had into one last blow. His sword connected with the side of Lew's head with a dull *thwack* and the recruit fell to the ground, unconscious.

James barely had time to read the notification before he, too, fell to the ground and sunk into blissful darkness.

> YOU HAVE GAINED 2 SKILL RANKS IN SWORDSMANSHIP.
>
> YOU ARE NOW SKILL RANK 15.
>
> Look at you, swinging your stick around! Enjoy your nap.

James bolted upright to a splash of icy water across the face. Lamia stood above him, grinning. She reached down and grasped his hand, helping him to his feet. "Excellent swordsmanship," she praised him, brushing a spot of loose dirt off his back. "I've taught you everything I can. You're ready for some real-world experience."

James nodded seriously. "Thank you," he said, holding out his hand for her to shake.

Lamia pressed a silver coin into his palm. "No, thank you. I had a feeling you might win today." She winked at him. "Now, I have a quest for you if you're interested."

"Sure!" James had been too busy to get bored, but after about three weeks of training without a break, he was ready for something different.

"Every week, the guard sends someone to clean Nana Rasner's herb garden. Would you be willing to do it for us this week?"

"Sure." James nodded. He'd barely had time to talk to her over the past three weeks due to his constant training, and he still had so many questions for her.

> You have completed the quest: Help the Helpless II
>
> *+ 3 experience*

> YOU HAVE BEEN GIVEN A QUEST: HELP THE HELPLESS III
>
> Help the Helpless III: Clean Nana Rasner's Herb Garden.
>
> (0/3 Star Moles) (0/1 Moonshadow Moth).
>
> Suggested level: 3 - 5
>
> Reward: Unknown.
>
> Penalty for failure or refusal: Unknown.

James felt like he was forgetting something, but he couldn't concentrate over the hammering from the smithy.

The smithy! James still had to talk to Kyrwin, the smith, before heading to Nana's place.

The smith was a burly man. He stood at the forge, hands on his hips, staring distractedly at a naked blade laying on the anvil in front of him.

Kyrwin didn't look up when James walked into his shop, so James coughed politely. When the smith still didn't respond, James coughed louder.

NAME: KYRWIN PRICE

RACE: HUMAN

LEVEL: 37

CLASS: SMITH

The smith blinked twice, then looked up. "Oh, hey there." He held out a hand, thick with callouses. "Name's Kyrwin."

"Nice to meet you," James said, accepting the handshake. "I'm James."

"Well met, James. How can I help you?"

"Actually, I was hoping I could help you out." James smiled. "Nana sent me to check in with you."

The smith nodded in appreciation. "I'm glad she remembered." He gestured at the blade laying in front of him. "I'm making a blade for my daughter's promotion. Youngest to become a Legion Captain in over a hundred years." He wiped a tear of pride from his eye. "She's only 20 years old and already choosing her Advanced class. But anyway, I'm rambling." He stopped to scratch his head. "What was I talking about? Right. The sword. I'm making a sword for my daughter's promotion, but the ceremony is in a week and I need to wrap the handle in ironweed. Now, normally I'd get it myself, but I don't have time to finish this sword and get the handle wrap.

"So, you need me to get you some ironweed?" James asked.

The Smith nodded. "Pretty much."

"Where can I get it?"

"Oh, Nana said I could stop by and grab some from her garden. I need it by the end of the day tomorrow if possible."

YOU HAVE BEEN GIVEN A QUEST: PICKING PLANTS

Picking Plants: Bring Kyrwin 5 Ironweed by the end of the
day tomorrow.

Suggested level: 3 - 5

Reward: Unknown

Penalty for failure or refusal: Unknown

James accepted the quest, reassuring the smith that he would be back in time with the ironweed. The quest seemed simple enough, and he might be able to get both of his quests done at once. He had a suspicion Nana had arranged it that way.

When James arrived at Nana's house, he found it locked and dark. He tried knocking anyway, but nobody answered. She was probably out for the day, so James approached the greenhouse and pushed open the door.

ENTERING DUNGEON: THE GARDEN (GROUND FLOOR).

RECOMMENDED LEVEL: 1-3.

Hot, humid air rushed out of the open doorway, sticking to his skin. He peered into the greenhouse before stepping inside, but he couldn't see through the thick vegetation. Drawing his sword and taking a deep breath to steel himself, he took a step inside.

By the time James was five steps into the greenhouse, he couldn't see the door through the thick brush behind him. It felt like he'd stepped into a different world. Well, another different world.

The garden was alive with the chirping, rustling, and chattering of various animals. It was dark underneath the canopy of dense trees, much darker than he'd expected, considering the building was made of glass. But any light coming into the greenhouse barely penetrated the dense foliage.

Cautiously, James crept forward, his shirt stuck to his back with sweat as he tried to stay quiet as he followed a meandering path deeper into what looked like a tropical forest. It was clearly magical and unlike any greenhouse James had ever seen before.

James had no clue how he'd find *anything* in this thick brush. He wished this world had quest indicators, and he could follow a floating marker to find the ironweed. He didn't even know what it looked like.

A screech next to his ear caused James to jump backwards, sword raised, but nothing happened. Taking deep breaths to calm his jackhammering heart, he continued deeper into the jungle.

Partially into his walk, James noticed a bush overflowing with plump berries. Perfect, his harvesting skill was low, so hopefully he'd be able to harvest them without issue and level the skill up.

When James got closer to the bush, he realized that they weren't berries at all. They were deformed, purple fruit. Carefully, James picked a fruit and inspected it. It seemed to be rotten, because his fingers punctured the fruit with ease, leaving them coated with a sticky pulp.

Deadnettle:

Rank: Unusual

A strange plant usually found in swampy environments. Toxic when consumed, the Deadnettle bush sends creatures that consume its fruit into a never-ending sleep.

James noticed the corpses of a few small animals scattered around the base of the bush in various states of decay. Curious, James sniffed the fruit. A sickly sweet smell overpowered him, travelling up his nose and into his brain, where it descended like a fog.

- 1 Wisdom.

Don't sniff strange plants.

Coughing, James quickly tossed the fruit onto the ground and stumbled away from the bush. He tripped over a root and fell down, hard. He landed next to a cluster of seeds, surrounded by chunks of rotted fruit.

Deadnettle Seed:

Rank: Unusual

These seeds let off an unusual gas with anesthetizing properties.

With his last vestiges of consciousness, James scooped a handful of the Deadnettle seeds into his pouch.

A loud rumbling noise filled the area as the surrounding earth shifted. Two large, clawed hands poked out of the dirt, scooping it away as a mole the size of a Great Dane poked its head out, sniffing the air.

STAR MOLE (LEVEL 3)

It had a long, pink nose that twitched as it took in its surroundings. Its paws were wide and pail-shaped, with long white nails at the end of each digit. James didn't see any eyes.

Moving slowly as to not make a sound, James stood and drew his sword. He moved like molasses and got a few steps closer to the Star Mole as it continued sniffing the air.

He raised his sword.

And hesitated.

He'd never killed an animal before. And no, spiders didn't count.

He'd always thought he wouldn't have any issues hunting deer, but he'd never actually tried. It wasn't like he was a vegetarian. But none of that mattered now. He was in a dungeon and faced with a dangerous beast. Just because it hadn't attacked him yet didn't mean it wouldn't as soon as it noticed him.

James realized he'd let the sword dip slightly while he'd been thinking and raised it again. This time he didn't hesitate. He swung down full force.

Just as he'd started swinging, the Star Mole homed in on his scent. It let out an ear-splitting screech, its pink nose splitting apart into five segments to reveal rows of razor-sharp teeth.

So that's why they call it a star mole. James stumbled back, his sword biting deep into a nearby tree.

YOU RESISTED THE STATUS EFFECT [DEAFENED].

After it's failed screech, the Star Mole jumped into the air and flipped, diving back into the earth. The ground split for the mole, as if it were an Olympic diver and the dirt was its pool. Everything was quiet once again except for the sound of James' heart thudding in fear as he spun, searching for his opponent.

James stood stock-still in the clearing for a couple minutes, waiting for the Star Mole to re-emerge.

Nothing.

Eventually, he realized that the mole probably wouldn't reappear for a while, so he continued his quest, searching for the ironweed. But now, he was on edge, startled by every slight noise.

A faint light caught his attention, cutting through the shadows like a knife. A group of silvery stalks shimmered in the dim moonlight. He approached them and, after reassuring himself that he wasn't about to be attacked, he harvested the plants.

Ironweed (x10):

Rank: Unusual

Ironweed can grow from iron-ore in Mana rich environments. It is a strong and flexible form of refined iron and highly coveted by weavers.

YOU HAVE GAINED 1 SKILL RANK IN HARVEST.

YOU ARE NOW SKILL RANK 2.

Quest update: Picking Plants (10/5 Ironweed).

He'd only let his guard down for a second, but as soon as he did, the earth started rumbling. James instinctively jumped out of the way as the Star Mole burst from the ground.

It sniffed the air for a second before it turned towards James, opened its mouth, and roared. This time, the sound reverberated through his body, rattling his bones as if he were standing next to the speakers at a concert.

The roar slowly faded away, then... nothing. The chirping and chattering of the creatures faded away, replaced by a dull ringing in his ears. The ringing slowly faded to complete silence.

> YOU HAVE BEEN [DEAFENED].
>
> Deafened:
>
> Duration: 5 Minutes
>
> While Deafened, you will be unable to hear.

A small ear icon appeared in the corner of James' vision, with a small digital timer next to it, counting down.

5:00

4:59

4:58

James looked around wildly. Without his sense of hearing, he felt lost, unable to balance properly.

The Star Mole sprung towards him.

He reacted instinctively, the muscle memory from his sword lessons taking over as he caught the Star Mole mid-jump with a deep, bloody gash to the belly.

It wasn't enough.

The mole swiped at him, but this time, James was ready. He raised his sword and blocked the claws, then stepped back to create some room.

Once the initial shock of deafness had worn off, he'd realized that the debuff really wasn't that bad. He could still *see* the Star Mole. Even if it went underground again, he could feel for the rumbling that signified its approach.

James advanced on the enormous rodent, sword at the ready. The mole tried to dive back into the earth, but James didn't give it a chance, stabbing at it every time it got ready to launch itself. The mole dodged a few strikes, but it was blind and cumbersome. With a final thrust, James skewered it through the chest.

You have killed a Star Mole (Level 3)

+ 7 experience points

Quest Update: Help the Helpless III (1/3 Star Moles) (0/1 Moonlight Moth)

LEVEL UP! YOU ARE NOW LEVEL 4.

Jesus. I've got two more of those monsters to kill.

James assigned his stat points, settling on putting two points each into Strength and Constitution.

He checked his health. He hadn't sustained any large injuries, just glancing blows, and his health was now at 117/126. Since the regeneration rate was so slow, he'd have to keep careful track of that, but if things continued as they'd been going, then he'd have enough to take out the other Star Moles before moving on, and he could rest up for a few hours before taking on the moth.

James sat down on a rock to wait out the rest of his status effect. Slowly, sounds started filtering back to him. The timer flashed as it counted down the last few seconds of his deafness.

Before continuing through the dungeon, James took a minute to butcher the mole, figuring it would give him a bit of time to restore a couple of points of health and stamina. He pulled his dagger out of the sheath at his waist and cut into the corpse. He tried to cut nice chunks of meat to store in his pack, but he didn't actually know anything about butchering, so after a few minutes of hacking at the corpse, he ended up with five large hunks of meat. His cooking skill also increased.

Star Mole Meat (x5):

Rank: Common

A large hunk of poorly cut Star Mole meat. When eaten, this meat gives + 20 health regenerated/hour for 5 hours.

YOU HAVE GAINED 1 SKILL RANK IN COOKING.

YOU ARE NOW SKILL RANK 2.

YOU HAVE GAINED 1 SKILL RANK IN ANATOMY.

YOU ARE NOW SKILL RANK 5.

James stood up, his lower back protesting. He cleaned his dagger before sheathing it and drew his sword. It was time to kill some more moles.

He'd taken less than ten steps when the next mole attacked. It burst out of the earth and slashed at James with its claws. Startled, James didn't react in time and the creature's claws cut into his cheek, narrowly missing his eye. Before he'd even realized what happened, the mole already disappeared back into the earth. James was left standing in the clearing, confused, and with blood dripping down his face.

Chapter 10

James spent the few hours hunting down the last two Star Moles. It was frustrating. Every time he damaged one, it would hop underground and disappear for a while before erupting from the ground with another attack.

Between attacks, James tried to gather as many ingredients as he could. Since his Harvesting skill was so low, he wasn't able to pick most of the plants he encountered, but he'd managed to cut a few useable stalks. By the time he'd found and killed the other two Star Moles, James had added some soldier's nettle, roundleaf, and river maple to his inventory.

He butchered the other two Star Moles, netting him fourteen experience and ten Star Mole Meats. His skill was improving—one cut was a higher quality than the rest.

Star Mole Steak:

Rank: Common

+ 30 health regenerated/ hour for 5 hours.

A high-quality cut of meat off of the flank of a Star Mole.

His Swordsmanship Rank had also increased.

> *YOU HAVE GAINED 1 SKILL RANK IN SWORDSMANSHIP.*
>
> *YOU ARE NOW SKILL RANK 16.*

James had also, on an impulse, tried to harvest a Star Mole's nose. He'd failed to do it successfully on the two he'd just killed, so he wandered back to the first one and harvested it successfully.

> Star-Mole Star:
>
> Rank: Unusual
>
> The flower-shaped nose from a Star-Mole. Your knowledge of potions is too low to see potential uses for this ingredient.

It was deep into the night by the time James had finished harvesting and he was tired and hungry. He tried to retrace his steps out of the dungeon, but after almost a half-hour of walking in circles, he gave up. There was no way he could retrace his steps under the oppressive darkness of the thick canopy that obscured everything but the slightest beams of moonlight.

But it was *beautiful.*

Far more beautiful than anything he had seen back on earth.

James searched the area and found some loose stones, which he arranged in a circle. He dug a shallow pit in the center and piled some dry leaves and moss shavings in it. Once he had everything together, he got two sticks and wedged one inside of the branches of another. Hopefully this would work, he'd seen it in a survival television show.

James started rubbing the sticks together to create friction. A small tendril of smoke escaped, winding its way through the leaves as it rose. Heartened, James increased his speed until he created an ember. Gently, he blew on the ember until one of the dry branches caught. In the windless environment of the Greenhouse, James was soon sitting in front of a merrily crackling fire.

He set to roasting a nice bit of Star Mole meat on a stick, saving the steak for later. Normally, he was a medium-rare kind of guy, but he wasn't on Earth, and didn't want to chance food poisoning. So, he cooked himself a well-done cut of Star-Mole meat.

Star-Mole Meat (Cooked):

Rank: Common

A slightly burnt and poorly cut segment of a Star-Mole. Impressive, it's edible this time.

YOU HAVE GAINED 2 SKILL RANKS IN COOKING.

YOU ARE NOW SKILL RANK 4.

Two levels from one meal! James chuckled. It was probably because his first attempt at cooking was so bad. Or maybe because he was at such a low level that producing something edible was an achievement. Either way, James took a bite out of the meat. It tasted okay, but he wished it were juicier.

YOU HAVE EATEN STAR-MOLE MEAT (COOKED)

+ 20 health regenerated/hour for the next four hours

Belly full, James debated his next move. He could sit around the campfire for the rest of the night and try to stay awake, or he could wander around in the dark. Neither option particularly appealed to him. Sitting by the campfire would be boring, and the fire might attract more creatures.

A light breeze stirred, carrying a silvery powder around his campfire. Staring into the flames, James' eyelids felt heavy as a contented warmth filled his chest.

What more could I want? I'm in a beautiful forest with a full belly. What would be the harm in a brief nap?

His eyelids grew heavier by the second, his desire to sleep overwhelming his anxiety.

But something nagged at him.

James ignored the feeling, drifting deeper towards a comfortable sleep.

His eyes snapped open.

What was he doing? He was in the middle of a dungeon. He might *never* wake up if he wasn't careful.

YOU RESISTED THE STATUS EFFECT [SLEEP].

James jumped to his feet and drew his sword, looking around for whatever had caused the status effect. He strained his eyes, trying to pierce the darkness, but couldn't make out anything.

He wasn't sure what caused him to do what he did next. It could have been his sword training, or maybe his subconscious mind heard the barest whisper of wings in the darkness. One thing was certain—stepping to the side and raising his sword ended up saving his life.

A blade of wind sliced through the air directly towards him, impacting his sword and reflecting off into a nearby tree, cutting a deep gash into the wood.

James spun around, looking for the source of the attack. His eyes swept back and forth, falling on a patch of darkness.

Something shifted.

He stared, concentrating, trying to find form in the blackness when suddenly, an enormous moth appeared. Dappled spots of white on decorated its wings, reminding him of starlight leaking through the forest canopy.

MOONSHADOW MOTH (LEVEL 5)

The moth hovered, and a dim blue light cut with small streaks of white built up around its wings. Then, it beat its wings hard, sending another gust of razor-sharp wind at James. He parried it with his sword and followed with a lunge, trying to close the distance between himself and the moth—he needed to get inside its range. But the Moonshadow Moth flew towards the dense canopy overhead, the darkness seeming to reach out and envelop the moth. Before James could react, the it disappeared into the night.

Just like with the Star Moles. How annoying.

James realized that having a campfire had been a stupid move. He'd basically lit a beacon for anything living in the greenhouse. The campfire had acted as a signal flare to all the mobs in the area. *I'm here, come eat me!*

He got to work, scooping handfuls of dirt on top of the fire to extinguish it.

Darkness reclaimed the forest. James couldn't see a thing.

As his vision adjusted, basic shapes took form. At first everything was vague, blobbish. But as time wore on, the foliage slowly separated into distinct shapes. It was still dark, but the darkness was at least manageable.

YOU HAVE GAINED 1 SKILL RANK IN NIGHT VISION.

YOU ARE NOW SKILL RANK 7.

His Night Vision Skill gave everything a green tint, like a cheap pair of night-vision goggles back on Earth. He could see fairly well around the patches of moonlight, but the further he looked from the slivers of light, the worse his vision got.

James noticed a patch of darkness that pulsed and shimmered in the night air as he scanned the treetops. He drew his dagger and held it in his hand, feeling the weight in his palm. Holding it by the blade, James aimed at the suspicious patch and threw.

The dagger soared through the air beautifully.

Then landed with a solid *thunk* in a tree twenty feet to the left of his target.

YOU HAVE GAINED THE SKILL: KNIFE THROWING

Knife Throwing (Skill Rank 1):

+ 1% accuracy when throwing knives.

If what you did could be called knife throwing...

James barely had time to read the message before he had to dodge another blade of wind. He rolled out of the way and sprang up towards the cloud of darkness, which swooped towards him, taking the form of the Moonshadow Moth as it closed in. When it reached James, it hovered, beating its wings furiously, creating a heavy gust of wind that pushed him backwards. Again, its wings glowed a dim blue. The gale screamed in his ears, accompanied by the drone of hundreds of tiny wind blades.

But the moth was finally close enough to reach.

It was now or never.

James hunched his shoulders against the wind and pushed forward, ignoring the shallow cuts that formed on his body from the barrage of tiny, needle-like blades of wind.

His health bar flashed as James closed in on the moth and swung his sword at its abdomen. The glow around the moth's wings faded, traveling back up the body and into the moth's head. Briefly, the moth's eyes flashed a whitish blue. It fell from the air, landing on the ground with a soft *thud*. The howling gale that it had summoned faded away, leaving an ominous silence in its wake. James coughed, panting with exertion and covered with blood. His health bar hovered at 15% and flashed in warning. Before the moth could recover from being stunned, James stabbed down straight into the moth's head, killing it instantly.

You have killed a Moonshadow Moth (Level 5)

+ *13 experience points.*

Help the Helpless III: (3/3 Star Moles) (1/1 Moonshadow Moth).

You have completed the quest: Help the Helpless III

+ *21 experience.*

LEVEL UP! YOU ARE NOW LEVEL 5.

CONGRATULATIONS, YOU HAVE REACHED LEVEL 5 AND CAN NOW CHOOSE A CLASS FROM THE LIST OF AVAILABLE OPTIONS.

Maybe you won't be so useless now.

James read through his prompts as he retrieved his knife and sheathed it.

I leveled twice! And I can choose a class!

James quickly scanned the list of available classes.

ROGUE

You have started the path of the shadows. Rogues specialize in taking down stronger opponents while hidden.

WARRIOR

A straightforward fighter that focuses on melee combat.

EXPLORER

Dangerous wilds? Fiery Fields? Underwater Kingdoms? No land is too exotic for you. Explorers specialize in visiting new places and making their mark, all in search of epic loot!

After reading through the classes, James decided to close the list. He could make his choice later, after consulting with Nana. Instead, he reveled in his level up: He was sure he'd be leveling much slower without his ring decreasing experience he needed to reach new levels.

James spent the next few minutes debating where to put his stat points. He wanted to distribute them as evenly as possible per Nana's advice, but he couldn't see how Intelligence and Wisdom had helped him at all so far. But they were his only stats under ten, and maybe he'd stop making so many stupid decisions if he had more points in them, he wasn't sure exactly how that worked. He tried to raise his Charisma and Luck, but it looked like they couldn't be raised manually, so he gave up and placed two points in Intelligence and two points and Wisdom.

The cuts on his body slowly closed up over the next few hours while he tried to find the path out of the dungeon. It was fascinating how healing worked in this world. From his observations, he healed at a normal rate when it wasn't enhanced, but the Star Mole meat had multiplied his recovery time by twenty. As someone who had worked in the medical field before being pulled to Novis, this fascinated James.

In the morning, he waited for the smithy to open to turn in his quest. A few minutes later, Kyrwin left his house, which was next door to his forge.

He greeted James. "You have the ironweed?" He asked.

James handed over the plant.

You have completed the quest: Picking Plants

+ 11 experience.

LEVEL UP! YOU ARE NOW LEVEL 6.

I bet you're glad you have that ring now, huh?

James grinned. He was leveling way faster than he should be, but he wasn't going to complain. He placed two points each in Strength and Dexterity before waving goodbye to Kyrwin. "If that's all, I'm going to head over to talk to Nana," James said as he left the smith to his work and headed back up the forested path.

Chapter 11

Back at Nana's house, James sat at the kitchen table with a hot mug of tea. He'd just finished telling her about his training over the past month when a notification popped up.

You have completed the quest: Helping the Elderly II.

+ 5 experience.

Nana sat listening to him quietly and only spoke once he'd finished. "It sounds like you've learned a lot over the past month. But how are you feeling?"

James thought about it. He'd been too busy to really think about the fact that he'd been whisked away from his home and brought to Novis. If he were being honest with himself, he didn't want to think about it. So, James did what he always did when he had a lot of emotions. He pushed them down. "I guess I'm okay. Still confused about a lot of things, but I'm learning a lot about this world."

"That's good." Nana smiled kindly at him. "You can't expect to learn everything at once. Do you have any questions I can help answer?"

James nodded. He had a billion questions, but knew she wouldn't be able to answer everything he wanted to know.

A few questions weighed on him more than others. *What kind of lunatic has a dungeon for a garden? And why did your garden try to kill me?* He decided to play it safe.

"What class should I choose?"

"What options did you get?" Nana asked with a smile.

With a thought, James pulled up his list of available classes and read them out loud.

ROGUE

You have started the path of the shadows. Rogues specialize in taking down stronger opponents while hidden.

WARRIOR

A straightforward fighter that focuses on melee combat.

EXPLORER

Dangerous wilds? Fiery Fields? Underwater Kingdoms? No land is too exotic for you. Explorers specialize in visiting new places and making their mark, all in search of epic loot!

Nana listened to the options and nodded. "What class are you thinking?"

James tapped his chin. "Explorer sounds like a fun class. I'll probably be adventuring around a lot. But I also like the idea of a stealthy character. It'll help keep me alive."

"You make some good points, but I would suggest you choose the Warrior class."

James was surprised. "But the Explorer class looks amazing!"

Nana nodded. "I understand why you would think that, but it is a double-edged sword. When you choose your first class, you want to be as general as possible to give yourself room to grow. If you choose the Explorer class or even the Rogue class, you're boxing yourself into a specific build. You want to choose a general first class and let yourself develop naturally."

That made sense to James. If he chose something like the Rogue class, then he'd have to be stealthy for the rest of his life. If he was fighting a Warrior head-on, he would always lose. "So how do classes work?" James asked.

Nana Rasner stirred her tea for a silent moment before she spoke. "I guess I'll start from the beginning: From the time they are born until they reach the age of fifteen, children don't level. On the day of their fifteenth year, then they can gain experience. Once they gain their first experience point, they level up to two and can start assigning points. When they reach level five, they can take a Basic class. That is what you are about to do."

"Okay. But then what?"

"The next class upgrades come at level twenty-five, when you can choose your Journeyman class, level fifty when you can choose your Advanced class, level 100 when you can choose your Master class, level 250 when you can choose your Grandmaster class, level 500 when you can choose your Sage class, and level 1000 when you can choose your Divine class. Once a person reaches the Sage levels, they must choose a unique, never before chosen path. There are under a hundred sages currently in existence, and less than ten known Divines."

"Are the Divines the Gods?" James asked. "Is one of them the one who branded me?"

Nana laughed. "A good guess, but no. Divines are equal in power to the Gods, but they were born mortal." She tapped her chin. Some are worshipped as gods, but most prefer to work on their own goals that mortals like us can't comprehend. But enough about them. The chances that you encounter any of them in your lifetime is laughably small." She stopped short. "I guess not as much for you," she muttered, more to herself than to him. Looking up, she shook her head. "I don't know what Sytar wants with you, but if you ever see a Divine, run."

James nodded in somber agreement. "I'm not looking to die anytime soon."

"That's good." Nana smiled at him. "Anyway!" She clapped. "Back to classes. You get to choose your specializations at—"

"What's a specialization?" James interrupted.

Nana glared at him. "I was getting to that. A specialization is another way to customize each class, adding your own unique flare. For example, if you are a Warrior and only fight with swords, then you can choose the Swordsman specialization to change your Warrior abilities so that they apply to swords only."

"Why would I want to do that?"

"The more specialized the Ability, the more powerful it is. It is a way of increasing your power without boxing your progression. Your choice in specialization doesn't affect your future class choices."

"So, when can I specialize?"

"As I was saying." Nana stared at James, daring him to interrupt. "You specialize at levels ten, forty, seventy-five and level 200. Once you reach Grandmaster, you start to develop your own unique path which will lead to Sagedom." Seeing the lost look on James' face, Nana tried again. "Let me explain with an example. I started at level five with the Planter class, a class specialized in growing things. Then at level ten I specialized in herbs, making my abilities more powerful when I grew herbs. Then at level twenty-five I chose the herbalist class. After that... well, that's too much to talk about. Do you understand?"

James nodded. "I think so. Thank you for explaining." He was glad to have Nana around. Choosing a class sounded incredibly complex, and he appreciated the guidance. He thought about what else to ask and remembered the herbs he'd picked. "Do you have any Herbology books?" He asked. He'd been interested in how medications worked on Earth and thought it would be cool to review a basic Herbology book to see how things worked in Novis.

Nana Rasner got up and quickly rifled through her shelves while giving James a stern look. "If you ruin this book, I will tan your hide and use your skin to bind a new one."

James gulped an agreement and carefully accepted the proffered book. "This will give you a description of some common potion ingredients, and a few basic recipes. It's a good place to start."

Potion Making for Dummies:

Rank: Common

This manual has some basic pictures and descriptions of
    useful plants and a few introductory potions.

After handing James the book, Nana looked at him grimly. "We need to talk about your Brand."

Well, that was ominous.

James was about to ask her what she meant, when a loud knock on the door interrupted them. James jumped in his seat, nearly tumbling to the ground.

Ferko entered the house and grinned when he saw James. "Are you ready to go?" Ferko asked him.

James glanced at Nana Rasner questioningly. She looked back at him innocently and turned to Ferko. "He's ready. Can you explain it to him while I go grab the charms?" She got up and left the room. James let out a heavy yawn. His sleepless night was starting to catch up with him.

Ferko turned to James and explained. "My farm has been plagued by a group of Rabbans lately. Normally I can deal with them on my own, but something is different about these, and I needed Nana's help to deal with them. She was making me a few charms to undo whatever curse is affecting them. She suggested I have you place the charms."

YOU HAVE BEEN GIVEN A QUEST: RABID RABBAN I

Rabid Rabban I: Take care of the Rabbans plaguing Ferko's gardens.

Suggested level: 5-10

Reward: Unknown

Penalty for failure or refusal: Unknown

James wasn't sure how he felt about being voluntold to go with Ferko, but he supposed it would be a good experience.

As he waited for Nana, he chose his class, following her advice.

YOU HAVE CHOSEN THE CLASS: WARRIOR.

New Level-up bonus:

+ 4 Free Stat Points

+ 1 Endurance

+1 Ability point

> You have unlocked the class tree! You have one unused Ability point. Would you like to spend it?

James selected 'Yes' and his vision was overlaid with a skill tree. The tree was divided into Tier I, Tier II, and Tier III Abilities, but only the Tier I Abilities were visible. The only way to see the higher tier Abilities was to unlock the previous abilities that led to it.

WARRIOR I

Increased Damage (0/10):

The strength of your body flows through your weapon, increasing your damage.

WARRIOR I

Immovable Object (0/5):

Your iron will flows through your armor, bolstering its defense.

WARRIOR I

Raging Bull (0/3):

+Requires Shield

Charge forward like a raging bull, pushing enemies aside.

He also had the Ability that he'd gained when he appeared in the cave; Death's Stare, but for some reason he couldn't put any points into the Ability. When he tried, a notification let him know that he lacked the requirements to increase it.

Disappointed but not surprised, James thought about it for a second before assigning his point to the Increased Damage ability. He would have preferred the Raging Bull ability, but he didn't have a shield and wasn't sure when he would get one.

YOU HAVE GAINED THE ABILITY: INCREASED DAMAGE (WARRIOR I)

Increased Damage (1/10):

+ 10% damage to all weapons

The strength of your body flows through your weapon, increasing your damage.

As soon as he made his selection, two Tier II Abilities appeared, attached to the Increased Damage node.

WARRIOR II

Split Weapon (0/10):

*Requires Increased Damage 5

Your weapons have a chance to shatter your opponent's weapons

---

WARRIOR II

114

Sharper Tools (0/5):

+*Requires Increased Damage 3*

In the hands of a master, even iron can cut through diamond.

James briefly wondered what "tiers" meant in the Sharper Tools ability, but after thinking about it for a bit realized that it was probably talking about different material strengths. He wasn't sure what the tiers of material were, but remembering how his iron dagger had barely scratched the spider carapace in the cave, he knew he needed the Sharper Tools ability.

James closed his windows and browsed through his new book while he waited for Nana to return. She came back a few minutes later carrying a stack of parchment slips. She handed the stack to James, and he examined them. Each was about four inches long and an inch wide, with arcane symbols scribbled across them, glowing a soft golden white.

Charm of Cursebreaking (x50):

Rank: Rare

A charm infused with life magic that has been primed to break curses.

As she handed them to him, Nana gave James instructions. "You must place the charms around the edges of his garden. Makes sure to place them no more than 100 feet apart. They will emit an aura that removes the curse of any Rabban that enters the area of effect."

Ferko thanked her and told James to meet him at the front gate of the village in the morning, then headed out.

Once he left, James looked at Nana. "Thank you for helping me," he said sincerely. "I don't know where I'd be if you hadn't decided to help me as much as you have."

She smiled. "Of course. Now get some rest, you have a lot to do tomorrow."

James took the hint and left, heading back to the inn to spend the rest of the afternoon relaxing, his first day off in a while. This world was strange, terrifying at times, but he couldn't get over the wonder of living in a world filled with magic.

Chapter 12

James met with Ferko at his cart in front of the city gates the next morning. He waved at Lamia as they pulled away and headed down the road to Ferko's farm, bumping over small potholes in the road as they transitioned from the nice cobbles of the village to the rougher dirt of the path. They wound along the river toward the Crimson Mountains, painting the horizon ahead.

They spent the rest of the morning chatting companionably as James enjoyed his first full free day in a while. Ferko told James about his family. It was hard for him and his wife because their son had recently left for Fallmire to undergo his initiation. Experience could only be gained once a person turned 15-years old. When people turned 14, they underwent a ceremony called initiation, where they were brought to the capital for two years of mandatory military service. Without his son, Ferko and his wife had to do all the farm work themselves. Their daughter wasn't old enough to help out yet.

"Hang on a second." James hopped off the cart to inspect an interesting patch of flowers on the riverbank.

> Dragon Ditch Weed:
>
> Rank: Common
>
> Come on... We both know that you know what it's used for.

Ignoring the item description, James compared the plant to its picture in his book. Both plants had pastel purple petals and a slight red tint to their leaves.

Dragon Ditch Weed:

A more common and less effective version of the plant Dragon Weed, Dragon Ditch Weed is a necessary component in both the Potion of Thirst, and the Drought of Dizziness.

Continued on next page...

James chuckled at the item description and slipped a few flowers into his pouch, when he felt an uneasy shiver run down his spine. He glanced nervously at the foggy forest across the river.

He'd heard stories about the Witchwood in town, which was rumored to have led to the death of many overconfident adventurers who tried to brave its secrets.

The Witchwood was actually one reason that Riverside, a border town, was garrisoned so heavily. The Goblin clans living in the forests constantly launched attacks on the town in an attempt to expand their territory.

James didn't know much about Goblins, other than what he'd heard from people in Riverside. But from what he understood, they didn't have a cohesive government. Rather, they followed a hierarchical society where the strongest Goblins would create and lead different clans, the largest of which was the Shrieker clan.

A particularly heavy bump brought James back to the present. They were at a farmhouse in the center of an expansive field filled with cinderstalks poking their leafy heads out of the ground.

A young girl of five or six ran out of the farmhouse as if shot from a cannon. "Daddy!" she cried out in excitement, wrapping Ferko's legs in a hug.

"Look how big you are!" Ferko responded as he scooped her up and started walking to the house. James waited for a second, unsure what to do, before following.

A plump, motherly woman holding a spatula greeted Ferko with a peck on the cheek before introducing herself to James.

NAME: MARY LASSEN

RACE: HUMAN

LEVEL: 29

CLASS: FARMER

James smiled and introduced himself. "I'm James. You have a lovely home."

"Aww, well thank you, honey." She turned to her husband. "You brought home a polite one this time."

Ferko smiled. "Let's grab some dinner to warm our bellies before you get to work." James agreed easily. He wasn't going to argue with a nice warm meal.

He sat down at the table while Mary served up a savory pie filled with meat, vegetables, and cinderstalk bits. While they were eating, James made polite conversation, talking about what life was like on the farm and how he'd met Ferko.

On James' first bite of pie, he felt relief in his travel-weary bones, and all the built-up tension in his body relaxed. An energy built up, but not the nervous energy from drinking too much coffee. Rather, this was more the type of energy you get during the peak of an intense workout. He could almost feel his muscles tightening, his lungs strengthening, his mind quickening.

A small icon popped up into the corner of his vision, and he focused on it.

You have eaten Mary's Cinderstalk Pie

24:00:00 duration

+ 5 *Strength*

+ 5 *Constitution*

+ 5 *Endurance*

+ 5 *Wisdom*

+ 5 *Dexterity*

+ 5 *Intelligence*

For someone of James' level that was an insanely powerful buff, and he smiled gratefully at Mary. Curiously, he asked her how she got her name on the prompt.

"I won the cooking competition in the fair at Carden last year, and the prize was that the system accepted my recipe as an official recipe," she said with pride. Mary went to the other room and returned with a small index card, which she handed to James.

Mary's Cinderstalk Pie:

Rank: Common

This recipe teaches you how to make Mary's Cinderstalk Pie.

YOU HAVE FOUND A RECIPE. WOULD YOU LIKE TO LEARN THE RECIPE?

James tried to hand the card back to her, but she shook her head. "It's yours. I have a whole box full of them. Consider it thanks for helping us out."

"In that case, thank you," James responded, mentally accepting the prompt to learn the recipe.

YOU CANNOT LEARN THIS RECIPE: MARY'S CINDERSTALK PIE.

Your skill in cooking is too low to learn an Advanced level recipe.

James sighed in disappointment and slipped the card into his pouch. He'd use it when his cooking level improved enough.

After dinner, she showed him to a room upstairs and set him up for bed.

The next morning after a delicious breakfast of eggs and sausage, Ferko approached James. "So, ready to do this?"

James nodded. The buff from Mary's Pie was still going strong, and James felt confident.

"Good. Head around the border of the farm and place one of those charms down every hundred feet." James removed the stack of parchment from his pouch. "It shouldn't be too hard, but call out to me if you need me."

"That's it?" James asked.

"Yep. Watch out for the Rabban though. They normally don't come out during the day, but they've been acting strange recently."

Ferko's farm was massive. Neat rows of green poked out of the earth as far as the eye could see. It wasn't all cinderstalks. There were tons of other plants that James had no name for scattered all over the farm in organized chaos. James couldn't help his amazement at the power of a high-level Farmer. He wondered what he would be able to do once he got his second or third class.

A warm breeze blew across the farm, rustling the tops of the vegetables and carrying the scent of nature to James' nose. But there was something else—an energy to the air. It smelled like adventure.

James suspected he was feeling the high ambient Mana levels of the Fertile Expanse. Ferko's farm perched on the edge of the expanse, but the Mana levels were still significantly higher than they were in Riverwood.

It was one of the reasons that the plants and animals in this area were so large and powerful, and according to Ferko was the reason he'd chosen this land. It wasn't deep enough in the Fertile Expanse that the farm was in danger from high-level enemies, but the ambient Mana *did* have a heavy effect on the vegetation.

The edge of the farm was easy to discern. There was a stark contrast between the organization of the farmland and the chaotic overgrowth of the land surrounding it.

Over the next few hours, James walked around the border of the farm, placing the charms on the ground as he went. Each time he placed one, it sank into the soil and a golden bubble expanded outward. All James had to do was walk until he found the edge of the previous bubble, walk a little longer, and repeat the process. It was slow, methodical work, mostly because of the massive size of the farm, but James enjoyed it.

About half an hour into his work, a rustling noise in the foliage interrupted him. He froze and strained his eyes, staring into the darkness for a glimpse of whatever was there. The rustling got closer until James could just barely make out a pair of long, fuzzy grey ears poking out of a nearby bush. He crept towards the ears, trying to make out the full creature.

YOU HAVE GAINED 1 SKILL RANK IN STEALTH.

YOU ARE NOW SKILL RANK 5.

With his bonus from the Cinderstalk Pie, the equivalent of over seven additional levels of stats, James was finding it much easier to sneak up on his prey. Once the creature's full face was in view, he could see its information.

RABBAN (LEVEL 13)

The Rabban was adorable. Weird, how what was in essence an enormous rabbit could be causing so much trouble. An enormous, cuddly, fluffy rabbit. If James had been paying attention, he might have wondered how such a cuddly prey animal could have reached level thirteen. Instead, he wondered if he could pet the Rabban.

James approached the Rabban, taking extra care to remain sneaky, but unfortunately, a life in the city didn't exactly lend itself to a high level of skill in sneaking through the woods. Life as a prey animal had, however, lent itself to excellent reflexes on the Rabban's part.

Before James had even taken ten steps, he stepped on a branch. Immediately the Rabban's ears perked up, and its head swiveled to stare directly at James, who had frozen in place in an attempt to hide in plain sight. Needless to say, it didn't work.

Slowly, James backed away from the fluffy beast, maintaining eye contact. He may have been a city boy, but he had seen enough nature documentaries that he had an inkling of what to do when facing a wild animal.

YOU HAVE GAINED THE SKILL: SIXTH SENSE

Sixth Sense (Skill Rank 1):

You don't know how you know. You just know. Keep listening to that feeling! It is said that Masters of the Sixth Sense can predict an enemy attack before their enemy has decided on it.

The Rabban interrupted James' reading as a crimson glow filled with pinpricks of black light surrounded it, temporarily obscuring it from sight. It blew outwards from the Rabban in a wave of force that pushed James back a few steps. The light faded away and James rubbed his eyes, trying to clear the bright spots from his vision.

When his vision cleared, the Rabban still stood in the same spot, only now it was in the center of a small crater of upturned earth and decayed vegetation. The creature was *transforming*. Bones splintered as the creature grew and reformed, its flesh melting and molding to the creature's new skeleton.

TWISTED RABBAN (LEVEL 13)

Malevolent eyes stared back at James, maddened by pain. The cute bunny was no more, replaced by a chest-height, broad-shouldered creature with a malformed mouth crammed with teeth that jutted in all directions. James eyed its two enormous white tusks nervously as he stepped back and drew his sword. The Rabban took a few steps forward but yelped in pain as its foot overlapped the golden dome created by the Charm of Cursebreaking.

It took another step towards James, golden sparks flashing off its body as the Charm of Cursebreaking attempted to either repel the creature or reverse the curse. But aside from the light show, the charm did nothing to stop the advancing creature.

It charged at him with a roar. James took a calming breath and sidestepped, swinging his sword and cutting deep into the Rabban's flank.

The beast screamed in rage, spinning around to face James, who was feeling much more confident after the successful strike. *Time to have a little fun.*

James mimed waving a cape, like a matador taunting a bull. With a screech of rage, the Rabban charged at him again.

Again, James stepped to the side, attempting another cut to the Rabban's flank. This time, the monster was expecting it and tossed its head to one side, driving a tusk deep into James' thigh. A red-hot pain lanced across his side, driving away all thought. He'd gotten overconfident, and he'd paid for it.

For the past month, James hadn't been sure how to feel about being brought into this world. Sure, he missed his life back on Earth. He missed his family.

But Novis was full of wonder. It was the land of magic he'd always dreamed about. For the past month, he'd floated through a dream. But the pain along his side hit like a bucket of ice water, the rudest of awakenings reminding him that the dangers of this place were all too real.

James stumbled back, clutching his wound as the Rabban pawed at the ground, preparing for another charge. He looked around for a place to dodge, but there was nowhere to go. He was trapped, the tree against his back blocking him from any evasive maneuvers. Not that he really had any in the first place.

As the Rabban charged, James braced himself and leapt, grabbing a branch a couple feet above his head. The Rabban crashed into the tree directly below him, the reverberation almost causing James to lose his grip. He hung there in silence, fresh blood flowing from his side and down his leg, where it dripped onto the Rabban's head.

The Rabban was clearly stunned from the impact. When it recovered, it would most likely be able to jump high enough to reach him. It was basically a rabbit, after all. Even if it couldn't, James wasn't sure how long he could hang from the branch, especially at the rate he was losing blood. He was already starting to feel lightheaded.

As he saw it, there was one option—attack the Rabban before it recovered. James shifted his grip on his sword, so it pointed towards the ground. Taking a deep breath, he let go of the tree and wrapped his other hand around the handle over the first.

James fell straight down, his sword severing the beast's spine, piercing through its body and into the dirt below. The Rabban had seen better days. James, on the other hand, was perfectly fine—he'd landed in a nice soft carpet of fur.

Well, mostly fine. Groaning, he pulled his shirt off and used it to bandage his side, tying it tight enough to hold pressure on the wound and hopefully staunch the bleeding until his health regenerated.

YOU HAVE GAINED THE SKILL: MEDICINE

Medicine (Skill Rank 1):

Not all healing requires magic, but it helps.

The corpse withered before his eyes, something he hadn't seen from any of the other creatures he'd killed. There was a soft *thud* as something hit the ground next to the shriveled corpse.

You have killed a Rabban (Level 13)

+ *2 experience points*

Well, that's disappointing. James wondered why he hadn't gotten much experience from the Rabban, when it was so powerful and high leveled.

The corpse was withered and dry, but James was pretty sure Nana would be interested in it, and as it had shriveled to the size of an actual rabbit, he stuffed it into his pouch to show her later.

He rooted around the ground, looking for whatever the creature had dropped, and found a black crystal hiding in a clump of grass.

The crystal emanated such a strong malevolence that James almost dropped it. It swirled with the same crimson and black light that had surrounded the Rabban when it had transformed.

Cursed Soul Gem:

Rank: Rare

A black gem crafted for an unknown purpose. You can feel the evil energies swirling inside.

Shuddering, James tossed the crystal into his pouch to show Nana.

Help the Helpless III: (37/50 charms placed) (1/1 Rabban Corpse)

James made it back to the farmhouse before collapsing from the blood loss. The last thing he remembered was Mary and Ferko lifting him up and placing him on a cloud.

The next morning, James woke up with his leathers folded at the foot of his bed and a bandage wrapped around his side. He sat up and stretched, testing his range of motion. Everything felt great, and he'd healed up nicely.

He unwrapped the bandage and saw unmarked flesh. Mary must have given him a potion or something.

James removed the bandage and got dressed, then headed downstairs. Ferko and Mary were glad that he was okay. He spent the rest of an uneventful day placing charms with the farmer, and they left for Riverside as the sun was setting behind the blood-red mountains to their backs.

Chapter 13

They arrived with the moon high overhead and made a beeline for Bartram's inn. The revelry of villagers relaxing after a long day's work filtered out of the swinging doors as they pulled up in the cart. Ferko unhitched the horse creatures—James still didn't know what they were called—and brought them to the stables.

The slow melody of a harp drifting out from under the door. "Good night to stay at the inn," Ferko commented as he returned. "Sounds like they have a bard." James hadn't heard music in forever. Although he'd never been particularly into music back on Earth, he still missed it.

Bartram greeted them when they walked through the door with his ever-present smile. "James! Ferko! Welcome, welcome. Can I interest you in some dinner?"

Ferko nodded. "That would be great, Bartram. Two rooms for the night, too. And two stables for my mounts." He handed Bartram some coins and smiled at James. "Consider dinner and the room part of your payment for completing the job."

Bartam chuckled. "James never needs to pay to stay here. Not after all the work he put in for me."

"Thanks Bartram. Good to hear. Let me know when I can taste some of it! I'm saving the stuff you gave me until it ages more."

"Let me see if I have a bit in the back.'"""""" He grinned and turned to go to the back room of the bar. "Find yourselves a table while I'm looking."

James thanked him and they waded through the crowded bar until they found a small table shoved into the corner, near a table of drunken guardsmen swapping stories.

If James had to guess, the first guard was in the middle of a raucous retelling of the last dungeon he'd been in. "So anyway, we walk through the door to the boss room and there's a baby dragon—"

"It wasn't a dragon," another guard interrupted. "It was a big lizard."

"It was a dragon," the first guard insisted.

"Was not."

"So anyway, the *dragon* turned to me and inhales. I think I'm toast, but—"

"Lizard. Not a dragon. I don't even think it was a dungeon monster. Yer story is a load of dung, and you know it. You've never seen a dragon, let alone fought one."

The first guard's tone turned dangerous. "I don't need to stand here and take these insults." The loud scraping of a chair silenced the chattering inn as the guard stood up and angrily slammed his fist down on the table. He made as if to push the other guard, but tripped over his chair and went crashing to the ground.

Bartram was there in an instant. "If you can't hold your liquor, then get out," he said angrily, grabbing the offender by his collar and tossing him out the door before coming back to glare at the other four guards at the table. "Anyone else wants to be kicked out?"

The rest of the guards took a keen interest in the contents of their drinks, which Bartram seemed to take as acceptance. He winked at James and disappeared, returning a moment later with a bottle of amber liquid and two glasses. "I couldn't find any fully fermented Bleufruit Cider, but here's something I've been working on."

James took a large sip of ale and coughed as the drink passed his throat. It tasted like cinnamon with a hint of pepper, but it went down smoothly after the initial shock.

> *YOU HAVE DRUNK CRIMSON MOUNTAIN SPECIAL ALE*
>
> 01:40:00 duration
>
> + 5 *Strength (-1 every 20 minutes)*
>
> - 10 *Intelligence (+1 every 10 minutes)*

The front doors opened, and a strange silence fell over the inn. A cloaked figure stepped into the bar, carrying with him a cool breeze that sent the dying firelight into a frenzy. That was odd; James hadn't remembered it being cold out. The day had been rather warm.

The cloaked figure stepped forward, his footsteps cutting sharply through the silence. He walked towards the hearth where the bard was hurriedly packing his equipment. Every eye in the room was on the stranger as he took the stage, tossing his hood back dramatically.

The stranger was almost handsome, if not for a scar that ran from his earlobe to the corner of his mouth, setting his face in a permanent grimace. He had golden hair and deep blue eyes that glowed softly as they raked over the crowd. They fell on James and stopped for a second before finishing their circuit.

> *NAME: ???*
>
> *RACE: ???*

When he was sure that he had everyone's attention, the stranger spoke with a rich, velvety voice. The kind of voice you wanted to hear read you a story. As he spoke, the firelight responded, brightening until the figure was a shadow framed by firelight. The air in the inn stirred as if from a gentle breeze.

The tale of a man who lost his sight

Stained with blood from an endless fight

Caught by the Fae

He lost his way

And now he rules in the night

Prince of thieves and lord of lies

Better watch out for his endless eyes

Magic of old

No hero too bold

To stop him before he can rise

The death of a brother

Replaced by another

All he can do is despise

The stranger's words reverberated through the air after he finished speaking, nobody daring to say a word. Silently, he pulled his hood back up and walked out the way he'd come. Beside James, Ferko gasped. It was as if the entire bar had been under a spell.

YOU HAVE RECEIVED A DIVINE MESSAGE.

YOU HAVE BEEN GIVEN A BRAND: DIVINE QUEST (MINOR).

+ 3 *Strength*

+ 3 *Endurance*

+ 3 *Willpower*

+ 3 *Constitution*

+ 3 *Intelligence*

+ 3 *Dexterity*

+ 1 *Charisma*

+ 1 *Luck*

+ 1 *Resilience*

Given to all who hear the warning. Good luck.

James clawed at his chest as the intense pain of the magical branding sent waves of heat through his body. He could almost smell the burned flesh, although he may have been imagining it. Again, as quickly as the pain started, it was gone. He looked around and saw that everyone in the inn wore the same pained expression.

James peeked under his leather shirt and saw the symbol of a sun branded directly over his heart. He took a moment to process what had happened, and his jaw dropped. He'd just received a level's worth of stat points in each category. Everyone in the inn had, too.

But why did everyone look so freaked out? What the hell had just happened?

The blinking notification symbol in the corner of his vision alerted him he still had a few notifications to check, so he focused on them.

YOU HAVE UNLOCKED A HIDDEN STAT: RESILIENCE.

Resilience describes your ability to resist all forms of damage and altering effects.

WORLD QUEST — CALAMITY

Calamity: An event with the potential to destroy hundreds of thousands of lives approaches. Help prevent it.

Suggested level: Any

Reward: Based on contribution

James had never been good at interpreting cryptic messages from the gods when he played games or read books. He usually understood the prophecy or riddle towards the end of the book, right around when the author explained it directly. But from the looks on the faces of the people in the room, this was bad news...

James made his way to Bartram. "What just happened?"

Bartram stared, pale faced, at the empty hearth. "That was..." he said, then trailed away in shock. "I never thought... not in my lifetime..."

James stared at Bartram. The man was terrified.

Bartram nervously scrubbed his hands on his apron. "That… That was the Makrien."

"The Makrien?"

"Nobody knows who he is, or where he comes from," Bartram explained. "Legends claim he wanders from hearth to hearth, warning people before a major disaster. Why he does it is a mystery. Maybe to warn people to evacuate, maybe because somebody around could stop it. I don't know. All I know is that the last time he appeared was almost four-hundred years ago, before the War of the Crimson Peaks."

James opened his mouth to ask another question, but the innkeeper just shook his head. "I need to pack," he said, quickly walking away without another word. James turned to look for Ferko, but the farmer was gone. So was the rest of the inn. James was alone.

I need to talk to Nana. Now.

Fragment of Divinity

Chapter 14

James was panting when he arrived at Nana's house, having sprinted the whole way. Ignoring the darkened windows and silent house, James pounded on the door so loudly that he was worried he might wake the smith who lived a half-mile away.

After a full minute of pounding, Nana still hadn't answered. James peered through a window.

Nothing.

Suddenly, a hand grabbed his shoulder, almost causing him to jump out of his skin. Nana's eyes were baggy, and her hair was disheveled, her usually calm demeanor replaced with a worried energy.

"We need to get inside, now," she said, dragging James through the door and into the main room of her shack. She sat him down at the table and stood in front of him, tapping her hand nervously against her thigh. "What exactly did it say?"

"What's going on?" James asked, concerned by the change in her behavior. "Are you talking about the Makr-"

"Don't speak its name in my house. The last thing I need is the kind of luck that comes from mentioning such creatures. Now please, what did it say?"

James decided not to press his luck. Nana hadn't steered him wrong yet— he trusted her to tell him more later when she was ready to tell him. So, he repeated the prophecy, word for word. She scribbled it down in a small notebook.

James tried his questions again. "What is… it? Why is everyone so worked up? The way Bartram explained it, a disaster is coming, but is it coming immediately?"

Nana signed, holding her face in her hands. "You don't understand. Of course, you wouldn't understand. You're a stranger." She raised her head and looked directly into James' eyes, bright yellow energy swirling around her irises. "You need to understand what it means to us. It is an omen. That creature has appeared approximately one year before the start of every major disaster in recorded history. Every time it appears, it follows the same pattern, traveling the world and spreading news."

"But why? And why does he spread the news in such a vague way? Couldn't it just say what the disaster is? Also, if the disaster is a year away, why did everyone bolt?"

When James paused for breath, Nana tried to answer his questions. "Nobody knows why or how it knows or why it spreads the news the way it does. Some people believe that it is to stop the disaster, but he has never averted one before."

Before she could continue answering his questions, James pulled down his shirt and revealed his new Brand. "And what is this? Why did everyone get these?"

"Again. Nobody knows." Nana snapped, annoyed now. "I don't have time for these questions. His sudden appearance isn't a coincidence."

"What do you mean?"

"I mean that, somehow, *you* are involved in this."

James couldn't comprehend why he'd be involved in something on a scale this massive. "Me? But I'm a level six nobody." He looked at her worried face. "Besides, I wouldn't do anything that could harm so many people."

"I know that," she reassured him. "Not intentionally, at least. But we need to figure out what your connection to this is. It will take some time." She took a deep breath and calmed down slightly. "We have time. For now, I need to research this, and you need to get stronger."

> YOU HAVE BEEN GIVEN A QUEST: GAINING POWER I
>
> Gaining Power I: Reach level 25 and upgrade your class
>
> Suggested level: Under 25
>
> Reward: Unknown
>
> Penalty for failure or refusal: Unknown

Nana Rasner walked to the sink and filled a bowl with water, then set the bowl in front of James. She removed a small vial of liquid from her robes and held it up to the light, producing a rainbow of unique shades and hues. "What is that?" He asked in wonder.

"This," Nana said, "is Mana Primer."

"It's beautiful," James remarked as Nana took a tiny dropper out from another pocket and very carefully added a single drop to the bowl of water. "What's it for?"

"It's for you." She stirred the bowl with the dropper and pushed it in front of James.

"Do I drink it?" he asked.

"If you want to overload and burn out all your Mana channels, then sure."

James pushed his chair back a few inches. "What do I do with it?"

"Place a finger inside the bowl and remove it." James followed her instructions. "Next, place your wet finger on this paper." James did, and the droplet of water soaked into the paper, but it wasn't rainbow anymore.

It was jet black.

"Whoa! What just happened?"

"Mana Primer is created by injecting a tiny amount of every type of Mana into Mana Water. The water absorbs the Mana but, since each type is represented equally, no one type of Mana can overwhelm any other type, which leads to the beautiful mix you saw. Then I diluted a slight amount of the Mana Primer into water. When you dipped your finger into the water, your primary Mana type tipped the scales enough that, when you placed a droplet onto the Mana Expression Sheet, it took the form of your Mana type." She took a breath. "Does that make sense?"

"I guess? What's a Mana type?"

Nana sighed again. "To explain what a Mana type is, first I have to explain what a Spell is. A Spell is simply a manipulation of Mana to accomplish a task. There are two ways to learn Spells, with a Spell book or through class Abilities. You with me?"

James nodded, and she continued. "Your Mana type changes how a Spell accomplishes that task. For example, if you were to read a Fireball Spell book, but you had a water affinity, then you would learn the fireball spell, but when you tried to cast it, it would come out as a ball of water and probably wouldn't be nearly as powerful as a water Spell could have been."

"Wait, so the spell would still be called Fireball? But it would shoot water?"

"In most cases. Unless someone has exceptionally dense mana, in which case the spell could actually change to reflect the new magic type. But that's very rare."

"So, what is my Mana type?"

"Your Mana type is Shadow," she said, smiling. "It's a Tier II mana, which is very powerful."

James was reaching levels of confusion he hadn't experienced since high school. "What are Mana tiers?"

"Mana types are divided into are five overarching categories of magic— Tier I, Tier II, Tier III, Divine, and Vile. The first three are simple, with Tier I as the weakest and Tier III as the strongest. The last two, Divine and Vile, are different. Both are much stronger than the Tiered magic and are only inherent to the Fae, the Fallen, and to a lesser extent, dragons."

Nana's lecture on magic tiers made sense to James so far, but he still had more questions. "So, my Mana is darkness, a Tier II Mana type? Can I see a list of the rest of the Mana types?"

"Sure," Nana said, pulling a small chunk of chalk from inside her robes. She drew a constellation chart, with clusters of magic types surrounding each race. "Here's a very basic overview of the distinct Mana types."

James looked at the chart. He focused on the cluster of magic around the Human section. He noticed something odd. It looked like every race except for Humans only had two or three connections. Humans had eight. "Why is there so much variety to Human magical talent?"

"Interesting question." Nana glanced at the chart. "But there's one other discrepancy you missed. Look and see if you can figure it out."

James couldn't see any other pattern in the Mana Tiers.

"It has something to do with… no, maybe…" Then, it was as if a switch clicked in his brain. "It's opposites!" He exclaimed.

"Right!" Nana replied. She tapped the Human node with her chalk. "If you look at the Human node, you can see that Humans can be born with Life, Death, Darkness, Light, Fire, Water, Earth, or Air affinities. Four pairs of opposites. Other races can only learn synergistic magic types." She tapped the

Elven node with her chalk. "Take the Elves, for example. They have a powerful connection to Life, Nature, and Water affinities, but that's it."

"So, there would never be an Elf born with another type of affinity?" James asked.

Nana shrugged. "It's rare, but it happens. Those children are usually left alone, unless they're unlucky enough to have a completely opposite affinity, like death, in which case..." She shook her head. "I wouldn't worry about it."

James nodded, too distracted by thoughts of magic to understand the meaning behind her words. "What exactly can I do with a Darkness affinity? Can I cast spells?"

Nana chuckled at his eagerness. "I have a Dark magic spell book that you can have. I'll go get it." She retreated to a back room and returned a short while later holding a book bound with black-scaled leather. The book absorbed light, forming a black nimbus around it, and when she handed it to him, he felt a chill, as if the air enveloping the book was slightly cooler than the rest of the house.

There was a symbol pressed into the cover, a series of symmetrical curvy lines that spiraled into the center. It was like looking into a void. "What's this mean?" He asked, pointing at the symbol.

"Oh, that's just the symbol for Darkness. Don't worry about that."

James nodded and examined the prompt that had appeared when he took the book from Nana.

Shadow Step:

Rank: Rare

Durability: 100/100

> This book will teach you the spell Shadow Step, a basic teleportation spell for Shadow casters.

WOULD YOU LIKE TO LEARN THE SPELL: SHADOW STEP?

James stared at the book, emotions roiling in his stomach.

My first spell! Yes, I'd love to learn it!

The book dissolved to ashes in his hand, producing a cool breeze and a whiff of burnt paper.

Nana's mouth twitched with annoyance as she watched the ashes blow around her shack and get everywhere. She smacked James in the back of the head. "Do that outside next time. I just swept."

YOU HAVE GAINED THE SPELL: SHADOW STEP

Shadow Step (Level 1):

Teleports the caster to a nearby shadow.

Range: 5 Meters

Cast time: Instant

Cooldown: None

Cost: 55 Mana

"This is amazing! Thank you!" Before she could react, James gave Nana a hug and turned to run outside and practice.

"Wait!" Nana called after him just as he reached the door.

James stopped, slowly turning. "What's up?"

"We have more to discuss. What did you find out at Ferko's farm?"

"Oh, right!" James had forgotten about that. He pulled the shriveled Rabban corpse and crystal out of the bag and handed them to Nana. Luckily it seemed like things didn't rot inside of his pouch, and the Rabban corpse was just as fresh as it had been when he killed it. He wasn't sure what he would have done if the rabbit had rotted inside his pouch.

Can you even clean an extra-dimensional pocket?

"I found this strange crystal next to the Rabban after I killed it. I'm not sure what it is, but it feels awful."

You have completed the quest: Rabid Rabban I

+ 9 experience

LEVEL UP! YOU ARE NOW LEVEL 7.

While Nana looked over the dead Rabban and the crystal, James debated where to put his points. He definitely needed to put points into Intelligence and Wisdom now that he could cast spells, so he put two points in each. His free point in Endurance was nice, but not a huge deal. His final decision was where to put his Ability point. James decided to put the point into the Increased Damage Ability. He wanted to unlock the Tier II: Sharper Swords Ability as soon as possible.

While he was assigning points, James realized that he hadn't given his character sheet a look since level 3, so he pulled it up to review it.

JAMES

HUMAN (WARRIOR)

LEVEL: 7

HEALTH: 163/163 REGENERATES 2.8/HOUR

MANA: 149/149 REGENERATES 2.4/HOUR

STAMINA: 190/190 REGENERATES 2.8/HOUR

STATS

STRENGTH: 15 DEXTERITY: 17

CONSTITUTION: 15

INTELLIGENCE: 16 WISDOM: 16

ENDURANCE: 14 CHARISMA: -2 LUCK:

2 RESILIENCE: 1

SPELLS

SHADOW STEP (LEVEL 1)

ABILITIES

DEATH'S STARE (1/7)

INCREASED DAMAGE (2/10)

BRANDS

MARK OF SYTAR

DIVINE QUEST (MINOR)

ACHIEVEMENTS

DUMB LUCK

While James was fiddling with his character sheet Nana was busy inspecting the crystal, her face growing grim. "Madness," she muttered softly. She snapped her fingers towards James, "Once you're done in the dungeon, can you go into the Witchwood and investigate where this came from?"

> YOU HAVE BEEN GIVEN A QUEST: RABID RABBAN II
>
> Rabid Rabban II: Investigate the Witchwood for the source of the cursed soul gem
>
> Suggested level: 30
>
> Reward: Unknown
>
> Penalty for failure or refusal: Unknown

"Dungeon?" James asked.

"Right." Nana rubbed at her temples. "Sorry, it's been a long day. While exploring, I found a dungeon that seemed appropriate for your level. Can you take care of it?"

> YOU HAVE BEEN GIVEN A QUEST: TOO MANY ANTS
>
> Too Many Ants: Clear the Dungeon of the Lion-Ant
>
> Suggested level: 10
>
> Reward: Unknown
>
> Penalty for failure or refusal: Unknown

James was a little annoyed at the lack of information, but she'd given him a lot today, so he didn't complain. "What type of dungeon and where?"

"Actually," Nana grinned, "it's somewhere you're quite familiar with."

James sighed and accepted both quests. It wasn't like he could say no to Nana, not after she'd saved his life and given him a magic book. He hadn't asked, but he was sure the book was expensive. "Fine… I'll head out in the morning."

Fragment of Divinity

Chapter 15

James had been walking for the better part of the day when he recognized a bend in the path. It was around where the bandits had accosted them on their journey towards Riverside. A journey that felt like years ago, not a little over a month. James had laughed when he'd realized that Nana was sending him to the dungeon that he'd seen in the back of the cave he'd started in. He was excited to return to the cave to see how much he'd grown. With his upgraded stats, James was making much better time than he had on the way to Riverside. Judging by the position of the sun, he'd probably have a few hours of daylight left by the time he arrived at the cave.

James smiled, enjoying the sun on his face and the breeze against his skin as he kept up his light jog. Days like this were rare back on Earth. Temperatures had risen with global warming until the average day was closer to ninety degrees.

But this? This is perfect.

A rustling in the branches next to him set off James' warning bells and he stopped, peering into the foliage. After a minute of fruitless searching, he shrugged to himself.

Probably just a bird, or whatever this world's version of a deer was.

Still, James couldn't keep the hairs on the back of his neck from standing up as he continued his jog.

Over the next hour the feeling continued to grow stronger, and James constantly glanced over his shoulder to make sure he wasn't being followed. Every once in a while, he'd catch a glimpse of fur flashing through the foliage, but never enough to trigger a status screen.

James tried to focus on his peripherals as he ran, trying to not alert whatever was stalking him. It made for awkward running, but after a couple minutes he caught a good look at the predator moving through the shadows.

> GREYMANE WOLF (LEVEL 7)

James didn't know much about wolves, but he knew that if there was one stalking him, then there had to be at least a few more. He knew enough to know that wolves were vicious pack hunters. James also knew that he wouldn't be able to take out an entire pack of wolves by himself. If he didn't think of a way to take out these wolves, he'd be dead.

James' breathing quickened. The sunlight, which had felt so good earlier, now did nothing to combat the chill running down his spine. He was going to die.

No. Focus. You're not going to die.

James spun, but the wolf had vanished into the tree line. He was alone again, the only sound the beating of his heart. He thought he saw a flash of yellow eyes staring back at him, but that could have been his imagination.

He resumed his jog and thought about what he had on hand that he could use to protect himself. He wished he could sit down and go through his pouch. Trying to remember what he had while running wasn't working.

To his surprise, when James wished to see the contents of his pack, a small screen appeared that listed everything inside. James smiled as he scrolled down the list, a plan forming in his mind. He'd forgotten about some stuff in there. His mood lifted as he realized he might not die after all, and he pulled ingredients from his pack as he ran.

First, James pulled out three sizeable chunks of Star Mole Meat. Working quickly, he pulled out some Deadnettle Seeds from his bag. He pressed the Deadnettle seeds into the meat, dispersing them evenly among the three pieces. He'd remembered that they let off an anesthetic gas that had knocked him out with only a small whiff, and he was hoping the effect would be even stronger if he fed the seeds to the wolves. After that, he pulled the Cave Spider Matriarch Poison Gland from his bag and pricked a small hole in it with his dagger. He dripped the poison over the meat, thoroughly coating it.

James wasn't sure how smart the wolves were, but he really hoped they fell for this, because he was out of options. If they didn't take the bait, then he was in for a very painful death unless he could outrun them, which was doubtful.

A short while later, James stopped running. An enormous wolf had stepped on to the path in front of him. The wolf let out a low growl as it advanced towards him, hackles raised, a predatory gleam in its eyes.

> ### GREYMANE ALPHA (LEVEL 11)

If it had been just the one wolf, maybe James could have fought it, even though it was a higher level, but low growls from behind him caused him to turn. Four other wolves stepped out of the trees.

James was surrounded.

The alpha was larger than the others and had patches of white around its eyes and muzzle. There was a long scar running across its snout, and more covering its body.

Unable to focus in two directions at once, James tossed two of the pieces of meat behind him and one in front of him. He heard the sound of flesh tearing behind him and gave a relieved sigh as he turned to see the wolves behind him ravenously devouring the meat. Hopefully, he'd added enough poison to affect them.

He turned forward just in time to see the older wolf lunge at him, just barely missing him as it snapped down with its teeth. James stumbled backwards and tumbled to the ground, his heart pounding in his chest. He'd been lucky. He needed to pay attention, or he'd get killed.

Spitting out a mouthful of dirt, James stood and drew his sword. His trick clearly hadn't worked on the Greymane Alpha, who'd ignored the meat completely.

A quick glance over his shoulder informed him that the rest of the wolves were feeling the effects of the poison. One of the wolves stumbled drunkenly before collapsing and another tried to join its alpha by advancing on James, but couldn't make it more than a few steps. Soon they were all on the ground, twitching as the poison ravaged their bodies.

> YOU HAVE GAINED 2 SKILL RANKS IN POISON.
>
> YOU ARE NOW SKILL RANK 3.

James felt bad for the wolves. He loved dogs, but he knew that they would have torn him to shreds without a second thought. Steeling himself, he faced the Greymane Alpha, who was staring back at him in fury, it's gaze darting between James and its pack. A low whine escaped its lips as it circled around James, purposefully putting itself between him and the rest of the wolves, who lay unconscious on the ground.

The wolf didn't attack, but stayed low to the ground, growling. It was obvious that the wolf wanted to go check on his pack, but was worried that James would attack him if he dropped his guard.

James considered his options. He could attack the wolves and earn experience. He was pretty sure he could take the leader by itself, especially since it was busy worrying about its pack, but something about that didn't feel right. The wolf wasn't a threat to him anymore; it didn't want to fight, and James didn't want to kill an animal that wasn't trying to kill him.

"It's all right," James said in a soft voice, sheathing his sword. "Go to your family. The poison wasn't enough to kill them. They should be fine once they've healed up." He knew that the wolf couldn't understand him, but hoped his tone would convey his feelings.

It might have been his imagination, but James could have sworn that the wolf dipped its head towards him in thanks before turning to check on its pack.

YOU HAVE GAINED THE SKILL: BEAST BONDING

Beast Bonding (Skill Rank 1):

You've learned that not all animals are mindless beasts. This skill allows you to attempt communication with beast class monsters.

James smiled and turned, continuing his journey to the cave, hoping he may have made a friend.

When he reached the cliff above the cave, he steeled himself for the climb down. Trying and failing to ignore the drop, he crawled backwards, awkwardly bracing one of his legs against the rock face. He was glad it was a nicely angled slab and not a vertical face, but still, it sucked. Carefully he descended, moving slowly hand-hand, foot-foot and trying to keep the weight in his feet instead of his arms. The levels he had gotten while climbing trees for Bartram were really paying off, and he felt much steadier climbing down the cliff-face than he had climbing up. Soon, he was on the ground in front of the cave entrance.

Dropping into Stealth, James entered the cave cautiously and scouted around, looking for anything that may have made the cave its home, since he had killed its previous inhabitants. Luckily, nothing seemed to have moved in.

After losing some time with the wolves, it was no longer the early arrival he'd hoped for. It was getting dark, so James decided to camp out, then tackle the dungeon the next morning.

Chapter 16

In the morning James went through a series of stretches before heading to the dungeon entrance. He was already feeling a lot more limber than he had back on Earth, though that could be due to his increased Dexterity.

James was excited for his first real dungeon dive. He didn't count the half-attempt at Nana's garden, because he'd only killed four monsters on the first level. This would be his first attempt at clearing a full dungeon, the first real test of his powers since coming to Novis.

People who didn't play video games could never understand the excitement of delving deep into a dungeon in search of rare and exotic treasures, of reading through prompt after prompt of item stats. Or maybe that was just James. Either way, he'd been disappointed that he hadn't gotten any loot from the garden dungeon. Although he probably shouldn't get his hopes up. Lion-Ants didn't seem like the type of creatures who collected mythical swords.

James walked over to the back of the cave and considered the dungeon. At level six, he was in the middle of the level range, so he was hoping that it wouldn't be too hard. On the other hand, maybe the suggestions was for the average level of a party. In that case, he was screwed.

ENTERING THE DUNGEON OF THE LION-ANT.

RECOMMENDED LEVEL: 5-9.

A low rumbling echoed through the cave as a section of wall slowly slid down, revealing a grey tunnel leading into darkness. A cool, damp breeze wafted out, carrying the stale smell of trapped air as the depths of the dungeon opened to the world for the first time in what smelled like ages.

The walls and ceiling of the tunnel were smooth, dark-grey stone. James ran his hand along the surface. It was almost unnaturally smooth, as if he were touching a granite countertop.

Behind him, the rumbling started up again as the door rose, closing with a sense of finality and trapping James in pitch-blackness. Normally he would have freaked out, but he was prepared for the darkness. Nana had handed him five potions as he left, explaining that he would probably need them for the underground dungeon.

Potion of Darkvision (x5):

Rank: Unusual

This potion gives dark vision up to 100 meters for five hours

---

Each potion would last him five hours, which meant that, as long as he could clear the entire dungeon in less than a day, he would be okay.

Pulling out the stopper, James drank the first potion in one swig, almost choking as the foul liquid touched his tongue. It tasted like the pink Tylenol his mom made him drink when he was sick as a kid.

There was a tingling sensation behind his eyes as the potion took effect. Slowly, shapes in the darkness took form, outlined in a greenish tint that gave the whole dungeon an otherworldly appearance.

He dropped into Stealth and crept deeper into the dungeon. He advanced cautiously for the first five minutes, but then his ADHD took control and his mind drifted to the Lion-Ants.

What would they look like? Would they be lions with ant heads? Or ants with lion heads? Or just big ants? What if they're furry!?

He didn't have to wait long to find out.

James was so lost in his thoughts that he almost missed the scuffling sound approaching from the other end of the tunnel. Something was out there. He couldn't see it yet, but there was no mistaking the rhythmic tapping of too many legs on stone. He pressed himself tight against the wall of the cave and drew his sword. Hopefully, the creature wouldn't be able to see well in the pitch-blackness, but if it did, he would be prepared.

A dull, violet light bobbed up the tunnel towards him. When it was close enough, James could see it for what it really was.

A Lion-Ant.

It was as large as James and scuttled on six legs that stuck out from an ant-like thorax. Its head was that of a lion, with a mane made from the same purple crystals that lit up the cave James had spawned in. But oddly, a crystal the dungeon lacked. The dim violet glow wasn't bright, but this close and to James' enhanced eyesight, it was uncomfortable to look at directly.

When it got closer, he could read the text floating above its head.

LION-ANT SCOUT (LEVEL 5)

The Lion-Ant stopped and sniffed at the air. James held his breath, his heart pounding loudly in his chest. He wished he could make it quieter.

YOU HAVE GAINED 1 SKILL RANK IN STEALTH.

YOU ARE NOW SKILL RANK 6.

With a snort, the Lion-Ant Scout continued its march, satisfied there wasn't anyone in the vicinity. Just as the beast passed him, James swung his sword in an arc down directly into the creature's abdomen His sword hit its jet-black exoskeleton with a loud clang, scoring deep but not enough to cause heavy damage.

You have gained the skill: Sneak Attack

Sneak Attack (Skill Rank 1):

+ 210% damage while hidden

The Lion-Ant roared in pain as deep blue ichor dripped from its wound. It lunged at James, it's lion's maw closing on the air where he'd been a second before.

After it missed it seemed confused and it sniffed around the air again, like the Star Mole had. That was odd. James could see the creature clear as day. It was close enough for him to touch with his sword if he wanted to.

Why can't it see me? It must be blind, just like the moles were.

But that didn't seem right. It had eyes, and they were darting around as if it could see something.

Realization struck like a hammer. *The mane!*

Living underground with a constant light source right next to its eyes probably wreaked havoc on its night vision. It probably couldn't see anything further out than a few inches from its eyes. *But why did it have eyes then? What was the point?*

His best guess was that the creatures were built as predators for outside of the cave. They hunted in the daylight and retreated to their cave after.

James shook his head. He couldn't focus on useless questions right now. He was in the middle of a fight. The takeaway here was that the creatures couldn't see very well. He needed to use that to his advantage.

To test his theory, James waved the point of his sword inside the ring of light emitted from the creature's mane. Immediately the Lion-Ant growled and lunged at the sword, almost tearing it from James' grip. James smiled to himself.

This just might work.

Carefully, he crept around the Lion-Ant until he was directly in front of it, but still out of sight. He lunged forward, stabbing into the beast's unprotected lion head.

His sword bit deep, piercing the monster's left eye and emerging out the back of its skull. It collapsed to the ground, the light from its crystal fading as blue ichor dripped from the wound.

> YOU HAVE GAINED 1 LEVEL IN SWORDSMANSHIP.
>
> YOU ARE NOW LEVEL 17.

> You have killed a Lion-Ant Scout (Level 5)
>
> + 15 experience points

> LEVEL UP! YOU ARE NOW LEVEL 8.

James placed two points each into Intelligence and Wisdom again, bringing them both up to 18. He also placed his Ability point into the Increased Damage Ability, bringing it up to 3. It now boosted his sword damage by 30%

and he was only two points away from unlocking the coveted Sharper Swords skill.

After assigning his points, James rubbed his hands together in excitement. It was time to get gruesome. He pulled out his dagger and stabbed at the carapace, testing its durability. Because his Sharper Swords ability didn't apply to daggers, the dagger could barely scratch the chitinous material. In contrast, James could easily cut into the skin of the Lion head. Intrigued, he tried to cut the creature's neck to separate the crystal mane from the head. When he did, he found out that the crystals only extended partly into the Lion-Ant's neck and were fairly easy to remove.

He pulled on one and it slid out easily. When it was free of the Lion-Ant's body its purple light stopped fading, and its remaining energy swirled around inside the gem. Working quickly, he tried to pull out the rest of the crystals, but only pulled out two more before the color had completely drained from the rest, leaving them dull and lifeless.

Ignoring the dull crystals, James inspected the three he'd pulled out. They were double-ended crystals in the shape of a six-sided prism coming to a point on either end.

> Weak Mana Crystal (x3):
>
> Rank: Unusual
>
> You can feel weak pulses of energy coming from this crystal.

James felt it, a low thrumming energy radiating from the crystals in his palm. Unsure as to their use, he placed the crystals into his bag in case they were dangerous, then moved on to the rest of the body.

James had heard that insects didn't have a circulatory system like Humans and other animals. He wasn't sure what they had instead, and he was interested to see what its insides looked like. Specifically, he was interested in how the ant's circulatory system meshed with the lion part of its body. Upon inspection, the ant didn't have a heart, veins, or arteries, but rather an odd muscle floating around inside that looked like it pushed around the insect's ichor. He also found a series of long tubes filled with air instead of lungs.

When James finally finished with the Lion-Ant's body and made his way up to the lion head, he stopped for a second, considering the best way to examine it. There were still a few dull crystals left that he hadn't removed, and he decided to cut around them to see how they attached inside. James was surprised when he didn't find veins, arteries, or insect parts. Instead, the inside of the Lion-Ant's head was filled with tendrils of purple Mana that connected the lion's brain to the mane, almost as if the crystals had been powering the creature, like arcane batteries.

> YOU HAVE GAINED 1 SKILL RANK IN ANATOMY.
>
> YOU ARE NOW SKILL RANK 6.

James finished his inspection and wiped off his weapons before moving on. He was disappointed that he hadn't had the opportunity to use his Shadow Step Spell in the fight. He hadn't tried it yet, and his Mana regeneration was slow enough that he needed to be cautious about using any spells. He only had 163 mana, with a regeneration of 2.8 per hour, which meant that after using it twice, he'd only have 53 Mana left. He'd have to wait almost an hour for a third cast.

With some quick math, James calculated that recharging his entire Mana pool would take around two-and-a-half days. Why Mana regenerated so slowly was a mystery to him. It led him to wonder how mages could be viable fighters if Mana regeneration was so slow. Maybe they got special class skills, or maybe they just knew something he didn't. He'd have to research that, because there had to be a way to use magic without draining his Mana away for days. Otherwise, nobody would want to become a mage.

While he was thinking about magic, his nose wrinkled in disgust. He'd just walked into a deeper part of the tunnel and been hit with a wall of stench that almost caused him to turn back.

James groaned. It was a smell he recognized.

No matter how often he'd had to smell it at work, James had never gotten used to the smell of decomposing bodies. It overpowered everything else and got stuck in his nose for days.

The first time he'd been called to a long-dead patient, James could smell him from outside the house. His partner had placed a hand on his shoulder to stop him from entering and handed him a few sticks of gum. The senior paramedic told him to chew that specific gum for dead bodies because it would overpower the smell. Other tricks, like Vaseline in the nose, would allow the smell to linger. The specific black packet of gum was James' tried-and-true method for blocking the smell of a body. Unfortunately, they'd stopped selling it in grocery stores, which meant he had to order it online.

James found himself patting his pants habitually, looking for gum, and realized that not only did he not have gum, but that he didn't have pockets either.

Shaking his head in an effort to clear his thoughts, James returned to the present. The smell was strongest around a side tunnel off the center passage, so ignoring it wasn't a difficult decision. James had no intention of encountering whatever disgusting, decomposing body was creating the smell. No, he'd avoid it if it could.

As he continued down the passage, James noticed that the tunnel sloped downward, but not in a straight slope like a tunnel should. Instead, it was bumpy, as if whoever created it gave up halfway through, poured a bucket of concrete down some stairs and called it a day.

"Man, this tunnel must have been designed by the laziest contractor ever," James muttered to himself, kneeling down to inspect the stone. A flash of white caught his eye, and he examined a tiny crack in the corner of the path. A bit of white peeked through.

It wasn't something James would normally notice. He wasn't the most observant, but the tunnel had been so uniform and boring that his mind jumped on the first miniscule out-of-place detail.

James chipped away at the stone with his dagger, working to reveal the floor beneath it. After a few minutes, James cleared about an inch of stone, revealing white marble tile.

Interesting. Why was there marble underneath the stone? How had the stone gotten there? The longer James was in this tunnel, the more questions he had. Hopefully, he'd be able to answer them by the time he finished delving through the dungeon. He thought about chipping away more of the rock, but his dagger was looking worse for wear, and a few nicks marred its edges.

James left the strange tile behind and continued down the tunnel into a sizable room, dominated by an enormous fountain, guarded by two Lion-ants. A trickle of water leaked out from the broken base of what had once been a statue, but was now just a pile of rubble. James tried to make out what the statue may have once represented, but he couldn't even tell if it was supposed to be a human or animal. Whatever the statue had been was long gone, lost to time. On the far side of the cavern, past the guards, three tunnels lead deeper into the dungeon.

LION-ANT GUARD (LEVEL 7)

LION-ANT GUARD (LEVEL 7)

James wearily eyed the two Lion-Ant guards. They were built slightly differently than the scout he had seen earlier, with larger crystals in their manes and an additional crystal set in their foreheads. These glowed brighter than the others, an almost blinding violet with James' enhanced vision. The most disconcerting change was probably their eyes, or lack thereof. Instead of eyes, they simply had one large mouth. They still looked like lions, only oddly proportioned with a mouth that had stretched and widened in a grim resemblance of a crocodile's face, but covered in golden fur. They stood slightly taller than James.

Fighting multiple creatures at once would probably end up killing him. James wasn't even that experienced fighting enemies one at a time. But he was smart, and that was his advantage. Every problem had a solution. He just needed to figure out what it was.

The Lion-Ants had strong armor and dangerous attacks. Those were their strengths. The trick was finding out their weakness, if they had one.

Their eyesight was a pretty big weakness. And they didn't have armor on their faces.

Hmm.

James grinned as he stated to formulate a plan.

James pulled one of the Weak Mana Crystals out of his bag and tossed it into the center of the room, the soft crack when it landed sounding like a gunshot in the silent cavern.

Immediately, the guards turned their heads towards the noise, but instead of rushing to investigate, they let out a pulse of violet light from the crystal set into their foreheads. The light pulsed out of the Lion-Ants in an expanding ring, covering the cave and passing harmlessly through James.

James breathed a sigh of relief. He'd been worried that the light would damage him. But his relief was short lived, as the two guards turned their eyeless faces towards him.

James reacted instinctively, all thoughts of Skills and Spells leaving his brain as pure terror took over. He bolted, footsteps echoing off the walls.

The first Lion-Ant quickly caught up with him, its sharp teeth piercing his leather and penetrating his skin. James screamed and reached down for his dagger, as there was no time to go for the sword. When he felt the familiar hilt, James yanked the dagger from its sheath and plunged it downward repeatedly into the creature's face, but to minimal effect. The beast kept its jaws stubbornly clamped shut.

He plunged the dagger down again, and this time it hit the gemstone in the Lion-Ant's forehead, cracking it and causing the beast to roar in pain. There was a solitary flicker of violet light from the crystal and it exploded, shaking the tunnel and launching James into a wall.

When the smoke cleared, James saw the second Lion-Ant stepping over its still-twitching comrade. But now James was prepared. He raised his sword to block the oncoming attack, but instead of rushing forward, the Lion-Ant raised its head into the air, the gemstone glowing green.

It almost looked like…

Oh no.

James jumped to the side just as the Lion-Ant let out a breath attack, blasting grey liquid over the tunnel. James avoided most of it, but not all. His left hand was coated with the liquid, which was quickly drying and transforming into the same stone as the walls of the cave.

At least he'd solved one mystery.

As the Lion-Ant advanced, James reacted without thinking, punching it in the face with his rock-covered fist and following up with his sword, skewering the beast through the skull.

> You have killed a Lion-Ant Guard (Level 7)
>
> *+ 21 experience points*

> *LEVEL UP! YOU ARE NOW LEVEL 9.*

Before James could finish reading his prompt, the first Lion-Ant leapt towards him, cyan ichor streaming freely from its wounds. It landed slightly to his left, snarling, and snapped at him, missing completely. James stepped back and it turned, homing in on the sound of his movement. Before it could react though, James sliced through its head with ease. Fighting creatures that couldn't think was... different. *Great XP, though.*

> You have killed a Lion-Ant Guard (Level 7)
>
> *+ 21 experience points*

> *LEVEL UP! YOU ARE NOW LEVEL 10.*

> *CONGRATULATIONS ON REACHING LEVEL 10, THE FIRST REAL MILESTONE IN YOUR JOURNEY.*

> Your Ring of Sytar has expired. Experience required to level has been returned to normal.

> HIDDEN EFFECT: YOUR RING OF SYTAR WAS SUPPRESSING THE POWER CONTAINED IN YOUR BRAND. OTHER CONTESTANTS MAY NOW RECOGNIZE YOU.

A crystalline aura surrounded James' ring, and it crumbled to dust, releasing a nova of energy.

James frowned when he read the notification, he'd gotten used to the easy levels. He sighed. It looked like things would get harder from here on out.

James felt a disturbance in the energy flowing through him as it suddenly reversed its flow, expanding outward. Before, it had felt like all the Mana in his body was travelling towards his core. Now, it felt as if his core were cycling the Mana through his body.

As the mana flowed out of his core, it flooded his body. When the Mana reached his skin, it burst out, sending a sharp pain throughout his body as if he were being pricked with millions of needles at the same time. Briefly, a thick layer of Mana surrounded him, leaving him empty, before it pulled back, leaving him with a thin shell coating his entire body. James looked down, but he couldn't see the thin aura around himself. He could feel it, though. It felt like the warmth of a ray of sunlight suffusing his entire body.

James shivered, then grinned. He hadn't realized how cold he'd been until he was suddenly warm again. His Mana seemed to drive away the damp and cold of the cave.

> PLEASE CHOOSE YOUR PATH.

A new screen popped up.

PATH OF THE SWORDSMAN (COMMON)

You focus exclusively on the sword, ignoring all other weapons. You rely on your skill to masterfully dismember your enemies. Choosing this path will grant you either the Strongest Sword or the Hardest Armor passive Ability.

PATH OF THE MAGE (RARE)

The first step on a long journey. Mages harness the unnatural powers of the land. Use your Mana to lay waste to kingdoms or vaporize your enemies. Choosing this path will unlock a random Tier I - III affinity.

Path of the Beast (Uncommon)

You are more at home in the forest than in the cities. Choosing this class will grant you a single-use Ability to permanently bind a beast as your Animal Companion.

PATH OF THE THIEF (COMMON)

You prefer to live in the shadows, sneaking around and attacking from behind. Choosing this class will give you the opportunity to add a passive Bleed or Poison debuff to your weapons that can be upgraded through Abilities.

PATH OF THE SHADOW (EPIC)

Flashy elemental magic isn't for everyone. You prefer to hide in the darkness, striking at the most opportune time.

James knew what Nana would tell him to do. And what he wanted to do. From what he could tell, most of the classes would pigeonhole him into a particular style of fighting, which Nana had warned against. The only class that didn't seem to do that was the path of the Shadow, which seemed to specifically strengthen his connection to Shadow Magic and nothing else. But the Path of the Mage was tempting. James would love to unlock two extra affinities. He could see himself as a powerful caster, throwing chain lightning around and destroying swathes of enemies on the battlefield. But he knew it was the wrong choice. With maybe a touch of hesitation, he selected the Path of the Shadow.

YOU HAVE CHOSEN THE PATH OF THE SHADOW.

New Level-up bonus:

+ 5 Free Stat Points

+ 1 Wisdom

+ 1 Intelligence

+ 1 Endurance

+1 Ability point

Your Warrior class abilities have been modified.

As James watched, a shimmer of black energy appeared and sunk into his skin. He admitted to himself that he'd made the right choice and clapped his hands together, excited to see what had changed. His jaw dropped when he read his new Ability descriptions.

WARRIOR OF DARKNESS I

Imbue Darkness (3/10):

> *+30% shadow damage added to weapon damage*

Your dark Mana flows through your weapons, imbuing them
with some of your power.

WARRIOR OF DARKNESS I

Arcane Armor (0/10):

Shadows flow freely through your armor, bolstering its
defense.

WARRIOR OF DARKNESS I

Pierce the Veil (0/10):

Your connection with the shadows allows you to see through
attempts to hide.

WARRIOR OF DARKNESS II

Ephemeral Weapon (0/10):

> **Requires Imbue Darkness 10*

Your weapons can take on the properties of shadow,
completely passing through an opponent's armor.

Warrior of Darkness II

Stronger Shadows (0/5):

*Requires Imbue Darkness 5

The bond between your shadow magic and weapon deepens, strengthening your ability to imbue your weapon.

WARRIOR OF DARKNESS II

Knife in the Dark (0/3):

*Requires Imbue Darkness 3

Costs:

- 15 Mana,

- 10 stamina

Throw a weapon at your opponent, creating 2 shadow copies per skill level.

From what James could tell, Increased Damage had turned into Imbue Darkness, Immovable Object had turned into Arcane Armor, and Raging Bull had become Pierce the Veil. For his Tier II abilities, Split Weapon had turned into Ephemeral Weapon and Sharper Tools was now Stronger Shadows, but was functionally the same skill. He had also gotten a new Tier II skill branching off from Imbue Darkness, Knife in the Dark.

After looking over everything, James could see why so much changed at level 10. It was a huge milestone.

He had two points to spend. He could put both points into Imbue Darkness to continue with his plan, but he could also get Knife in the Dark and finally have a Tier II skill. In the end, James put one of his points into Knife in the Dark. He remembered his fight with the Moonshadow Moth and wanted a ranged attack.

He placed the other point in Imbue Darkness. As soon as he placed the point, he felt the Mana flow through his body change once again, extending past his hand to incorporate his sword, as if it were just another part of his body. Strands of umbral energy swirled across the blade.

Finished with his abilities, he turned his focus on his stats. Unfortunately, leveling to 10 hadn't given him the bonuses that his class promised, so his Intelligence and Wisdom were still 18. James put two points in each, which increased his Mana enough to cast Shadow Step three times instead of two.

James placed his last four points into Strength and smashed his hand against the cave wall, shattering the solidified liquid-rock that encased it. He flexed his hand, then smiled.

He had corpses to study.

Chapter 17

Before moving on, James harvested the Lion-Ant crystals. Unfortunately, he'd wasted too much time playing with Abilities and Skills after the fight, and the energy in the crystals had almost drained completely. In total, he recovered three Weak Mana Crystals from the Lion-Ants before moving on to his new favorite hobby, studying monster corpses.

James had learned most of what he needed to know from the first Lion-Ant corpse that he'd taken apart. Now it was a matter of looking for anything interesting he may have missed on the others. In particular, he was looking for weak spots. This was a novel idea for him, but after the fight was over, James realized he shouldn't test for weak points during a fight. It would be smarter more productive to find the weaknesses in a dead creature's defenses, then apply it to the living.

On initial examination, James didn't see any glaring weaknesses. No areas of thin armor, no automatic kill switches. Even the creature's lion- head was tough, with extraordinarily thick bones. They'd been tough enough to take a brutal beating from his daggers. But when he started manipulating the Ant-Lion's legs, he realized that the armor around their joints was much weaker than the exoskeleton surrounding their bodies. He could target their legs to cripple them, something he hadn't considered earlier.

Looking for weak points was proving fruitful, and the system apparently agreed with him.

> YOU HAVE GAINED 3 LEVELS IN ANATOMY.
>
> YOU ARE NOW LEVEL 9.

James didn't have long to celebrate before his enhanced vision vanished, leaving him in the center of the tunnel, unable to see. James conjured the next potion from his pouch and downed it, shuddering as the thick, foul liquid crawled down his throat.

James considered the three paths ahead of him. Normally he would choose the left one. Everyone knew the old trick—always pick the left turn in a maze.

But this wasn't a maze, and there was a… *presence*… drawing him toward the central passage. He could feel an energy flowing out of the passage and knew he needed to go see.

James trekked down the featureless tunnels, lost in his thoughts. He'd thought dungeons would be more interesting and action-packed, but here he was, moseying through featureless rock rooms. There weren't even any enemies for him to fight. No chests. Video games had led him to believe that even the most senseless, brain-dead creature would have barrels and boxes full of gold and rare items lying around, but the reality was disappointing. He hadn't found a single copper, much less a barrel full of gold.

Busy commiserating about the lack of treasure, James tripped over a raised section of the floor. He careened forwards and caught himself just before he hit the ground.

What the…

James examined the stone floor. A raised section stood out in stark contrast to the otherwise seamless tunnel. He scowled. The ants hadn't demonstrated enough brainpower to set traps.

He pulled out his dagger and chipped away at the rock, revealing hints of silvery metal. Excited, James dug faster, revealing a thin, shimmering metal chain. He tugged on it, releasing it from the rock.

The necklace was beautiful. A silvery-blue metal chain attached to a small crystal pendant that housed a sliver of blue and red opal. The opalescent shard shimmered, glowing with a pale blue energy that sent crackles of lightning dancing over the crystal pendant.

His hands shook in excitement as he examined the necklace clutched tightly in his hands. The information displayed in his interface was the telltale green hue of a legendary item.

> Fragment of Syreus:
>
> Rank: Legendary
>
> Crafted from the remains of the God Syreus, this necklace
>   allows the wearer to call down a storm once per day.

> YOU HAVE GAINED A QUEST: SPLINTERED PAST I
>
> Splintered Past I: You have found the remains of a god. Find
>   out what happened to Syreus.
>
> Suggested level: Unknown
>
> Reward: Unknown
>
> Penalty for failure or refusal: None

The first thought that ran through James' mind was disappointment. For a legendary artifact the effect was underwhelming.

It called down a storm. That was it?

He'd been hoping for invisibility or invulnerability or something. Something worthy of a Legendary rarity item. Still, thinking about the rewards he might get from a quest chain that *started* with a legendary item, James salivated. As soon as he placed the pendant around his neck, it heated up and he gained a notification.

YOU HAVE GAINED THE SPELL: SYREUS' WRATH

Syreus' Wrath (N/A):

Range: Self

Cast time: 10 minutes

Cooldown: 24 hours

Cost: None

Summons a storm centered around the caster

The promise of future rewards put James in a great mood. Even the fact that the tunnel had looped around and led him back into the room with the fountain hadn't dampened his spirits. Normally, he would have been pissed to realize that he had just spent almost an hour walking in a large circle through a gloomy cave and wasting his potions. Instead, he hummed quietly to himself as he skipped down the last remaining passageway until, remembering he was in a dungeon, he dropped back into stealth.

James really wanted to try his new spell, but something told him that summoning a storm underground could go one of two ways. Either he would be successful, summon a storm underground, and drown when the deluge flooded the tunnels. Or he would be unsuccessful, wasting his only cast. There was no possible way anything good could come from using the spell here.

He'd also been itching to try Shadow Step, but was waiting for the right moment to use it. He was the type of video game player who waited to use all of his powerful Spells and items until the final boss fight—a strategy that didn't necessarily work all the time. Still, it was a valid strategy. He didn't want to end up stuck in a situation where he needed his magic but didn't have any mana. Still, James admired his restraint in waiting to use his spell.

Over the course of the next few hours, James encountered six more Lion-Ants as he delved deeper into the dungeon. He dispatched them without incident, netting him a total of 68 experience, two Skill Ranks in Swordsmanship, and three in Stealth. Unfortunately, his anatomy skill hadn't leveled. Probably because he was examining the same creatures repeatedly.

James frowned in annoyance as he looked at his experience bar again. His progress had slowed to a crawl when he'd hit level ten. Prior to level ten, each ant individually had given him almost enough experience to level up. Now he was six ants in and still hadn't gained enough to level.

James was so focused inward on his thoughts that he almost tripped when the tunnel suddenly leveled out, bringing him back to the present.

ACHIEVEMENT UNLOCKED: CLUMSY I

Clumsy I:

- 1 Dexterity

You really should be looking where you're going.

He let out a small noise of annoyance—his ADHD would be the death of him if he couldn't stop drifting into daydreams, especially in dungeons. To be fair, he hadn't been able to take his medications with him into this world, but still, he should be able to focus in a literal deathtrap. It wasn't his fault caves were so boring.

James shook his head to clear away the thoughts. He'd done it again. He needed to focus.

The surrounding dungeon was becoming less homogeneous as James passed bits of tile and exposed wall sconces. *Interesting. Maybe the ants hadn't had time to finish coating this area yet?*

James turned a corner and saw the end of the passage. Two massive oaken doors lay shattered into splinters around the cavernous entrance to the boss room.

I mean, come on. A room at the end of a long passage, guarded with enormous doors? It's practically screaming 'boss fight'.

James activated Stealth and peered into the room. There was a large, misshapen, golden altar in the center of a raised platform, but that wasn't what commanded James' attention. He strained his eyes upward, trying to make out the art on a faded fresco on the ceiling. The details had faded with time… and ant-related damage, but he could vaguely see what it used to look like: an altar rising out of a rough body of water with a heavy storm surging overhead.

One thing James didn't see was the boss, and that worried him. Maybe he'd been wrong, and this wasn't the boss room. He would have to enter the room to find out.

Before entering the room, James checked the timer on his Darkvision buff. About an hour left. He didn't want to risk getting caught in the dark again, so he pulled out the third potion and quaffed it. He'd have to head back to Nana's and restock if this wasn't the last room.

James would rather fail the quest than risk getting caught in the oppressive darkness of the tunnels with no light again. It wasn't that he was claustrophobic. There was just something about being eaten to death by enormous ants with lion heads that James really didn't want to happen to him.

Actually, would it be worse to be eaten by ants with regular ant heads? James shook his head no. *Focus.*

As soon as James stepped into the room, the ground rumbled and an enormous Lion-Ant burst out of the ground, showering him with rubble.

LION-ANT QUEEN (BOSS: LEVEL 10)

Instead of a lion's head on the body of an ant like the others had been, the queen looked more like a centaur, but with the head and torso of a humanoid lion and the lower body of an ant. The queen had no mane, but five long crystals jutted out of her head like a morbid crown. She clutched a long, thin lance in one of her massive paws and advanced towards him, the point of her lance pointed directly at his heart.

James drew his sword. "Let's dance."

The Queen halted her advance, staring at James with what he assumed was an incredulous expression. Her eyes narrowed in anger and she spoke, her words coming out in a low rasp. "You come into my home, kill my children and now you want to *dance*? How dare you!" She resumed her charge.

James was so surprised at her response that he almost forgot to dodge, but he barely avoided the lance. He landed awkwardly on his right foot and tripped, rolling to the ground. Luckily for James, he'd spent an entire day with Lamia practicing falling, specifically how not to impale yourself with your sword when you trip during a fight. According to her, it was one of the most common ways to die. James wasn't sure he believed her.

Rolling to his feet, James held out his hand to stop the charging queen. "Wait!"

Maybe I can clear the dungeon diplomatically. Is that a thing?

Unsurprisingly, she ignored him, continuing her charge.

James spun to the side and repeated the move he'd used on the Rabban, slashing across her flank. But unlike the Rabban, the queen was armored. His blade skittered along her flank, flashing with sparks of dark energy as his Ability worked to penetrate the carapace. At the end of his swing, James brought the sword back, slicing through the middle joint on one of her legs.

The queen roared in anger as she swiped at James with her unencumbered paw and scored three deep claw marks across his chest. The force of her blow threw him hard into a nearby section of the cavern wall. It crumbled under the force of his blow, revealing an unexplored cavern, but James couldn't focus on that. He needed to keep his head in the fight.

James stood up, coughed, and looked down at his chest. Three claw marks scored deep into the leather, but he was relieved to see that they hadn't gone through to the flesh.

James prepared to dodge as the queen charged towards him, a little slower than before. As she closed in, she turned on a burst of speed, throwing off the timing of his dodge. Her lance scored deeply into his side and his health dropped precipitously, flashing around 45% in the corner of his vision.

Swearing, James grabbed his dagger and flung it at her face, activating Knife in the Dark just as she raised a paw to block it. The dagger flashed black, then two shadowy copies split off from the main dagger as it flew through the air. One dagger impacted her outstretched palm, another in her abdomen, while the original hit directly in her eye. The shadowy daggers stayed in her body for a second before disappearing with a flash of black light, leaving two bloody wounds.

> YOU HAVE GAINED 1 SKILL RANK IN KNIFE THROWING.
>
> YOU ARE NOW SKILL RANK 2.

James couldn't tell who was more surprised by that throw, him or her, but he didn't have time to think about it. He launched himself towards the queen, ready to deliver the final strike, when she roared.

A pulse of energy left her mouth and James changed his strategy, stepping back and bracing himself to block with his sword. The pulse passed harmlessly through James, leaving him confused. He didn't see any status effects, so he wasn't sure exactly what the queen could have done.

That was when the ground started rumbling.

Oh no.

Two enormous Lion-Ants scrabbled out from the rocky ground and charged at him.

> LION-ANT ROYAL GUARD (SUMMON: LEVEL 9)

> LION-ANT ROYAL GUARD (SUMMON: LEVEL 9)

Frantically looking for an escape route, James held up his sword to ward off the two new threats. Then he remembered his Shadow Step spell. Wishing he'd practiced, James concentrated on the shadow underneath the queen's body and disappeared, reappearing in the darkness underneath her abdomen. Thankfully, the crystals on her head cast enough light for her to have a shadow in the dark cave.

James stabbed his sword upwards, straight into her abdomen. The carapace held strong for a second as the black energy around his sword burned at it, but it quickly gave, sending James' sword deep into the queen. He yanked it backwards, coating himself in bloody ichor.

She shrieked, then collapsed. James rolled from underneath her, barely escaping in time as her full weight slammed into the ground, cracking the stone.

He spun, ready for the two guards to attack, but they didn't react. They had collapsed with their queen.

James coughed again. It hurt to breathe.

That was a win in his book.

Chapter 18

After missing out on quite a few Mana crystals because he'd been too slow to harvest them, James went for the queen's crystals first. Since he'd wasted so little time, he was able to harvest all five.

> Average Mana Crystal (x5):
>
> Rank: Unusual
>
> You feel stronger pulses of energy coming from this crystal.

Each of the crystals he'd collected was average quality and gave off pulses of energy that even James, with his limited experience, could tell were much stronger than the pulses coming off from the weak crystals in his pouch.

James placed the new set of crystals in his pouch alongside the others, then reviewed his notifications from the fight. Once he'd finished checking his notifications, he would investigate the hidden room and examine the anatomy of a Lion-Ant Queen.

> You have killed a Lion-Ant Queen (Boss: Level 10).
>
> *+ 82 EXPERIENCE POINTS*

> Congratulations! You have killed your first boss. Boss monsters are much more powerful than similarly leveled monsters, and give bonus experience.

That was a lot more experience than anything he had killed before. Over 10 times as much as a level 3 Lion-Ant Scout. James was pleased with that, even if he hadn't leveled up.

> *ACHIEVEMENT UNLOCKED: SOLO DUNGEONEER*
>
> Solo Dungeoneer:
>
> + *10% damage when fighting alone.*
>
> + *3 Resilience*
>
> + *3 Strength*
>
> - *1 Wisdom*
>
> You came. You saw. You conquered. And you did it all by yourself. Impressive.

Awesome! A permanent percentage boost to damage and a huge stat boost completely negated any negative feelings James may have had regarding the drop in Wisdom.

Surprisingly, that was it. He'd been expecting more notifications, maybe some Skill Ranks. Maybe he was getting to a point where his combat skills would start to level slower. He tried to ignore his disappointment - he couldn't expect his skills to increase every time he fought something. That would be ridiculous.

After he finished dealing with his notifications, James retrieved his dagger and got started on the carcass. Grabbing the loot after an epic battle was his favorite part of any RPG, and he'd been looking forward to it.

While James worked, he thought about his fight. The Lion-Ant queen had spoken to him.

Did that mean she was sapient?

When he'd started learning to fight, he thought he'd have more of an issue killing anything, especially sapient creatures. But he'd just killed something that had spoken to him, and honestly, he felt nothing.

Well, no use dwelling.

James pushed his worries down, trying to enjoy himself as he butchered the Lion-Ant. His mind wandered to the earlier fights and how his blade had penetrated the Lion-Ants much easier after he had imbued his weapon with shadow magic.

After an hour of gruesome work, James harvested a Lion Pelt and a Monster Core from the Lion-Ant Queen. He wasn't sure what the Monster Core was for, but he'd harvested it from a boss monster, so it would probably end up being useful at some point.

Lion Pelt:

Rank: Common

The pelt from a Lion-Ant Queen. It feels soft.

Monster Core (Earth):

Rank: Unusual

The core of a level 10 Lion-Ant Queen.

The prompt was right; the pelt felt soft. James wasn't sure how he felt about burying his head in the fur of a being he'd just slaughtered, but he shrugged it off and focused on the Monster Core. He thought it was a sphere, but on closer examination, it was actually a multi-faceted gemstone. The entire thing glowed light green, but not enough to hurt his eyes. When he held it, he could feel energy swirling around inside. But it felt alien to him, not like the Mana Crystals where the energy felt like he could conjure it at a moment's notice.

Shrugging, James placed both items in his pouch and moved on. He only had one potion left, and he still needed to find his way out of the dungeon after he'd finished looting.

James inspected the broken wall. It looked like a thin layer of stone had been covering a secret doorway. When he'd been flung into the wall, he'd hit the thinner secret door instead of the reinforced wall next to it. It had been a one in a million shot.

The majesty of the room struck James like a hammer when he entered. It was the first room he'd seen that the Lion-Ants hadn't reached, and as such was the only one that wasn't mostly covered in stone. The room gave him his first glimpse at what the dungeon might have looked like back when it was a temple, before the Lion-Ants had desecrated it. By this point, he was pretty sure he was in a temple dedicated to a storm god, probably Syreus if he went by the amulet.

The room was well preserved, with bookshelves lining the walls. One of the shelves held a small chest, but James wasn't paying attention to that. His eyes were on the carved banisters that lined the edges of the room. Wooden burls, carved so that their twisting patterns tumbled around the room like the surge of the tide, decorated the outskirts of the room while a ring of intricately carved chairs surrounded a central table. In the middle, a yellowed, stained parchment, held down by a staff. A thin layer of dust coated everything in the room.

James lifted the staff and examined it, blowing dust off of the wood to better visualize the arcane carvings flowing over the weapon.

Keeper's Staff:

Rank: Rare

+ 50% damage when channeling Water, Fire, Air, and Lightning spells.

- 50% Mana cost to Water, Fire, Air, and Lightning Spells.

Given to the Keepers of the temples of Syreus, the Keeper's Staff was a symbol of the power wielded by his followers. The crystal at the top was designed to channel small amounts of Mana to create a storm in its center. The storm would be individualized based on the caster's Mana types and power level. It was a great point of pride.

Crafted from gnarled wood, the staff was topped with a large crystal sphere. When James touched the staff, he could feel it pulling his Mana upwards, towards the crystal, which filled with a black energy. The energy built up in the staff, dark sparks flying around the gemstone as James felt his hand burn with an icy heat.

Your Mana type [Dark] is incompatible with this item. Only [Fire], [Water], [Air], [Lightning] can be channeled through this staff. You really should be more careful with magic items.

"Aughhhhhh!" He screamed, trying to release his grip on the staff.

Nothing happened. His hand wouldn't respond, and the pain increased. It felt like he'd stuck his hand inside a vat of liquid nitrogen.

The crystal, now filled with black mist, let out a pulse of magic, blowing James back and causing him, thankfully, to let go of the staff.

Breathing heavily, James cradled his hand and sat on the floor, letting relief wash over him.

When the pain subsided, he gingerly used a rag to grab the staff without touching it and deposited it in his pouch.

With an abundance of caution, James picked up the paper, careful not to damage the fragile page.

Today I inherited the position: Keeper of the temple. This should have been the day of my greatest triumph, but instead it was the darkest day of my life. All those years dedicated to the service of the temple. Dedicated to Syreus, Lord of the Storm. My heart sits heavy in my chest as I write this message, but someone needs to know the truth in case I disappear. I have stumbled upon a conspiracy of epic proportions. Everything I believed… a lie.

I guess I should start from the beginning.

My Journey started as an orphan, raised in the temple of Syreus, Voice of the Wind. As I grew older, so too did my devotion to my god. The Keeper at the time took notice, and helped me rise through the ranks of the temple, preparing to replace him when he died. On the eve of his death I was brought to the temple of fire and the Rite of Listening was performed. I meditated for three days at the eye of the world, but heard nothing. The wind failed to whisper in my ear. I was crushed. Why wouldn't Syreus, Bringer of Rain want me? Was I not devoted enough? When I shared my shame with the Elder of Fire, he told me that it was okay, that I would make a fine Keeper, anyway. Surprised, I asked him what he meant. He told me that nobody actually heard the Voice, that we merely performed the Rite for tradition.

Blasphemy! I couldn't believe what I was hearing and reached out to the temples of Water and Air but got no reply. I traveled across the continent to the temple of Lightning and spoke to the Watcher himself. He refused to give me a straight answer, telling me that Syreus, Face in the Mist had not spoken to a Keeper in years. I returned to my temple and pretended to accept their explanations while secretly doing my own research. I was shocked to find that there had been no accounts of Syreus, Ruler of the Sky speaking for over three hundred years. Three hundred years ago, when the previous Warden died, and the new Warden took over his position. I wrote a letter to the other Keepers, detailing my suspicions. Not a single one answered me.

I believe Syreus was betrayed by his followers. I do not know what manner of being could harm a god, but I fear the worst. Lately I have felt a Presence watching me, and I fear that my time on this world will come to an end soon. I am leaving tonight and sealing the temple. My life is in danger and I must find answers. I will be heading towards death, but I must do my part. I do not know who to trust anymore, so I leave this letter for you, adventurer. If I die, someone needs to take over my quest. Please find out what happened to my god.

- Darious, 415th Keeper of the Cloud Temple.

QUEST UPDATE: SPLINTERED PAST I

FIND OUT TO WHAT HAPPENED TO DARIOUS, THE PREVIOUS KEEPER OF THE CLOUD TEMPLE.

James stared at the paper. How had he stumbled upon a legendary quest chain of this magnitude so soon after arriving on Novis? He couldn't imagine that every single person living in this world had God-given quests or Legendary objects. Sure, he was special in that Someone had brought him to Novis, but James was unsure if it was luck, or something more sinister.

Before leaving, James took another look around the room to make sure he hadn't missed anything, and realized that, with all the pain and intrigue, he'd forgotten about the chest.

Mentally chastising himself, James walked towards it, rubbing his hands together greedily. *This was what it was all about.*

He pulled at the lid.

Locked.

Of course it was.

James sighed and looked for a key. He checked every corner of the room, to no avail. Maybe the key was somewhere else in the dungeon, or not. Either way, he didn't have the time to search. He needed to head to the surface before his last potion ran out.

It was time to do things the old-fashioned way.

He placed the chest on the ground, pulled out his worn dagger and, using the pommel, he hammered at the wooden chest until it burst open. A pile of gold, silver, and copper coins spilled out, along with a half-smashed glass bottle. Whatever had been in the bottle had gotten all over the coins and melted them, leaving most of them unrecognizable. Cursing his impatience, James gathered the 3 gold, 9 silver, and 10 copper that weren't malformed.

When James examined the broken chest, he realized that the bottle had been hooked up to a mechanical contraption that he couldn't figure out. Probably something nasty, whatever it was. He gulped, resolving to be either more, or less, careful in the future. He honestly wasn't sure which had saved him. The system seemed to agree.

YOU HAVE GAINED THE SKILL: TRAPS

Traps (Skill Rank 1):

   + *1% to trap detection.*

Sometimes the dumb decision is also the smart one.

James let out a yawn as he checked the timer on his Darkvision potion. It had been a long day, and he was ready to go home.

The rest of his journey was straightforward. He'd walked through the tunnels past groups of dead Lion-Ants that looked like they were in the process of rushing to help their queen when they died. There wasn't a single living thing left in the cavern, as far as he could tell.

Stepping into the cave, James blinked at the sudden brightness and held his hand up to cover his eyes. Shutting his eyes completely, he waited the last five minutes of the potion duration and opened them again once it wore off. It was nighttime. Too late to head back to Riverside.

James sighed, resigning himself yet again to sleep on the cold, hard stone of the cave instead of the warm soft covers of the inn. He needed to get some sleeping gear and wondered why he hadn't already gotten any. It's not like it would have been difficult to carry around. He had a pouch that could fit anything as far as he knew, and it didn't even weigh anything. Why wouldn't he want to lug around some camping supplies?

Before heading to sleep, he took out his book, *Potion Making for Dummies*, and started to read.

Chapter 19

James woke up feeling surprisingly limber, considering he'd just spent the night on another cave floor. Maybe his body was getting used to sleeping without a memory foam mattress. He stretched as he stood and put away his book. He'd fallen asleep learning more about the native plants and their uses.

Apparently Roundleaf, one of the plants he'd found in Nana's garden, was an ingredient for a healing salve. He'd also found entries for the other herbs he'd picked. He could use River Maple to create a water-breathing potion, and he could chew Soldier's Nettle to give himself a huge stamina regeneration boost. According to the book, if he were a higher level, then he could refine the Soldier's Nettle into a potion that would allow someone to "Run for three days and three nights without rest." The plant got its name from its popularity with soldiers, who would pick it off of the side of the road as they marched. James had been excited to try some until he'd read that it was technically banned for soldier use because it produced an incredibly addicting euphoria. He decided to forego the herb unless he really needed it. The last thing he needed was a magical cocaine addiction.

All that reading had given him a new skill, Alchemy, which allowed him to use raw ingredients to create potions, salves, pills, and elixirs. After staying up most of the night and reading through a quarter of the book, he was Skill

Rank 5 in Alchemy, which gave him a +5% chance of success when crafting potions. It also gave him a 1% chance to discover a new use for an ingredient when harvested. He'd also gotten a quest to create a basic health potion.

YOU HAVE BEEN GIVEN A QUEST: LEARNING TO BREW I

Learning to Brew I: Create one basic healing potion

Suggested level: None

Reward: One Health Potion

Penalty for failure or refusal: None

James accepted the quest, and it had prompted him to find one Roundleaf and two measures of Red Silkweed before he could brew the potion. Since he already had the Roundleaf, all he needed was the Red Silkweed which he knew, from an illustration in his book, was a group of long red strands that grew in cracks along the Crimson Mountains.

After packing up his book, James pulled up his status page. It had been a long time since he had reviewed it, and he wanted to see how things were looking after the dungeon.

JAMES

HUMAN (WARRIOR OF DARKNESS)

LEVEL: 10

HEALTH: 121/169   REGENERATES 3.4/HOUR

MANA: 175/175   REGENERATES 3.0/HOUR

STAMINA: 109/220   REGENERATES 3.4/HOUR

STATS

STRENGTH: 22   DEXTERITY: 17

CONSTITUTION: 15

INTELLIGENCE: 20   WISDOM: 19

ENDURANCE: 16   CHARISMA: 1   LUCK:

2   RESILIENCE: 4

SPELLS

SHADOW STEP (LEVEL 1)

SYREUS' WRATH

ABILITIES

DEATH'S STARE (1/7)

IMBUE DARKNESS (4/10)

KNIFE IN THE DARK (1/10)

BRANDS

MARK OF SYTAR

DIVINE QUEST (MINOR)

ACHIEVEMENTS

DUMB LUCK

CLUMSY I

Not bad.

His stats were a bit uneven, but he'd collected three Spells, which he was excited about.

James scrambled up the rock face, nimbly placing his feet on small outcroppings that would have escaped his notice a month ago. Intuitively, he bent his knees to keep the weight on his legs and used his arms for balance. Once he reached the top of the ravine, he hopped to his feet and started along the path to Riverside, humming a tune. He was excited to turn in his quest and see what Nana would have for him next.

A few minutes into his walk, he felt a strange sense of unease. It was like the feeling he'd gotten from his Sixth Sense ability—a general feeling that there was something wrong, but nothing to tell him what it was. He looked around for the cause of his unease. He was sure it wasn't wolves. When they stalked him, he'd heard the slight shifting of the brush as they moved through it and their panting as they loped through the forest. He'd seen flashes of their pelt as they slunk through the trees.

This was different. James extended his senses, but he couldn't feel anything. But it was more than that. It was a distinct nothing, as if all the surrounding creatures had abandoned the forest. It was silent.

Walking faster, James frequently checked over his shoulder, hoping to catch whatever or whoever was following him. Still, nothing. A fog crept in, growing noticeably thicker by the second. He quickened his pace.

YOU HAVE GAINED 1 SKILL RANK IN SIXTH SENSE.

YOU ARE NOW SKILL RANK 2.

It's not really useful if you can't figure out how to escape.

The fog thickened until James couldn't see the path underneath his feet. "Whoever's out there. I'm not afraid of you," he called out with false bravado.

Silence.

He pulled out his sword and stood, waiting for the inevitable attack. He could feel the prick of eyes against the back of his neck. It was coming.

He waited for five minutes, but nothing happened.

James waited another five minutes and still nothing happened

Weird. The fog seemed to wrap around him, caressing him and creating odd patterns that danced across his mind. James couldn't tear his eyes away. It twisted. Twirled.

Beautiful...

YOU HAVE BEEN [MESMERIZED]

James tried to fight a sudden sleepiness as the fog caressed him, but his limbs grew heavy and darkness overtook him.

Chapter 20

James groaned. His head was killing him. His mouth was dry as if he'd drunken an entire bottle of tequila before bed. He pried open his eyes, rubbing at the crust around them. He groaned again. It felt like he was lying on his back on the deck of a ship. Slowly, he looked around. He was on a cart rumbling across a dirt road. More importantly, he was in a cage. He groaned again. His head really hurt.

"Wha—"

"Shhh," a voice hissed.

"Where—" James tried again, his mind still full of fog. It felt like one of those mornings where he'd taken a few Benadryls to sleep and woken up more tired than when he'd gone to bed.

"Shhh." This was accompanied by a hand across James' mouth that got the message across, shutting him up. Head slightly clearer, James tried to sit up and look around, but before he could, the speaker hissed at him again. "Keep your head down and pretend you're asleep. We can talk tonight."

James wasn't sure what was going on, but listening to the other guy in the cage was probably a smart idea. He dropped his head back down and cracked an eye open, looking for the speaker. His eyes roved around the cage, stopping on a graceful, dark-skinned woman with pointed ears. She wore bright red robes, suggesting she was a mage. At first, her appearance confused him. She looked human, aside from the ears. But then he read her status page.

> NAME: NIDRA FORREN
>
> RACE: WOOD ELF
>
> LEVEL 22
>
> CLASS: FIRE MAGE

An elf!

Why did she look so much like a human? And why couldn't she escape with a fireball or something? As he stared at her, her eyes opened, and she glared at him with a look that said, "Dude. Stop being creepy."

He glanced away, embarrassed, before scanning the rest of the cart. Aside from the elf, there were two teenage humans, and what looked to be a cross between a panther and a human. The panther lay alongside the bars of the cage, projecting the image of a sleeping animal, but James could see how tense he was as his tail flicked and his ears twitched.

> NAME: ORREL FLEETFOOT
>
> RACE: BEASTKIN-PANTHER
>
> LEVEL 24
>
> CLASS: ANCESTRAL WARRIOR

James wanted to stare longer, but he didn't want to alienate any more people in the cart. The Elven woman, Nidra, was still glaring at him through half-closed eyes. He would need to apologize to her when he got a chance.

James' eyes fell on the two tall Humans sprawled across the floor of the cart. As far as he could tell, they were twins.

> NAME: OPHEL SERENO
>
> RACE: HUMAN
>
> LEVEL 13
>
> CLASS: ROGUE

> NAME: LUCIEN SERENO
>
> RACE: HUMAN
>
> LEVEL 15
>
> CLASS: BLADE

When James met Lucien's eyes, the youth winked at him and made the shushing gesture again. He had a friendly expression on his face and mouthed two words. *Talk Later.* He then mimed closing his eyes.

"Audun, I swear to Vither. Your spell's wearing off." A sharp, cruel voice cut through the silence.

"It's not wearing off. They're just shifting in their sleep."

James cracked his eyelids and peeked at the speakers.

> NAME: AUDUN STROMMEN
>
> RACE: ORC
>
> LEVEL 27
>
> CLASS: HYPNOTIST

NAME: VEGAR HEZIEL

RACE: HALF-ORC, HALF-DWARF

LEVEL 30

CLASS: SLAVE TRADER

James cringed when he saw the orcs. They looked nothing like Ferko. Their tusks weren't trimmed and jutted from their lips, ending in fine points. When one of them opened their mouth to yawn, James saw a jumble of sharp, mismatched teeth.

When Vegar turned to glance at the slaves, James caught a glimpse of his face and shuddered. Vegar had a cruel face with a scar running across his right eye. He somehow looked pinched and sallow, even though he stood twice as wide and almost a half-foot shorter than James. He rode at the head of the group of slavers with confidence, leaving James no doubt as to who was in charge.

Audun was steering the cart, lazily flicking the reins of two large lizard-beasts as they trundled across the path. He was tall and wore a voluminous robe that hid most of his body. The parts that James could see were covered in tattoos of arcane symbols that *crawled* across his skin. The longer James stared at the tattoos, the heavier his eyes felt, as if someone were stacking weights on his eyelids. He tried to fight the feeling, but fell back into a dark and troubled sleep.

YOU HAVE BEEN [MESMERIZED]

James woke up to the darkness of the night sky. The cart wasn't moving, which helped with his pulsing headache, but he still felt awful. Apparently magically induced sleep caused hangovers. He shook his head, trying to clear the fog.

"Morning, sleepy!" Lucien greeted him cheerily.

"How's it going?" Ophel asked.

"What's going on?" James whispered. "Where are we?"

Ophel and Lucien exchanged glances. "I don't know if you've noticed, but we're in a cage." Lucien said.

"And as for where we're going, no clue," Ophel finished.

"Then why are you so cheery?" James snapped. He knew they were trying to be helpful, but he couldn't understand how they could be so bubbly given the situation.

Lucien grinned at him. "Well, we aren't dead yet! Besides, I'm sure someone's coming to rescue us."

Ophel smiled. "And we're still together."

James was flabbergasted. How could these two be so cavalier about being kidnapped and caged? He looked around. The rest of the prisoners were sitting quietly, watching their conversation, curious about the newcomer, but unwilling to speak.

James kept the emotion from his voice. "Do you guys have any idea where we're going?"

The Elven woman, Nidra, looked up. "Can you all quiet down a bit? I'd rather not wake them." She gestured at the orcs.

James peered through the bars and saw three canvas tents. An Orc woman sat close by, leaning against a tree stump as if on guard duty.

NAME: SINEW BRUTSBANE

RACE: HALF-ORC, HALF-TROLL

LEVEL 30

CLASS: BARBARIAN

Sinew was built like a truck, and an enormous wooden club lay by her side. As James watched, the half-orc let out a loud grunt and shifted, scratching her face. James froze, but after a second realized that she was asleep and snoring.

James shuddered. He did not want to fight that.

"So, when's your rescuer coming?" James whispered, quieter, to Lucien.

"No idea," Lucien said. "We ran away from home, our dad's probably sending someone to hunt us down now."

"Huh." Unless they were nobles, he had serious doubts about their parent's ability to hire someone who could take out a party of slavers single-handedly.

James reached for his pouch, but it was gone. Frantically, he patted himself down. He was still wearing his leather armor and his necklace, but he was missing his weapons and pouch. He wondered why they hadn't removed the armor and jewelry.

James noticed multiple notifications flashing for his attention, so he opened them.

A Slave Trader with the skill Chains of Oppression has captured and branded you.

YOU HAVE BEEN GIVEN A BRAND: PROPERTY.

Property

- 20% penalty to all stats and skills when fighting your owner.

+ 20% to all stats and skills when following orders

James looked down, examining his body and searching for the brand. It must have appeared while he had been sleeping because he hadn't even realized that he had a fresh one. He searched his body and found the brand on the top of his left foot. It looked like a pair of wings framing a keyhole. "No, no, no," James whispered. His mouth went dry, and he sucked in deep breaths. The other slaves were looking at him with a mixture of pity and resignation. Even Nidra's glare had turned into knowing sympathy.

Scared to continue looking through his notifications, but even more scared not to, James kept reading, knuckles white as he gripped the bars of the cage.

YOU HAVE BEEN GIVEN A QUEST: LIBERTY OR DEATH

Liberty or Death: An hour of fighting for your freedom is worth a lifetime in chains. Will you die alone as a slave or fight for your freedom?

Suggested level: n/a

Reward: [Property] will change to [Liberated]

Mandatory quest: Unable to refuse

The quest gave James hope, and he turned to the other slaves, his mind racing with ideas.

"Has anyone tried to escape?" He asked desperately.

Nidra replied first. "Don't bother. Even if you could use magic, which you clearly can't, the cage is warded against it."

"Okay, I don't need the attitude. I'm just trying to help."

As soon as he snapped, he regretted it. He knew she was probably just as stressed as he was, if not more, and that it wasn't an excuse for him to snap.

In a nicer tone, he apologized. "Sorry. I'm just stressed." He gestured around at the cage. "Obviously."

She nodded, accepting his apology. "We all are."

James decided to move the conversation away from escape, which was clearly a sore subject. "I've never met an elf before. Where do you all live?"

She sighed. "I live in Fallmire."

James had thought Fallmire was a human city, but from the way Nidra responded, he could tell she didn't want to elaborate. "Oh." James turned to Orrel. "How about you?"

Orrel glared at him for a second before turning away. The Panther-kin's eyes were orange and slitted, similar to Lamia's, but more pronounced. More importantly, they dripped with hatred. Of what, James wasn't sure.

"Don't bother." Lucien chimed in.

"Yea, he hasn't spoken since we got caught, and we've been here for weeks." Ophel agreed.

"How'd you get captured?" James asked the twins.

"Great story," Ophel said.

"The best," Lucien agreed.

Ophel started the story. "It started on a dark stormy night. We—"

Lucien cut him off. "No, it didn't. It was a clear day."

"Shut up, it adds drama." Ophel argued.

Lucien ignored him. "It started on a nice temperate evening. We—"

A sudden noise shut him up and all the slaves immediately dropped to the ground, pretending to sleep, with James following their cue.

Sinew groaned loudly, stretching her arms as she stoop up, glaring at the cart. They all lay there, motionless. James wasn't sure what would happen if she realized they were awake, but he didn't want to find out.

While James lay quietly in the cage, he planned an escape. He had an idea, but he needed to make sure everything was in place before he filled the others in.

The rest of the night passed in relative silence, none of them wanting to risk waking Sinew again.

The next morning started with the sharp sound of metal against metal as Vegar struck at the bars of the cage with a crude, rusty sword that looked like he'd stolen it from a pirate film. Each strike of the sword created an unpleasant metallic ringing.

Once he'd made sure all the slaves were awake, Vegar doled out a ladle of water to each of them. When Vegar got to James, he held out the ladle the same as for the others. James reached for it gratefully, but when his lips touched the metal, Vegar slowly tilted it, letting the water spill to the ground.

"Oops," he said, grinning maliciously.

James could have screamed, but looked down quietly. He knew Vegar was waiting for a reaction so he dish out some punishment. It was a classic way to show who's boss.

James spent the rest of the day daydreaming about having a drink of water and a bite of food. That night Vegar repeated the same trick, tipping the ladle over and pouring out James' serving of water, a cruel glint in his eyes.

Over the next few days, James observed the group of slavers as they set up and tore down the camp. They'd stored all their gear underneath the cart, so they would pull it out every night, pick someone to stand guard over the slaves, and set up camp.

In total, there were five slavers, the three he'd already seen and two others. Sinew had a brother, Butcher, who was just as large and twice as mean. Both of the Half-Orcs were the definition of brute, and looked like they had been injecting steroids since they were two. They spent their days arguing over who was stronger and which one of them had more giant blood, to the point when one would inevitably pull out their club and smash the other alongside the head. That was usually when Vegar told them to cut it out, although sometimes he let them fight for a while. Even though they were both close to eight feet tall, it was obvious they feared him.

There was also Mandra. James hadn't noticed her until the fourth day when she emerged from the trees on the side of the path and whispered something to Vegar.

> NAME: MANDRA SALIEN
>
> RACE: ORC
>
> LEVEL 23
>
> CLASS: BEAST TAMER

While James was watching her, a falcon swooped down from the clouds and landed on Mandra's shoulder briefly, before taking off again. She turned to Vegar and whispered something to her. He nodded.

James wondered if the rest of the slaves knew what was going on. He turned to look at them, but they were all feigning sleep.

"What's happening?" James whispered.

"Another poor soul is about to be captured," Lucien whispered back sadly. "But seriously, do us all a favor and shut up during the daytime."

James shut his mouth and watched with mounting horror as the Orcs pulled the cart into the undergrowth, and Butcher and Sinew hid on opposite sides of the path. Vegar grabbed an arrow from the cart and stabbed it into his own shoulder, hissing in pain before laying on the ground near a dense part of the forest where Audun was hiding behind the undergrowth.

A few minutes later James saw a Dwarf walking down the road, whistling.

NAME: ARIK FORGEBORN

RACE: DWARF

LEVEL 26

CLASS: HAMMER

When the Dwarf saw Vegar, collapsed and calling for help with an arrow in his shoulder, he stopped and pulled a large war hammer off his back, then crouched next to him.

"What happened?" he asked.

"Bandits attacked me. They stole—"

While Vegar talked, an ethereal blue mist gathered in the surrounding forest. The spell took hold, and Arik froze, staring blankly into the mist. As soon as he froze, Butcher and Sinew jumped out of the forest and grabbed him, holding him in place.

Audun walked out of the forest, sweating profusely and breathing heavily. He approached the slave's cage and fog started billowing out from underneath the cart. James felt the fog surrounding him, pulling him into unconsciousness.

Chapter 21

James was the first one up, followed by Orrel, then Nidra and then the two humans. He lay there, pretending to sleep while trying to figure out how long he had been asleep for. Based on the position of the sun, he was fairly confident that he had absolutely no idea what time it was. He also wasn't sure where they were.

He lay awake for the next few hours, trying to fall back asleep. There wasn't really a point to staying awake. Still... The bright sun hitting his eyelids made it almost impossible to sleep. Eventually he gave up and just lay against the bars, thinking.

His mind eventually wandered back to the prophecy he'd heard in the inn. He wondered what it meant. How it applied to him. After all, there was no way it was a coincidence that he'd been brought to this world at the same time as an apocalyptic-level event.

Am I here to save the world, or to destroy it? Maybe it wasn't about me at all?

That a deity of death had brought him to Novis was telling, and he resolved to fight against anyone, or anything that would try to make him commit whatever evil acts the prophecy foretold.

In a stroke of luck, Butcher took guard duty that night. It meant they could talk, because he always fell asleep before his butt hit the dirt. Arik hadn't woken from the spell yet, so James turned to the other captives. "So, where do you think we're headed?"

"Probably Iruek-Vrul." Lucien speculated.

A low moan interrupted him as the recently captured Dwarf started to wake.

"Shhhh," James hissed at Arik.

"My head," The Dwarf moaned, massaging his temples. "How much did I drink?"

Butcher interrupted with a loud snore, and James grabbed Arik over the mouth to shut him up.

The Dwarf struggled for a second, his eyes widening as he processed his surroundings. He tried to get up, but Lucien helped James hold him down. It worked for a second, but when James felt a slimy substance on his palm, he stared at the Dwarf in disbelief. "Are you licking my hand?"

A muffled "yeff?" squeezed between James' fingers.

He groaned. "Disgusting. Fine, I'll let go of your mouth, but you have to promise to shut up and listen to us, okay?"

Arik nodded in agreement, and James took his hand off of the Dwarf's mouth and wiped it on his leg. Lucien let go of his arms.

Looking extremely disgruntled, Arik sat silently on the floor of the cart and waited for an explanation. James took the time to examine the Dwarf. He was fascinated, like he had been with the elf, Nidra. Arik was around four and a half feet tall, well-muscled and extremely hairy. He eyed James with hostility.

Oh, right. I'm being creepy again.

He kept forgetting that he shouldn't stare at the fantasy creatures around him, but it was hard not to. Trying to ignore the fact that this was the first Dwarf he'd ever seen, James explained their predicament.

The longer James talked, the tenser the Dwarf got, until he sprang to his feet with remarkable agility and started yanking on the bars. The others tried to stop him, but they were too late.

He'd woken Butcher.

With an angry grunt Butcher stood up, his angry shadow looming over the cage. He lumbered towards the slaves and slammed his wooden club against the bars so hard that they bent. Alerted by the noise, the rest of the slavers woke up and came out of their tents to see what was going on.

Vegar approached, a cruel smile splitting his face. "What do we have here?" He asked. "An escape attempt?"

Arik swore at Vegar and tugged harder against the bars. "Orcish scum!" he spat, giving up on his futile attempt to free himself, and stood, facing Vegar. "Invoking the name of Vyher, I formally challenge you to a Duelo-Rai." Time seemed to freeze for a second and the words hung in the air, as if the universe were registering what had just happened. An almost imperceptible energy crackled in the air between Arik and Vegar.

Orrel growled an almost imperceptible, "No."

Vegar laughed, his mouth twisted into a cruel smile. "All right, Dwarf. I accept your challenge." In a louder tone of voice that had the air of a ritual he continued, "Invoking the name of Vither, I accept the terms of the Duelo-Rai."

James glanced between the two of them, with no idea what had just happened. By the look on everyone's face, this 'Duel of Rye' was a big deal.

Vegar and Arik's eyes misted over as they read notifications that James couldn't see, while the rest of the slavers were excitedly clearing a wide circular area in the center of the camp. It was the fastest James had seen any of them move. When James turned to ask his fellow slaves what was going on, he saw that they were waiting in excited anticipation. The only people who weren't excited were himself, who was just confused, and Orrel, whose mouth was locked into a grim frown.

"What's going on?" James whispered to the twins.

"A Duelo-Rai!" Lucien exclaimed excitedly but quietly, clarifying when he saw the confused expression on James' face. "A soul-duel. They're fighting for his freedom."

Can I do that? Maybe he'd request one after he watched Arik's.

Vegar and Arik's eyes returned to focus. Vegar was the first to speak, calling Audun over to the cage while Arik waited patiently.

The mage scrambled to obey his leader and met Vegar at the door to the cage.

"Put the mage to sleep before we open the door." Vegar ordered the hypnotist, referring to Nidra, who glared back at him.

Audun looked embarrassed. "I can't. My Mana hasn't regenerated from earlier."

James recalled how tired the mage had looked after casting the spell on Arik earlier. How much Mana did that mesmerize spell take? If he could only use it once, that would make the ability less overpowered. James could use that to his advantage. Another puzzle piece fell into place in his escape plan.

Vegar's sharp voice cut through James' thoughts. "What exactly am I paying you for if you can't put the slaves to sleep whenever I need it? It's not like you're cheap."

Stoically, Audun replied, "You pay me to help you capture them with minimal bloodshed so you can run with a skeleton crew. I probably save you five times the gold I cost you."

Vegar's mouth twitched into a frown, and he turned away from the mage. He gestured to Butcher and Sinew. "You two. Let the Dwarf out of his cage."

He then turned to Nidra, who was glaring at him. "Watch yourself, Elf," he hissed before stepping back. "You'll regret any funny business."

As soon as Butcher and Sinew opened the doors, to the surprise of no one, Nidra started casting. A fiery glow surrounded her body and she let off a bolt of crackling fire, targeting Butcher's head. The bolt hit dead-center and the Orc burst into flames. He screamed in pain and rushed off looking for water, leaving the exit unguarded.

James tensed, getting ready to run. The gate was open. He could cast Shadow Step and be gone within seconds. They wouldn't be able to follow him if he used his spell to get across the river. But James couldn't leave the other slaves behind.

There was a black flash, followed by a scream as Orrel slashed Nidra across the face with his paw, carving three deep furrows into her skin and interrupting her next cast. The glow surged back into her body and she fell, writhing in pain from magical feedback. Orrel stepped back. "I'm sorry. I had no choice," he whispered.

Sinew pulled Arik out from the cage and slammed the door shut.

Silence.

Then Vegar spoke. "You absolute fool! Do you understand how much gold you just cost me? You better hope that doesn't scar."

Orrel stared at Vegar, his expression unreadable, unwilling, or unable to reply.

Vegar pointed at Orrel, then turned to Arik. "That will be your fate. A soulless husk. You'll belong to me for all eternity. Even death won't break our bond."

Arik ignored him and held out his hand. "Give me my hammer."

Vegar laughed and handed the Dwarf his enormous war hammer as the other slavers encircled them. "Let's begin."

The two fighters circled each other. Vegar made the first move, drawing his cutlass and pointing it at Arik. A spectral chain extended from his sword and wrapped around Arik. It slithered down his body and squeezed before vanishing.

Arik retaliated, swinging his hammer at Vegar. It arced slowly, as if it were being swung through molasses. Arik frowned and tried to move faster, but to James it looked as if the Dwarf were pushing through honey. But as the hammer moved it changed shape, lengthening so that Arik could hit Vegar without closing in.

Vegar easily stepped under the blow and smiled. "Can't do much with your movement speed slowed, can you?" He taunted, raising his sword in the air. An orange aura surrounded his body and James got a notification.

YOU ARE INSIDE THE AREA OF EFFECT OF THE CRUSH UPRISING SPELL.

You have been affected by the status effect [Aura of Ogses]

- 50% to all stats to all enslaved beings in the aura

James felt his body weaken as the aura's effect took hold. Vegar stepped forward and spun, slamming the butt of his sword into the back of Arik's head.

A desperate "How?" escaped the Dwarf's lips as he fell into unconsciousness.

Vegar quirked an eyebrow. "You really think I don't have a way to put down rowdy slaves?" He laughed, tossing Arik's limp body into the cage. Nobody moved when the door opened.

Chapter 22

Arik didn't speak for the rest of the night.

He ignored the food and water that the slavers laid out for him. He just stared blankly out through the bars of the cart.

He didn't even crack a smile when Sinew attacked Butcher because she thought he had cut himself a larger piece of bread than her at dinner. Their fistfight had levelled two trees before Vegar put a stop to it, telling them they would pay if anyone heard the racket and investigated the camp.

James gave up on his attempts to console Arik, and his thoughts drifted to the escape plan that had been brewing at the back of his mind. He thought about how magic affected the cart, how slowly Mana regenerated, how at least two of the slaves were bound to the slavers and wouldn't be able to help. Slowly, he assembled the bones of a plan, but he needed to wait for the right moment to pull it off.

That night James had the best rest he'd ever had while stuck in the cart. He dreamt of freedom.

When dawn broke over the slaver camp, Lucien started to hyperventilate. The cumulative stress of the past few weeks had built up to a boiling point. He freaked out, rocking on the floor of the cage and moaning as he held his head in his hands. "I don't think anyone is coming for me."

Ophel tried to comfort his brother, but nothing he said reached Lucien. Eventually Lucien stopped moaning and, with a wild look in his eyes, shook the bars of the cage just like Arik had done. The noise woke the slavers and Vegar stormed out of his tent, fire in his eyes. He wasn't smiling this time.

"Do you know who I am?" Lucien screamed. "I'll kill you."

Vegar approached the bars and placed his face against them, staring directly into Lucien's eyes. "I know who you are," he scoffed. "A dirty, pathetic slave."

Lucien growled and spat directly into his captor's eye. Vegar stumbled back, rubbing at his eyes. He glared at Lucien and pulled out his cudgel, advancing on the cage. Before he'd taken two steps, he stopped. An evil grin spread across his face and he gestured for Audun to join him.

Vegar pulled a crystal out of the pocket of his robes and handed it to the mage as he approached. It looked like the Mana Crystals that James had picked up in the Lion-Ant dungeon, but much more complex. Its geometry was difficult to look at, and it glowed much brighter than the Average Mana Crystals that James had.

Audun took the crystal hesitantly and stared at it. "Are you sure?" he asked. "I used one a few days ago, and—" He stopped speaking, cut short by the expression on Vegar's face. "Of course, sir." Without further hesitation, he crushed the crystal between his fingertips, releasing a blue energy into the air. He inhaled deeply, pulling the energy into his body and held his breath for a second, as if exhaling would allow the energy to escape. Then he started chanting, his fingers contorting into arcane shapes.

A cloud of energy engulfed Audun's body. Through the haze, James could see the mage's tattoos dancing frantically as if they were trying to escape his skin. Before James realized what was happening, it was too late.

James watched helplessly as the slavers entered the cart. But to his surprise, they pulled out Ophel instead of Lucien. They dragged him to a nearby stump and forced him down into a kneeling position.

Spit dripping slowly down his chin, Vegar spoke. "You think we don't know about your nightly chatter? Do you think we're stupid? Do you think we put you to sleep instead of punishing you for stepping out of line because we don't like to hurt people? Do we seem like pacifists to you?" The more he spoke, the redder his face got. "We don't hurt you because we don't want to deliver damaged goods. You're worth more to us uninjured, but sometimes," he sneered, "sometimes we need to teach you slaves a lesson."

By the end of his speech he was spitting out every word, and his eyes were bugging out of his head. Then, like a summer rainstorm, he calmed. His face smoothed out and his smile reappeared, but the evil glint remained behind his eyes. He gestured to the slavers holding Ophel, and they pushed his head down, so he was kneeling with them, holding his head to a tree stump.

"Ophel!" Lucien screamed. Somehow, in his grief, he mustered the strength to break the Mesmer debuff and move. He stumbled to the bars and shook them, sobbing. "He didn't do anything. Take me instead." But his pleas fell on deaf ears.

Vegar's voice had the ring of ceremony to it, as if it were a ritual he had performed many times before. "We have gathered together to witness the execution of the slave Ophel. He has been found guilty of insubordination and insurrection."

At those words, Lucien collapsed to the floor of the cage, sobbing.

Vegar lifted his sword above Ophel's head. "I, Vegar Heziel, execute this slave, severing his bond with this world for eternity. May he find peace in the next world."

An ominous orange glow gathered around his sword, then he brought the sword down on Ophel's head with a meaty thwack, followed by a thump as the head hit the ground.

James' eyes snapped to the stricken man's brother. A grey glow built up in Lucien's eyes and faded, streaming away like smoke in the wind.

Vegar sheathed his sword. "Time to get going. We don't know who might have heard us." There was no trace of a smile left on his face as he turned and looked each of the remaining slaves in the eyes.

Lucien threw up and promptly passed out, while the rest of them just sat in stunned silence at the horror they'd just witnessed.

Over the next three days, nobody spoke. Each slave was lost in their own thoughts, imagining the personal hell that would be the rest of their lives. Every once in a while, one of them would try to comfort Lucien, but he never reacted, staring at the ground with dead eyes.

The slaves weren't the only ones on edge. A few days ago, they'd crossed the river and entered the Witchwood. A constant, thick fog surrounded them, caressing them with its cool touch. It made it impossible to see over ten feet away, and the slightest noise caused the slavers to twitch. As they walked, James could see the tension in the slavers backs as they tried to move the cart through the fog as silently as they could. But who, or what, the slavers were worried about still remained unclear to him.

A few nights later, James had had enough. Making sure that Orrel and Arik - the two soul-bound slaves - couldn't hear him, he pulled Nidra and Lucien aside and whispered to them. "I think I can get us out of here. If I unlock the cage, will you fight?" Lucien ignored him and turned away, but Nidra looked interested.

"How exactly are you planning on getting us out?" she asked skeptically.

"Let me handle that," James said. "I'll let you know when it's time."

As more days passed, James watched and waited. He made a mental note of everything he saw and heard, planning for the moment of escape. A raven flew by, and James had a strange feeling of déjà vu. James tried to put the bird out of his mind but couldn't. For some reason, he had this *feeling* in the back of his mind that something was wrong with the bird. He examined it, trying to figure out what was bothering him. That's when he noticed the runic symbols on the tips of its wings.

The symbols were subtle, and he wouldn't have noticed them if he weren't looking for something off. He tried to interpret the symbols, but he couldn't recognize any of them.

Suddenly, the bird gave a loud caw before turning and staring directly into James' eyes. It held the gaze for a second, then turned and flew away, disappearing into the mist.

That night James decided it was time to put his plan into action. He should have done it earlier, before Ophel died, and that would haunt him, but he couldn't let his mistake keep him down. There were other people that needed saving.

The first step was to test to see if it was possible. He needed to be discreet; he still didn't understand the soul-binding, and he was worried that Arik or Orrel would be obligated to try to stop him. Once he'd made sure that everyone, including the other slaves, was asleep, James cast Shadow Step. He disappeared and in a flash of darkness reappeared on the outside of the cage.

YOU ARE AFFECTED BY [PROPERTY]

-20% to all stats while disobeying orders or attempting to escape.

James was elated.

When Nidra had explained that the cage blocked magic, James had initially lost hope. But when he thought about the practical implementation of magic, something hadn't seemed right to him. It was only after a few days of wondering that he realized what had been bothering him.

How had Audun used magic to mesmerize them while they were in the cage if it blocked magic?

Now, James didn't know much about magic, but he had an extensive history of playing magical role-playing games. With his gaming background, James assumed there had to be some rules behind how the cage worked. He came up with two possible theories. Either the cage blocked all attack magic, or it blocked magic coming in one direction.

Of those theories, the first one was much more likely. James figured that blocking magic one-way would be much harder than just targeting damage-dealing spells. He wasn't sure why he'd figured that, but it felt right.

He stood in the shadow of the slave cart. As soon as his legs touched the ground, he collapsed. Groaning softly, he glanced around to check if anyone had seen him. Once he'd made sure that he was still hidden, James arduously worked his way to a standing position. It had been almost a week since he'd last stood or walked, and his legs were killing him.

James took a step, reveling in the bliss of extended legs. After a few minutes of experimentation, he felt confident enough to walk again and hobbled to the cart where he rifled through the slaver's possessions, looking for anything useful.

The slavers had stocked the cart with bags of rice, vegetables, and stewed meat on top and less immediately useful items deeper in the pile. There was no organization, and finding anything was a challenge, but eventually James found a set of brutal looking curved daggers crafted from a shimmering orange metal. Each dagger had a gemstone pommel, one brown and one white.

Orichalcum Dagger of Density:

Rank: Unusual

+ 10% Armor penetration.

This dagger has been forged from Orichalcum; a dense metal found in deep in the Crimson Mountains.

Orichalcum Dagger of Speed:

Rank: Unusual

+ 20% Attack speed

This dagger has been forged from Orichalcum; a dense metal found in deep in the Crimson Mountains.

Perfect! James had been looking for a replacement for his broken dagger, and now he had two! Even better, both of them were much stronger and more durable than the iron dagger.

James tested the daggers by swinging them around, bravely driving back a force of invisible slavers. Or at least that's what he thought he looked like. In reality, he just kind of flailed around a bit. James wasn't used to the Orichalcum Dagger of Speed and kept mistiming his swings. It was hard to control and felt like someone was pulling on his hand when he attacked with it. At one point while swinging, he almost slashed a gash across his thigh.

After liberating the daggers, James stuck them under his leather clothing and used Shadow Step to return to the inside of the cart without waking anyone else. He'd thought about sneak-attacking the slavers, but decided against it in favor of waiting for an opportune moment. He wasn't confident in his ability to kill six Orcs that were all much stronger than he was without Nidra's help.

The next morning came and James realized that he'd made a mistake. Stuffing two sharp daggers securely into his clothing was very uncomfortable. In fact, he would even say that hiding unprotected daggers in his clothing was a poor decision. It was around the fifth time he poked himself by shifting his weight slightly when he did something about it. Carefully, without letting the other slaves see, he slipped the Orichalcum Dagger of Speed out from his jerkin and handed it to Nidra.

Her eyes widened in shock, and she mouthed a word. *How?*

James grinned. "Don't worry about it. We're going to get out of here. We—" He was interrupted by a prickle on the back of his neck. He turned to Nidra, rubbing at the spot on his neck. "Do you feel that?"

"Feel what?"

"That twinge on the back of your neck, like you're being watched."

Her eyes drifted up and to the left as if she were thinking about something. "You know what? I think I do."

James glanced around nervously. *Is it just me, or is the fog getting thicker?* A raven cawed and swooped overhead. James shivered. "I hate this fog."

Nidra nodded in reply, still looking around nervously.

James pointed at the raven. "That bird's been following us for a few days. Do you know anything about it?"

Nidra stared at the bird for a second. "It feels… wrong. Unnatural. But I don't know what it could be."

As the cart trundled along the dirt road through the Witchwood, James lay back against the bars and closed his eyes, breathing deeply. He imagined that the air he pulled in was cool and crisp, while the air he exhaled was hot and humid. That part didn't work particularly well because they were in the middle of a fog so thick that he felt like he was trying to breathe in water, but he still liked the exercise.

Five minutes of meditation later and James was awarded a prompt.

> YOU HAVE GAINED THE SKILL, MEDITATION.
>
> Meditation (Skill Rank 1):
>
> + 1 Mana regenerated per minute while meditating.
>
> Wow. Clearing your mind is pretty easy when there's nothing in there.

James grinned. Regenerating one Mana per minute would helpful. His current regeneration was around three Mana per hour. He would never have Mana problems again as long as he could meditate between battles. This new skill answered his previous question about the viability of mages in battle.

Hours passed as James sat, Meditating, listening to the creaks as the cart wound its way along the muddy road through the fog. By midday he'd hit Skill Rank 5 in meditation, boosting his Mana regeneration to one-and-a-half per minute. More importantly, he'd fully recovered his Mana from the previous night.

A short while later, Vegar directed Mandra to steer the cart along a tall rocky wall. They followed the overgrown path for an hour, eventually reaching a well-protected clearing next to the riverbank. The only way in was through the small path that they'd taken.

"Stop here!" he shouted to the group.

A loud caw sounded above them as the raven flew overhead.

Nervously eying the bird, Vegar turned to the other slavers. "Weapons ready. They're here."

Chapter 23

Vegar was on edge. Why did the slaves always act up? He thought hiring a mage to subdue them would lower overhead costs because he wouldn't need to chop off a slave's head to prove a point with every trip, but it hadn't worked. He glared at Audun out of the corner of his eyes. The mage wasn't what he'd been promised by the guild. He'd paid a fortune for a mage with a Sleep affinity, which was an abnormality for orcs. Normally Orcs could only specialize in Blood or Metal magic, but after almost a year of searching, he'd found Audun. Why exactly was he paying the guild so much when Audun couldn't use magic when he needed it? Ridiculous.

He took a deep breath, trying to find his Zen. His mother had told him he needed to relax more. Besides, he had more important things to do. He glanced up at the raven.

The Shriekers were coming.

The Shrieker clan had once been subordinate to the Bonebreaker Orc clan—Vegar's clan. They had been the first Goblin tribe to join the Orcs in their quest to escape the Howling Wastes, over the Crimson Mountains and into the East. But when they had encountered resistance from the Dwarves of the Crimson Mountains, the Shriekers had abandoned them. Now, they were sworn enemies.

Vegar ground his teeth and narrowed his eyes as he stared into the forest, trying to make out movement.

There!

A Shrieker stepped out of the tree line, and Vegar shuddered. Disgusting creatures. No matter how much he looked at them, he couldn't get over their large eyes with fully black sclera. Their skin was green, a proper color, not like the pink-skinned Humans, but unlike his own tough, leathery hide, the Goblin was covered in scales. Scales! Like a common beast. He spat in the dirt.

"Til." He greeted the Shrieker Shaman with the correct honorific, ducking his head slightly. No matter how much he hated the creatures, if he could get out of this without a fight, he would. Especially against a group with a Shaman. Shrieker shamans wielded powerful magic, gifted to them from their dark goddess. Fighting against a group of Shriekers led by a shaman was foolhardy. The more you killed, the stronger they got. Truth be told, he wasn't a hundred percent confident that he could win against the shaman.

"Sssslavemasterrr," the Goblin hissed in greeting, struggling to speak in the common tongue as it dipped its head.

"Is there any way we can end this peacefully?" Vegar asked. He didn't have time to make small talk.

The Shrieker let out a barking laugh. "Sssstraight to the point. Very well. Give ussss the marked one, and you can go."

Vegar followed the Goblin's gaze to the cage, his eyes flitting from slave to slave. "Marked one?" He had no idea what the Shrieker was talking about. Aside from the slave brand, he hadn't seen a mark on any of his slaves, but then again, he hadn't really checked. It was so much easier to just toss them in the cart without removing their armor and risk of breaking the sleep spell.

The shaman's eyes widened. "You don't know?" it hissed in surprise.

Vegar's eyes stopped on one of the humans. This one didn't flinch when Vegar met his eyes. He locked gazes with the orc until finally; it was the slaver that looked away.

That one would be a problem, but there was something about him. A strange energy. Vegar was surprised he hadn't noticed it before, but now that he was looking for it, it was obvious. "Why do you want him?" Vegar asked curiously, fishing for information.

"Our goddessss has questionsss." The shaman replied. "Sssso. Do we have a deal?"

He could hand over the slave and head home without a fight. He'd still collect a tidy profit from the three remaining slaves, especially the Elf. It was almost impossible to find an elf roaming through human territory, and their lands were too well defended for him to even consider entering. With the money he made, he might even be able to hire a more competent mage. But something felt wrong. Why did the Shrieker want the slave so badly?

No, he wouldn't give the Shriekers anything. His eyes hardened, and he spat on the ground before turning to the shaman to refuse his offer.

Before he could speak, a crossbow bolt sped out of the trees, catching Vegar in the shoulder, a crimson arc of blood fountaining out as he spun from the force of the blow. Vegar let out a pained howl, pointing to the trees where the arrow had come from. "Kill them!" he screamed, frantically backing away from the fight. His skills were great for dealing with slaves, but not as useful in direct combat. That's what the others were for.

He retreated to the cart, dodging Sinew and Butcher as they barreled toward the shaman, a red glow surrounding them as they activated their berserker rage. He smiled. Hopefully, they'd overwhelm the shaman before he could cast. Normal berserkers were dangerous. Berserkers with hereditary troll regeneration were deadly. Even as Vegar watched, cuts appeared on their skin, caused by their own damaging auras, before healing instantly.

His smile turned into a frown as a wave of Shriekers leapt out of the forest and formed a wall between the shaman and the two slavers. Vegar flinched at the crunch of bone as the two slavers careened into the line of terrified Goblins.

Turning his attention away from the orcs Vegar focused on the shaman. Purple light pulsed at the tip of his staff as the shaman chanted, holding his staff high in the air. For the first time in a long time, Vegar felt fear's icy grip on his heart. He knew that spell. To confirm his suspicions, he glanced at the minions. They were all small, without the normal physiological changes of higher leveled beings. He'd estimate they were between levels five and twelve. To confirm, he cast Appraise on three of them.

LEVEL 9 (GOBLIN)

ESTIMATED VALUE: 13 GOLD

LEVEL 7 (GOBLIN)

ESTIMATED VALUE: 7 GOLD

LEVEL 11 (GOBLIN)

ESTIMATED VALUE: 23 GOLD

Well, he'd confirmed it. They were all low level. That was bad. "Butcher! Sinew! Kill them before the shaman finishes casting!" He could see the two of them look at each other in confusion, then at the swarm of Goblins on top of them, then at the shaman. Realization struck and the two of them redoubled their efforts. Butcher grabbed a Goblin that had been on his shoulders stabbing him in the back and threw him into a tree.

Vegar returned his attention to the shaman who was still casting his spell. Spirit of Vengeance was a powerful death spell. It would trap the souls of every one of the Shrieker allies who died and use them to create a monster.

Nearby, Mandra burst from the undergrowth and raised her longbow. Above, her falcon screeched as it fought with the shaman's dark familiar, the midnight raven.

Vegar looked around.

Where was that blasted mage?

Cowering next to me. Of course.

Annoyed, Vegar roughly pushed the mage towards the shaman. "Go. Use your magic," he hissed.

"But it's not really—"

"Go!" Vegar ordered.

Audun's eyes widened in fear, then he squeezed them shut in concentration. A dim purple glow built up between his hands, like he was rolling a ball of dough. Tendrils of mist enveloped him, taking on the same purple tint as his magic. Slowly the mist swirled into the ball between his hands and condensed into a thick cloud.

He released his spell at the same time that Mandra released her arrow, sending the orb through the air towards the shaman.

Vegar felt his heart lift as the spell joined Mandra's arrow on a collision course towards the Shrieker shaman. Maybe this wouldn't be the massacre he thought it would be.

But life never works out the way you want it to. Before the two attacks hit the shaman, he slammed his staff into the ground. A bubble of purple energy expanded from its tip and surrounded him. Mandra's arrow shattered on the barrier, and Audun's mist exploded harmlessly into a cloud of violet vapor. The wretched beast was already chanting the words to his next spell. The big one.

Vegar stared at the shaman, his hope fading, then turned to Audun. "Do it again. Stronger this time." He knew it wouldn't work, but he needed a distraction. It was time to get serious. He hadn't wanted to use his trump card because it took so long to charge, but if he didn't...

Audun stared back at him, fear in his eyes. "I... I can try. That staff is powerful, and my spells aren't designed for combat."

"It's fine. Do it."

Audun sent more of the purple mist swirling around the shaman's shield, obscuring his vision.

While Audun and Mandra distracted the shaman with their attacks, Vegar rifled through the cart.

Where was it?

He briefly wondered why someone had rifled through the cart, but didn't have time to interrogate his fellow slavers. There'd be time to talk later. He let out a cry of triumph as he pulled a large crossbow from under a bag of rice.

Drakefire Crossbow:

Rank: Epic

Enchantment School: Fire, Air

Durability: 1,975/1,975

Charge time: 1 minute

> Ammunition: 2/2
>
> Recharge Rate: One bolt every two weeks.
>
> This crossbow was lovingly crafted from the wood of a redfire tree and enchanted to produce bolts of pure Drakefire.

Vegar looked at the crossbow in his hands. It was exquisitely carved from a red-hued wood with gold trimmings. Two high-level monster cores had been carved and placed on either side of the catch. The fire core produced the destructive energy while the wind core helped stabilize the shape into a bolt and launch the projectiles. The devastating weapon had cost him over ten thousand gold, but it was worth it. Nothing could withstand the force of the crossbow.

Returning his attention to the fight, Vegar was pleased to see it was going well. Butcher and Sinew were covered in large gashes, their regeneration unable to keep up with the damage they were taking, but they were still standing. The corpses were piled high around them. They stood back-to-back, fighting the last two Shriekers.

The battle with the shaman was not going as well. Arrows littered the ground around his shield. The occasional flash of violet light through the fog would let them know that the shield was still active. Deep inside the fog there was an almost blinding violet light as the shaman neared the end of his spell.

Unable to wait any longer, Vegar stepped out from behind the cart and pointed his crossbow at the shaman. He stepped on the strap, cocking the string to the creaking protest of the rarely used mechanism. As soon as it locked behind the catch, bright orange energy engulfed it. The energy built up and lengthened, taking the form of a flaming arrow.

The shaman cried out in triumph, raising his arms and letting loose his spell. A pulse of violet light radiated from his body, washing over the battlefield as Vegar let loose his bolt. The flaming projectile let out a deafening roar as it punched through the shield and struck the shaman in the shoulder. The arrow exploded, engulfing the shaman in fire.

You have killed Saru-Til (Level 39).

+ 3,467 experience points

Vegar grinned. Getting enough experience to level up at his level without having to tackle high level dungeons was difficult, so every chunk he received was worth celebrating.

His joy was short lived.

An ominous howl pierced the mist as the violet light settled on the Shrieker corpses that littered the ground. For a second, the universe stood still. Then, a stream of light flowed out of every corpse and attached itself to the one still standing.

With a screech, Mandra's falcon plummeted from the air and landed in a crumpled heap on the ground. She screamed and ran to it, her longbow forgotten on the ground. The raven swooped down and attacked Butcher, pecking at his eyes. The Orc stumbled back, swatting at the bird, leaving Sinew to finish the last Shrieker.

The sole remaining Shrieker glowed with an eerie violet light, and Vegar screamed. "Kill it! Kill it now!" He was already charging another bolt on his crossbow and he pointed it at the monstrosity that was taking form, a 15-foot-tall behemoth that Dwarfed even Butcher. Spines crawled down its back, and the Goblin's thin scales had thickened and hardened into a powerful armor. Six arms poked out from its lizard-like body and two cruel, curved horns erupted from its forehead.

A tag appeared.

SOUL COLLECTOR (BOSS: LEVEL 75)

Vegar let out a fearful roar, letting loose his flaming bolt. It flew true, striking the creature mid-chest. The flame penetrated deep, charring the creature's flesh, but the flames didn't consume it like they'd consumed the shaman. All of its energy had gone into penetrating the monster's armor. The creature roared in anger and swung a massive clawed fist at Sinew, throwing her into a nearby tree with enough force to topple it. That terrified Vegar—nothing could move Sinew. She was a hunk of pure muscle, over seven feet tall and built like a brick wall.

He backed away. Maybe he could escape and save himself. But Butcher rejoined the fight, blood leaking from his empty eye sockets. The raven had pecked his eyes out.

Together, Butcher and Sinew held back the beast while Audun used the last of his Mana to cast debuffs on the monstrosity to slow it. Mandra rejoined the fight, sending arrow after rage-filled arrow streaking towards the beast. The bolts from her powerful longbow barely scratching its armor, but they drove it back. Vegar stopped retreating and tossed the spent crossbow to the side. He unsheathed his sword.

They could win this.

Over the next hour, they slowly whittled down the monster's health. The longer they took, the harder the fight as it got used to its new body. But finally, Vegar's sword penetrated the patch of scales that he'd weakened with his Drakefire bolt. The sword slid in, driving deep into the monster's heart.

You have killed Soul Collector (Boss: Level 75).

+ 67,454 experience points

Basking in the glow of his kill, Vegar allowed Mandra to harvest materials from the beast while Audun, Butcher, and Sinew searched the Shrieker corpses. It didn't matter. Vegar only had eyes for one body. Approaching the corpse of the shaman, he picked up the still-glowing staff. It was carved from wood with a powerful violet core embedded in the tip. Vegar ignored the shaman's burnt clothing in favor of two rings and a bracelet that gave off a soft orange glow. He left the rest of the loot to his crew.

Wishing he had the ability to identify items, Vegar put them away in the cart, and waited for the other slavers to finish looting. Once they were done, he called them over to gather around the cart. They all looked like hell. Butcher and Sinew were covered in large cuts and bruises. Sinew was missing an ear and had a little nub where it was already starting to grow back. Butcher was missing both eyes—how he was able to finish the fight was beyond Vegar's understanding. Audun had spent all of his Mana and lay half-dead on the ground. Mandra had disappeared into the forest with the corpse of her bird the second the fight had ended. Vegar didn't understand, but he didn't begrudge her some alone time.

They all stared silently back as Vegar looked them over. He'd wanted to put some distance between them and the battlefield before more Shriekers found them, but seeing the state his people were in, he couldn't. He may rule through pain and fear, but as a leader he still had to know when he was going too far. That was just pragmatic. "Let's set up camp here tonight." He said, to the relief of the other slavers.

Once they had warm food in their bellies, they relaxed, as much as they could with what they'd been through. Every once in a while, Vegar would turn to see the eyes of the slave on him. The one the Shriekers had wanted. *What was his name again?*

An ominous wind cut through the forest, tossing leaves and small branches in the air. Vegar looked around nervously. The sky darkened, and the trees shivered as the gale built up into a full storm. Raindrops the size of his fist fell through the air as bolts of lightning smashed into the ground in explosions of pure power.

This storm wasn't natural. Vegar looked around frantically. *The shaman! He must still be alive! But how?*

His eyes fell on the slave, who was now standing outside of the cart, chanting. A rainbow of light surrounded him as his fingers wove through an intricate spell form. *How had he gotten out? Where could he have possibly learned a spell this powerful?*

Vegar didn't have time to answer those questions as he dodged a piece of hail as big as his head that left a crater when it hit the earth. "Kill him!" Vegar screamed at the others, pointing towards James.

Chapter 24

James watched Vegar's eyes widen as the slaver noticed him casting. He had been so distracted by the fight that he hadn't noticed when James used Shadow Step to escape the cart.

> YOU ARE AFFECTED BY [PROPERTY] -20% TO ALL STATS WHILE YOU GO AGAINST YOUR OWNERS
>
> You are attempting to escape. Stay free for 24 hours or kill your owner to lose your [Property] status.

Once James had escaped, he moved to a slightly better hidden area and started to cast Syreus' Wrath. Wind whipped around him as he spoke, picking up small branches and flinging them around the camp. The more he spoke, the stronger the wind and the larger the radius of the storm. Vegar stepped towards him, arms outstretched, but it was much too late to stop him.

James stood motionless, his entire being focused on casting the spell. The raw power of a god flowed through him as he channeled the power of the God of Storms, using his body as a conduit for the energy of the amulet.

"Vyas Etero Vicie!" With those last three words James completed the spell and the storm burst forth in a raging maelstrom of energy. Thick columns of

lightning struck the ground, blasting up clumps of dirt and creating craters in the earth. Droplets of water the size of his fist intermingled with hail the size of his head, barraging the ground as snowflakes floated down peacefully. With a small expulsion of will, James set up a safe zone around the slave cart, creating a hole in the storm to keep the other slaves safe.

The violence of the storm had taken the slavers by surprise, and they paid for it as they were barraged by wind, rain, and hail. Sinew tried to crawl towards him but couldn't make any headway in the raging storm, her strong muscles bulging as she pushed against the headwinds.

James had no such issue. Surrounded by a cone of stillness, he advanced on Vegar. The slaver tried to raise his sword to defend himself, but a chunk of ice slammed into his arm, breaking it with a crack. The slaver screamed in pain, dropping his sword, but James didn't slow, advancing on his enemy with his Orichalcum dagger drawn.

Vegar tried to speak, but James couldn't hear him over the sound of the storm. With another small exertion of his willpower, he extended the clearing around him to cover the head slaver.

"How dare you! I am your master and you will obey me!"

James ignored him and advanced further. The slaver pointed a finger at James. "Stop immediately!" he screamed.

> YOU HAVE BEEN GIVEN AN ORDER: STOP IMMEDIATELY. FAILURE TO OBEY WILL RESULT IN PUNISHMENT.

James ignored the slaver and took another step forward. This time he felt a pinprick of pain in the center of his skull as he stepped forward. With every step, it intensified. After three steps it was the worst pain he had ever felt. After five it was unbearable. Still, he soldiered on, taking slow methodical step after step towards Vegar.

He reached a point where no matter what he tried, he couldn't make himself take another step. He tried to will his body forward, but it wouldn't obey. James collapsed to the ground and with his last remaining shred of consciousness he removed Vegar from his protection, allowing the storm to ravage the slaver. He'd wanted to be the one to drive his dagger through the slaver's heart.

James woke up to a deep silence, hanging heavy after the noise of the storm. Through the fog James could see indistinct figures slowly picking their way through the wreckage of the camp, illuminated by the strange purple glow that emanated from the fog.

YOU HAVE GAINED 1 SKILL RANK IN STEALTH.

YOU ARE NOW SKILL RANK 10.

You have killed Audun Strommen (Level 27 Orc Hypnotist).

+ 297 experience points

LEVEL UP (X2)! YOU ARE NOW LEVEL 12.

You have killed Sinew Brutsbane (Level 30 Orc Barbarian).

+ 315 experience points

LEVEL UP! YOU ARE NOW LEVEL 13.

Three levels!

After casting that spell, James understood why the Fragment of Syreus was a legendary object. Still, he wished it had taken out all the slavers, not just two. James cautiously dropped into Stealth and crept into the thick undergrowth, taking care not to step on any branches or disturb any plants. Once he was hidden, he took a look at his character sheet to figure out where to put his points. He had fifteen stat points in six ability points to assign. In the distance he could hear moans of pain from Vegar as he called out for help, but he ignored the slaver.

After seeing the power of magic, James decided to focus more on his spellcasting ability. Keeping that in mind he put three points into Wisdom and two into Intelligence, bringing them both up to 26. He put six of his remaining ten points into Constitution because he kept almost dying, and the last four into Dexterity, bringing it up to 21.

Once he had assigned his attribute points, James took a look at his abilities. He brought imbue darkness up to level 5 and his dagger responded, flaring briefly with a dark light. James then spent two points in Stronger Shadows. When he purchased the Stronger Shadows ability, some of the black energy that surrounded the dagger sunk into it, darkening the metal. Sadly, purchasing Stronger Shadows didn't reveal anything new in his ability tree.

After purchasing Stronger Shadows, James thought about what to put his last three points into. He decided that he wanted to reveal more of the class tree, so he put one point into Arcane Armor.

WARRIOR OF SHADOW I

Arcane Armor (1/10):

> +10% Shadow Defense.
>
> Shadows flow freely through your armor, bolstering its
> defense.

James watched as shadows escaped his skin and flowed over his leather armor, turning it from a tan color to a darker grey, with shadowy light playing over it. Two new nodes popped up.

WARRIOR OF SHADOW II

Shadow Armor (0/5):

*Requires Arcane Armor 5

Darkness wraps around your armor, cloaking you.

WARRIOR OF SHADOW II

Silent as the Night (0/10):

*Requires Arcane Armor 5

Your aura condenses into darkness, padding the joints of your armor and muffling the sound of your movement.

James wanted them. Even though James wasn't a stealth-based character, he had gotten good use out of his stealth skill. Both of those skills would be insane for a stealth-based rogue, but still useful for him. At Skill Rank ten in Silent as the Night he could move completely silently! Maybe revealing more of the map hadn't been the best idea, as he couldn't decide what to get.

Oh, well. In for a penny, in for a pound.

He put his next point into Pierce the Veil to finish revealing all of his Tier II abilities.

WARRIOR OF SHADOW I

Pierce the Veil (1/10):

+ 5% chance to see through stealth effects

Your connection with the shadows allows you to see through attempts to hide.

James then looked at the new ability that had been revealed.

WARRIOR OF SHADOW II

Fearsome Visage (0/10):

*Requires Pierce the Veil 2

Your aura emits a malevolent energy that has a chance to cause a Fear effect on enemies

---

He didn't know what to do. Every one of those abilities was amazing. He put the remaining point into Arcane Armor to bolster his defense, as he was turning into a glass cannon. With that, he was ready to continue the fight.

James carefully picked his way through the trees, following the noise of Vegar cursing.

He finally found the slaver pinned underneath a large tree that had fallen on his legs, cradling a broken arm and crying out in pain. He approached the slaver silently, dagger drawn. With surgical precision, he plunged the blade into the back of the Orc's neck, severing his spine and paralyzing Vegar.

James turned Vegar over and watched the panic in the slaver's eyes as he saw his own blood on James' blade, then realized he couldn't move, or even take a breath.

"Goodbye, asshole." James plunged the dagger into the slavers eye. As the light left of the slavers eye, a globe of crimson energy rose out of the slavers body. The globe pulsed once before exploding into a red liquid that splattered all over James. The liquid flashed one more time, before disappearing into his skin.

> You have killed Vegar Heziel (Level 30 Half-Orc, Half-Dwarf Slave Trader).
>
> *+ 291 experience points*

> *LEVEL UP! YOU ARE NOW LEVEL 14.*

> You have completed the quest: Liberty or Death
>
> *+ 31 experience.*

> *VORGAK THE VILE HAS PLACED THE MARK OF DEATH UPON YOUR SKIN. THIS MARK CAN BE SEEN BY ALL EVIL-ALIGNED INDIVIDUALS.*
>
> You are now [Wanted].
>
> *Current Bounty: 100 Gold.*

> *YOU HAVE GAINED 1 SKILL RANK IN SMALL BLADES.*
>
> *YOU ARE NOW SKILL RANK 3.*

James grabbed at his foot as a burning pain spread across it. With a small ding, a new notification popped up.

> *YOUR BRAND: PROPERTY HAS EVOLVED.*
>
> You have gained the brand: Liberty
>
> *+ 1 to all basic stats while not enslaved*

James was glad to be rid of his slave brand. He could feel the difference in his movement, in his strength, and in the clarity of his thoughts now that he didn't have a 20% reduction to all stats. He was also worried about the implication of the bounty on his head, but there was nothing he could do about it. It wasn't like he been planning a picnic with someone called Vorgak the *Vile*.

Not wanting to spend more time deciding where to put points, James put one point in each of his stats, except endurance. Raising them evenly had been working out well for him so far, so he wanted to continue that trend. He put one point in Arcane Armor and another in Imbue Darkness.

He turned to the cage. Now that Vegar was dead, James could let out the rest of the slaves.

Cautiously he looked around, making sure that none of the remaining slavers were in his vicinity. He couldn't see anyone through the thick mist as he crept to the cart and looked through the bars.

"Hey," he whispered as he approached. "You all okay?" He was a bit worried that his protection had waned when he had passed out. The possibility that he had accidently hurt the other slaves was very real, but the fact that the cage looked unharmed was a good sign.

"What was that?" Nidra asked, looking a little windswept but no worse for the wear.

"How did you do that?" Arik asked, shock evident on his face. He let out a huge grin and shouted, "I'm free!"

"Shhhh," James whispered. "They aren't all dead yet. I wanted to get the rest of you out first."

Arik mimed zipping his lips, but he grinned all the same. "So, how are you getting us out of here?" he whispered.

James chuckled. The Dwarf was much more animated now that he wasn't soulbound to a sadistic slaver.

James tried to pull open the cage door, but it was locked tight. When he tried to smash the lock with the pommel of his dagger, the metal clanged, but when he examined it afterwards, he didn't see any marks on it.

He cringed. That had been too loud.

Maybe his Stronger Shadows ability would let him cut into this strange metal.

"You aren't going to manage that," the Dwarf chuckled. "Trying to cut through *Darksteel* with Orichalcum!" He burst into laughter again.

James sighed. "Then how do I get you out of here?"

The Dwarf stroked his beard. "Where I come from, we have these magical talismans we call 'keys'."

I should have thought of that. Way to go, Brainlord.

James crept back to Vegar and searched his corpse. He went through the slaver's pockets. There were a few odds and ends, but no key. He searched inside Vegar's coat and found hispouch attached to Vegars belt. Pumping his arm in victory, he retrieved his pouch, leaving the belt. There would be time to loot the corpse later when there wasn't a rather hefty chance that he would be attacked by an orc.

After about five minutes of getting way too comfortable with the dead slaver's body, James finally found the key hanging from a necklace. He yanked the chain, breaking the necklace, and retrieved the key.

Darksteel Key:

Rank: Rare

A key crafted from Darksteel

Once he had unlocked the cage, James received a notification.

You have completed a hidden requirement of the quest:

Liberty or Death

Requirement: Free all the slaves

Reward: Higher Brand

James felt the now familiar pain in his forehead as his brand shifted, changing into something new.

YOUR BRAND [LIBERTY] HAS EVOLVED.

You have gained the brand: Liberator

+ 10 to all basic stats

YOU HAVE BEEN GIVEN A QUEST (REPEATABLE): FORGING FREEDOM

> Forging Freedom (Repeatable): Find and free as many slaves as you can
>
> Suggested level: n/a
>
> Reward: Varies depending on group size and difficulty
>
> Penalty for failure or refusal: none

As James read through the quest prompt, he finally realized why he'd been brought to Novis. He would eradicate slavery from the land. He didn't care what some God wanted with him, this was his true purpose.

"Thank you!" Arik exclaimed, wrapping James in a bear hug.

"Now what?" Nidra asked.

"Now we hunt." Orrel said. "Who is left?"

James stared at the group, unsure what to say. Finally he settled on "Well... Butcher and Mandra are the last two slavers." He thought for a second. "Umm, lets-"

"Right." Nidra interrupted. To James' relief, she'd seen that he was struggling and taken pity on him, taking command. "Let's split up into groups of two and search for the last two." She spat on the ground after saying their names. "If anyone finds one, call out and we can attack together."

"I work alone." Orrel said simply.

"Me too," James said. In reality he didn't care if he had to work with a partner, but he wanted to cut up an orcish corpse to boost his anatomy skill, and he wasn't sure how the others would feel about him butchering a sentient in the name of "science."

"Suit yourself." Nidra said. "Arik and I will be a team. Let's go."

When she looked up, a dark orange light burned in her eyes as pent-up Mana swirled through her body.

Someone was going to burn tonight.

Chapter 25

After they split up, James stopped for a second and looked around. He couldn't help feeling like he was missing something. He patted at his waist and felt the familiar weight of his sword. Luckily, it had been inside his pouch.

He patted the sheath on his calf. His dagger was still there. What else could he be missing? He mentally counted the slavers.

Yep. Two left. What else?

All the former slaves had been freed, so that couldn't be it.

Wait, was that right?

James couldn't remember if Lucien had been at the talk. Actually, he was having trouble remembering the last time he had seen Lucien.

Probably in the cage with the rest of them.

James found Lucien still sitting in the cart. The teenager sat quietly, staring into the distance. His eyes were hollow, as if he hadn't really seen what had gone on around him. It was an expression that James had seen many times in people experiencing shock.

James opened his mouth to reassure the teenager, then closed it. He wasn't good at this. He glanced around, looking for help, but realized he was it.

James gently put his hand on Lucien's shoulder, and the teenager jumped.

251

"Sorry," James said, pulling his hand back. "You okay?"

The teenager looked up at him with red-rimmed eyes. "It was my fault."

"No, it wasn't," James said firmly. "Vegar killed him."

"It wasn't that," Lucien said, voice breaking. "I… I was the one who convinced him to—"

The snap of branches interrupted Lucien, who looked up in fear. James couldn't see anything through the dense fog.

"Hang tight, I'll be right back," James promised, heading into the fog.

James tried to pinpoint any noises that might clue him in to his enemies' position, but he couldn't hear a thing. He dropped into stealth and crept towards where he had last heard the noise, drawing his sword. Finding his sword had been a relief, because even though the dagger was enchanted and crafted from a high-grade material, James didn't really know how to use it well. Chasing down a high-leveled enemy didn't seem like a great time to learn.

A gust of wind blew in, dissipating some of the fog and giving James a slightly better line of sight as he crept through the forest, keeping his eyes and ears open. A twig snapped in the distance and James crept towards it, keeping stealth active as he moved. A fox ran by, startling him and breaking his stealth. That was all it took.

Suddenly an arrow hit him in the shoulder. He let out a yelp of pain and threw himself to the ground as another arrow sped over him, which made a loud thwack as it struck the tree behind him.

Without stopping to think, James rolled over as another arrow slammed into the ground where he had been. He didn't know what to do. He needed a second to think. He executed the first thought that came to mind and Shadow Stepped behind a nearby tree.

Quickly, he dropped back into stealth and peered around the tree, looking for whoever had shot him. That small movement sent a jolt of pain through his shoulder, which still had the arrow stuck in it. James knew better than to pull out an impaled object. Instead, he snapped the shaft so that it wasn't sticking out of his back.

James thought about where he would hide if he were attacking from range with a bow and realized he'd been searching in the wrong place. He had been looking for opponents on the ground, when the most likely place to find an archer would be in the treetops.

He scanned the trees, looking for the archer.

There!

A shadow moved between the trees above. Once he focused, the darkness faded away, leaving Mandra exposed. She was crouched in the branches of a tree not too far from James. Her body was still as a statue and her head swiveled like an owl. He never would have noticed her if she hadn't changed positions.

James considered calling for help, but her stealth ability was insane. If he lost sight of her in the forest, he would never find her again. For all he knew, she could go back into stealth while he was watching her.

His best course of action was to stay silent and not let her know that she'd been exposed. Now all he needed to do was figure out the best way to get to her.

Climbing the tree was out. James was used to climbing trees, but he was pretty sure that she would notice. He wasn't exactly a master of silence.

Maybe I could attack from above. Climbing another tree would be too noisy, but maybe he could Shadow Step. He checked his mana—190 left after the first cast. That was enough to cast Shadow Step three more times, which would get him fifteen meters.

He glanced up at Mandra. The woman was up there. Shadow Step probably wouldn't get him as high as he wanted to go, but sneaking up on her would be incredibly difficult without it. That meant he should probably save one of his three casts to make sure that he could get in range before she noticed him.

James looked at the trees. Their branches were closer together towards the top, but narrower. He could make this work if he were careful.

James closed his eyes and whispered a quick prayer. Not that he was religious, but if someone were watching over him, now would be the time to help.

He cast Shadow Step and landed in a large cluster of branches about 5 meters off the ground.

YOUR SPELL SHADOW STEP HAS RANKED UP!

Shadow Step (Spell Rank 2):

Teleports the caster to a nearby shadow.

Range: 10 Meters

Cast time: Instant

Cooldown: None

Cost: 60 Mana

When James saw the extra range, he almost cheered. James had been wondering when the spell was going to level up. It looked like spells leveled slower than skills did. As far as James could tell, abilities didn't level at all without assigning points.

He looked around for branches. His plan was to climb as high as possible to conserve mana. Luckily, there were a few well-positioned branches in reach.

James climbed up the tree at a sloth's pace, careful not to break any branches. After another minute, he had managed five more meters. He felt like a superhuman climbing with his boosted stats. There were no other branches in reach, so he cast Shadow Step again. That left one cast, with enough extra Mana to cast Knife in the Dark if he wanted to.

After that last cast, James stopped, pressing his palm to his forehead. An unexpected side effect of using almost all of his Mana so quickly was a splitting headache. He hadn't realized that casting would create so many issues for him.

But he was close. Very close. Five trees away, and roughly her height. Up high, he could see much clearer than down on the ground where the fog clung to everything. Praying she didn't turn and see him, he crawled along branches from tree to tree until he was about 10 meters away. Once he was in range, he cast his final Shadow Step.

He landed silently in the branches directly behind Mandra. For a second, everything seemed like it would work out perfectly.

With a resounding *crack,* the branch snapped under their combined weight.

For a second, time stood still as James watched Mandra's expression turn from shock to fear.

Then time sped up again and James reacted, his prior tree-climbing experience coming into play. As he fell, he dropped his sword and whipped out his dagger, slamming it into the side of the tree with all his Strength. With his Strength and the increased penetrating power of the blade, it sunk deep into the wood. His shoulder wrenched as he jolted to a stop, breathing hard. Branches snapped below him as Mandra plummeted to the ground.

With a groan, James grabbed a nearby branch and pulled himself up until he was sitting. His right arm hung limply at his side, and any movement sent agonizing pain into his shoulder.

Yeah, that's dislocated.

James sighed. He wouldn't be able to get down without two hands. He knew what he had to do, but every fiber of his being strongly suggested he didn't.

Reducing a bone wasn't usually something paramedics did, but he had watched a few doctors reduce shoulder dislocations in his clinical shifts, and had even helped in one. This was going to suck.

It was also going to be extremely difficult. Dislocations could cause the muscles around the injured area to tighten up, making it almost impossible to reduce without a liberal dose of muscle relaxers.

James wished he hadn't given all the Deadnettle seeds to the wolves. Its anesthetic properties would have been helpful right then.

With his left hand, he grabbed his right wrist and pulled the dislocated arm forward, positioning it in front of him. James' vision darkened and he let out a loud scream as, with the grinding of bone on bone, his arm popped back into socket.

James collapsed onto the branch, sighing with the immediate relief.

He wanted to give his body time to relax. He hadn't received any notifications.

Mandra was still alive.

Carefully, he used his iron dagger and the orichalcum dagger to climb down the tree.

He found her laying on the ground not far from the base. Her body was broken, with her arms and legs pointing in unnatural directions.

James stared at her for a second before sighing, bending down, and slitting her throat.

You have killed Mandra Salien (Level 23 Orc Beast Tamer).

+ 181 experience points

James retrieved and sheathed his sword, then looked around cautiously. Their fight had made a lot of noise and was bound to attract attention he didn't want. Carefully, he dragged Mandra's corpse deeper into the woods.

A quick frisk produced a few useful items.

A small carved wooden whistle that was useless to him but probably useful to someone who had a beast tamer class.

Beast Tamer's Whistle:

Rank: Unusual

Blow into this whistle and all bonded creatures within 5
kilometers will hear it

A small copper band that gave one dexterity.

Ring of Dexterity:

Rank: Common

+ 1 Dexterity

It's a ring. And it gives +1 dexterity. Not much to say about
this one.

James was pretty happy about this find, because he didn't have any rings other than the strange one he'd spawned with. He equipped it and smiled when it resized automatically to fit his finger. That was probably one of the coolest features of items in this world. James loved watching them resize.

The final item was a green and brown patchwork cloak that gave him a small boost to stealth while in a forest. Again, probably not a game changer, but it was nice. He'd been a little cold lately, so the cloak would be nice to warm him up.

> Cloak of the Forest:
>
> Rank: Unusual
>
> + 5 *Skill Ranks in stealth when in a forest.*
>
> This cloak has been woven in a pattern designed to hide the wearer in forested areas.

James dumped the rest of her possessions into his pouch, including a tinder box and some rope.

Now for the fun part.

He studied her anatomy, testing the bones and joints for weak points. What he found was interesting. The front of the Orc's skull was thick, but the back was much more fragile.

> *YOU HAVE GAINED 1 SKILL RANK IN ANATOMY.*
>
> *YOU ARE NOW SKILL RANK 10.*
>
> You know, this doesn't make you dragging a dead woman's body into the forest to study it any less creepy.

James ignored the notification and continued his examination until he heard voices calling his name, moving towards him. Quickly he moved away from the body and called out to them, leading them towards the camp and away from the corpse. He was sure "for science!" was not going to fly if they questioned him about the corpse.

Chapter 26

Back at the destroyed camp, James started a campfire to drive away the chill of the fog. Then he got started cooking up five large pieces of Star Mole Meat. He was lucky he'd harvested so many. He only had five left. He was also lucky that food placed in his pouch didn't spoil because none of them had been fed anything near a full meal since they'd been captured.

> YOU HAVE GAINED 1 SKILL RANK IN COOKING.
>
> YOU ARE NOW SKILL RANK 5

As James cooked, Lucien moved closer to the fire and sat down, saying nothing as he stared into the crackling flames.

Eventually the rest of the group made it back. Arik was limping, but Nidra and Orrel seemed unharmed.

When James asked Arik what happened, he winked. "I've had worse. Big brute put up a fight, but we got him."

Nidra leaned in and whispered in James' ear. "Don't listen to him, he tripped on the walk back."

James laughed. "So what happened?"

Arik grabbed a hunk of meat and bit into it, moaning in pleasure. Through a mouthful of food he started to regale James and Lucien with the tale of their fight with Butcher. James noticed Lucien watching Arik talk with rapt attention and smiled. Maybe there was hope for him.

Later that night, after everyone had gone to sleep, James leaned against a tree keeping watch, when a tap on his shoulder startled him. His hand went to his sword before realizing that it was Orrel. The Beastkin stood in front of him, almost indistinguishable from the darkness of the night except for his large, shining pupils. James wondered how he'd gotten so close without breaking stealth.

"Human." Orrel inclined his head to James.

"Orrel," James replied. He had only heard the Beastkin speak once, so he was curious to hear what Orrel had to say that couldn't be said around everyone else.

"Thank you for saving me from a fate worse than death," the Beastkin said. "*Aeris vitro et-tu*. I owe you my life. If you ever need anything, come find me." He grabbed James' hand with one paw and pressed something hard and metallic into James' palm.

> ORREL FLEETFOOT HAS FORMALLY PRONOUNCED THAT HE OWES YOU A LIFE DEBT.

James looked up, confused, to ask Orrel what the prompt meant, but by the time he had finished reading it the Beastkin had disappeared into the darkness as silently as he had come.

James shrugged and looked down at the object in his hand—a blue coin about the size of a half dollar. A paw print was carved into one side and a spear on the other.

Token of the Panther:

Rank: Rare

Symbolizes a great deed in service of the Panther tribe.

James slipped the token into his pouch before settling in for a long night of watching. While he watched, he decided to start going through the items and pick out what he wanted. Everything that Audun, Vegar, and Sinew owned technically belonged to him because he was the one who killed them, but he also didn't want to fill his pouch up with random junk. When James played video games, he liked to keep a minimalistic inventory, and the same was true here.

He walked over to Vegar's corpse. The slaver wore a rough leather tunic that glowed a soft brown. There was no visible core on the tunic, which was interesting, but James realized that his Ring of Dexterity didn't have a core either. He would need to ask an enchanter why some items had a core and others didn't.

Leather Tunic of Toughness:

Rank: Unusual

This leather tunic is enchanted to enhance its toughness and durability.

James put on the tunic and it shrunk to fit him perfectly. He moved on to the belt.

Slick Goblin Skin Belt:

Rank: Rare

Not only will you look slick wearing this belt, you'll be slick. Grants the spell Slick Skin, which causes you to excrete an oily substance from your pores.

James shuddered, but put the belt on anyway. Maybe it would come in handy.

YOU HAVE GAINED THE SPELL: SLICK SKIN

Slick Skin (n/a):

Causes the user to excrete an oily substance from their pores. (WARNING: Flammable)

Range: Self

Cast time: Instant

Cooldown: 5 minutes

Cost: 35 Mana

The only other item that James was remotely interested in was the bracelet Vegar had taken from the Shaman. It still gave off a dull orange glow that James had never seen before. On closer examination, he realized why.

It was a unique item.

Bracelet of Last Breath:

Rank: Unique

Grants the user the unique ability: Dying Will. Each time the ability is triggered, this bracelet has a chance of being destroyed.

> CLASSLESS (ITEM)
>
> Dying Will:
>
> Leaves you alive with one health left when an attack would otherwise kill you. Be warned, any damage you receive at one health will kill you. This includes damage over time effects such as bleeding, burning, drowning...

That was an amazing ability. No wonder Vegar had survived the storm. James immediately equipped the amulet before moving on.

Next moved on to Audun's corpse.

He wore one of the other rings that the slavers had gotten from the Shaman. It looked like it had been crafted from darksteel, and it was set with a deep blue gemstone that housed a pulsating red light set in its center.

> Cursed Ring of Flowing Thought:
>
> Rank: Epic
>
> + 1,000 Mana
>
> + 100% Casting Speed
>
> -90% Health
>
> -90% Stamina
>
> Was it worth it? Not for Audun.

James would have to think long and hard about whether he wanted to wear that ring. Sure, he was always complaining about his lack of mana, and he would probably never have Mana problems again if he wore that ring. But he was still a front-line fighter, and sacrificing that much health and stamina would be a bad idea. It would work much better for a pure caster who was able to shield themselves with magic, like the Goblin shaman. Or a mage who could put their enemies to sleep instantly like Audun could.

James tossed the mage's ring in his pouch before moving on, leaving the rest of the mage's gear for Nidra.

Sinew's corpse was a disappointment. None of her gear was usable because, unlike everyone else, she hadn't looked for cover and tried to weather the storm in the open. Her body had been torn apart by enormous chunks of ice that had smashed her gear to pieces, leaving nothing salvageable.

James moved on to the cart where he found a serviceable bedroll and a pillow and slipped them into his pouch. With any luck, his days of waking up with a stiff neck were over.

James then looked through the cart for the crossbow that Vegar had used to kill the shaman. He knew it was incredibly powerful, but no matter how hard he looked, he couldn't find it. Orrel must have taken it without telling anyone. He shrugged and pulled out the last two interesting bits of loot: A chest full of coins and the shaman's staff.

The chest of coins contained a few hundred gold. James dumped a hundred into his pouch and left the rest for the group to fight over, then pulled out the staff.

Deathrattle:

Rank: Rare

Channeling death spells through this staff greatly increases their power

---

James shuddered and slipped the staff into his bag. It wouldn't be useful to him, but maybe he could sell it for some coin. He still wasn't sure how much anything was worth.

Once he finished taking his pick of the loot, James sat down to finish his shift. The rest of his watch was spent practicing knife throwing and meditating.

> YOU HAVE GAINED 3 SKILL RANKS IN KNIFE THROWING.
>
> YOU ARE NOW SKILL RANK 5.

> YOU HAVE GAINED 2 SKILL RANKS IN MEDITATION.
>
> YOU ARE NOW SKILL RANK 7

> YOU HAVE GAINED 1 SKILL RANK IN NIGHT VISION.
>
> YOU ARE NOW SKILL RANK 8.

Lightly, James shook Nidra's arm. She woke up with a start and immediately channeled her mana. The orange glow faded from her eyes when she realized it was only James.

"Sorry," she whispered. "Little on edge."

"No worries, we all are."

She stretched. "Did anything happen while I was sleeping?"

"Nope." James paused for a second, thinking. "Well, Orrel left."

"Left?" She asked incredulously.

James shrugged. "Walked away."

"Where did he go?"

"No idea. He gave me this though." James pulled out the token and showed it to her. "It looks like it can get me to a tribe called the Panther Tribe. Any idea what that is?"

She took the token from him and examined it, turning it over and running her finger over the designs carved into the coin.

"No idea. They're probably one of the beast tribes that live in the glades, but I don't know much about them."

James sighed, slipping the coin back into his pouch. "Shame. Neither do I." He pulled his newly acquired sleeping roll out of his pouch, watching Nidra's eyes widen when she saw it. "By the way, I got a start on the looting, but I left you a bunch of stuff. Take what you want." He frowned. "I think Orrel took the crossbow."

She nodded in appreciation. "Thanks."

James smiled and climbed into his bedroll, asleep before his head hit the pillow.

Chapter 27

James woke to a scream.

He rolled out of his bedroll and leapt to his feet, drawing his sword.

Nidra was trying to hold off a small green-skinned figure wielding a spear and shield.

A Shrieker.

NAME: VASILI ORREN

RACE: GOBLIN (SHRIEKER CLAN)

LEVEL 14

CLASS: WARRIOR

Nidra had grabbed a discarded spear from the fight earlier and was waving it around erratically in an attempt to ward off the Goblin. She may have been good at magic, but close combat was clearly not her forte.

James watched as she made a poor attempt at a feint and tried to stab the Goblin with the spear. He easily batted the weapon away with his shield and taunted her. Whenever she tried to cast, another attack would make her lose focus.

The goblin seemed to be having a great time toying with her. His fighting style was reminiscent of a cat toying with a mouse. First, he knocked her spear to the side with his shield and retaliated with a quick, shallow jab that just barely drew blood.

But there was only one Goblin.

Where were the others? Why was the Goblin making so much noise? Wouldn't stealth have been better?

He shoved those thoughts aside. His friend was in danger.

Lucien and Arik had also woken up to the clamor and joined him, staring in confused silence. The presence of his companions brought James back to the present.

"Come on!" he shouted, taking off towards Nidra. "We have to help her!"

The others followed James as he sprinted towards the Shrieker.

When the Goblin turned and saw three humans running towards him with weapons drawn, his eyes widened, and his expression turned from glee to fear. He jabbed at her ferociously, his spear scoring deeper as she barely dodged lethal blows. Until she didn't. The Goblin saw an opening and, with a cry of excitement, plunged his spear towards her heart.

James, not knowing what else to do, cast Shadow Step. He appeared next to the Goblin and tackled the creature from the side. The surprised Goblin dropped its spear, and the pair tumbled through the low grass. James had the weight advantage and quickly pinned the thrashing creature. It bit and scratched at James, covering him with small wounds.

James swore and headbutted the Goblin, caving its nose, then drew his dagger and stabbed the Goblin in the eye.

YOU HAVE GAINED 1 SKILL RANK IN SMALL BLADES.

> *YOU ARE NOW SKILL RANK 4.*
>
> Wow. You're getting really good at not stabbing yourself.

> You have killed Vasili Orren (Level 14 Goblin Warrior).
>
> *+ 45 experience points*

A war horn sounded in the distance. James looked up to see a long line of Goblins advancing from the trees where they had been hiding.

There were no potential escape routes, as the Goblin had maneuvered them too close to the cliff face. They were trapped.

Angrily, James kicked at the now-dead Goblin as plans churned through his mind. He could always use Shadow Step to escape, but he didn't want to abandon his friends.

A singular Goblin stepped forward, clad in full plate. He held up his hand in a tight fist, and the line of Goblins stopped.

> *NAME: EROI-TUL*
>
> *RACE: GOBLIN*
>
> *LEVEL 19*
>
> *CLASS: EARTH WARLOCK*

He pulled off his helm and grinned, revealing sharp teeth. "Hello, Jamesss," he hissed.

"How do you know my name?"

"Oh, I know all about you," The Goblin said, tilting his head so that James could see a flash of red glowing underneath his armor. James felt a twinge in his own brand as the goblin revealed his "I know that you come from another world." At that, a few of the other Goblins shifted uncomfortably. "I know all about your brand." His smile would make a dentist hang up his drill. "And your quest."

James spared a glance at his companions. He could tell they wanted to talk about the revelation, but also knew that it wasn't the time. James was annoyed. This smug Goblin acted like he knew all the answers, while James was still in the dark. James snapped. "Well, that's great! Maybe you can tell me, because they forgot to clue me in."

Eroi-Tul ignored James. "So, will you come with us peacefully?" He asked.

James grinned and gave him the finger.

The Goblin smiled. "That's what I was hoping for."

His eyes glowed green as he channeled his mana, conjuring a magic circle of green energy. Ancient runes swirled around the circle, creating a light breeze that picked up loose dirt and leaves. The movement sped up until all James could see was a twister of dust and green energy.

It stopped as suddenly as it had started. A massive Humanoid creature made of dirt and rock stood in the center of the circle. It was twice as tall as James, with short stubby legs and lanky arms. Veins of the dark green energy pulsed ominously over its surface.

"Attack!" the warlock ordered, pointing at James. The creature obliged, stepping out of the circle and advancing on the small group.

EARTH ELEMENTAL (LEVEL 24)

The Elemental advanced, step after slow plodding step, each footfall accompanied by a small tremor.

The rest of the Shriekers followed the elemental, advancing on James.

He looked around. There was nowhere to go.

A bolt of flame shot past James, targeting the warlock. The Shrieker snapped his fingers and a shell of rock bubbled up around him, connected to the Earth Elemental by a thread of green mana.

The fireball impacted against the shield and burst apart, leaving a star-shaped scorch. The shield quivered and shook, sloughing off its outer layer before stilling. When James looked back at the Earth Elemental, the thread of Mana was still connected to the shield, but the elemental had shrunk.

That gave him an idea.

"Attack the shield! It damages the elemental!" James yelled back to Nidra. He then turned to Arik and Lucien. "On me! Protect Nidra! Backs to the wall!"

The three adventurers backed up against the cliff wall and formed a semicircle with Nidra in the center. Arik held his hammer and Lucien wielded a spear taken from a Goblin's corpse. Nidra's eyes danced with energy.

The warlock's shield let out a quick pulse of green light. A war cry went up from the Goblin horde and they charged, overtaking the Elemental and mobbing the trio en masse.

The next five minutes were pure hell. James, Arik, and Lucien hacked and stabbed at any Goblins that got too close while Nidra continued her spell.

Every so often, James would realize that he had lost focus, intent on watching Arik. The Dwarf's weapon had a mind of its own. As Arik blocked a slash from one Goblin's sword, the upper half of his hammer liquified, flowing around the Goblin's weapon and countering. Watching the Dwarf work was so interesting that James almost failed to block a spear thrust towards Lucien's unprotected flank.

The kid clearly didn't know how to fight with a spear, but he was holding his own. Lucien stabbed a Goblin with his spear and, using its momentum, flung the Goblin into one of its brethren.

> *YOU HAVE GAINED 1 SKILL RANK IN SWORDSMANSHIP.*
>
> *YOU ARE NOW SKILL RANK 20.*

The notification brought James back to the present as he brought his sword down on a Goblin's head, its dark energy sizzling as it sliced the creature in half.

> You have killed Kiros Helev (Level 17 Goblin Warrior).
>
> *+ 28 experience points*

Why did I gain so little experience? And why haven't I gained experience for the other people's kills? James didn't have time to wonder as another Goblin stepped forwards to take the last one's place.

With an explosion of magical energy, Nidra finished casting. Eight bolts of fire blasted from her palm, each one targeting the warlock's protective barrier.

As the bolts of energy connected, a pulse of Mana flowed from the Elemental back into the shield as the Elemental shrunk by half. It was now around James' height and covered in small cracks. It had also just reached them.

The Elemental slammed a fist into the ground, sending a shock wave of earth straight at Arik.

The Dwarf jumped into the air, but was caught by the creature's other fist, which sent him flying. He landed in a crumpled heap on the ground.

"Arik!" James shouted. He cast Shadow Step and appeared next to the dwarf, dropping down to check his pulse. It was faint, but present.

He turned back to the battle. They were getting absolutely wrecked and there was nothing he could do about it. His storm pendant was still on cooldown, and he didn't have any area of effect attacks. It was time to take a risk.

He cast Shadow Step.

James disappeared, leaving a confused Goblin in his wake. He reappeared on the other side of the Goblins, directly next to the warlock's shield, and started attacking. Each blow from his sword sent a pulse of energy from the Elemental into the shield, healing the shield but damaging the Elemental.

James Mana was flashing low. *Seventy-two. One more cast.*

His plan was working. The Elemental had turned and was rumbling towards him. Back by the cliff face, his friends fought fiercely as they tried to push back the waves of Goblins. But it wasn't enough. Nidra had long since run out of Mana and was fighting with a discarded spear. Lucien was covered in blood, and Arik was holding back the entire force basically on his own. As James watched, the Dwarf's eyes turned silver. He pulled a second hammer off his belt and let off a rapid series of attacks, pushing the Goblins back.

"Hey, wasn't I your target?" James called out to the Goblins as he cast his last Shadow Step.

James reappeared by the tree line, then immediately took off and ran towards the dense undergrowth. Maybe he could take the heat off of his friends and lose the Goblins in the woods.

A heavy rumble accompanied the warlock's shield breaking down. The Elemental reformed into a mound of earth and the warlock stepped on it, riding it like a surfboard.

Shit. Why was the Elemental suddenly so fast?

James sprinted through the undergrowth, ducking a branch to avoid poking his eye out.

He leapt hurdled a fallen log but landed poorly, twisting his ankle.

Stumbling to his feet, James kept going. He could feel the rumbling of the earth as the Elemental gained on him. James started to slow down. There was nowhere else to go.

Breathing heavily, James held up his hands in defeat.

The Earth Elemental came to a halt and sunk into the ground, leaving Eroi-Tul standing in front of James, wearing a nasty grin.

"Giving up so soon?" he asked. "I was just getting started."

"If I go with you, will you leave the others alone?"

The Goblin tapped his chin, a dark glint in his eyes. "Nope."

"Wait, what?" James was flabbergasted. "You need to let me give myself up for my friends. It's the noble sacrifice of the hero. It's an important plot point."

The Goblin stared back, unimpressed, and pulled a cruel black broadsword from a sheath behind his back. "Then goodbye, hero," he snickered.

"I'm sorry?" James asked as he backed away slowly, hands in the air. "Aren't you going to take me back to your leader or something? This seems rather final."

Eroi-Tul raised an eyebrow in confusion. "We want you dead. Why would I give you the chance to escape?"

"Don't you at least want to start a long-winded explanation on why I'm here and how you're going to stop me?" James threw out desperately.

"I'm good," the Goblin said, swinging his sword.

James closed his eyes as the sword descended, throwing his hands out in a reflexive attempt to save himself as his life flashed before him.

Wait.

The Mana Crystals.

James remembered Audun cracking a Mana crystal and becoming infused with power.

With movement reinforced by desperation, James grabbed a fistful of the crystals out of his pouch and cracked them all at once.

You have used an Average Mana Crystal.

+ 500 Mana for 5 minutes

WARNING: EACH CONSECUTIVE CRYSTAL WILL LOSE A LARGE PORTION OF ITS POTENCY. USING MORE THAN ONE CRYSTAL IS DANGEROUS AND CAN CAUSE PERMANENT DAMAGE.

You have used an Average Mana Crystal.

+ 250 Mana for 5 minutes

WARNING: EACH CONSECUTIVE CRYSTAL WILL LOSE A LARGE PORTION OF ITS POTENCY. USING MORE THAN ONE CRYSTAL IS DANGEROUS AND CAN CAUSE PERMANENT DAMAGE.

You have used an Average Mana Crystal.

+ 125 Mana for 5 minutes

WARNING: EACH CONSECUTIVE CRYSTAL WILL LOSE A LARGE PORTION OF ITS POTENCY. USING MORE THAN ONE

CRYSTAL IS DANGEROUS AND CAN CAUSE PERMANENT
DAMAGE.

You have used an Average Mana Crystal.

+ 62 Mana for 5 minutes

Are you stupid? Can't you read?

WARNING: EACH CONSECUTIVE CRYSTAL WILL
LOSE A LARGE PORTION OF ITS POTENCY. USING
MORE THAN ONE CRYSTAL IS DANGEROUS AND CAN
CAUSE PERMANENT DAMAGE.

You have used an Average Mana Crystal.

+ 31 Mana for 5 minutes

Was it worth it?

With a rush of power, James' Mana bar filled up, but not with its usual blue color. The bright violet energy bar showed 968 mana. A blinking timer appeared in the corner of his vision, counting down the five minutes before his Mana bottomed out again.

Ignoring the confused warlock, James cast Shadow Step.

And kept casting it.

Eventually he made it back to the battle, leaving the warlock far behind.

James appeared behind a Goblin who was standing over an unconscious Lucien. It was raising its club for the finishing blow when James stabbed him in the back of the neck, dropping him instantly.

Before any of the other Goblins could process what had just happened, James moved on to the next Shrieker. He teleported around the battlefield in this fashion, appearing in each Goblin's shadow and alternated stabbing each Goblin in the neck with his dagger, or skewering them on his sword.

You have killed Goblin x 13.

+ 396 experience points

LEVEL UP! YOU ARE NOW LEVEL 15.

YOUR SPELL SHADOW STEP HAS RANKED UP!

Shadow Step (Spell Rank 4):

Teleports the caster to a nearby shadow.

Range: 20 Meters

Cast time: Instant

Cooldown: None

Cost: 70 Mana

YOU HAVE GAINED 7 SKILL RANKS IN SMALL BLADES.

YOU ARE NOW SKILL RANK 11.

> *YOU HAVE GAINED 3 SKILL RANKS IN STEALTH.*
>
> *YOU ARE NOW SKILL RANK 13.*

> *YOU HAVE GAINED 4 SKILL RANKS IN SWORDSMANSHIP.*
>
> *YOU ARE NOW SKILL RANK 24.*

> *YOU HAVE GAINED 9 SKILL RANKS IN SNEAK ATTACK.*
>
> *YOU ARE NOW SKILL RANK 10.*

The blinking timer in the corner of his vision hit zero just as James killed the last Goblin. He felt the power rush out of his body, replaced with a numb pain. Ignoring it, James tried to use Shadow Step to reach Arik and Nidra, who lay unresponsive a short distance from Lucien.

His Mana bar flashed black, and a notification appeared.

> *YOU HAVE USED (5) AVERAGE MANA CRYSTALS*
>
> This has caused extensive scarring, preventing you from accessing your Mana.
>
> You should've listened to my warnings.

The message was accompanied by an intense headache. James clutched his head as he collapsed to his knees and vomited bright red blood.

That can't be good.

Determined to check on his friends, James stumbled towards them. Just in time to see Eroi-Tul emerge from the forest.

The enraged Goblin saw James standing in a field of corpses and grinned evilly.

"Nowhere to run now, James." The Goblin hissed.

James frantically looked around, but the Goblin was right. He couldn't abandon his friends, even if he wanted to.

The Goblin cackled. "After I kill you, I'm going to kill your friends. Sytar should've picked a better champion. you're an embarrassment to your God."

James didn't have time to think about the goblin's words . He pulled out his sword and braced himself for the fight. He wouldn't let this vile Goblin hurt his new companions.

How strong can he be? He's a mage, after all

Chapter 28

The Goblin's first blow carried more force than the small creature seemed capable of, battering James' blade with the force of a truck. Without his increased strength, James doubted he would have been able to block the blow. It collided with James' sword with a sharp *clang,* sending a shower of sparks into the air.

With surprising dexterity, the Goblin disengaged with a smooth step back and unleashed a flurry of sword strikes that hammered at James' defenses.

Each blow sent a shockwave of pain down his arms as the blades clashed. Stumbling back, James parried as much as he was able. Each time a blow landed, James felt his arms weaken further. Offense wasn't even a thought on the horizon as James struggled to breathe under the onslaught.

As the fight wore on, James had increasing trouble lifting his sword, the tip wavering as his muscles quivered like Jell-O. His stamina was hovering dangerously close to zero.

With a particularly ferocious overhead chop, the warlock sent James' sword to the ground at the Goblin's feet. He backed away, defenseless, as the warlock advanced.

"It's over," Eroi-Tul hissed.

James pulled the dagger from his belt and threw it. He tried to activate Knife in the Dark, but a blinding pain brought him to his knees.

Eroi-Tul casually batted away James' dagger and advanced.

"Nice try, but it's time to die."

The warlock raised his black sword.

A howl cut through the fog, and an enormous wolf appeared from the mists, launching at the warlock.

> ### GREYMANE ALPHA (LEVEL 15)

The Greymane Alpha collided with the warlock, knocking him down as it tore at his armor.

The wolf had grown since James had last seen him and was now bigger than James was.

Four other wolves joined the assault, attacking the off-balance warlock, who was barely visible under the combined assault.

A burst of green energy pulsed underneath the wolves and the warlock slowly stood up, picking the wolves off of him, throwing them aside as if they were nothing.

Unfazed, the wolves continued their harassment of the warlock. Whenever he turned to focus on one of them the other four would attack from the sides and rear.

James could tell the Goblin was getting frustrated, his blows getting increasingly sloppy. Eventually Erok-Tul gave up.

The mage stared at James with hate in his eyes. "I'll be back. And next time… next time these *pups* won't be able to save you."

He jumped into the air, calling out to his elemental, which formed underneath him as a vaguely horse-shaped mount of dirt, then rumbled off into the forest.

The Greymane Alpha gave James a nod as if to say, "Our debt to you has been paid." The pack took off into the forest, chasing after the quickly dwindling form.

James wanted to call out in thanks, but he was too tired. When he tried to stand, he found that his limbs were made of lead. But he had to get up. He had to save his friends. Groaning, he stumbled to his feet.

He must have blacked out for a second, because the next thing he knew he was by his companions.

James bent and checked them each individually, making sure they had a pulse and were breathing.

They couldn't stay where they were. More Goblin ambushes were sure to follow. That meant they needed to travel. But James was exhausted. He could barely stand as it was.

He didn't want to do it, but James rifled through his pouch and pulled out a few doses of Soldier's Nettle. This time only one of the doses was for him. He had learned his lesson on moderation from the crystals.

He popped a pinch of the herb into his mouth and chewed.

Minty.

After the first swallow, a warm, soothing feeling spread from his stomach across his body, easing his muscular pain and the burning numbness in his Mana channels.

You have used Soldier's Nettle

+ 1,000% Stamina Recovery

James' stamina bar climbed steadily higher. His muscles twitched with a nervous energy. He needed to move.

This stuff is amazing! He had already forgotten his exhaustion and was bouncing in place. No wonder it was addictive. He felt like he could run for hours, and he hated running.

James grabbed Arik by the shoulders and shook him. "We need to go. Now!"

"Are we dead?" Arik groaned, opening his eyes and blinking slowly. He looked around. "Where did the Shriekers go?"

"There's no time," James said, repeating the process with the other two. He ignored their questions and handed each of them a heavy pinch of Soldier's Nettle.

"We need to go now. The Goblins are going to be back soon." James said, getting up and jogging towards the woods. He beckoned for the others to follow him, his movements quick and spastic.

The others exchanged glances but, trusting their companion, pushed themselves to their feet, groaning. One by one, they popped the Soldier's Nettle into their mouths and jogged after him.

"So, where are we going?" Nidra asked between breaths.

"Away," James replied. "The warlock is going to be back soon." James explained what had happened after they went unconscious.

When she heard about the Mana Crystals, Nidra gasped. "You used five Mana crystals at once?"

"I know," James sighed. "It was a bad idea."

"Probably a little more than a bad idea," she said. "What happened?"

James explained that his Mana channels were burnt and that he wasn't able to use any mana. He asked if she knew a way to fix it.

She shook her head. "Unfortunately, the damage is permanent."

James swore. "Perfect. Just what I needed."

An hour later, James heard the howl of wolves. His friends glanced around nervously, but James reassured them that the wolves were there to help.

The Greymane Alpha burst out of the trees ahead, letting out an earsplitting howl. It looked at James dead in the eyes and a notification popped up.

> *A GREYMANE ALPHA IS ATTEMPTING TO ESTABLISH A TELEPATHIC LINK WITH YOU*

James waited patiently to see what the wolf had to say.

> *YOUR SKILL LEVEL IN BEAST BONDING IS NOT HIGH ENOUGH TO COMMUNICATE WITH THE GREYMANE ALPHA*

Why can't anything work the way it was supposed to?

The constant struggle for his life was starting to wear on James and had put him in a terrible mood. "Sorry. I can't understand you."

"I don't think it speaks common," Arik chimed in helpfully.

James didn't respond to the Dwarf other than to glare at him before he looked back to the wolf and shrugged his shoulders helplessly.

The wolf gave him a baleful glare. It tossed its head back and howled again in clear frustration.

James stared at the beast in confusion.

Pawing at the path, the wolf sniffed the ground and looked back to James.

James had no idea what it was trying to say. He finally settled on simple. "Thank you for your help."

He could almost see the creature roll its eyes in annoyance. It pawed at the path again, letting out a soft whine. This time the wolf walked over to the edge of the path and nosed the plants.

A war horn blared from the tree line in the distance.

James cursed. "How did they find us so fast?"

The Greymane Alpha stared at James in what could only be called astonishment at his inability to grasp the simplest concepts. It pawed at the path again, this time staring at James pointedly while it did. Suddenly, James realized how stupid he was. He looked around. They had been so busy trying to put distance behind them that James hadn't even noticed that they were running on a well-tread path. Not a great place to lose pursuers.

"Shit." He turned to the others and gestured at the ground. "We're idiots. We've been following the path."

His statement was at first met with blank looks as the group processed what he had just said, their eyes widening when they came to the same realization as James and understood just how stupid they had been.

"Off the path! Now," James told them, hacking into the dense undergrowth. He nodded his thanks to the wolf, who gave him one last exasperated glare before disappearing back into the woods.

> *YOU HAVE GAINED 1 SKILL RANK IN BEAST BONDING.*
>
> *YOU ARE NOW SKILL RANK 2.*

The path forward was difficult. He was covered in shallow scratches from clinging thorns as he attempted to clear a path for the party through the thick brush. With each stroke of his sword he let out a low curse, the noise dampened by the fog. His only saving grace was the thick leather that protected him from the worst of the brambles.

"Why does... this have to... be so damned thick?" he huffed between strokes. "All I wanted... was to shoot lightning."

"So, what's the plan?" Nidra asked, ignoring his complaints. How she wasn't covered in blood was a mystery to James, but she seemed to move through the forest with grace as she casually slipped through the branches without a sound.

"Run," James wheezed. "We run far."

"Where are we running?" Nidra's ability to move through the forest with ease was annoying James more than he cared to admit. He was constantly being whipped by branches and stumbling over roots while the elf looked as if she were on a casual stroll.

"No idea," James growled.

"That's a crappy plan," Nidra replied snippily.

Enough is enough.

James stopped abruptly and snapped at the elf. "I'm sorry, but why am I suddenly the leader?" He gestured wildly. "I got us out of the cages! I saved us from the goblins! It's someone else's turn to figure this out." He turned around and continued his assault on the bushes.

"Great. You got us out of the cages. And we're in such a great place, now. I think—"

"I might have a suggestion." Arik interrupted, snapping them out of their argument.

"Fantastic," Nidra said. "Let's hear it."

"The Iron City," Arik said proudly.

"The Iron City. That's your plan?" She scoffed.

James wanted to ignore them and keep running, but his curiosity got the better of him. "What's the Iron City?" He asked.

"The largest Dwarf stronghold in the world!"

"It's also hundreds of kilometers away. We would have to cross the entire Crimson Mountain range to get there, and *none* of us are even close to the zone level requirement." Nidra interrupted.

James looked at Arik. "Is that true?"

Arik rubbed the back of his head nervously. "Yes."

James sighed in annoyance. "Great. Anyone else have a plan?"

"I can get us there in less than a month." Arik said.

"Really?" James could hear the sarcasm mixed with disbelief in Nidra's voice as she challenged the Dwarf. "You can get us from here to the top of the mountains in two weeks. Impossible."

Arik crossed his hands across his chest and glared at the elf. "Possible."

"Fine. How?"

"I can't tell you," Arik said.

"Great." She threw her hands up in the air in defeat and turned to James. "He can't tell us. Sounds like a great idea."

"You have a better idea?" James asked. "Seems to me that you haven't really contributed much."

She held her hands out, calling on her mana. Flames licked her arms and warmed the group, casting dancing shadows across her face and darkening it. "I contribute this." She growled. "I light shit on fire. If you don't like it then you can go fuck yourself." Suddenly she burst into tears and her fire winked out, leaving them especially aware of the cold and damp of the fog.

James was shocked. He had no idea how to react.

Was it something I said?

Lucien mumbled something, and James jumped on the opportunity to change the subject. "What was that?"

"I said we should trust Arik."

James sighed and turned to the Dwarf. "Fine, but can you at least tell us why you can't tell us where we're going?"

Arik nodded, rubbing his beard. "If one of you gets captured before we get there, then the Shriekers could torture the information out of you."

James sighed. "Lead the way."

Arik grinned at him. "You won't regret it."

The distant sound of a horn spurred them onward, this time following Arik as he wound his way through the forest much more deftly than James had. Probably due to the spinning metal blades that he had formed from his war hammer to clear the forest ahead.

"I really hope you know what you're doing," James called out as they picked up speed. Forest travel was much easier when it wasn't him leading the way.

Over the course of the next few hours, whenever one of their stamina bars depleted, the others would slow, taking the time to rest and recharge before continuing.

It was during one of their rests that Nidra finally brought it up "So, what did that Goblin mean when he said you were from another world?"

James talked as they walked. He explained how he'd woken up in a cave and been attacked. He hesitated before bringing up his brand, but decided that if he couldn't trust these people, who could he trust. They'd been through a lot together.

Nidra rested a hand on his shoulder, "I'm sorry. We'll figure this out."

Arik grinned, "yeah, you're not alone anymore."

James spared a glance back to check on Lucian, who hadn't reacted to the revelation, but couldn't read the teenager's face. Before he could comment on it though, a horn sounded in the distance and the group sped up. The chase was back on.

**

As time wore on, the sounds of the war horns faded. With the benefits of the Soldier's Nettle, they were leaving the Goblins behind. But still, they ran.

About four hours into their run, the trees grew sparser as the soil changed from a rich brown to a loose, dirty red.

The Crimson Mountains loomed over them, casting a dark shadow.

Arik thumped his chest proudly. "Majestic, eh?"

"A bit ominous," James replied.

"Nah." The Dwarf smiled at him. "You smell that?"

James sniffed the air. Now that the Dwarf mentioned it to him, he could. The damp smell that permeated the forest had given way to a dry, dusty smell. "Yea, I smell it."

"That's the smell of home!" The Dwarf chuckled.

"So how much farther?" He asked.

"Not far now."

The forest abruptly ended, giving way to a narrow meadow that ended in a steep drop into a chasm of red stone. James stopped his run just in time and teetered on the edge before Lucien grabbed his arm and pulled him back. James thanked the teenager and Lucien nodded. James looked around the meadow. It was a grassy field with the forest behind them and the chasm in front of them. To either side, more forest and more chasm. They were stuck.

He was about to ask Arik what was going on when the Dwarf held a finger to his lips and shushed him. He got a rope out of his bag and looped it around a tree. Then he gestured for the group to follow and they descended into the chasm.

The bottom of the chasm was dark and wet, filled with a red mud that sucked James' feet down to the ankles. Arik held out a hand for silence and pointed to his feet, showing the group how to wade through the mud without making a sound.

As they wound through the chasm James glanced back at the rope and looked to Arik. "Won't the Goblins know where to find us if we—"

"Shhh," Arik hissed. "This isn't the place to talk."

James nodded. While they walked, he checked his notifications for the run. After scrolling through a bunch of stamina depletion notifications, he found that he had unlocked a new achievement.

ACHIEVEMENT UNLOCKED: MAD DASH

Mad Dash:

+ 5 *Endurance*

+ 5 *Constitution*

A red plant growing out of the chasm wall caught his eye, and he stopped to examine it. It was a rich red color and long and slimy, reminding him of seaweed. He touched one of them and quickly wiped his hands off against his leather tunic. It was disgusting.

Red Silkweed (x5):

Rank: Unusual

This weed can be used in a healing potion.

It was Red Silkweed! James smiled to himself as he plucked all five strands of the plant out of the chasm wall and stored them in his bag.

Quest Update: Learning to Brew (5/2 Red Silkweed)

Sweet!

When he found a place to rest, he would try to brew up a health potion.

James was so focused on his harvest that he hadn't noticed that they stopped, and he ran into Lucien's back. The youth glared at him before returning his gaze to Arik.

"Stay quiet," the Dwarf whispered. James didn't see anything especially interesting about this particular wall, but he trusted Arik, so he watched and waited.

The Dwarf held his war hammer over his right palm and concentrated. A silver glow built up around his hands and a tiny droplet of metal formed on the tip of the weapon. It slowly ran down the length of the shaft and dripped into Arik's hand. He pressed his palm against the dirt wall and the silvery droplet expanded, spreading more than it should have been able to. Dirt rained from the wall as the droplet exposed a circular carving with three inner circles of runes. The droplet sank into the carvings, which glowed silver for a second, then the runic circles spun like the lock on a safe. *Click*.

A segment of the wall detached, revealing a hidden doorway into darkness.

One by one, the group entered the tunnel.

Chapter 29

With a quiet thud, the door closed behind them, leaving them in a pitch-black corridor inside the chasm wall. With his Night Vision, James could just barely make out the silhouettes of his companions clustered together as they all read the prompt that had just popped up in the corner of each of their visions.

YOU HAVE ENTERED THE DUNGEON: ABANDONED
AQUEDUCTS

RECOMMENDED LEVEL: 25-35

Great. It wasn't enough that they were in a dungeon. They were in high-level dungeon. James glared at Arik. Not that his ire was visible, but it was the thought that counted.

James was looking forward to spending some relaxing time in the Dwarven city and learning more about this world. Sure, he had nearly died a few times and been captured and put into slavery, but Goddamnit, there was magic here, and that was *awesome.*

Thinking about magic reminded him of his burnt Mana channels, which sent him into a spiral of depression. The only reason he hadn't figuratively lost his mind after being plucked from Earth and dropped here was because of the wonders of magic. *If I can't use magic, what's the point?*

With a soft *whoosh* a small sphere of flame appeared, slowly rotating around Nidra's head, startling James out of his thoughts. The orb gave off a warm, red light, illuminating the long passageway into the darkness. Blood red droplets leaked eerily from the tunnel walls and ceiling. Arik explained it was only water, dyed red from the iron in the soil. Whenever one of the droplets dripped into Nidra's flaming light, it would let out a hiss and tiny cloud of steam. Somewhere in the distance James could hear the rushing of water.

Nidra looked at Arik curiously. "What is this place?"

Arik ignored her question, addressing the group first. "Before we go any further, I need each of you to swear by the System that you won't tell anyone about this. You won't mention it in passing, you won't write it down, you won't send a coded message. You won't try to reveal your knowledge of this to anyone." He paused. "Unless they already know about it. Then I guess it's okay."

A system message that James hadn't seen before popped up.

> Arik has asked you to swear to never reveal your knowledge of the Dwarven Aqueducts to anyone. Do you accept?

He thought about it for a second, wondering what the implications of the promise were. Clearly, there would be consequences if Arik was willing to use it as a way of swearing a secret that he seemed so serious about.

"Why is this so important?" Nidra insisted, interrupting James' musings. "I'm not going to agree without more information." She crossed her arms and glared at the Dwarf.

Arik met her gaze. "This isn't a negotiation," he said firmly. "Either submit the pledge, or I'll kick you out."

"You'll kick me out?" She replied angrily, orange light building up around her fingertips. "I'd like to see you try."

Arik stared at her for a second before completely ignoring her and turning to the others. "How about you two?" He asked.

Lucien nodded. "Better here than dead."

James took a few more seconds to think about it. On one hand, he didn't know what he was signing up for, but on the other hand it couldn't be worse than what was currently going on.

OATH ACCEPTED:

Never speak of the Dwarven Aqueducts to anyone who doesn't already know about them.

Nidra's expression softened, and she sighed. "Fine. But this better be worth it." She turned to Arik. "Now can you finally tell us what's going on?"

Arik nodded. "Thank you, everyone for agreeing. Knowledge of the Aqueducts is guarded fiercely by my people. You'll understand why in a second, but first some history." He stopped to take a sip of water from the flask at his hip before continuing. "The Dwarven kingdom used to span the entire mountain range. Our cities overflowed with gold and drink, and these tunnels were the key to it all." Arik patted the wall sadly. "They allowed us to quickly and safely transport goods between our cities and the outside world without braving the harsh environments of the mountains."

"You're not saying..." Nidra stared at Arik in astonishment. "No. That would be impossible."

Arik nodded, clearly proud of his race. "These tunnels span the entire range of the Crimson Mountains. From these tunnels you could enter any of the dead cities."

At that, Lucien's eyes widened. "The dead cities? They're real?" he asked, fear evident in his eyes.

Arik nodded. "Real as you or me."

"The dead cities?" James questioned.

"Do you know anything?" Lucien snapped at James.

"I must have missed that lesson back in *my world*," he replied drolly. He waited for Lucien to continue explaining, but clearly the youth wasn't in a talkative mood. James felt sorry for him. Clearly Lucien was still having trouble coping with his twin's death, which made sense. Still, James was curious about Dwarven history, so he turned to Arik to continue the discussion. "What happened?" James breathed. With the way the group was talking about it, it was clear that the Dwarven history was tumultuous and grim, but he had no idea what the dead cities were, or why these tunnels were so amazing.

"War." Arik replied, almost too softly for James to hear. It was difficult to see in the dim light, but James thought he could make out a teardrop run down the Dwarf's face and into his beard. James shut up. He wasn't amazing at picking up social cues, but even he knew when it was time to leave a subject alone.

"Well, let's go." Arik said with an embarrassed cough.

"Hang on," Nidra said. "I don't understand. Even walking straight to the city, it would take months. How are you planning on getting us there in less than two weeks?"

Arik winked at her. "You'll find out soon. Now keep your eyes peeled. We don't know what's moved in here since this place was abandoned."

"Months?" James asked. "Just how large are these tunnels?"

Arik proudly replied. "From where we are to the Iron City is about 3,000 kilometers."

"That's impossible." James said. If Arik was telling the truth, then this tunnel system ran under a mountain range for almost the distance of the entire eastern United States. And that was just one tunnel. "How many tunnels are there?" James asked.

Arik thought about it for a second. "Well, right now we're in a small branch off of one of the main tunnels, but there are six main tunnels, and too many branches to count."

James gave up on comprehending the sheer scale of the tunnel system. If someone had gone up to him and told him the United States government had decided to create an underground metro system across the entire country, he would have laughed in their face at the sheer impossibility of a project that large. Now this Dwarf was telling him that they had done the equivalent project without modern technology. It was incredible. Even with magic, James couldn't imagine how a project like this worked. And to keep it secret from the rest of the world. "This is amazing."

The Dwarf grinned at him with genuine appreciation. "Glad you like it. It's our crowning achievement." His face went grim when he next spoke. "Saved a lot of lives when the Orcs attacked."

James, putting two and two together, surmised that there had been a conflict with the Orcs leading to the Dwarves abandoning a bunch of their cities. "So, can you tell me a little more about your people's history?" James asked.

As the group continued through the dungeon, Arik obliged. About the first city, the expansion, the endless war. James listened with rapt attention, holding back the barrage of questions that he wanted to ask as he tried to put the information together into a cohesive picture of the world's history.

They were just getting into detail about the fall of the first Dwarven city and the undead plague, when Lucien held up a hand and the party came to a sudden halt.

"Hang on," he whispered, interrupting Arik. "There's something up ahead."

James stared into the darkness but couldn't make out anything, even with his Night Vision skill. "I can't see it." he said. "What level is your night vision?"

Lucien gave him a rare smile. "Level 53. I used to go out at night with my brother and—" At the mention of his brother, Lucien went back to his usual sullen silence.

"I'll go check it out." James offered, dropping into Stealth. Quietly he made his way forward, glad they weren't walking through ankle-deep mud anymore.

As James got closer to the shapeless form, he caught the stench of rotting flesh. James coughed, choking on the putrid air.

When he got closer, James started to make out bits of bone and patches of matted, oily hair. It was the corpse of some sort of Humanoid, covered in a dense black fur. Its top half was completely picked bare, with small fragments of fur left on the bottom half and bones scattered across the passage. James picked up the creature's skull and examined it. It was vaguely Human, but thicker and with horns.

A minotaur!

Upon further examination, the Minotaur's bones were picked clean and covered in deep gouges that appeared to have been made from two sharp incisors. Whatever had killed the minotaur was clearly carnivorous, and judging by the state of the corpse, not a tidy eater.

At least it's not bugs this time.

James turned back to his companions. "We have company. Not sure what, but I'd wager it isn't friendly."

"That's disgusting," Arik said, his voice muffled as he spoke with a hand over his mouth.

"Suck it up," Nidra laughed, seemingly unaffected by the smell. Maybe elves had a natural immunity.

"Let's move on," James said, trying to hold back another cough. "Lucien is looking a bit green."

They continued their trek, and James jogged to catch up with Arik. "So, what do you think made those bites?"

"Not sure." Arik replied. "Hungry bugger."

The group proceeded through the tunnel cautiously, with James scouting ahead. After about five minutes, the tunnel walls widened, changing from red dirt to yellowed bricks. The sound of rushing water also got louder as they approached the source.

They exited the tunnel into a new, much different passage. This new area was a semicircular tunnel made from a yellowed brick that ran in both directions for as far as the eye could see. They were standing on a raised platform that ran parallel to a slow-moving channel of water. The thundering sound of the rushing water was much closer, but James still couldn't see its source.

As one, the group turned to Arik, waiting for him to lead the way. The Dwarf took one step into the room when they all heard a slight *click*. Arik scowled at the brick under his foot. He swore.

James slapped his forehead. "We forgot to check for traps."

"Thank you for that *insightful* observation," Arik replied. "Nothing gets by this guy, does it?"

"Hey, you didn't think of it either," James pointed out as he bent down to examine the trap. "Sorry man, looks like you're stuck there forever." James grinned at Arik.

"What do you mean?" The Dwarf looked panicked. "We need to—"

His speech was cut short by James, who launched himself at the Dwarf, grabbed him around the waist, and tackled him into a pool of water.

The sputtering Dwarf rose out of the water, swearing and yelling at James for being so irresponsible. A metal contraption that reminded James of a bear trap shot out of the mortar surrounding the brick and snapped shut on the spot Arik had recently vacated.

There was a brief moment of silence as everyone processed what had just happened and then Arik resumed his tirade, punctuating it with angry swats at James' kneecaps.

"Why didn't you just replace Arik's foot with a rock or something?" Nidra asked.

Examining the trap, James guessed he probably could have stopped it from working if he had jammed his dagger into the mortar around the brick. It would have prevented the bear trap from being able to spring open. The system seemed to agree, because James got a skill notification.

> YOU HAVE GAINED 1 SKILL RANK IN TRAPS.
>
> YOU ARE NOW SKILL RANK 2.

The notification reminded James he still had points to assign. He hadn't wanted to risk assigning his points while running - he was clumsy enough as is.

"Hang on a second." He said to his friends. "I still have to assign some points from the fight earlier."

James had five stat points and two ability points to assign. He ended up putting three in Endurance and two in Constitution, because both of those stats were lagging behind. That brought Endurance up to 20 base, 33 with bonuses and Constitution up to 21 base, 34 with bonuses. After assigning his stat points, James debated where to put his ability points. It was tough, because he was already level 16. He only had 9 more levels until he chose his advanced class, which meant that he would only get 18 more ability points total. If he wanted any of the Tier III abilities, he would need to start planning.

James wanted to put his points into damage because his fighting style had been quick attacks and fast kills, but now that he couldn't access his mana, it seemed like a bad idea. Luckily his injured Mana channels didn't seem to be affecting his passive abilities like Arcane Armor and Imbue Darkness, but he still decided to hold off on spending his points until he figured out if they could be repaired. If he got lucky and they were fixable, he would invest in damage. If not, he would invest in armor.

"Does he know we're in the middle of a dungeon? What's taking so long?" Nidra whispered to Arik, who walked over to James and slapped him, bringing him back to the present.

"Right. Sorry," James apologized. "I forgot where we were for a second." He closed his status sheet, smiling at his progress, and rejoined the group as they marched deeper into the dungeon.

Fragment of Divinity

Chapter 30

They were still walking along the same tunnel two hours later. The scenery hadn't changed, and James was starting to get hungry. "Can we stop to eat?" He asked the group. "This is the most boring dungeon in existence."

"I wouldn't mind," Nidra agreed. "I'm pretty hungry."

"That might be a bad idea," Arik said ominously. "I would hold off on the food for a few hours."

"Why?" James asked suspiciously.

"You'll see," The Dwarf said mysteriously, waggling his eyebrows.

James pondered the Dwarfs words. He could only think of a few reasons that he would need to stay hungry and none of them pleasant. James really hoped they weren't going to ride something fast. He hated fast rides with a passion.

"Come on, we're getting close." Arik said, motioning for them to follow.

Lucien gestured for them to stop. Initially, James couldn't tell why, but then he heard it too. A low scraping sound, barely discernible above the roar of the water. It sounded like nails on stone. Without further warning, three enormous rats crawled out of the darkness ahead of them.

> PLAGUE RAT (LEVEL 24)

Each was covered in a coat of dirty grey fur stained rust-brown, with patches of skin that peeled loosely off of their bodies, revealing sections of bone. Yellow pus dripped from numerous sores all over the Plague Rat's bodies, sizzling when it hit the ground. James was pretty sure he could get smallpox just by looking at them.

Disgusting.

"Lucien get behind me. Nidra behind Arik," James said, drawing his sword.

"But I can fight," Lucien said, surprising James.

"Can you?" James asked. All he had seen of the teenager fighting so far was his awkward flailing with the spear against the Goblins.

"With a dagger I can."

"How about the one I gave you, Nidra?" James asked. "Since you don't really do close combat, anyway."

"Good idea." Nidra tossed Lucien the Orichalcum Dagger of Speed.

He caught the dagger effortlessly and slashed at the air a few times, judging its weight and speed. Nodding in approval, he said, "This'll do," and thanked Nidra. By the way he moved, it was clear he knew what he was doing.

James almost smacked himself. He had known that Lucien was a Blade, and he probably should have thought to ask if Lucien wanted a dagger. James wasn't sure exactly what a Blade did, but it sounded like the type of class that would use a dagger.

"Okay, so Lucien and I are under-leveled. Can each of you handle a rat while Lucien and I team up against the third?" James asked Nidra and Arik.

Arik nodded, but Nidra took a while longer to decide. She thought for a second and shook her head. "I'm going to need someone to distract it while I cast. I don't do well in one-on-one fights."

James remembered her trying to fight the Goblin without being able to use Mana and realized his mistake. "Right. Lucien and I will each distract one while you deal damage to them." He turned to Lucien. "Focus on defense. We don't need to hurt them, just distract them until Nidra can burn them up." He then addressed the whole group. "Everyone cool with the plan?"

Arik nodded, cracking his knuckles. "I'm always down for a good fight."

Nidra gave him a thin-lipped smile and stepped back, conjuring her mana.

Lucien spun the blade around his hand dexterously and grinned. "With a dagger I am!" James hadn't seen him show this much emotion since before his brother died.

Together the group moved into formation. James, Lucien, and Arik each targeted a rat while Nidra chanted, orange light bathing the group. But before any of them could attack, each of the plague rats breathed out a cloud of noxious green fumes.

James stumbled back, holding his breath as he tried to escape the cloud, but he ended up inhaling a lungful.

James vomited. He'd thought that nothing would be worse than the smell of a decomposing body, but he was wrong.

YOU ARE AFFECTED BY [BILE PLAGUE]

00:00:30

- Fever

- Nausea

- Malaise

The cool air of the tunnel grew uncomfortably hot, and beads of sweat dripped down his body as James' skin grew flushed. It felt like a molten ball of lead had appeared in his stomach, and he collapsed to his knees in agony.

Through his tears he saw Arik collapse next to him, also vomiting. Nidra was luckily outside of the range of the attack, and Lucien was somehow still fighting, advancing on one of the Plague Rats with a quick series of dagger strikes.

James' chosen Plague Rat was advancing on him, but a wall of fire sprung up, sending the rats into a panicked retreat. James used the opportunity to vomit profusely. It helped a little, and he was able to return to his feet as the fire died down and the Plague Rat started advancing again.

Wiping his mouth on his sleeve, James met the Plague Rat's gnashing teeth with his sword, preventing what would have probably been an incredibly painful and necrotic bite. Antibiotics probably didn't exist in this world, and James didn't want to lose an arm, so he didn't try to attack the Plague Rat even when it gave him an opening. Instead he focused on defense, blocking its attempts to bite and scratch while he waited for Nidra to cast.

> YOU HAVE GAINED 1 SKILL RANK IN SWORDSMANSHIP.
>
> YOU ARE NOW SKILL RANK 25.

> CONGRATULATIONS! YOU HAVE REACHED JOURNEYMAN
>
> RANK IN SWORDSMANSHIP. :

> AS A JOURNEYMAN, YOU MAY CHOOSE ONE OF THE
>
> FOLLOWING BONUS ABILITIES

HEART OF THE SWORD

Your sword is reinforced by your own iron will and will never shatter.

SPIRIT OF THE SWORD

The power of a sword's past owners flows through you, giving you guidance as you fight.

BODY OF THE SWORD

You and your sword are one. Metal Mana flows from the sword into your body, reinforcing it.

James barely had time to read the notification under the onslaught of attacks from the rat, but he managed to skim over the notifications and consider his options. Heart of the Sword was the same as Stronger Shadows. Both skills strengthened his sword, and there was probably a limit to how strong a sword needed to be.

He absentmindedly parried another lunge from the rat. With that option eliminated, he debated between the other two. Body of the Sword sounded interesting; James would love to have impenetrable metal skin, but it also sounded similar to his Arcane Armor ability. Spirit of the Sword, on the other hand, was nothing like any ability he already had and would probably be useful to him if he had to fight other humans. On the other hand, Spirit of the Sword was the only skill that had an ill-defined bonus.

What exactly did guidance mean? Was I going to become a Grandmaster of Swordsmanship overnight?

He wouldn't know unless he tried. James picked Spirit of the Sword.

JOURNEYM. IN SWORDSMANSHIP BONUS

Spirit of the Sword:

Every sword has a story to tell. Starting with the first beat of the blacksmith's hammer, the saga evolves every time it changes hands. Each chip on the blade is full of the hopes and dreams of its previous owners, and now you are able to glean a small piece of their understanding, so listen well. You may be surprised at what you learn.

With a start, James realized that his grip was slightly off. He adjusted his grip and tested its weight, noting that it was slightly off balance. He didn't know how he knew, he just did. When he moved to block the Plague Rat's next strike, his movement was more fluid and more self-assured than it had been before. It was nothing major—he still didn't have enough skill to attack the creature, but it was gratifying to feel adept while fighting instead of feeling like he was on the edge of dying every time he was attacked.

A fireball passed over his shoulder, snapping James out of his daydream. It slammed into the Plague Rat, igniting its oily fur. It screeched in pain and convulsed, trying to paw the flames away. Its health plummeted as the flames consumed the creature until it collapsed, burnt and unrecognizable.

James waited for a notification letting him know the creature was dead, but nothing flashed across his vision. That was odd. He should have at least gotten *some* experience. He walked up to the corpse of the Plague Rat and poked it with his foot. It didn't move. There was no tag above its head letting him know what it was. All the signs pointed to dead, so why hadn't he been notified?

"Focus, James!" James snapped back into the present in time to dodge an errant strike from the Plague Rat that was fighting with Lucien. The Plague

Rat seemed to have noticed James' inattention and tried to take advantage of it by clawing at him while his back was turned. Unfortunately for the rat, its strike opened it up to Lucien's blade, which slashed across its side with a lightning-quick series of cuts. He ended the combo by sinking his dagger deep into the Plague Rat's side.

Trying not to repeat his last mistake, James turned to help Arik only to find that the Dwarf had made short work of his Plague Rat and had been about to join their fight. Now that everyone had finished, James approached Nidra to ask her about the experience.

"Hey, Nidra?" James called.

"What?"

"How come I didn't get experience or a notification from the Plague Rat we just killed?"

She raised an eyebrow in annoyance. "Seriously? How don't you know that?"

James scowled at her. "I had a sheltered childhood. Please."

Nidra sighed, then proceeded to speak slowly, emphasizing words as if talking to a simpleton. "Only the person who kills a creature gains any experience from it. If someone else helps you kill the creature, then the experience you get is reduced proportionally."

"But why?" James asked.

"You really didn't know," Nidra realized. "But everyone knows. It's a rule."

James realized that Lucien and Arik were listening closely. He turned to address the group. "Look, there are a few things about me I'm not ready to talk about, but for now, let's pretend I know very little about the System. Just answer my stupid questions."

Nidra gave him a suspicious glance before eventually acquiescing.

"So anyway," James said in the silence. "Is there a way to share experience?"

"Yes." Nidra sighed. "You need to hire a life-mage with the Create Party skill, but most people won't go that far."

"That doesn't sound too bad," James said.

"I don't understand the magic behind it, but it's difficult, and extremely hard to undo," Nidra said.

James nodded. "Thanks for the information."

"You know, you're going to need to explain yourself if you want me to keep helping you."

"I know."

A sparkle inside one of the Plague Rat corpses caught James' attention, and he bent down to pick it up, taking care to avoid as much of the creature's fluids as possible.

Cursed Soul Gem:

Rank: Rare

A black gem crafted for an unknown purpose. You can feel the evil energies swirling inside.

James picked up the familiar black crystal from the center of the Plague Rat and showed it to his companions. "Has anyone seen anything like this before?"

Arik and Lucien shook their heads, but Nidra took a step back and made an odd sign with her fingers as if she were pushing something away.

"Nidra?" James asked.

She shook her head. "I don't know what that is, but I can feel the malevolent energy inside of it." She shuddered. "Get rid of it. It has the touch of madness."

"Madness?" James asked.

"One of the Vile magics. Dangerous and evil," She replied, shuddering, "only used by the Fallen and Dark Elves

James nodded. "Then I'll get rid of it somewhere safe, not here where anyone could find it." He slipped the gem into his pouch and examined the other two Plague Rat corpses. He found a Cursed Soul Gem in each one and slipped it into his pouch before motioning to Arik to proceed.

As they continued through the dungeon James scouted ahead, trying to spot more Plague Rats. This time, he paid much more attention to the noises around. They were coming up on an intersection in the tunnel when he heard the click of nails on stone. Shrinking against the wall, he waited to see how many Plague Rats were coming. This time, almost a dozen Plague Rats crossed the intersection, scampering past James without sparing him a glance.

> YOU HAVE GAINED 1 SKILL RANK IN STEALTH.
>
> YOU ARE NOW SKILL RANK 14.

James breathed a sigh of relief when the Plague Rats were out of sight and turned, creeping back to his group.

Back with his companions, James expressed his worry that there were too many rats in the dungeon. The group couldn't take them all on.

"Don't worry," Arik assured him. "We aren't here for the dungeon. We're here for something else."

"I'd still like to know what we're looking for," Nidra grumbled good-naturedly. She had grown to accept the mystery of it all and was as excited as everyone else was for the grand reveal.

"We're not far," Arik assured them.

"You've been saying that forever," Lucien pointed out.

"Listen to the water," Arik replied. "That's our destination."

"Do you have a boat waiting for us?" James joked.

Arik winked. "Something like that."

That didn't inspire confidence in James. He spent the next half hour imagining various water-themed roller coasters as they delved deeper into the tunnels.

Chapter 31

Everyone but Arik stared at the underground river far below them as it cut across the cavern, creating a deep furrow in the solid stone wall. Fresh water sprayed upwards with enough force to reach the group, soaking them even though they stood at least twenty feet above. Nidra opened her mouth to speak, but all sound was drowned out by the crashing of the waves against rock, so she tried again, shouting to be heard over the roar.

"Is that water travelling uphill?"

"Good eye," Arik shouted back.

"How is this possible?" Her voice conveyed amazement even through the shouting.

"Welcome to the Aqueduct, pride of the Dwarves." Arik called back, puffing out his chest.

"How did you do this?"

"Runic script."

"Runic?" Nidra gasped. "How old is this?"

"Over a thousand years," Arik said.

"What's runic?" James asked, butting into their conversation.

"A lost form of magic," Nidra answered.

Arik nodded sadly. "A loss as great as any."

"So where to now?" James asked, looking around for the path. As far as he could tell, there was nowhere else to go from where they were.

Arik gestured for the group to follow him as he made his way to the edge of the tunnel overlooking the water. Carefully, he grabbed on to something under the lip that James couldn't see. He turned, slowly lowering his foot over the edge. Then he was gone, followed by Lucien, then Nidra.

James gathered his courage and crawled to the edge of the tunnel, peering over the ledge to see how his friends had descended. Thick iron bars had been pounded into the stone in the shape of a makeshift ladder that ran down the cavern wall to a thin walkway next to the river. His three companions were waiting for him on the walkway, holding on to a thin chain as they braced themselves against the spray. Suddenly, the world tilted and James felt like he was falling, his body pitching forward. Hands shaking, he quickly crawled back from the ledge.

"I can't do this!" James shouted down to Arik.

There was a muffled reply from his companion, but he couldn't hear it over the water. Cautiously shuffling closer, James lay on the ground about five feet behind the ledge and stretched his neck out. "I can't do this." He repeated. "I hate heights."

This time he was able to make out the Dwarf's reply. "We all made it." Arik shouted back. "It's either this or the rats. Your choice."

James looked back down the tunnel. He could probably make it back to the entrance if he stayed in stealth the whole time. The only question was whether the door would let him exit or not without Arik's metal magic. While James was debating whether to go down the ladder or not, a lone Plague Rat passed by the passage entrance. It stopped, sniffing the air for a second, before turning to see James standing by himself with no way to escape. The Plague Rat squealed in joy and advanced on James. Two more rats joined it.

There was no way out. James doubted he would have been able to fight off one Plague Rat without his magic, and now there were three advancing on him. He sighed. He knew what he had to do.

James turned and bolted for the ladder, the Plague Rats close on his heels. James tried not to look down as he launched himself towards the ledge, sliding across the slick rock. Just as he went over the ledge he spun his body in midair and grabbed the first rung of the ladder.

James hung by one arm for a second, breathing heavily while he listened to rats angrily complain about losing their meal. One of the rats cautiously made its way to the edge and tried to bite at James' fingers. The creature's needle-like teeth closed on air, barely grazing the hair on James' knuckles. James grabbed the next rung down.

Don't look down. Don't look down. Don't look down.

James climbed down the ladder, muscles trembling in fear. Suddenly, with a screech, one of the rats launched itself off of the edge. As it fell, it swiped at James with its claws, cutting a wide furrow across his back.

YOU ARE AFFECTED BY [SEPSIS I]

Sepsis I

- 5% to max HP

- 2 Strength

- 2 Constitution

- 2 Endurance

- 2 Dexterity

THE INFECTION IN YOUR BLOODSTREAM IS SPREADING. YOUR DEBUFF [SEPSIS I] HAS UPGRADED TO [SEPSIS II]

Sepsis II:

- [Delirious]

- 15% to max HP

- 8 Strength

- 8 Constitution

- 8 Endurance

- 8 Dexterity

James groaned in pain as he felt the infection spread from the burning wound on his back. His grip weakened marginally, and he felt heavier on the bars. Black veins angrily swelled to the surface of his arms, carrying death throughout his body.

The Plague Rat plummeted into the river, its joyous screeches turning into terrified squeals as it struggled to stay afloat in the rapids. Another Plague Rat launched itself off of the edge, this one missing its target, plunging straight into the river. It splashed into the water and thrashed around, using the drowned corpse of the first Plague Rat to hold itself above the water. The third Plague Rat followed the first two, again missing James and landing in the river with the others. Mechanically, James climbed down the ladder, dropping the last few feet onto the path.

The walkway was about as wide as his shoulders, slick with water and algae from the constant barrage of waves crashing over it. "Why don't Dwarves know what handrails are?" he grumbled to himself, grabbing on to the chain handrail to help keep his balance. Slowly he slid one foot in front of another, heading to a small door at the end of the pathway that his friends had disappeared into. He kept focused on the stone doorway ahead, trying to ignore the cold spray of the water that seemed dedicated to knocking him off the ledge. Halfway to the door, a surge of water slammed into him, lifting his feet off of the path. James screamed and held the chain in a death grip, knuckles white with effort, while his feet flailed in the water searching for a place to rest. After what seemed like an eternity, the swell died down and James gasped ragged breaths of relief.

When he finally reached the doorway, James was soaked, his hands numb. When he tried to let go of the chain, his hands wouldn't respond, so he banged on the door with his foot in an attempt to get the attention of his friends.

As if in a dream, James heard voices and felt his friends grab his wrists and haul him into the room, slamming the door shut behind them.

James fell to the floor, gasping.

He heard footsteps approach. A worried voice said, "We need to get him to a healer right away."

What was the voice talking about? He was fine. "I'm fine." He said, pushing himself to his feet. He was slightly unsteady, but he could stand up on his own. James opened his eyes but couldn't make anything out. Everything was dark and fuzzy. Rough hands caught him as he stumbled and fell , guiding him to the floor.

He heard a voice, distorted as if it were coming from underwater, "He isn't looking too good. We need a healer."

That was the last thing James remembered before darkness claimed him.

The infection in your bloodstream is spreading. Your debuff [Sepsis II] has upgraded to [Sepsis III]

Sepsis III:

317

- *[Delirious II]*

- *50% to max HP*

- *20 Strength*

- *20 Constitution*

- *20 Endurance*

- *20 Dexterity*

Rough hands grabbed him, forcing him down into a seated position. James fought against them, weakly pushing at the offending limbs. He tried to tell him to stop, but all that it came out of his mouth were unintelligible syllables. Then the darkness came again.

The next thing James remembered was a gentle hand holding his head and guiding him to cool sips of water. James pushed his eyes open a crack and he could see Nidra's concerned eyes looking down at him.

James briefly regained consciousness as the rocking motion stopped. His eyes widened as he saw a dwarf pointing the crossbow directly at him. "Don't move, Demon,"

A new notification popped into view.

THE INFECTION IN YOUR BLOODSTREAM IS SPREADING. YOUR DEBUFF [SEPSIS III] HAS PROGRESSED TO [SEPSIS IV]

Sepsis IV:

- *[Delirious III]*

- *75% to max HP*

- *50 Strength*

- *50 Constitution*

> *- 50 Endurance*
>
> *- 50 Dexterity*

James tried to respond, to tell the Dwarf that he wasn't a demon, but his mouth wasn't working. When he pulled up his stat screen, all of his stats were set to zero. He tried to unbuckle his seatbelt. Why was he belted in? What was going on?

James' breath started coming out in ragged gasps as he descended deeper into confusion.

From somewhere close by he heard a female voice, urgently pleading. "Please... He needs a healer."

Who needs a healer? Poor guy.

He felt someone unbuckling the straps holding him up and tried to stand, but nothing would move. He collapsed to the ground like a ragdoll and felt strong hands lifting him off of the ground.

Then, blackness.

Chapter 32

James slowly returned to consciousness, blinking blearily as he took in the surrounding room. He was lying on a comfortable cot in a windowless stone room with an iron door set in the wall. Cautiously, he tried to move his body and found that, with some effort, he was able to sit up.

A blinking notification in the corner of his vision got his attention, and he opened it.

THE INFECTION IN YOUR BLOODSTREAM HAS BEEN HEALED. YOUR DEBUFF [SEPSIS IV] HAS REGRESSED TO [SEPSIS I]

Sepsis I:

  - 5% to max HP

  - 2 Strength

  - 2 Constitution

  - 2 Endurance

  - 2 Dexterity

Without the threat of death looming over him, James felt much better. He took in his surroundings, which didn't take long. The room was practically empty, occupied only by the cot he was lying on and a bucket in the corner. James didn't want to think about what the bucket was for.

He examined the cot, checking under the mattress to see if he could find anything hidden. In video games there was usually a helpful item hidden somewhere in jail cells, and that's what this felt like. No dice. James continued examining every inch of the room. He wasn't sure what he was looking for, but he figured he would know it when he saw it.

The sound of metal on stone outside his door alerted James that someone was coming, and he retreated to the bed, pretending that he hadn't moved. "Dinner." A rough voice came from outside the door, followed by the creaking of a rectangular slot on the bottom of the door as whoever was outside slid a tray of food through it. James rushed over to the sound, trying to get a good look at whoever had slid him the food, but all he could see was a retreating pair of steel boots.

"Wait!" James called out desperately. "Where am I? Why am I here?" The last thing he remembered was climbing down the ladder with Arik

The guard ignored his questions, disappearing from James' sight.

Sighing, James sat down to eat. His tray was laden with an odd-colored mush that he poked at. It was the worst thing he had eaten since coming to this world, but he devoured it with gusto. After he finished his meal, he sat on the bed, swinging his feet in boredom. *This place needs a bookshelf or something.*

Over the next few hours, his boredom progressively worsened. Without his pouch he had nothing to do, otherwise he would have tried to read his potion making book. Annoyed, he tried to meditate. When he closed his eyes and focused inward, he could see the Mana traveling sluggishly through constricted channels throughout his body, but it felt pointless when he couldn't use it.

YOU HAVE GAINED 3 SKILL RANKS IN MEDITATION.

YOU ARE NOW SKILL RANK 8.

Once he grew bored with meditation, James tried to think up more to do. He tried pacing around the room, but quickly grew bored with that. He wished he had a book. Locking someone in a room like this was cruel, especially when they had ADHD. God, he was bored.

James sat on the bed.

He got off the bed.

He scratched his nose.

Eventually he couldn't take it anymore. James didn't know how long he had been in the cell, but it couldn't have been more than a few hours. James pounded on the door. "Let me out. Let me out! *Let me out!*"

Nobody came.

"Fine. If nobody will talk to me, I'll get out myself," James shouted to nobody. He would escape using Shadow Step. Sure, his Mana bar was still completely black and read *n/a*, but he could feel the Mana moving when he meditated. There was no reason the spell shouldn't work. James drew on his mana.

Pain unlike he had ever felt permeated his body, driving away all other thought. It felt like someone had taken a funnel and poured liquid fire directly into his brain, letting it trickle down his body. He collapsed to the ground, screaming and shaking, then blackness.

James woke up a short while later to the sound of soft footsteps outside his door. A key turned in the lock and the cell door creaked open. He heard a worried voice next to him. "What happened?"

James cracked his eyes open just enough to see a young Dwarven man kneeling by his side, looking at him in concern.

> NAME: THON MUNSEY
>
> RACE: DWARF
>
> LEVEL 35
>
> CLASS: HEALER

Thon was around four feet tall, with a long beard that separated into two braids which were connected to his mustache, giving him the appearance of having one very long mustache. If James wasn't in so much pain, he probably would have laughed.

"What happened, James?" the Dwarf asked softly, helping him to his feet and sitting him back on the bed. "The Sepsis debuff shouldn't have caused pain like that."

"Not Sepsis," James croaked. "Something else."

The healer looked at him closely. "Something else?"

"Mana burns." James said.

The healer raised an eyebrow in surprise. "At your level? How?"

"Crystals." James groaned. "Please. The pain."

The healer frowned, rifling through his robe and muttering to himself. "Now where is it?" Finally, he handed James a blue leaf. "Chew this."

Popping the leaf in his mouth, James felt an immediate cooling sensation spread across his body, washing away the pain.

> YOU HAVE EATEN [WIZARD'S COOLANT]
>
> Wizard's Coolant:

- 100% pain from Mana burns

James sighed in blessed relief, finally free of the pain that had been plaguing him since the fight with the Goblins. He wondered where he could get more of the plant.

While James giggled giddily with the sweet relief of the potion, and the healer turned to one of the guards. "Fetch Eugenius."

The guard clapped a hand to her chest and marched off.

"By the way, how do you know my name?" James asked curiously. Abilities like his Death's Stare ability were very rare. Most people didn't see names hovering above everyone else's head like he did.

"Your friends." The Dwarf replied. "They've been quite helpful." He chuckled to himself. "So far, you've been the politest prisoners we've ever had." As he was talking, Thon pulled a clay pot from his robe, handing it to James. "Drink this."

James' head was starting to feel a little fuzzy from the painkiller, but one word in particular stuck out from the healer's statement. "Prisoners?"

"Focus on getting better," the healer said, nudging James' hand. "Drink."

James drank, almost spitting out the disgusting fluid. "What is this? Brake fluid?" He sputtered, trying to choke it down.

"Break fluid? No, just the opposite. It's made to heal."

"Never mind."

As soon as he finished drinking the potion, James got a welcome notification.

The infection in your bloodstream has been healed completely. [Sepsis I] debuff has been removed.

James sighed in relief. "Thank you."

"Of course."

"Please tell me why one of my students is so incompetent that they cannot handle a simple case of Sepsis?" A stern voice called from the doorway.

Name: Eugenius Tomic

Race: Dwarf

Level: ???

Class: Lifegiver

Eugenius was dressed in snow-white robes with dark green accents and had an immaculate white beard that stretched from his chin to his toes. It was meticulously braided, without a single hair out of place.

"There better be a good reason you interrupted my work for a simple case of sepsis," Eugenius grumbled. Somehow, he managed to look both annoyed and bored at the same time while he glared down his nose at the quaking apprentice.

"Sir... It's not that," the terrified healer mumbled.

"Speak up," Eugenius snapped. "I can't hear a word you're saying."

"Sir, his mana. The channels."

Eugenius pushed the healer aside and approached James. "Never mind, boy, I'll do everything myself." Kneeling, he grabbed James' hand, examining his palm. Green light shone on Eugenius' fingertips and questing tendrils ran along James' hand. Pulling a bright blue monocle out of his robe, Eugenius stared at James.

James shifted uncomfortably under the Dwarf's piercing gaze. "You have the same class as someone else I know," he told the Dwarf.

Eugenius froze, slowly looking up at James' face for the first time. James fearfully met the Dwarf's eyes, wondering what he said wrong.

Eugenius raised an eyebrow. "You know Lillian?"

"Nana?" James responded, equally surprised. "How did you know I was talking about her?"

Eugenius chuckled. "Lucky guess."

"So how do you know Nana?"

"Know her? She taught me. How's the old bat doing?"

"She's doing well." James responded, wondering how old Nana must be if she had taught Eugenius, who looked old even by Dwarven standards.

"How do you know her?" Eugenius asked James curiously.

James settled on a partial truth. "She was teaching me when I got caught by slavers. My group and I escaped here. That's why we came up through the tunnels."

Eugenius second eyebrow shot up. "You're a healer?"

"No, she was teaching me how to fight."

"Really."

James could tell that the Dwarf didn't believe him. "So how did you do this much damage to your Mana channels?"

"I used five Mana crystals at once," James mumbled, embarrassed.

"Five!" The Dwarf exclaimed. "It's a blessing you're still alive. Can you channel at all?"

"No. Every time I try, I collapse in pain."

Eugenius sighed. "As Mana flows through your body, it lets off energy. Abilities, even ones without an active or passive Mana cost, feed off of this energy. Luckily for you, the trickle of Mana that still flows through you is enough to support your Abilities, although I wouldn't recommend picking up new ones or else you could cause a manaspasm. Your Mana channels could constrict and completely close off. Without any Mana flowing through your body, you'd die."

James took a moment to process the news. "So. There's no way you can heal me?"

"I'm sorry, but no. It is impossible to heal damage this extensive. You will never be able to use Mana again."

With that grim pronouncement, Eugenius got up to leave. At the door, the healer gave James a knowing glance. "We will speak more about Lilian later. I would like to hear more about the specifics of your meeting."

"Wait. Before you go, what's going to happen to me?" James asked, worried.

Eugenius spared James one last sad glance as the cell door slammed shut behind him, leaving him alone in the cell.

Chapter 33

O nce Eugenius left there was nothing to do. James cursed, wishing he had asked Eugenius for a book or something. He was bored. James pulled up his character sheet. He hadn't checked it in a while and didn't have anything better to do.

JAMES

HUMAN (WARRIOR OF DARKNESS)

LEVEL: 15

HEALTH: 243/243   REGENERATES 4.1/HOUR

MANA: 0/0   REGENERATES 0.0/HOUR

STAMINA: 340/340   REGENERATES 4.2/HOUR

STATS

STRENGTH: 33   DEXTERITY: 33

CONSTITUTION: 34

INTELLIGENCE: 38   WISDOM: 38

ENDURANCE: 33

CHARISMA: 1   LUCK: 2   RESILIENCE:

4

SPELLS

SHADOW STEP (LEVEL 1)

SYREUS' WRATH (N\A)

SLICK SKIN (N/A)

ABILITIES

DEATH'S STARE (1/7)

DEATH'S STARE (1/7)

IMBUE DARKNESS (4/10)

ARCANE ARMOR (3/10)

PIERCE THE VEIL (1/10)

STRONGER SHADOWS (2/5)

KNIFE IN THE DARK (1/10)

DYING WILL (N/A)

SPIRIT OF THE SWORD (N/A)

BRANDS

MARK OF SYTAR

DIVINE QUEST (MINOR)

LIBERATOR

ACHIEVEMENTS

DUMB LUCK

CLUMSY I

SOLO DUNGEONEER

MAD DASH

James was proud of his progress. Other than the loss of his mana, he had managed to hit level 15 in around two months, a feat which he thought was impressive. Too quickly, James finished looking over his status sheet and found himself with nothing to do once again.

He wondered what his friends had gotten up to. Arik was probably in the most trouble for bringing them into the city, but apparently the rest of them were in trouble too. Lucien had been having a very rough time lately, and James hoped the teenager wasn't giving the Dwarves any trouble. The best way out of this situation was probably staying calm. After all, they hadn't actually done anything criminal. Hopefully.

There was a quiet knock on his door, and James shook his head, clearing his thoughts. "Come in," he called out hesitantly.

A female Dwarf entered the room. She was dressed in black, baggy clothing that hid her features along with a face-covering that masked everything but her eyes, which were a nondescript brown. She entered the cell silently and sat down facing James on a chair that one of the guards had quickly slipped behind her. Calm and impassive, she waited, not saying a word, just staring directly into James' eyes as he read the lack of text floating above her head.

> NAME: ???
>
> RACE: ???
>
> LEVEL: ???
>
> CLASS: ???

James had never seen a nametag without any information before. That would probably make her some kind of rogue or other information-gathering class. Perhaps a spy. Either way, he didn't have enough information to work with, so staying quiet would probably be his best bet. Time stretched on as neither of them spoke, staring intently at each other.

Five minutes.

Ten minutes.

James' eyebrow twitched in annoyance.

Twenty minutes.

Finally, he couldn't take it anymore. "I'm James." He introduced himself, holding out his hand for her to shake.

"James." She stared at his hand for a second, but ignored it, leaving James sitting on the bed with one hand stretched out awkwardly.

He held it out for another couple of uncomfortable seconds, but realized that she wasn't going to shake it. With a sigh, he dropped his hand back down. "Can I help you?"

"You tell me."

"I don't know." He shrugged. "Why am I in here?"

"Why do you think you're here?"

"No idea." James knew better than to admit anything. He had seen enough cop shows to understand that this was an interrogation, and that anything he said would only hurt his case. With his limited knowledge of this world, he would probably end up giving away something he shouldn't.

They continued staring.

Another five minutes passed. It didn't look like she was going to move at all.

Was she going to sit there all day? That would be uncomfortable. It might be better than the boredom though. Still, maybe she could get him a book or something to pass the time.

Ten more minutes.

"Hey. Would you be able to get me my pouch?" James asked. "I'm very bored and have a book in there that I would like to read."

She ignored his question and continued to stare.

James was starting to go from feeling uncomfortable to feeling annoyed. *What was her problem? I haven't done anything wrong.*

Finally, after almost an hour, James burst out, "If you have a question to ask then ask it! I don't even know why I'm here. First, I get caught by a bunch of slavers, but I get free and save one of your people, but then you all lock me up without even a trial. Fine. But you know what, I don't deserve this. I helped Arik. That's another thing. Arik doesn't deserve this kind of treatment either. He helped us escape from a bunch of Goblins. We would have died if he hadn't taken us though those tunnels. Even then, he almost didn't do it. He made us promise not to tell anyone, so what's the issue? It's not like I can talk about it, anyway." James paused to take a breath and realized what he had done. He had been rambling and ended up revealing much more than he had planned.

The mysterious Dwarf stood up. "Thank you, James." She turned to leave. The guard followed, dragging the chair out of the room after her.

"Wait, can I please get my book or something?" James called after her. "I told you what you wanted to know." But the door closed with no response.

James screamed in frustration, pounding on the door. "Let me out!" he shouted, pounding on the door until his fists bled.

As the adrenaline faded, James could feel pain beginning to bubble up in his hands. He looked down at them and felt a lump in his throat. He had been moving constantly since he had appeared in this world and now, with time to rest, all the emotions he'd been holding down bubbled to the surface. Alone and broken, James sobbed. It was all too much for him. He didn't know how long he cried, but by the time he was finished, he felt much better. He couldn't give in to hopelessness. No matter what happened, he would be okay.

Resolved, James decided to spend his time in this jail cell as productively as he could. He needed to train his skills.

James sat cross-legged on the cot and closed his eyes, breathing in through his nose and out through his mouth. This time, instead of solely focusing on his Mana channels, James tried to understand his body on a deeper level. Using his knowledge of anatomy, he delved into himself and followed the pathways of his blood vessels and internal organs. When James focused on his entire body, the experience he got for the meditation skill drastically increased and the skill shot up in levels.

YOU HAVE GAINED 17 SKILL RANKS IN MEDITATION.

YOU ARE NOW SKILL RANK 25.

CONGRATULATIONS! YOU HAVE REACHED JOURNEYMAN RANK IN MEDITATION.

As a Journeyman, you may choose one of the following bonus abilities

OF BODY AND MIND

No longer does meditation only affect your mind. With your knowledge of anatomy, you can use your meditation to heal your body as well. The amount you heal increases based on your Anatomy and Meditation skill levels (Requires Skill: Anatomy).

PASSIVE MEDITATION

You understand the inner flow of Mana through your body. The Meditation skill becomes a passive skill, increasing the flow of Mana through your body and drastically improving your Mana recovery rate.

SPIRITUAL AWAKENING

Unlocks the Spirit stat

James cracked his neck and stood up, rubbing the sore spots on his butt. He had no idea how long he had been meditating, but as he looked over the potential upgrades, he knew it was worth it. The first upgrade would help him heal much faster, allowing the skill to affect his health in the same way it affected his mana. If he understood it correctly, the next Ability would boost his Mana regeneration rate an insane amount. The final option, Spiritual Awakening, was more nebulous. James had no idea what the spirit stat did, and he wasn't in a good position to find out. He wished Nana were here to help.

The smartest option would be to close the window and pick his Ability when he had more knowledge, but when he tried, he got a new prompt.

> Do you want to forgo your Journeyman bonus for the Meditation skill? This is a permanent choice.

He quickly cancelled. There was no way James wanted to give up a bonus this good. Instead, he decided to choose the most useful skill for him right then. If he were in a better position, he might have taken a chance on Spiritual Awakening, or if he had his Mana, he would have chosen Passive Meditation, but since he would never be able to use spells again, he decided to choose Of Body and Mind.

> *JOURNEYMAN MEDITATION BONUS*
>
> Of Body and Mind:
>
> With your knowledge of anatomy, you understand that everything is connected. Mana and blood coexist, flowing through your body in parallel. By feeling the flow of energy through your body, your meditation skill will boost health regeneration as well as Mana regeneration.

James pulled up his meditation skill to see what the boost was.

> Meditation (Level 25):
>
> + *3.4 Mana regenerated per minute.*
>
> + *3.4 health regenerated per minute*

Amazing!

It looked like the amount of health that he would regenerate every minute was equal to his skill level in Anatomy. Eager to try out his new skill, James concentrated. Sinking into a trance, he watched his hands heal, bones sinking back into place and tendons reattaching at an impossible speed. When his body had finished healing, he was hit with a wave of exhaustion, much more than anything he had ever experienced before. He sunk back onto the cot and fell asleep almost instantly.

Fragment of Divinity

Chapter 34

The next day passed uneventfully as James continued working on any skills that he could work on in his cell. To train his climbing skill, he mantled around the room, using the stones as climbing holds. Leveling was much slower than when he was using the skills against actual enemies, but he still managed to gain a few levels in each.

> YOU HAVE GAINED 3 SKILL RANKS IN CLIMBING.
>
> YOU ARE NOW SKILL RANK 12.

> YOU HAVE GAINED 1 SKILL RANK IN MEDITATION.
>
> YOU ARE NOW SKILL RANK 26.

James also tried to level up his Stealth skill, but after about an hour of stealthily pacing around the room with no experience gain, he gave up. But by the end of the day James was happy with the progress he had made, and he hadn't been nearly as bored as the previous day. That night as he lay in bed falling asleep, James wondered when he would even be let out of the cage. He didn't know the rules in here-maybe they would leave him to rot forever. Or maybe not. With those dark thoughts running through his mind, James fell asleep.

Later that night, he woke up to the sound of heavy boots outside his door. A series of guards filed into his room, standing at attention. They were followed by the most richly-dressed Dwarf he had ever seen, wearing a rich red robe accented with gold trim.

NAME: FLORIUS AMESRY

RACE: DWARF

LEVEL: ???

CLASS: GRAND CHANCELLOR

When Florius got close enough, James realized that the Dwarf had fine tendrils of gold thread woven through his beard to match the gold accents on his robe. Based on the smooth confidence with which he walked, James could tell that the Dwarf was either royalty or incredibly important. With a class like Grand Chancellor, James guessed that it was the latter. He would have to play this right if he didn't want to upset someone who looked like he could make James' life very hard.

Remembering his conversation with the mysterious figure the day before, James wondered how best to deal with the Grand Chancellor. He had already told the Dwarves how his group had gotten to the Iron City, so he wasn't sure exactly what Florius was here for. Still, he should probably be polite to the person who had him in jail, even if he didn't really want to. In the end, James decided to introduce himself, but when he stood up and held his hand out to the Grand Chancellor, one of the guards stepped forward and drew his sword.

Waving his hand, Florius stopped the guard and addressed James, voice dripping with distaste. "Do you know why I'm here?"

"To let me go?" James said hopefully.

A brief look of surprise flashed across the Grand Chancellor's face. "How could you... no, never mind."

It was James' turn to look surprised. "Wait, you're letting me go?" A small flash of hope wormed its way into his heart. He'd been worried that they were planning on keeping him here forever.

The Grand Chancellor ground his teeth in annoyance. "Yes, but do you know why I specifically am here?"

"You're in charge of letting people out?" James asked.

"You think that the Grand Chancellor, right hand to the king, comes all the way down to this...place," he looked around distastefully, "just so that I can give you a sweet roll and let you out of prison?" His eyes flashed with anger. "No. I'm here because I disagree with my King's decision to allow you to roam the city while we decide how to deal with you. Letting a Human, and even worse, an Elf, free with the knowledge that you have is foolhardy. But I live to serve, so here we are." Florius leaned in so close that their noses almost touched, and James could feel his hot breath on his face. "Just be warned that I will be watching you very closely. One slip up and you may just... disappear." The Grand Chancellor strode out of the room, leaving a very conflicted James in his wake. It would probably be a good idea to get out of the city as fast as he could.

Soon after Florius left, there was another knock on the door. This time, his guest was a younger Dwarf, carrying all of James' possessions.

NAME: DANFORTH SAND

RACE: DWARF

James wasn't sure how to tell a Dwarf's age, but Danforth's beard was much shorter than any of the other Dwarves that he had seen so far. For a servant, it looked like he was treated well. He wore a red tunic with a golden fox printed on the back.

"Hey there. I'm Danforth." The Dwarf gave him a shy smile. "I'm here as your guide."

Danforth handed James his gear and turned around to allow him to change back into his leathers. Once James was dressed and equipped, the Dwarf escorted James out of the room and into a long hallway filled with doors just like his. Each door had a cell number carved into the rock next to it. James had been in cell 1,328. The two continued walking through a maze of identical hallways while James chatted with his guide.

"What's going to happen to my companions?" James asked.

"They're fine. We're actually heading to them in a bit."

"Where are we headed now?"

"To clean you up. You smell worse than an orc's backside." The Dwarf chuckled. "With how dirty you are, I'm not sure they'd even let you enter the outer ring."

"That would be much appreciated." He smiled at Danforth, "lead the way."

The pair walked in silence for a bit before James asked something else he'd been wondering about. "So, What's the symbol on your shirt?" James gestured at the golden fox emblem on the back of the Servant's tunic.

"Oh, this?" He smiled proudly. "It's the sigil of house Stricken. It shows everyone that I'm a member."

"You're a noble?" James asked, surprised that the nobles would use family members as servants. Maybe it was an outer family and inner family deal, where the outer family served the inner family?

Danforth looked confused for a second before realizing what James meant. Immediately he shook his head in denial. "No, in our culture the people who live with you are considered part of your house, but I don't have noble blood and could never inherit the throne."

"Gotcha. So how does the throne get passed down?"

"The throne goes to the youngest child at the time of the King's death." Danforth explained.

"Really?" James raised an eyebrow. "Why the youngest? In my... country, the eldest always inherits."

Danforth raised a curious eyebrow. "Why? The eldest child gets the least prepared parents. The youngest children make for more balanced leaders. And they live longer."

"Interesting," James said. He'd never thought about it that way. "Wouldn't that make the kids more likely to assassinate their parents if they thought they were going to lose the throne?"

Danforth shook his head quickly, "Don't say stuff like that."

"Right. Sorry."

There was an awkward paused before James asked, "So how far away are we?"

"We're almost out of the prison. We're going to come out in the outskirts and head straight to a bathhouse, then I can show you around the city."

"So why do they call this place the Iron City?" James asked. He had been wondering for a while but hadn't thought to ask anyone.

"It used to be an iron mine off of the Old City, but when..."

Danforth stopped talking as they came to a heavily guarded thick iron door. He spoke a few words to one of the guards, who nodded and opened the door for the two to pass. But when James stepped up to the door, another guard blocked it. "Watch yourself, Human," he growled, spitting on the ground. Without another word, he stepped back.

James exited the jail into a series of much wider tunnels, filled with a hodgepodge of living spaces, tents and bags of meager possessions scattered among ramshackle stalls filled with dirty looking Dwarves. When they saw James, some of the Dwarves made rude gestures, spitting on the ground, while others ignored him.

"Do Dwarves not like Humans?" James asked when he caught up to Danforth.

Danforth rubbed the back of his head awkwardly. "I probably should have warned you."

"About?"

"I may not have been entirely honest with you earlier. I'm not just here as a guide. I'm also here as an escort to make sure you stay safe. Some Dwarves have… issues… with Humans."

"Why?"

"They resent you for not helping us during the desolation."

"The desolation?" James thought, trying to remember if he'd heard the term before. "Is that related to why this is the only Dwarven city left?"

Danforth nodded sadly. "Our cities were once spread across the Crimson Mountains, but we were attacked. Orcs came from the other side of the mountains, from the Howling Wastes. Now our people are a fragment of what they once were."

"How could they have taken over so much? From what I've seen, you Dwarves are powerful."

Danforth shook his head, lowering his voice and whispered, "The Tei'zir."

"What are the — " James started to ask, but before he could finish, Danforth clapped a hand over his mouth, drawing admonishing stares from passersby.

"Quiet." The Dwarf hissed.

"Sorry. What are the… they?"

"Have you not heard the story of the Elder Races?" Danforth asked James.

"The Elder Races?"

"Hang on." Danforth smiled. "This is my favorite story." As if reciting from memory, he spoke.

"In the beginning there was nothing. From that nothing emerged two opposing forces, Chaos and Order. The conflict between the forces of Chaos and Order has been going on since long before time began, and still rages today. Over the course of the war, the Angels, scions of Order, created the First Elders. The creation of the Kieva marked the start of time itself, while the Hiken were given the power of the written word. Their script has been lost to time, forgotten but for a few blessed fragments. In direct opposition to the forces of Order, the Demons created them. We do not speak their name, but we all know it, and it strikes fear into our hearts."

"So that's who the Orcs have leading them?" James asked, trying to understand.

Danforth glared at him, annoyed at the interruption, but nodded before continuing. "The three races fought, leaving a devastating trail of destruction across the land, but all was equal for a time. Until Zephyr betrayed the other angels and descended into darkness. Zephyr was the first of the Dark Angels, and he worked with the demons to create a new race, the Oroi, but the Oroi were neutral, neither Chaos nor Order. Some Oroi took up the mantle of Chaos, while others rejected their creators and sought peace. But the ability to choose in such a powerful race was too much. Over many millennia, the Elder Races wiped each other out through their constant war. They vanished, gone forever, but we, their descendants, live on."

"Hang on a second, if there are no more, then how are the Orcs led by one?" James pointed out.

Danforth shrugged. "I don't know, but my grandfather fought in the war. He saw It. He said it was a nightmare he would never forget." The dwarf shuddered; eyes lost in memories of his grandfather's story.

"Hey, don't worry about it." James said, patting the Dwarf on the back. "We're safe here, right?"

"Yea." The Dwarf smiled. "We have the Seven protecting us."

"The Seven?" James asked, glad his guide was so chatty.

"The Seven Sisters!" Danforth said excitedly, forgetting all about his grim mood earlier. "They're the reason we still have this city. Seven Saint-level fighters, each specializing in a different weapon!"

"What's a Saint-level fighter?"

"Man, they don't teach you Humans much. Someone who reaches level 500 in a skill is considered a Saint in that skill. Do Humans not have Saints? Is it because you don't live very long? I heard Humans only live 50 years!"

"Sometimes we can live longer, up to a hundred if we're lucky."

"A hundred years! How do you get anything done?" Danforth asked in amazement. "I would be half dead."

It took James a second to process that. "Wait, how old are you?"

"I'm 47."

That took James by surprise. He thought Danforth was 18 or 19. They continued chatting amicably for a while until they reached a door with a picture of a bed next to a bath carved into it. Danforth escorted him in and exchanged a few words with a surly Dwarf sitting behind the counter. They seemed to be arguing before Danforth turned to James. "One gold."

"A gold?" James said incredulously, looking around the dingy establishment. "How could this place possibly cost a gold?"

Danforth said something to the owner, who looked at James, nodded, and said something in return.

Danforth sighed. "He said you're right. Humans get a special price. Two gold."

James was about to argue, but saw the Dwarf reaching for something under the table and thought better of it. He already had the Grand Chancellor after him and didn't want to give him any new reasons to lock him up again.

"Fine. Here's your gold." James pulled two gold out of his pouch and threw it on the counter. The Dwarf grinned and pulled a curtain back, directing the two of them to some baths. As they passed, James was pretty sure he saw Danforth place a single copper coin on the counter.

"What language was that?" James as they headed down the hallway.

"Old Dwarvish." Danforth replied. "But don't worry, in the city everyone speaks common." He gestured to a shelf on the wall. "Undress and put your stuff on the shelf. Someone'll come and wash it."

James stripped down and followed Danforth through the building, hopefully towards his friends.

They eventually arrived at a stone room off the side of the bathhouse with a few steps that descended into a pool of water. Danforth sat on a bench that ran along the outer edge of the bath, while James, after realizing the water only came up to his bellybutton on the bench, moved to sit on the floor in the deeper area of the water.

Clouds of steam rose off of the water and exited through a hole cut into the rock ceiling. Water constantly flowed through the room, coming in a tunnel on one side and exiting out the other.

"Ohhhhhh. That's nice." James closed his eyes and settled into the warm water. He couldn't remember the last time he'd cleaned himself, as evidenced by the streams of filth flowing off of him in the bath. He nodded in appreciation to Danforth, who was making a point to sit upstream, well out of range of the fetid pool surrounding James. Grabbing a bar of sweet-smelling soap, James set to scrubbing himself vigorously.

"What's up with that hole?" James asked, pointing. "Is it to get rid of the steam?"

Before Danforth could answer, a familiar voice responded. "That, my friend, is how we don't all die from your stink!"

"Arik!" James exclaimed as Arik and Lucien entered the bath. He half-stood to hug his friend before he realized that they were both naked. He sat back down in embarrassment and laughed. "I'm glad you're okay, what happened?"

"I got tossed in a dungeon, just like you."

"But why are we free?"

"From what I've heard, once he verified our stories, the King decided that my actions were necessary and that it was cruel to keep us locked up when we hadn't broken any laws."

"So, we're free to go?" James asked.

"Not exactly." Danforth chimed in.

"What do you mean?" Lucien said angrily.

"We're still technically prisoners. The King just recognized that there's a little nuance to the situation and decided that since your stories match and have been verified that none of you would be a threat walking around the city while you wait for your trial. But you cannot leave the city. If you do, you will be presumed guilty and treated accordingly."

"I hate Dwarves. First one prison, then another." Lucien muttered darkly, glaring at Danforth. "I don't need a babysitter."

"I'm here to help you, not babysit you," Danforth interjected, raising his hands defensively.

Lucien said nothing, instead electing to sit in angry silence and glare at the Dwarf.

"I'm very happy to see you guys." James said, trying to break the awkward silence.

Arik laughed. "Not as happy as I am to see you taking a bath."

"Walking next to him through the tunnels was rough," Danforth agreed.

Arik looked at him seriously. "You didn't share a capsule with him."

Fragment of Divinity

Chapter 35

The next morning, the group met up with Nidra, who had been escorted to a separate section of the bathhouse for women. Together they sat and talked, relaxing luxuriously around a table heaping with bacon, eggs, and other things that James couldn't identify but was happy to eat. It felt like he hadn't gotten a good meal in months.

The sound of Danforth coughing politely cut through the conversation, and the Dwarf looked at the group seriously. "While you're in the city, make sure that you aren't causing any trouble."

"We know," James said, waving him off. "We're in a tight spot."

"I don't think you understand how tight of a spot you're in," the Dwarf said grimly. "Letting you go was not the king's most popular decision."

"What do you mean?" Nidra asked.

"You've seen our people's reaction to you guys as you've walked through The Outskirts. They aren't exactly fans. The King was well within his right to leave you imprisoned until trial, but he recognized that it might take years before it makes it to court, so he decided to free you out of pity, considering your short life spans."

That was interesting and James was grateful, but he was focused on one part of the conversation in particular. "Years?"

"Our system is…"

"Let me explain this," Arik interrupted. "I have more experience with Humans and they'll probably understand me better."

Danforth nodded and gestured for Arik to proceed.

"You know how Dwarves live much longer than Humans?"

James and Lucien nodded.

"Well, our government follows a strict set of rules and regulations to ensure that everything runs smoothly, but because we live so long, certain procedures, like trials, take much longer to process here then they would in your human kingdoms."

James raised an eyebrow in confusion. "So how long will it take to get us our trial?"

Arik chuckled awkwardly and rubbed the back of his neck. "Normally it would take between twenty-five and fifty years, but…"

"Fifty years!" James interrupted. "I don't have fifty years!"

"Oh, it won't take fifty years."

"They're speeding it up for us?"

"Just the opposite." The Dwarf steepled his fingers. "How long did you say Humans live?"

"Maybe a hundred years, if we're lucky."

"Yeah. The trial probably wouldn't happen in your lifetime."

"Why not?"

"Think about the position that the King has been placed in," Danforth said. "Why would he want to postpone your trial?"

James talked to himself, trying to figure it out. He started with the obvious point. "We came in via tunnels we shouldn't know about." Then he moved on to a few inferences. "Clearly the King is benevolent, seeing as how he released us instead of leaving us to rot, but at the same time he can't have us leaving and telling people about the tunnel because it's a huge security risk. He needs to do something to stop us from leaving the city with that information. If he delayed our trial, we would probably die first, which would solve his problem nicely."

Arik smiled. "Got it in one."

"So why don't we just leave?" Lucien said.

"What?" Everyone turned to look at him.

Lucien shrugged. "What's stopping us from just leaving the city and going back home?"

Danforth paled and opened his mouth to reply, but before he could, Arik answered. "You don't want to do that. The King would take that as an insult to his generosity in freeing you. He'd send the Ironguard after you."

"The Ironguard?"

"They deal with secretive matters that the King doesn't want made public. They're strong, and they wouldn't rest until they captured you. And once they brought you back, well, let's just say the King wouldn't let you wander freely anymore."

"So I would rot away in a jail for the rest of my life if I don't stay in the city?" James clarified.

"That sounds about right," Danforth confirmed.

Angrily, James stood up and pushed away the table. Plates crashed to the ground and food spilled everywhere as he stormed away.

Arik caught up with him and put a hand on his shoulder. "Think about it before you do anything. Do you want to spend the rest of your life in that cell?"

"No," he admitted, "but I have a quest given to me by the Makrien."

Arik's eyebrows shot up in surprised, and he paled. "The Makrien?" He whispered in fear, then he shook his head. "Now isn't the time. We can talk later. For now, don't tell anyone."

Before James could ask what had gotten into his friend, the rest of the group caught up.

"You doing okay?" Nidra asked Arik, putting her hand on his shoulder. "You're looking a bit pale."

"I'm fine," he said. "Just ate some bad breakfast."

She seemed to accept his explanation and, as one, the group turned to exit the bathhouse.

About an hour into their walk, James turned to Danforth. "So how far are we from the city?" He asked. The glares had gotten more hostile now that their party consisted of an additional Human and Elf. James was starting to feel uncomfortable.

"Just a few more hours," Danforth reassured him. "You'll know we're close when you see the statue of Ozure. Look for a mage standing on a pile of skeletons."

James nodded. "Do you think they'll attack us?" He asked Danforth, gesturing around them.

"Not as long as I'm with you. Don't wander off, though." He pointed at Nidra. "Especially you."

"Why her?" James asked.

"Elves and Dwarves don't typically get along," Arik said.

"Do you guys get along with anyone?" James asked, annoyed. Constantly worrying about his safety was wearing thin. Hopefully, it would get better in the city, otherwise he might lose his mind.

Arik thought for a moment. "The Gnomes."

James sighed, "So why do Dwarves hate Elves more than Humans? I thought we abandoned them or something."

"You're partially right. In Dwarven eyes, Humans are cowards who abandoned us when we needed them, but Dwarven hatred of Elves goes back thousands of years. Our magical affinities are fundamentally opposed, which led to conflict."

James saw Nidra's expression darken and hastened to change the subject. "So, can you tell me about the city?"

"The city is beautiful." Arik said wistfully, "I can't wait to see my home again, but to answer your question, it's divided into three rings, the Outer Ring, the Inner Ring, and the Palace. The Outer Ring is inhabited by craftsmen and other laborers. Mages, skilled craftsmen and merchants live in the Inner Ring."

James thought about that. It sounded like the city was divided by class, with blue-collar workers in the Outer Ring and white-collar workers in the Inner ring. "So who lives in the palace? The king?"

"All the nobles live in the Palace. It's a huge compound surrounded by walls with noble houses clustered under the shadow of the palace. The higher rank a noble has, the closer they live to the king."

"So, what about where we are now? Is it not part of the city?"

"The Outskirts? Well, the Outskirts are interesting. People who've been banished from the Iron City, or people who can't afford the city live out here. Outside the city means outside its protection though, so people try to stay close to the walls. We're traveling through the prison square, but soon we'll arrive at the processing center."

"The processing center?"

"It's how we get into the city. You'll understand after you've seen it."

With that cryptic remark, the group continued in silence for a few minutes until they reached a long line of Dwarves seemingly waiting for nothing.

"What is this?" Nidra asked.

"The queue," Danforth replied.

Arik looked at the line and groaned. "I'd forgotten just how bad Dwarves can be."

"So how long is this line?" James asked.

"It'll probably take a week to get us to the center, then five or six months until we're fully processed," Danforth replied cheerily.

"Six months? I don't have six months! Isn't there a way to speed this up?" James exclaimed.

Danforth sighed in annoyance. "Man, you Humans are always in such a rush. Fine, how much money do you have with you?"

"A hundred and one gold, ten silver, and ten copper. Why?" James asked.

"Come with me."

Danforth escorted the group through the tunnel, completely skipping the line. When they reached the front, they saw two heavy iron doors, guarded by a pair of bored-looking Dwarves. The processing line led into the first door and was crawling along as the guard took a copper from each person and then let them through. The other door didn't have any line in front of it, and they approached the guard.

The guard looked over their group, counting each one on his fingers. Once he'd finished counting them, he held out his hand. "Five silver."

"You want a silver per person?" James said incredulously. "How much is it to get in that line?" He pointed at the other line.

"The regular lane is one copper, the express lane is one silver." The guard said, his tone of voice clearly indicating he didn't want to talk. "Either pay the fee or get in the other line, I don't care, but quit bothering me."

James was about to keep arguing with the guard, but Danforth pulled him aside and spoke. "Just pay him."

James considered arguing, but sighed and handed the guard five silver.

"Thank you! Have a pleasant time in the city." The guard said as they passed.

The group filtered through the door and into a much shorter line of people who'd also made it past the first gate. A sign in the corner read "Welcome to the Processing Center. We hope you have a pleasant day." The sign was stained, with chipped and peeling paint. All in all, it was a good symbol of how James felt right then. This was starting to feel like airport security.

Almost as if to prove his point, the guard at the next station stopped them and asked for identification. Arik and Danforth each handed over a stone card, about the size of a driver's license. He looked the licenses over and made a quick notation in his booklet. "These three are with me," Danforth said. "They've been granted entrance by the king."

The bored guard stared at Danforth drolly. "No identification, no entry."

"Now look here." Danforth pulled a piece of paper from a pocket within his robe. "A letter from the palace instructing you to let them in."

The guard took the letter, skimmed it with a purposeful slowness and handed it back to Danforth. "No identification, no entry." He repeated without a change in expression.

James sighed. He knew where this was going. "How much?"

The guard looked them up and down as if he were trying to size up how much he could ask for. "Two Humans and an Elf? You would have to pay the special processing fee. Ten gold."

"Ten gold? That's outrageous! That's—" James stopped his rant when Danforth elbowed him in the ribs. He put his head in his hands and took a deep breath before reaching into his pouch and pulling out the bribe.

"Thank you," the guard said, pleased. He handed each of them a paper card and instructed them to show it to the next guard.

"You know, we have a place like this in my home," James said to Arik. "It's called airport security, but they don't take bribes. They exist to make it look like things are safer, but it's been proven they don't actually do anything. They mainly exist to take away people's soap and sometimes their yogurt."

"Why would they take soap?" Nidra asked.

James shrugged. "Your guess is as good as mine."

The next area of the check-in process made the DMV look like a rave. Dwarves filled benches as far as the eye could see, sitting and waiting while they clutched slips of paper with a ticket number. Every ten or so minutes a mage would conjure up a flaming number above everyone and a Dwarf would scurry over to another desk for what James hoped was the final part of the check-in process.

Danforth took them up to a desk where an elderly Dwarf was waiting.

NAME: ELDORA STONEHEART

RACE: DWARF

LEVEL: ???

CLASS: BUREAUCRAT

With excruciating slowness, she took their papers and reviewed them, before setting them down next to her. She then handed James a ticket and instructed him to sit on a bench and wait for his number to be called. He looked down at the ticket.

Iron City Entrance Ticket:

Rank: Common

> This ticket allows you to enter the Iron City. #1,983,120

James looked at the most recent number called: 457,983. "Ummm, how long is the wait?" He asked.

"We are experiencing a high volume of immigration, but your ticket should be processed in three to five years." She smiled at him. "Have a pleasant day."

"Hang on a second." James put the ticket back on the desk. "Do you have an express lane or something?"

"Of course." Her smile grew wider, and she pulled a small sign out from under the desk and placed it next to her. It read 'EXPRESS LANE'.

"How much?" James asked, resigned.

"Ten gold," she said without missing a beat.

He gave her the money, and she picked up his ticket and concentrated. A flash of orange light lit the ticket and singed off the number, replacing it with the number 457,984.

> Iron City Entrance Ticket:
>
> Rank: Common
>
> This ticket allows you to enter the Iron City. #457,984

"Hey!" A Dwarf approached the counter and angrily pushed James out of the way. "I was next in line and my ticket just changed numbers to 1,983,120. This is my third year waiting! By Vither, you better fix this."

"Sir, please calm down. Swearing won't solve anything." The smile across her face didn't match the dangerous glint in her eye.

James and the others quickly backed away as the Dwarf continued screaming at her. The last they saw of him was two guards dragging him away as he cursed and thrashed.

Once at the next desk, they were greeted by yet another bored-looking guard. This one was idly playing with a metal puzzle formed from interlocking rings and spoke without looking up. "Please place your possessions on the bench." He gestured to a bench next to him. "All of your stuff will be returned in four to eight months after a contraband check."

"Excuse me?" James said. He was getting really annoyed at these guards and their clear disdain for their jobs.

The guard sighed and looked up from his puzzle ring. He gave James a droll stare. "If you would like express service, then I can process your equipment immediately. It's ten gold each." Satisfied that was the end of it the guard returned to his puzzle.

"Fine. Here." James threw the gold on the table angrily.

The guard sighed and slowly put down his puzzle and counted out the fifty gold. Once he'd confirmed that all the gold was there, he stamped their tickets and gestured for them to head in. "Welcome to The Iron City."

Chapter 36

The cold stone of the mountain was replaced by the warm kiss of sunlight against his skin as James stepped out of the tunnel and into full light for the first time in what felt like weeks. He shielded his eyes against the brightness. Once his vision cleared, he stopped walking and stared, taking in the amazing city for the first time.

He was standing at the boundary of a hollowed-out space inside a mountain, almost like a crater, and so large that he couldn't see the other side. The walls of the mountain rose high above, towering over them until they ended abruptly, revealing the open sky. Roads wide enough for two horses to walk abreast wound their way up the walls, allowing Dwarves access to the numerous tunnels dug through the mountain. If he focused into the distance, James could just barely make out the wall separating the Inner and Outer rings.

James felt the hairs on the back of his neck start to quiver. Something was up.

YOU HAVE GAINED 1 SKILL RANK IN SIXTH SENSE.

YOU ARE NOW SKILL RANK 2.

Someone, or something, was watching him. With all the grace of a confused tourist, James looked around, trying to figure out where the feeling was coming from, but with everyone looking at them, he couldn't pick out anyone in specific who triggered his skill. Giving up, he ignored the feeling and followed Danforth through the bustling crowd.

The group made their way to a building a few blocks away from the entrance. An old wooded sign above the door depicted a broken pot. Outside the door, a rotund Dwarf greeted them with a big grin.

> *NAME: TANNEN WILDFIST*
>
> *RACE: DWARF*
>
> *LEVEL: 54*
>
> *CLASS: INNKEEPER*

He greeted them with a friendly voice and a cheery wave. "Welcome to the Cracked Cauldron, home of the best stew in the Outer Ring."

"Morning, Tannen," Danforth greeted the innkeeper before he turned to address the group. "Tannen, here, is probably the only innkeeper in town that'll let two Humans and an Elf stay at his place."

"How much is it going to cost?" James asked cautiously.

"It's five of you, right?" Tannen asked, counting. "One silver and five copper will get you two rooms and two meals per day."

That was much more reasonable than James had thought it would be, considering his recent experiences. "Deal. Here's for the first week," he said, handing over the coins.

"How about I get you all some dinner?" Tannen suggested, leading the group to a table after handing them their keys.

"Actually, I'll take my own room," Nidra said, handing him a few coins and receiving her own key.

"Fair enough," James said, handing one of the keys to Arik. "You and Lucien stay in one room and I'll stay with Danforth in the other." James wanted to keep an eye on the Dwarf. Even though he'd been nothing but pleasant, James still didn't trust him. The Dwarf was working for the royal family, after all.

While they waited for their food, the group relaxed and talked about what they wanted to do the next day. Nidra wanted to head to the library and the Mage's Guild, but Danforth told her that she wouldn't be able to get into either, since both were in the Inner City. Apparently, the 'tax' to get into the Inner City was a hundred gold, or close to a thousand if they didn't want it to take years. Lucien wanted to practice fighting and earn some gold, so Arik promised to take him somewhere to learn. James wanted to go to a market and sell some of the items he'd acquired and replenish some of his gold.

That night, James sat down with *Potion Making For Dummies* laid out on the floor in front of him alongside the Red Silkweed and Roundleaf he'd need to make a healing potion. He'd borrowed a simple alchemy kit from Nidra and was determined to craft his first potion. Following instructions from the book, he put two strands of Red Silkweed into a bowl and added water. The mixture fizzed and warmed rapidly as he stirred, and the Red Silkweed dissolved into a dark red liquid that reminded him of that disgusting cherry cough medicine his mom used to make him drink when he got sick.

James then used a mortar and pestle to crush up a few leaves of dried Roundleaf and tossed a pinch of it into the red liquid. As he stirred, the solution started to glow. Once he'd finished, James poured the potion into a flask and examined his work.

Weak Health Potion (x1):

Rank: Common

-*Heals 100 health.*

A weak health potion crafted by a novice.

The potion wouldn't win any awards, but it was stronger than he'd thought a weak health potion would be. Either way, that wasn't why he'd made the potion.

YOU HAVE GAINED 1 SKILL RANK IN ALCHEMY.

YOU ARE NOW SKILL RANK 6.

You have completed the quest: Learning to Brew

+ 5 experience

Once he'd completed the quest, James stashed the potion in his inventory and stretched. It was time to head to bed.

The next morning, James woke up feeling refreshed and ready to take on the day. Lucien and Arik had already left to go train, so it was just him, Nidra, and Danforth at the breakfast table.

"So, what are we up to today?" Nidra asked.

"I was thinking we could go to the market?" James asked. "I have a few things to sell and wanted to see if I could find a few nice items."

"Sounds good," she said. "I'll probably just stay here."

"Do you want to come with me?"

She thought about it for a second before she nodded. "I guess it's better than hiding in the room all day."

"Great! It'll be fun! Maybe we can find something for your fire magic." James turned to Danforth. "So where's the market?"

"Just past the temple district."

They exited the inn and followed the cobbled roads through the city. James still couldn't shake the feeling that he was being watched, but try as he might, he couldn't find his stalker. By this point, he was sure it wasn't just his imagination and didn't want to ignore it, but there wasn't really anything he could do about it.

Danforth filled James and Nidra in on the history of the city. James had never been a history buff back on Earth, but the history of the Iron City was fascinating. It had originally started as an iron mine thousands of years ago, but a disaster in the old city had made it uninhabitable, driving the Dwarves deep into the mountains where they founded the City of Iron. It was the only Dwarven city completely dug into a mountain and the only Dwarven city to survive the Orcs due to its inaccessibility. There were only two entrances to the outside world, and both had been barricaded by the Orcs for over fifty years, which was why the Dwarves were so cut off from the rest of civilization.

When James heard about the entrance blockade, he got a quest notification.

> YOU HAVE BEEN GIVEN AN OPEN QUEST: FREE THE CITY OF IRON I
>
> Free the City of Iron I: Destroy the two Orc barricades blocking entry to the City of Iron. Report to Florius with results.
>
> Suggested level: 50
>
> Reward: Unknown

Penalty for failure or refusal: none

Another open quest. Interesting.

The gears in James' head started turning. Maybe he could earn the Dwarves favor by helping them in the war, maybe even win his freedom. That would be preferable to his current plan, which was nonexistent.

A chill ran down his spine, accompanied by a sharp burning in his hidden brand, the Mark of Sytar. He stumbled, then caught himself, but he wasn't in the street anymore.

James stood alone in a room, lit by only a candle, with *something* shifting in the surrounding darkness. He could feel his heart beating in his chest, and he shivered in the sudden cold. His brand burned hotter.

"Leave this place. You're in grave danger," a voice hissed from the shadows.

"Where am I? Who are you?" James called out into the darkness.

He blinked and found himself standing back in the warm sunlit street with Danforth and Nidra next to him. He squinted at the return of daylight.

"Are you okay? Nidra asked, concern written across her face. "You were just on death's door. Maybe you need a few more days to relax?"

"I'm fine." James said, looking around for an explanation as to what happened. He caught the eye of a Dwarf, standing on the stoop of a gothic temple built from black stone.

NAME: ENZO FIRETONGUE

RACE: DWARF

LEVEL: 55

CLASS: PRIEST OF SYTAR

Enzo shook his head, then disappeared inside the temple.

"What is that place?" James asked, pointing at the black building.

"That's the temple of Sytar," Danforth said. "Not popular for regular worship, but an important god of Order. He rules the underworld and is the God of Death."

"I thought the undead were evil?"

"He doesn't rule the undead," Danforth clarified. "Sytar hates the undead. They're souls who have been stolen from him."

"Oh," James said, hurrying to get out of range of the temple and its strange priests.

The sun had reached its zenith by the time the group finally reached the market. They stopped in front of a shop called Pitro's Pieces, an out of the way place off of the main road that Danforth assured them would have the best prices.

Inside, the shop was filled with teetering shelves and piles of gear organized seemingly at random. Behind the counter was the tallest Dwarf that James had ever seen. If Dwarves had football, this one would be a linebacker.

NAME: PITRO WIDEANVIL

RACE: DWARF

LEVEL: 41

CLASS: MERCHANT

The Dwarf's eyes widened when a Human and an Elf walked into his store, but without missing a beat he introduced himself. "Hello, I'm Pitro. Anything I can do to help you fine folks today?"

"I actually have stuff to sell," James said.

Pitro's expression fell slightly, but he gestured for James to approach the desk and show him what he had. James pulled out a few of the equipment pieces that he'd picked up—the Keeper's Staff, the Cursed Ring of Flowing Thought, and the Beast Tamer's Whistle.

The Dwarf examined James' items with a practiced gaze and nodded. "I'll take them all. I can give you five hundred gold for the staff, ten silver for the whistle, and fifteen gold for the ring."

"Why is the ring so cheap? It's rarer than the staff." James pointed out.

"Yes, but it's cursed, which means a mage would need to remove the curse before I could sell it. I'm sure you understand how costly that would be."

James thought about it for a bit and decided to sell everything but the ring, which might prove useful sometime in the future.

"Alright. What about store credit?"

"Store credit?" the Dwarf asked, unfamiliar with the concept.

"You give me a specific amount of gold that I can spend only in this store. That way the money returns directly to you."

"Ahhh," the Dwarf said. He thought about it for a moment. "I can bring the total up to five hundred and fifty."

James agreed and immediately got a new notification.

YOU HAVE GAINED THE SKILL BARTER

Barter (Skill Rank 1):

+ 1% price to buying and selling.

James wondered how high the merchant's barter level was. If each level gave a 1% boost to price, then he'd probably just lost a fortune. In the end it didn't matter though, he needed new gear more than he needed gold, especially if he was going to get out of here.

James browsed the shop, looking for something to buy. Eventually James found a few items that interested him.

> Orichalcum Sword of Embers:
>
> Rank: Uncommon
>
> A sword of medium length crafted from Orichalcum and enchanted with a weak fire core. Can be wielded with one or both hands.

The sword was priced at three hundred gold and would be a huge upgrade from his regular steel sword. When James drew it, instead of bursting into flames, the sword glowed with the same darkness that always surrounded weapons when James used them, except this time the edges were tinged red.

With only two hundred and fifty gold left to spend, James went for a more utilitarian item—a pair of shoes that would repel liquid. It seemed like something that would be nice in a world with lots of dank dungeons and putrid puddles.

> Hydrophobic Leather Boots:
>
> Rank: Uncommon
>
> These boots have been enchanted with a weak water core to repel fluid.

The boots were two hundred and fifty gold. Exactly how much he wanted to spend.

After buying the items he wanted, James commiserated with Nidra that they just spent all the money they'd gained in a single trip.

Pitro, overhearing their conversation, interjected. "You could always try your hand at the Colosseum."

"The Colosseum?" James asked.

Danforth quickly responded. "You don't want to do that."

James ignored him. "How much can I earn?"

"The grand prize is a million gold and a vial of Spirit Salve. For an intrepid adventurer like you, it shouldn't be a problem," the merchant said with a wink.

When she heard Spirit Salve, Nidra let out a small gasp.

"Spirit Salve?" James asked.

"It's a legendary healing salve that has been said to cure all wounds in addition to granting special skills to whoever uses it."

James thought about it. He'd could probably afford to push his trial up and get out of the city if he won. "Sign me up!" He exclaimed.

Chapter 37

That night, back at the inn, James told Arik and Lucien all about their adventures of the day. Including how he'd signed up for the Colosseum. Arik angrily turned to Danforth. "I thought you were here to prevent things like this from happening!"

"Woah, what's the big deal?" James asked. "He tried to stop me, but I didn't listen."

"Did you tell him?" Arik said, glaring at Danforth.

"Tell me what?" James asked nervously.

"The same person has won every year for the past fifty years. A hundred and tenth level Soulsmith!"

"So what?" James said. "I can just forfeit if it looks like I'm going to lose."

Arik put his head in his hands. "The fights are to the death, and you aren't allowed to forfeit."

"Why didn't you tell me that?" James asked Danforth angrily.

"I tried to warn you," Danforth snapped. "But no, why would you listen to me, the Dwarf sent here to guide you, when you could be listening to a sleazy merchant."

"Well, can I get out of it?" James asked.

Arik sighed and shook his head. "No, you can't remove your name once you've signed up. You're going to have to fight."

"Well, the fights aren't for a month and I have a bunch of materials. Can you make me some gear?" James asked Arik.

"I'll do my best, but it won't make enough of a difference to win. If you don't cheat somehow, you won't win against the champion. The level difference is too high."

James nodded, but he didn't like his chances. He didn't even have magic to back him up. This would be difficult.

The rest of the month was spent preparing for the fight. James trained constantly with his new sword, fighting against Lucien, Nidra, and any Dwarves Danforth could recruit that wanted to beat up on a Human. The night before the Colosseum, he was battered and bruised, but had managed to raise his Swordsmanship to 29. He also raised his Unarmed Combat to level 21, his Knife Throwing to 14, and his Small Blades to 23.

In a flash of Dwarven ingenuity, Arik had used the Cave Spider Matriarch Carapace, Lion Fur, and Rocksilk to create a nice set of armor for James. Each piece in the armor was crafted from shining black carapace plate and lined with lion fur, but the best part was the breastplate which had the Monster Core (Earth) implanted in its center.

Spider Carapace Breastplate of Stone:

Rank: Uncommon

+ 10% armor weight

+ 50% durabilty

> A strong breastplate crafted from the carapace of a Cave Spider Matriarch. This armor has been enchanted with a weak Monster Core (Earth) to harden it.

The extra weight wasn't great, but James would trade some mobility for a huge boost to his survivability.

In addition to the breastplate, Arik had also managed to craft bracers and greaves.

> Spider Carapace Greaves:
>
> Rank: Common
>
> Greaves crafted from the carapace of a Cave Spider Matriarch.

> Spider Carapace Bracers:
>
> Rank: Common
>
> Bracers crafted from the carapace of a Cave Spider Matriarch.

None of the items by themselves were amazing, but when James equipped all three, he got a new notification.

> YOU HAVE EQUIPPED (3/5) PIECES OF THE SPIDER CARAPACE ARMOR SET
>
> Spider Carapace Set (1/5):
>
> + 10% defense against Beasts.

> Spider Carapace Set (3/5):
>
> + 15% chance to detect traps.
>
> Spider Carapace Set (5/5):
>
> + 20% damage against Beasts.

The bonus was a worthwhile upgrade. He was happy to get rid of the ratty leather bracers and pants. Looking at himself in the mirror, he couldn't help but feel powerful and ready to take on the arena.

That was when the shouting started.

Dwarven voices echoed outside the inn, shouting, "The King is a coward! A Human-loving coward!"

James snuck into Nidra's room, where everyone else had already gathered.

"What's going on?" he whispered.

"It's a revolt," Danforth said shakily. "This was the worst time to let you go free."

"What do you mean?" James asked.

"The King's wife is pregnant," Danforth said, as if that explained everything.

"So what?"

"I told you, the King's decision to bring you in was unpopular. His youngest seized the opportunity to voice his dissent. It seems people are starting to listen."

"So, what do we do?" James asked.

"Well, if the heir is successful, then you're going to get thrown back into the prison."

"Then we need to get out of here," James said, his voice tinged with worry.

"That would be smart." A heavy banging punctuated Danforth's point as the angry mob outside attempted to get into the inn.

"We know you're in there!" a voice called out from the street.

James looked around, frantically searching for an exit. "Where should we go?"

"I don't know, but we need to go now," Nidra said.

Another loud knock on their door startled them, but when James peeked out, he saw only the innkeeper. He gestured for the group to follow him and brought them to the kitchen. "Quickly," he said, lifting a section of the wooden floor to reveal a hidden passageway. James hesitated, but climbed in, his companions not far behind.

They crept under the floorboards, bits and pieces of the innkeeper's conversation floating down to them. He was arguing with several people, explaining that he had no idea where the Humans had gone. There was a heavy thud, and a cheer went up from the mob. James stopped and looked back. "We need to go help him."

Nidra shook her head. "They'll kill us."

"He saved us." James argued quietly. "We owe this to him."

"We don't have time to argue," Danforth said. "James and I will attempt to rescue the innkeeper and we meet up with you three later." He tossed Nidra a smooth silver marble and handed James its twin. James rolled the marble around in his hands, examining it. It was a solid ball of silver with no blemishes or obvious marks. "This is a Seekstone"

> Seekstone:
>
> Rank: Rare
>
> This stone will always point the way to its partner.

"So how does it work?" James asked.

Danforth plucked the stone from James' hand and closed his eyes, concentrating. Nothing happened for a second, but then the stone started glowing on the side, pointing to Nidra. Danforth moved the stone around, but the light stayed pointed to Nidra. "Just concentrate and push your Mana through the stone. It'll light up and point the way to your companions."

"That's great, but I can't use my mana." James said.

"Don't worry, I can." Danforth grinned. I'll use it when we need it. He pocketed the stone and gave James a wink.

And so, against all common sense, the group split into two. Arik lead Nidra and Lucien through the escape route, while James and Danforth turned back to help the innkeeper.

Back at the entrance to the tunnel, James could hear talking above them. "What's the plan?" he asked Danforth.

"You stay down here, and I'll sneak up there. Cover me as I retreat." Danforth said. "Will that work?"

James nodded and watched as Danforth ascended the ladder and paused, listening to make sure there was nobody above. He gave James a thumbs up, pushed open the trapdoor, and clambered out of sight. There was a murmur of voices, and then a figure dressed in black-hooded robes jumped down and faced James.

NAME: KIRI ALLINE

RACE: DWARF

LEVEL: 61

CLASS: PRIEST OF SYTAR

The Dwarf, Kiri, was already chanting as she fell, violet light writhing around her fingers. By the time she hit the ground, she'd finished casting and a bubble of violet light shot towards James' chest. He tried to dodge, but wasn't able to get out of the way in time. The spell impacted his arm, and a notification quickly flashed by.

> *YOU ARE [SILENCED].*
>
> Silenced:
>
> For the duration of the effect, you will be unable to make any noise.

James tried to call out to his party, but nothing came out. He slammed his sword against the wall but, again, no sound came out.

James charged at the Priest and slashed at her with his new sword. She smiled and released the spell she'd been holding, and James was blasted backwards, silently slamming into the wall of the cavern.

Stunned, he slid down to the ground. He tried to get up, but three more Dwarves hopped down, led by Danforth. One of the Dwarves dropped a sack into his hand and patted him on the back. "I appreciate your work. I'll let you know if I need you for anything else down the line."

Danforth bowed to the Dwarf, who appeared to be the leader.

> *NAME: DEMI HEARTEN*
>
> *RACE: DWARF*
>
> *LEVEL: ???*
>
> *CLASS: PRIEST OF SYTAR*

"Any opportunity to serve." He turned to James, flashing a cruel grin. "Goodbye, Human. I'll be looking for your friends next." As he spoke, the words above his head changed.

NAME: DANFORTH SAND

RACE: DWARF

LEVEL: 49

CLASS: ASSASSIN

"Why?" James groaned; his voice barely audible as the effects of the debuff wore off.

"Money, mostly. But honestly, getting rid of Human *trash* is enough for me." Danforth punctuated his words with a gob of spit to the ground next to him.

"Bastard," James whispered, trying to push himself to his feet.

"None of that now." The leader, Kaster, waved his hands, and James collapsed into unconsciousness.

Chapter 38

James woke up, groaning when he tried to move. Everything hurt. He was alone in a well-lit room with walls made from reddish-brown stone blocks, each about the height of a Dwarf. Torches lined the walls, tipped with glowing crystals that emitted bright white light. Marble sarcophagi lined the walls, and a sinister stone basin sat in the center of the room, slowly bubbling with a deep amber liquid. Other than the low bubbling sound, it was eerily quiet. There was no sign of the priests who had knocked him out. Frantically, he patted at his belt, making sure that his pouch was still there. He breathed a sigh of relief at the familiar feeling when his hand touched it.

But then, where am I?

Maybe reviewing his notifications would help give him a clue as to what happened?

> ENTERING THE DUNGEON: PRISON OF THE FIRST
>
> RECOMMENDED LEVEL: 100-250

James' eyes widened when he saw the level requirement for the dungeon. There was no way he would survive it. Maybe there was something in here that could help him. Perhaps a hidden exit. At least the fact that he was dumped alone in a dungeon meant that the priests probably weren't watching him.

James brushed himself off and got up. He needed to explore this room before he could decide on anything.

He approached a sarcophagus and examined it. It was a rectangular block of dark marble with a lighter marble lid. James traced his fingers along a few scratches in the lid which created a long streak along the dust-covered marble. One of his fingers caught in a slight cleft in the stone and he followed it, stirring up ancient dust.

He blew away a cloud of dust from the surface. When it cleared, he was disappointed that the lettering on the lid had faded well past the point that he could make out individual letters. He thought about opening the sarcophagus to see what was inside, but this was a level 100+ dungeon. He wasn't *that* dumb. Based on how things had been going for him lately, a skeleton would jump out and slaughter him or he'd unleash an undead plague.

Instead, he moved on to examine the basin, bubbling peacefully in the center of the room. There was nothing unusual about it, except for a silver cup bobbing around in the liquid, tempting him. He thought about ignoring it, but couldn't. It was like leaving a big red button with "Don't Push" written on it right in front of him. Of course he was going to push it. Besides, it wasn't like his chances of survival were high at the moment. He'd die in this dungeon the second he encountered an enemy.

James knew what he was about to do was stupid, perhaps one of the stupidest things he'd ever done. But still, he dragged the cup through the liquid and brought it to his lips. Before drinking, he took a deep sniff of the liquid. A sweet earthy scent suffused his nostrils, rushing straight to his head, and setting it spinning.

James smiled and took a long drink of the liquid. It was sweet, but burned as it went down. A rumbling filled the chamber, clouds of dust coming out of the walls. The basin sunk down into the earth until it vanished, leaving a bare floor. The rumbling stopped.

Achievement Unlocked: Why not?

Why Not?:

+ 1 Luck

- 5 Intelligence

You thought it was a bad idea, but did it anyway. Why not?
This seems to be a pattern with you.

James ground his teeth in annoyance. His Intelligence was really taking a beating from all of these stupid decisions he kept making.

His annoyance lasted until he got the next prompt.

YOU HAVE GAINED THE ABILITY: BLOOD OF THE MOUNTAIN

Blood of the Mountain (1/1):

+ 100% base defense

+ 25% mental defense

The blood of the mountain flows through your veins, reinforcing your body and mind.

James could feel the liquid burning as it raged through his body. A red flashing in the corner of his vision indicated that his health was dropping precipitously. James realized that he was going to die if he didn't heal immediately, so he dropped to the ground and started meditating. His accelerated healing competed with the liquid in a desperate tug-of-war for his life.

Time stopped as James focused on his breathing, ignoring the pain as the strange beverage ravaged his system, occasionally flaring up and sending him into fits of pain so severe that he almost lost control of his mediation. But by controlling his breathing, James was able to keep his meditative state active and his health up.

The damage finally stopped, and James collapsed to the ground, breathing heavily. He lay there panting for a while, unable to move as he tried to ease away the tension in his spasmed muscles. His stomach growled, and, agonizingly slowly, he forced his muscles to move. His hand crept towards his pouch, reaching for food, but just when he was getting close, the world faded to blackness and he sunk into unconsciousness.

James woke up with a start, swinging his head around wildly.

Where am I? Are there enemies around?

Then he remembered. He'd been captured and tossed into a dungeon. He really needed to stop falling asleep while defenseless inside dungeons. Almost as if to punctuate that point, he got a new notification.

ACHIEVEMENT UNLOCKED: DUMB LUCK II.

Dumb Luck II:

  + 2 Luck

You really never learn, do you?

Well, at least it didn't take away from his intelligence this time.

James sat up; his motion accompanied by a popping sound as his body adjusted itself. He had to stop sleeping on the ground like this. He always felt awful the next morning. Mentally chastising himself for dropping his guard in a dungeon yet again, he started to stand up, but before he could, a rumbling from his stomach reminded him just how hungry he was. He searched through his pack and wolfed down some rations.

The room had two doors, one made of stone and the other of black marble with ornate golden patterns. The pretty one probably led deeper into the dungeon, so James decided to try the stone door first. It might lead to an exit. But there was no obvious handle, and when he tried to push the door open, it didn't budge.

James sighed, resigned. It looked like he'd have to delve deeper into the dungeon in search of an alternate exit. He was going to kill that Dwarf. Well, probably not. There was a huge level difference. But he would be very angry.

James examined the ornate door. It was divided into three parts that depicted a mythological scene. The top square showed an army of winged figures surrounded by light, fighting against a force of dark, twisted creatures. The middle square had one of the light figures turning on its comrades and attacking, devastating their ranks. The final square had a circle of the light creatures surrounding a dark creature, weaving a net of gold around it.

It was stunningly crafted, but James didn't have a clue what it was referring to.

James dropped into stealth and opened it a crack, peering down a completely empty corridor. The door opened quietly, and with the fountain gone, there was no sound whatsoever in the dungeon. It was eerie. As quietly as he could, James slipped through the door and snuck along the corridor. He was very careful where he put his feet. He scanned the ground for anything that looked suspicious, which is why he spotted a slightly elevated floor tile seconds before his foot hit it.

James crouched down to examine the tile. At first, he had no idea how to disarm it. He searched for a button or hole that would allow him to interact with its internal workings. Eventually, he spotted a thin gap underneath the tile, so he slid his Orichalcum Dagger of Weight underneath. At a snail's pace, he lifted the trigger tile and set it to the side, revealing a spring mechanism. A quick flick of his dagger severed the springs, and he received a notification.

> YOU HAVE DISARMED A FLASHFIRE TRAP.

James wiped the sweat off his brow and reached into the hole, pulling out a small vial of orange fluid that glowed with a soft light.

> Flashfire Vial:
>
> Rank: Epic
>
> - 200 Damage per second while ablaze
>
> Smash this bottle to release the fluid trapped inside. The Flashfire will stick to an opponent's skin and burn far longer than any normal fire should.

Very carefully, James slipped the Flashfire into his pouch. The insanely powerful magical napalm would have killed him in two seconds. Hopefully, he wouldn't have to use it, but if he absolutely had to encounter an enemy, then it might come in handy.

James continued down the corridor, moving with a glacial slowness. He didn't see any more traps, but that didn't mean there weren't any. He made it to the next room without incident.

It was empty, too.

What kind of dungeon is this? I should be encountering enemies left and right.

He was about to take a step into the room, when an overwhelming instinct strongly suggested he didn't. James took a closer look at the room. Everything seemed fine until he examined the doorway. A small gap between the stone blocks housed bits of iron that, when he noticed it, took on a distinctive red hue. James wasn't sure what would happen if he stepped over the threshold, but he knew it would be bad.

He needed to figure out a way to trigger the trap from a safe distance. With that in mind, he pried one of the torches off the wall and broke the glowing crystal off the end. He walked all the way to the other end of the corridor and threw the marble as hard as he could, so that it passed over the trapped door and into the next room. It flew through the doorway and hit the floor with a sharp crack, but nothing triggered.

James wondered how else he could trigger the trap, but realized that he was asking the wrong question. It wasn't how the trap was triggered that he really needed to know, but how it detected a person passing through. He retrieved a second crystal. On a hunch, he pricked his finger and dribbled some blood on it.

He hurled the bloody crystal, holding his breath in anticipation as it crossed the threshold, but again, nothing happened.

He was becoming annoyed. Maybe it was a mechanical trap and would go off if he hit a tripwire. He examined the bottom of the doorway and found a razor-thin strand of reddish wire that blended perfectly with the background.

Grinning at his genius, James jumped over the tripwire and into the room, but his elation lasted approximately a half second. Metal grates slammed shut on both exits with echoing *thunks*.

Then, silence.

He was trapped.

Chapter 39

James swore under his breath.

Of course I end up trapped in a dungeon! God forbid something good happened to me. Wasn't my luck supposed to be high?

At least there weren't any enemies around, but now he had to figure out how to get out of here. The room was small, probably ten feet square, and had two doorways, both obstructed by metal grates with wide-set bars.

James pressed himself against the bars and sucked in his stomach, trying to slip through them, but they were slightly too narrow for him to fit. He looked around for other ways out but couldn't find anything. There wasn't anything else in the room with him. But something about the wide bars gave him pause.

He spent a while thinking about the bars, but still didn't have any ideas. He reached for his pouch, and his hands brushed against his belt.

The Slick Goblin Skin Belt!

He'd received a spell from it that let him coat himself in a slippery substance. It was a bit of a gamble because of the injuries to his Mana channels, but maybe since it was an item-based spell it wouldn't be affected.

Concentrating, James felt the Mana move through his body and he focused on the Slick Skin spell. He could feel the Mana surge through his body, picking up speed, but the second the spell attempted to activate, everything went wrong. Pain racked his body, and he fell to the ground, unable to move. It felt as though liquid nitrogen was traveling through his Mana channels, burning him with icy fire.

The next thing James remembered was waking up with his face pressed on the cold stone of the dungeon floor with a splitting headache, with no idea of how long he'd been out for.

James groaned as he sat up, head in hands, and rubbed at his temples. "Not doing that again," he muttered to himself, trying to relieve the pain in his head. Then he noticed the thick oily substance coating his whole body. The spell had worked!

James tried to push himself to his feet, but no matter how hard he tried, he couldn't keep his balance with the slick substance under him, so instead he grabbed the bars and used them to pull himself along the floor and, with a bit of effort, through the gate.

Once he was outside of the trap room, James realized he wasn't sure how to get rid of the goo covering his skin. That would be a problem, because he straight up couldn't stand with it covering him. It felt like he'd just taken a bath in a tub of Astroglide.

With no other options, he pulled the bedding out of his bag and wiped himself off with a blanket. He tossed the dirty bedding back into the pouch—he'd wash it the first chance he got.

James continued down the passageway, still wary at the lack of enemies. He shrugged and continued. Maybe luck really was on his side this time.

Up ahead, the tunnel branched into two passages. There was no noticeable difference between them, but James stuck by his left turn role for mazes. After all, it had worked so well back in the spider cave.

James continued on until, for the first time in the dungeon, he heard a noise. It was a faint rattling sound that sent shivers down his spine. He knew he should probably retreat, but he wanted to see what type of monster inhabited the dungeon. Just a quick peek, then he would try the other passageway.

Making sure his stealth was still active, he crept towards the rattling. As he sneaked, he tried to stay close to the walls of the dungeon instead of going down the middle of the passageway. He wasn't sure why, but he felt like there would be more traps in the middle.

YOU HAVE GAINED 1 SKILL RANK IN STEALTH.

YOU ARE NOW SKILL RANK 15.

When he reached the doorway to the next room, James peered around it. A hulking skeleton patrolled the area, marching around the room, which was empty except for an ornate chest in the back.

DEFILED SKELETON (LEVEL ???)

The Defiled Skeleton was a terrifying sight to behold. It was composed of a variety of bones, clearly taken from many different races, haphazardly arranged in a bipedal shape. Every step the creature took made another rattle as bone met stone.

James was about to retreat when the Defiled Skeleton's patrol took it right up near the corner he was hiding by. Trying not to breathe, James pressed himself into the wall and prayed for the skeleton to move on, but it stopped and raised its head as if it were sniffing the air. His muscles tensed, and James prepared to bolt, but after a few seconds the Defiled Skeleton kept moving as the rattling of its bones faded away into the distance.

Almost as if to punctuate how close his call had been, James got another couple of ranks in Stealth almost immediately.

> *You have gained 2 skill ranks in Stealth.*
>
> *You are now skill rank 17.*

Heart beating rapidly in his chest, James peered around the corner again. The room was empty. The Defiled Skeleton must have moved on to another part of the dungeon for its patrol.

James wanted to leave, he really did, but the thought of treasure in a level 300 dungeon hidden underneath a Dwarven city made him pause. He needed to know. Besides, he'd hear the rattling noise if the Defiled Skeleton returned. With a greedy glint in his eyes, James crept across the room to the chest.

It was built from the same stone that the dungeon was built from, and was unremarkable except for a polished golden keyhole. James looked closer at the keyhole and saw tiny holes lining it, each glowing a dim red.

> *You have gained 1 skill rank in Traps.*
>
> *You are now skill rank 3.*

If he tried to pick the lock, he'd probably get stabbed with a poisoned needle or attacked with poisonous gas. It was so obvious that the keyhole might not even open the chest. James focused on the chest itself, feeling around its edges for anything abnormal.

He discovered a triangular indent on the side of the chest, about a quarter inch deep. He tried sliding his dagger into it, but nothing happened.

On the other side of the chest he found a piece of stone that stuck out slightly and wiggled when he touched it. He pulled it out, revealing a triangular cut of stone, perfectly shaped to fit the indent on the other side.

James lined up the two parts and pressed the triangular bit in until he heard a click. The stone key spun in place and with a barely discernible whirring, the chest opened, revealing a black swath of fabric, but nothing else. James picked it up to reveal a cloak that was so black it seemed to absorb the light.

Eses' Cloak:

Rank: Legendary

This cloak belonged to Eses, god of the night. If you are in stealth while wearing the cloak, you will become invisible. It also has many pockets, as all good cloaks should.

This was probably the coolest item James had ever seen. He might survive this dungeon after all. He took off his Cloak of the Forest and donned the new treasure, fastening the star and moon clasp at his neck. He watched as his body immediately faded away, leaving only a faint outline around the edges of his body. When he waved his hand in front of his face, he saw only a blur in the air. The invisibility wasn't total, but it was amazing.

The rattling of the Defiled Skeleton approached again, and James realized that he didn't have enough time to make it back to the hallway. He immediately shrunk into the shadow of the chest, as he didn't have enough time to make it out of the room. He hoped that the cloak would be enough to hide him from the Defiled Skeleton. It didn't have eyes, so he was worried that it would detect him with magic.

As the Defiled Skeleton paced around the room, seemingly unaware of him, James noticed a second triangular indent in the wall by the edge of the chest. If he hadn't been staring hard at the wall, he wouldn't have noticed it.

He knew it was risky, but once the Defiled Skeleton finished its patrol, he pulled the key out of the chest. It emitted a loud shriek, and he heard the Defiled Skeleton rush back to the room.

James realized that he had nowhere to retreat and, in an attempt to silence the shrieking, he jammed the key back into the small hole.

Blessed Silence.

Unfortunately, the Defiled Skeleton was almost to him, and he still didn't have anywhere to go. Hopefully, the cloak would prevent it from noticing him if he stayed still and quiet.

With a click and a soft grinding, the entire chest popped off of the ground and swung to the side, revealing a ladder leading into a hidden tunnel.

With the Defiled Skeleton almost on him, James grabbed the first rung and descended without hesitation. Above, the chest swung back into place, cutting off the light.

His feet hit the floor, and James stayed quiet, listening, but nothing stirred in the darkness.

Where was he? Was this still part of the dungeon?

James wasn't sure, but he needed to be careful. He placed his hand against the wall of the tunnel and slowly crept forward in stealth, listening for the slightest bit of noise. His thoughts drifted to his party. He'd worry about finding them if he survived. Hopefully, they'd managed to get away from Danforth.

After a half hour, James realized that the tunnel was sloping sharply downward, which worried him because down usually didn't mean exit. He'd avoided thinking about it, but there was a real possibility that he was just in a more dangerous part of the dungeon, and not in a path leading to the exit.

After what felt like hours of walking, James reached the end of the tunnel. A thick metal door blocked his way, engraved with a winding series of spidery letters that covered every inch of available space. As James watched, the letters seemed to flow across the door, undulating like a living thing. He slowly reached out a hand and brushed it softly against the door, causing a ripple of rainbow light to pulse out from underneath his fingertips. It was beautiful.

Before he knew what he was doing, James retrieved a piece of parchment and a quill from his pack and sat in front of the door, copying the lettering down. He felt the Mana in his body stir and pick up speed, but not enough speed to hurt him. It was hard to describe, but when he cast a spell, it felt like a raging torrent of energy going through him. This felt more like meditating, a calm river flowing through his body and energizing him. But instead of continuously swirling around inside, the river flowed through the pen and onto the paper.

When his last stroke ran across the paper, it burst into flames. His quill exploded, sending bits of feather everywhere. James dropped the burnt remains and cursed, wafting his hands through the air as he tried to cool his burnt fingertips.

What the hell just happened?

YOU HAVE GAINED THE SKILL: RUNIC

Runic (Skill Rank 1):

Some say the pen is mightier than the sword, and for you it's true. By writing in the language of the Elder Races, you can imbue permanent magical effects with your writing. But beware, mortal. Runic magic can be dangerous.

ACHIEVEMENT UNLOCKED: ANCIENT MYSTERIES

Ancient Mysteries:

+ 10 *Intelligence*

+ 10 *Wisdom*

You have taken your first step on the journey to unlocking
the power of Runic Magic. Usually this takes years of study
and hard work, but you seem to have a way of avoiding
that.

YOUR PARCHMENT DOESN'T HAVE THE MANA CAPACITY TO
SUPPORT RUNIC MAGIC.

YOUR QUILL DOESN'T HAVE THE MANA CAPACITY TO
SUPPORT RUNIC MAGIC.

A burning word appeared in the air before James, the one he'd been
copying down on the paper before it exploded. It hung in the air for a second
before fading away, but he knew he'd never forget it.

YOU HAVE LEARNED THE RUNE: XYDYL - BINDING.

YOU HAVE BEEN GIVEN AN OPEN QUEST: LANGUAGE OF
THE GODS

Language of the Gods: Learn the Runic Alphabet (1/5739)

Suggested level: N/A

Reward: Knowledge is its own reward. But there's also a
reward.

Penalty for failure or refusal: none

James took in a sharp breath. "What the hell just happened?" he said, this time out loud.

He remembered Arik telling him about Runic magic one night when he was explaining how enchanted weapons work. It was one of the four ascended branches of magic the Elder Races used. Enchanting used to be done through Runic magic back when the Elder Races still existed, but after they disappeared, Runic slowly started to fade away. The Dwarves tried to find it but couldn't, and eventually created their own method of enchanting weapons, using monster cores. But it was just a cheap facsimile of Runic enchanting.

Eager to learn more Runes, James pulled some more paper out of his bag and was about to copy the rest of the Runes on the door, when he realized that he didn't have anything to write with because his quill had exploded. But this could be his only chance to ever learn Runic.

Carefully James went through his inventory and searched for anything that he could use, but he couldn't find anything. When he was about to give up, James realized that he did have one more option, but it would be dangerous. He shrugged. Everything he did was dangerous, and this would be way more beneficial than the last few times he'd done something stupid.

He studied the script, wanting to make sure he understood how Runic worked. At first glance, it looked like hundreds of different Runes crawling across the door, but after carefully studying the language, he realized that it was the same five runes repeated over and over with slight variations. He wasn't sure what the variations meant, but he was able to figure out the base runes for each one.

James pricked his finger with his dagger and, using his blood as ink, sketched out other four runes. Each sketch was accompanied by a flash as the paper burned, but there was no issue with him using his blood to write.

> *YOU HAVE LEARNED THE RUNE: VYDIR - STRENGTHEN.*

> *YOU HAVE LEARNED THE RUNE: HEIYE - REPEL.*

> *YOU HAVE LEARNED THE RUNE ARTYN: - DRAIN.*

> *YOU HAVE LEARNED THE RUNE: KYROS - HARDEN.*

> *YOU HAVE GAINED 1 SKILL RANK IN RUNIC.*
>
> *YOU ARE NOW SKILL RANK 2.*

Each time he learned a rune, James felt the power burn into his brain, strengthening him. He wondered why those specific runes were on the door. His best guess was that they were there to keep people away, or to make the door stronger. Either way, it was time to see what lay beyond.

James placed his hand on the door and pushed, expecting to meet resistance.

It opened smoothly and silently.

Fragment of Divinity

Chapter 40

James stared into the room in shock. He didn't know what he'd been expecting, but it wasn't this.

YOU HAVE ENTERED THE HIDDEN AREA: THE LIBRARY

RECOMMENDED LEVEL: 500+

He gulped. He was standing at the entrance to a brightly lit library, but that wasn't what worried him. Whatever was in this area was much more dangerous than anything above, but he couldn't back out now. There wasn't anywhere to go. He hung on to the hope that this hidden area would have an exit he could take. Besides, how bad could a library really be. Books were awesome.

The room was filled with books, floor to ceiling. Books that weren't on shelves were stacked haphazardly in piles that looked ready to topple. The only area free of books was the ceiling, crafted from the same dark metal as the door and covered with the same scrawling script. Mouth agape, James picked up a book and examined it.

> Necrophilia: Is It Okay if It's Your Summon?
>
> Rank: Unique
>
> Durability: 100/100
>
> The only known copy of a peer-reviewed book documenting the ethics behind carnal relations with summoned undead. By R. Ichter

James dropped the book.

Why was it sticky? Never mind, I don't want to know. Before it could hit the ground, the book floated into the air and inserted itself into one of the many stacks around him.

A stern voice chastised him. "Careful with that. It's priceless."

James jumped, looking around wildly for the speaker. He stopped when he realized that nobody was there. "Hello?" he called into the seemingly empty library.

"I'm in the back. And hurry, I don't have all day."

Curious, James headed towards the voice. It didn't sound hostile, which was good. Better than the skeletons at least. Navigating through the maze of books was a difficult task, because sometimes paths would simply end and he'd have to backtrack to find a new opening, usually a small space between the shelves he'd overlooked, that he could squeeze through. Along the way, he stopped to read the covers of books that seemed especially interesting to him.

The Divine Dungeon. Gnomes and Why They Rule. A System Apocalypse.

Eventually James made it to the back of the room where he found a kindly, bespectacled old man, barely visible behind a desk stacked high with books and papers.

NAME: ???

RACE: ???

LEVEL: ???

CLASS: ???

"You're a person!"

The old man chuckled. "Of course I'm a person."

"You can call me Ozure. Welcome to my library."

"What is this place?" James gestured around the room.

"It is my home," Ozure answered simply. "Now, on to business, what have you brought me?"

"Brought you?" James asked, trying to remember where he'd heard the name Ozure before. It was something to do with the history of the Dwarves, but he couldn't recall what.

"Yes, a bit of original work, something to add to my collection."

"Oh," James said, looking through his bag. He really needed to stay on this guy's good side, because he was pretty sure Ozure could kill him with a glance. Something about the man emanated power. The book *Potion Making for Dummies* probably wouldn't work, it was just a Common item. "What about this?" He pulled out Mary's Cinderstalk Pie recipe.

Ozure smiled and took the parchment, reading over the recipe. "I've never seen this recipe before. Looks delicious. This'll work."

"So, why am I here?" James asked.

Ozure raised an eyebrow. "And what do you mean by that?"

"I mean that somehow, I made it through a chunk of a dungeon hundreds of levels higher than I could handle, and I barely encountered any enemies."

"I guess I felt your mark, and needed to see why Sytar's chosen wanted to enter my humble dungeon."

"I didn't come here on purpose," James said, trying to convey that he was harmless and didn't want to fight. "Honestly, if you'd let me out, I'd be happy to go peacefully."

"Oh, would you?" He laughed. "Don't you want to hear why you're here?"

"I… suppose."

"But first, I must apologize for being such a bad host." Ozure got up from his chair and approached James slowly. The Mana flowing around his body was so powerful that James could hear it crackle. "You brought me such a nice gift, and I haven't done anything for you."

James backed away, slowly at first, but then faster. This stranger locked away in the bottom of a dungeon wasn't his friend. Because that's what he was. It had taken James a while to figure out what the issue with the stranger was, but he'd just realized it.

Ozure kept referring to this as his library. His home. James had thought the runes around the door were to keep people from getting into the room, but perhaps they were to keep Ozure from escaping.

He recalled the dungeon name. Prison of the First. He didn't know what the first was, but he knew what a prison was.

Quickly, James turned and bolted for the door, only to find Ozure standing in front of it waiting for him. The old man raised an eyebrow and gave him a smirk. "Going somewhere?"

"Just… heading out. It was lovely to meet you, but I have to meet up with some friends."

"Oh, I'm sure they can wait. After all, I have to thank you for your gift." Quick as a snake, Ozure struck. He grabbed James by the head and flooded Mana into his body.

> *YOU HAVE BEEN [PARALYZED].*
>
> *DURATION: ???*

Questing tendrils of energy flowed into James, interacting cautiously with his broken Mana channels. "You really did a number on yourself, didn't you?" Ozure shook his head. "I think I can help, but you're going to have to let me."

What did he mean, let him? James was paralyzed. Ozure could do whatever he wanted.

Ozure must have seen the question in James' eyes, because he sighed in annoyance and waved his hands. With a rush, James felt the paralysis slip away, and he got up, backing away from Ozure. "Let me go," he said, trembling.

Ozure chuckled but didn't move. "Are you sure you want that?" He asked. "I could let you leave, but you'd be stuck back where you were; dead in a dungeon. You need me."

"You need me just as much as I need you," James said. "And if you want my help, you're going to have to answer some questions." It was a bold play, but James was running out of options.

Ozure sighed. "Fine. What do you want to know?"

"What were you going to do to me?"

"I was about to fix your Mana channels."

"Then why did you chase me down and paralyze me?"

"You started running. I didn't want you to leave before I could help."

James thought about that for a second. Ozure had just given up something that he probably hadn't meant to say. He'd inadvertently revealed that he couldn't leave this room. James filed that information away for later, but it wouldn't help him right now, because Ozure was clearly much faster than him.

"So, you were going to fix my Mana channels. Why?"

Ozure nodded.

"For no reason. Just out of the goodness of your heart." James wasn't buying it, and he hated dancing around an issue. "Just tell me what you want," he said, annoyed. "I thought you ancient beings were supposed to be wise and to the point."

"I'll fix your channels as a gesture of goodwill." Ozure gave him a smile that didn't reassure him at all. "After that, we can bargain."

"How do I know I can trust you?"

"You don't really have any other options," Ozure pointed out. "Feel free to try to make it out of the dungeon without my help. You won't."

James thought. As much as he hated to admit it, Ozure was right. James did need him. Even if he could make it out of this room, he'd still be stuck in a dungeon hundreds of levels too high. "Fine," he grumbled. "What did you need?"

Ozure grinned. "Delightful. I just need your permission to access your core. From there, I can work to repair your Mana channels. You'll be good as new."

James really didn't want to do this. Everything about this interaction was setting off alarm bells, but he didn't have much of a choice. "Damned if I do, damned if I don't," he muttered.

"Fine. Do it."

> WOULD YOU LIKE TO GRANT OZURE ACCESS TO YOUR
> MANA CORE?
>
> Warning: This can leave you vulnerable. Be sure you trust
> whoever you are granting access to.

James gulped, but he didn't have a choice. He agreed.

Ozure placed his hand back on James' head and reconnected his Mana tendrils. This time, the connection was much stronger, and James felt the wispy touch of a vast, alien mind swirling with thoughts. Powers he couldn't comprehend.

"You...you're not Human," he whispered as the world faded into darkness. The last thing he remembered was a dark glint in Ozure's eyes.

***

Once James was unconscious, Ozure smiled. Everything was going according to plan. It had taken thousands of years, but soon he'd be out of this prison, and he'd have his revenge. But he wasn't out yet. First, he had to fix this Human's Mana channels, a trivial task for him.

Tendrils of multicolored energy extended into James' core, the center of his being. The energy wrapped around it and ate away at the scar tissue that had built up inside. Slowly, it crept through James' body, following his Mana channels. Whenever the energy encountered scarring it cleared the damage away and widened the channels.

It was time for the real work to begin. James hadn't only caused scarring. He'd permanently damaged the core itself, making it impossible for the Mana to flow quickly. Fixing the Mana scars had made it so James wouldn't be in pain when he cast spells, but the Human would be weak as a kitten, unable to cast anything but the most basic spells.

Unfortunately, Ozure couldn't do anything to improve Mana flow through the core, even with James' permission. What he could do was work around it, but it would be dangerous. Even after all his years, Ozure had never tried to do this before. But he'd spent years meticulously planning it, and the Human had brought something in that could help make the procedure safer.

Ozure raised his hands and started chanting. His Mana control was perfect. He'd evolved past the need for spells long ago when he'd gained the Mana Manipulation skill, widely considered the start of any real mage's journey.

Tendrils of Mana wrapped around James' wrist and explored the Bracelet of Last Breath. The item was unique, a powerful artifact created through Runic magic, and it had taken quite a bit of energy for Ozure to tip the scales of fate to cause it to fall into James' hands. He'd spent weeks unable to see out of his cursed prison after the artifact fell into the damned slaver's hands. But it was all worth it.

His Mana thrummed as he sent a command into it, crushing the bracelet. For the briefest instant, the spell contained inside was freed, but before it could dissipate into the atmosphere, his Mana wrapped around it, trapping it. Using the trapped spell, Ozure wove a powerful stasis enchantment around James' body.

YOU HAVE CREATED A SPELL: STASIS

Stasis (Level 1):

For 24 hours, the target of this spell cannot move, breathe, speak, feel, or die.

Range: Touch

Cast time: Instant

Cooldown: None

Cost: 975 mana

His Mana level dropped almost a thousand points, but the bar in the corner of his vision barely twitched.

Once he knew that he would be able to perform the surgery without killing James, Ozure concentrated and condensed his mana, forming a razor thin scalpel. Carefully he cut into James' chest, the knife easily slicing through muscle, sinew, and bone. Eerily, because of the Stasis effect, no blood flowed from the wound. It stayed motionless inside of him as if he were a frozen corpse.

Ozure summoned more mana, flowing it into the wound in James' chest and pulling, cracking the chest open and leaving a gaping hole that revealed a heart frozen mid-beat.

Next, Ozure moved down to James' leg. With a few precise slashes, he exposed a long, thick vein.

Much slower now, he cut out two sections of the vein, taking care to include the tightly wound Mana channels that followed the vascular system around the body. Mana channels worked in a similar way to veins and arteries, transporting Mana around the body. The systems were tightly linked, but normally they never intersected. Ozure's theory was that if he connected the two systems, that the force of the blood moving through the body would be able to push the Mana along with it.

Setting aside the newly separated sections of vein, Ozure stretched the cut leg vein down and used Mana to repair the damage he'd caused and reseal the vein and Mana channels.

Once he'd healed the wound in James' leg, Ozure returned his focus to James' chest—it was time for the difficult part. He was going to have to connect the heart to the Mana channels. For it to work he would need to remove the Mana core completely and use the heart as the sole Mana pump.

He disconnected the input area of the core and, using the segment of vein he had harvested from the leg, connected the input Mana channel to the aorta, so that blood and Mana would be pushed through the heart and into the Mana system. Then he disconnected the output area of the core and connected it to the superior vena cava, so that the blood and Mana would drain back into the heart. He then carefully cut out James' Mana core and removed it, setting it aside.

Mana Core (James):

Rank: Unique

A Mana core belonging to the Human James. This core is unique to him and can be used in a variety of ways.

Finally, Ozure closed all the damaged areas and sealed James' chest, leaving him looking normal except for a thin scar on his chest and a much smaller scar on his leg.

Chapter 41

James groaned, grabbing his head. "Where am I?"

"Careful," a voice from behind him said as a hand on his back helped guide him to a seated position. "I repaired your Mana channels, but you need time to recover. Here, drink this." James felt a glass of water touch his lips and he drank greedily, barely noticing when the water sloshed out and over his chest and legs.

As he drank, the events of the previous day slowly filtered back to James. He was in a in a dungeon. He'd found a weird library prison where a strange man had offered to give him surgery, and he'd accepted. "What happened?" He asked shakily. "What did you do to me?"

Ozure came into view as James' eyesight returned. He was smiling pleasantly—maybe James had imagined the dark look in his eyes before. "The surgery was successful."

"I can cast spells again?" James was excited to finally be able to use magic again, he'd felt weak without it. He tried to stand up, but when he moved, he was hit with a wave of vertigo that left him nauseated.

"Be careful. I had to connect your Mana system to your circulatory system to fix everything, which means that for now, you'll have to fill up twice as much space with the same amount of blood. You'll be dizzy for a few days as your body produces more blood to compensate for the new space. Drink plenty of fluids."

James nodded. He didn't really understand what Ozure had done, but he understood the concept.

"How about you rest and check your prompts and let me know what changes there were." There was a hungry look in Ozure's eyes when he asked James to look over his prompts that James didn't like. He'd tried to be casual about it, but his tone was almost too casual. For the first time since arriving, James had a slight upper hand, and he wasn't sure what to do with it. He didn't know enough to make any decisions yet, so he nodded in agreement, which was a mistake. Another wave of nausea overwhelmed him.

James lay back and closed his eyes, pulling up his notifications.

> *YOUR MIND HAS ENCOUNTERED THE MIND OF A BEING OF POWER. IT WAS ONLY FOR AN INSTANT, BUT IT WAS ENOUGH.*
>
> *YOUR MANA TYPE HAS EVOLVED FROM SHADOW (TIER II) TO ARCANE (TRANSCENDENT).*
>
> *SPELLS AND SKILLS WILL CHANGE OVER TIME.*

James remembered the brief instant of contact he had with Ozure's mind. It had been alien and malevolent. The fact that a mere instant of contact with Ozure's mind had upgraded his magic to a new type spoke volumes about how powerful he... it was. James had never heard of transcendent magic and wasn't sure where it fell on the tier chart Nana had shown him.

> *YOUR BRACELET OF LAST BREATH HAS BEEN DESTROYED.*

That was a scary thought. He'd been counting on the bracelet as a trump card that would let him survive certain death. Even though he hadn't used it, with the bracelet gone he felt more naked and vulnerable. James shrugged mentally. It didn't matter. He was alive, and could theoretically use his Mana again. That was what mattered.

> YOUR MANA CORE HAS BEEN REMOVED. YOUR BODY CAN NO LONGER CIRCULATE MANA. SOME SKILLS HAVE BEEN MODIFIED TO REFLECT THIS.

> YOUR MAGIC AND CIRCULATORY SYSTEMS HAVE BEEN COMBINED. THIS HAS CREATED A NEW STAT: ESSENCE, A COMBINATION OF MANA AND HEALTH.

> YOUR ABILITY: BLOOD OF THE MOUNTAIN HAS GIVEN YOUR BLOOD A STRONG AFFINITY OF MANA.
>
> NORMALLY, BLOOD AND MANA CANNOT MIX, BUT BECAUSE OF YOUR UNIQUE CIRCUMSTANCES, YOUR BLOOD HAS A HIGHER AFFINITY FOR MANA THAN IT DOES FOR OXYGEN.
>
> YOUR BLOOD WILL NOW CARRY MANA THROUGHOUT YOUR BODY, AND MANA WILL FUEL YOUR CELLS.

> YOU ARE NO LONGER HUMAN. YOU HAVE EVOLVED PAST THE NEED FOR THE BASIC FORMS OF ENERGY. NOW YOU

> *SUBSIST ON PURE ENERGY. YOUR RACE HAS CHANGED TO*
> *REFLECT THIS.*

RACE CHANGE: SHAKTI

You have evolved into a being of energy. This is a unique race, and most changes will not reveal themselves immediately. They will evolve and grow with you. For now, here are a few immediate changes.

+ No need to breathe

+ 99% poison resistance

+ No need for food, drink, or sleep

+ Incoming spells do 50% more damage

- Your Stamina stat has been absorbed into the Essence stat

James closed his eyes and tried to feel for any changes to his body, but didn't feel anything. He still felt like a normal Human, albeit a Human who'd just been hit in the head with a hammer.

YOU HAVE GAINED THE ABILITY: SOLAR POWERED

Solar Powered (1/1):

Your body needs energy to survive. Luckily, there's a huge source of it in the sky. While in sunlight your essence will passively recharge at a rate of one per minute.

YOU HAVE GAINED THE ABILITY: ABSORB

Absorb (1/1):

Your body needs energy to survive. Although you don't need food or drink, you can still absorb essence by consuming mana-rich food or drink.

James was too tired to even begin to comprehend what he'd just read. Insufficient blood, combined with the bodily stress of recent surgery had addled his mind so much that when he was done reading through the prompts, his body crashed and he fell into a restless sleep filled with dreams of death and bloodshed.

When James woke up, he felt much better. His head had stopped hurting and he didn't vomit immediately when he tried to stand up. Both good signs. Waking up and not feeling the slightest urge to eat or drink was an off-putting sensation and reminded him of his prompts. To see what had happened to him, James pulled up his character sheet along with his Skills, Spells, and Abilities, paying special attention to what had changed.

JAMES

HUMAN (WARRIOR OF DARKNESS)

LEVEL: 15

ESSENCE: 1500/1500

STATS

STRENGTH: 33   DEXTERITY: 33

CONSTITUTION: 34

INTELLIGENCE: 38   WISDOM: 43

ENDURANCE: 33

CHARISMA: 1   LUCK: 5   RESILIENCE:
4

SPELLS

SHADOW STEP (LEVEL 1)

SYREUS' WRATH (N\A)

SLICK SKIN (N/A)

ABILITIES

DEATH'S STARE (1/7)

DEATH'S STARE (1/7)

IMBUE DARKNESS (4/10)

ARCANE ARMOR (3/10)

PIERCE THE VEIL (1/10)

STRONGER SHADOWS (2/5)

KNIFE IN THE DARK (1/10)

DYING WILL (N/A)

SPIRIT OF THE SWORD (N/A)

OF BODY AND MIND (N/A)

BLOOD OF THE MOUNTAIN (1/1)

SOLAR POWERED (1/1)

ABSORB (1/1)

BRANDS

MARK OF SYTAR

DIVINE QUEST (MINOR)

LIBERATOR

ACHIEVEMENTS

DUMB LUCK

CLUMSY I

SOLO DUNGEONEER

MAD DASH

WHY NOT?

DUMB LUCK II

ANCIENT MYSTERIES

James was a bit confused. He'd assumed his Spells and Abilities would have changed when his Mana type upgraded, but it didn't look like that had happened. Maybe he would see Arcane options with his next class choice.

As James puzzled over his character sheet, Ozure approached. "How are you feeling? You've been asleep for almost a week now."

"A week! I need to go!" In all the excitement, James had totally forgotten that he needed to get to his friends. They were probably worried sick. He needed to warn them about Danforth. If Danforth hadn't gotten to them, they were almost certainly looking for him.

"You can't leave yet." Ozure handed him a quill and a pad of parchment. "Before we talk about leaving, I need to write down everything you experienced and all the prompts that you received."

James didn't want to, but he knew that Ozure wouldn't let him leave and arguing with him would end in a stalemate. "Fine. But once I finish writing everything down, do you give me your word that you'll let me leave?"

"Of course." Ozure grinned at him with a smile that never quite reached his eyes. "I would never keep you here against your will."

"Mhm," James grunted, getting to work. He could reasonably assume that Ozure had a way to detect most of the changes already, but not all of them. Otherwise, why would he be so pressed about James writing everything down. Big things like the race change were obvious, and James would have to write them down, but he didn't want to tell Ozure everything, which begged the question.

What can I leave out?

In the end, James decided to write down everything except for his newfound transition to Arcane magic.

Once James had finished writing, he handed the parchment to Ozure, who quickly skimmed through it. "Can I leave now? My friends might be in danger."

"Of course. But the dungeon might be dangerous for you on your own. Surely you could take me with you, and I can protect you from all the nasty undead."

There was no way James was letting Ozure out of the dungeon, even if he'd fixed James' Mana core. "No, I think I'll be fine." He didn't really, but he was hopeful that he'd be able to escape with a combination of Teleport and Stealth. "I'll be fine," he repeated, more to reassure himself than anything else.

"If you say so. I know you think I'm evil, but I'm really not. As a gesture of good faith, you can take my sword. It should help you through the dungeon, even if you aren't nearly strong enough to make your way through it on your own." Ozure pulled a masterfully crafted sword from under his desk. Even before he saw the telltale purple of a Mythic rarity item, James knew that it was powerful. He could almost feel the energy coming off of the sword.

Tyrfing:

Rank: Mythic

Forged from pure mithril and enchanted by the first Elders, this sword can cut through anything. It will never dull, rust, or break.

The sword was made to be wielded with a single hand and had a straight blade with glowing blue runes running down it's center. The entire sword was made from a blue metal that looked almost purple when it caught the light.

Its handle was embossed with gold and carved masterfully into the shape of a wolf's head.

James took the sword reverently and was immediately hit by a wave of thoughts and emotions that threatened to overwhelm him. He saw himself as a powerful warrior clad in gleaming armor, standing in a clearing in the center of a battlefield surrounded by corpses. He watched in horrified fascination as he raised his arm and swung Tyrfing, sending an arc of crackling blue energy across the battlefield. The energy impacted a group of approaching enemies and incinerated them instantly.

He blinked, and suddenly James was in a heavily forested area, approaching a castle. He raised Tyrfing into the sky and a bolt of pure darkness exited the sword and flew into the air like a beacon. The sky darkened until there was no ambient light anywhere. That was when the screams started. James' vision took on a green hue and everything came back into view. People ran along the ramparts, frantically trying to escape. There was no thought of fighting back against him; he was a force of nature.

James blinked again and with a shuddering gasp he was back in the library with Ozure staring at him with a raised eyebrow. "What was that?" James asked, hesitantly strapping the sword to his belt.

Ozure shrugged. "It was probably one of your Skills or Abilities interacting with the sword." He stopped speaking for a second, tapping his chin in thought. "Maybe your Spirit of the Sword Ability?"

James shuddered. "But it's never given me visions of a sword's previous owner before."

Ozure shrugged. "No idea then. Either way, you're free to leave." He held his hand out, gesturing towards the door for James to exit.

"That's it?" James asked, surprised that Ozure was going to keep his word. "You aren't going to keep me here forever or anything like that?"

"Nope. I got what I needed from you." Ozure smiled. "I look forward to meeting again."

James hoped not. If he could avoid Ozure for the rest of his life, he'd die happy. He walked to the exit, but when he tried to leave the room, nothing happened.

"Sorry about that." Ozure approached, holding a glowing sphere filled with dancing shadows. "Let me get that for you." He placed the sphere close to the door.

The door opened silently and Ozure stepped to the side, holding out his hand to let James leave.

Chapter 42

James stepped into the darkness of the hallway and breathed a sigh of relief. Finally free from the Library. James grinned. He was armed with the ability to cast spells again, and hope of an escape bloomed in his chest.

The first order of business was testing out his Spells and Abilities, to see how they'd been affected by his change from Mana to Essence. Strangely, when he pulled up a window to view his skills, the window still showed that they cost Mana and not Essence, which made no sense. He didn't have Mana anymore.

His Essence pool was much larger than his Mana pool, which meant he could cast more spells, but since it was also his health pool, he would die if he spent it all.

James knew the first skill he should test out was Meditation. He'd need a way to recover Essence if he used too much.

With a deep breath, James dropped into a meditative state and concentrated on using the skill like he had before, by circulating Mana through his body.

He didn't feel anything.

He was missing something. Whatever he'd used previously to move the Mana through his body wasn't there. James remembered what Ozure had said about removing his Mana core and realized that it had probably been what was circulating the Mana before.

Ozure had explained the procedure to him—how he'd set up James' system to transport Mana using blood. So, James focused on his Body and Mind Ability, because it had boosted his healing before. To his surprise, it worked.

As James meditated, he felt the currents of energy flow through his body, and he let his mind sink into a relaxed state as he drifted along with the current. He was startled by a soft electric-blue light that brightened under his skin, following his vascular system. It surprised him so much that James lost hold of his meditation. The light faded away, and a notification popped up.

YOUR SKILL MEDITATION HAS EVOLVED INTO A NEW SKILL:

ESSENCE CIRCULATION.

Essence Circulation (Skill Rank 26):

Cost: 10 Essence/second

Using this skill, you speed up your Essence circulation to bring essence to your cells much faster. While in a state of Essence Circulation your body expends much more Essence to do normal tasks, but you will have a 32% boost to all stats.

Interesting.

This skill wasn't the Essence recovery skill he was hoping for, but it was still powerful. If he could maintain his concentration while fighting, he'd be able to perform at a much higher level. It could give him the edge in a fight.

To test out his new skill, James ran around the cavern while concentrating on circulating his Essence. He'd originally worried that he wouldn't be able to adapt to the quick movement, but his increase in Dexterity allowed him to nimbly run around the room and hop off the walls. After a few minutes, he checked his Essence—he was down almost a quarter already. If he wanted to use the skill in combat, he'd need to keep an eye on it or risk dying from overuse.

He tried Shadow Step. When he concentrated on his Essence, his veins glowed again with the electric blue light, but he shrugged it off as a side effect of his new race. For a second, nothing happened, then the world froze around him. A bright blue 3D grid appeared in a thirty-foot dome around him.

Slowly, James through the grid. He passed easily through the blue bars and wondered what they were for. There was a small timer counting down from five in the corner of his vision. When he got to the end of the grid, he turned around and walked back. On his way back his foot caught on a small rock and he tripped, instinctively grabbing at one of the grid lines. Instead of passing through it, the bar solidified in his grasp and he managed to steady himself.

Interesting.

He was able to interact with the bars if he wanted to. To test his theory, James gripped the bar with both hands and clambered up. When the timer hit zero, the grid disappeared and James fell, hitting the ground with a dull thud. He didn't care. His new spell was amazing.

YOUR SPELL SHADOW STEP HAS EVOLVED INTO A NEW

SKILL:

ARCANE TELEPORT.

Arcane Teleport (Spell Rank 4):

Allows the caster to teleport anywhere within 30 feet.

Cost: 200 Essence

Cast Time: Instant

Cooldown: None

James grimaced at the Essence cost of his new spell. It wasn't cheap. When he'd stopped time with the spell he'd hoped that he could use it during fights to position himself better, but with a 200 Essence cost he wouldn't be able to cast it more than five or six times.

James checked his Essence levels to make sure he'd have enough to test out a few more abilities, but all of his abilities were gone. Instead, he was greeted by a deep red notification.

ERROR: UNKNOWN MANA TYPE. RESETTING CLASS.

YOUR WARRIOR OF DARKNESS CLASS HAS BEEN REMOVED DUE TO A LACK OF NECESSARY PREREQUISITES.

ERROR: YOU HAVE SKILL POINTS ASSIGNED TO SKILLS YOU NO LONGER HAVE. THESE SKILL POINTS CAN'T BE REASSIGNED.

YOU HAVE GAINED A NEW CLASS: ARCANE WARRIOR

Current level up bonus (Arcane Warrior):

+ *3 Intelligence per level*

+ *3 Wisdom per level*

+ *1 Strength per level*

+ *2 Endurance per level*

+ *1 Dexterity per level*

+ *9 Free points per level*

+ *3 Ability points per level*

James couldn't decide whether he was upset or not. He'd just lost all of his Warrior of Darkness skills, and the points he'd assigned to them wouldn't be refunded. That was a huge blow. On the other hand, he'd just gotten a much more powerful class.

With a start, he realized that he'd forgotten to assign two of his points, which meant that he still had two Ability points left. Excited, James opened up the Ability tree to see his new Abilities. Just like with the Warrior of Darkness tree, there were three Tier I abilities. Unlocking them would reveal some of the higher-tier abilities.

ARCANE WARRIOR I

Arcane Mastery (0/30):

Your control of Arcane magic increases, granting increased control, damage, and casting speed when using arcane spells.

ARCANE WARRIOR I

Arcane Missile (0/5):

You let loose a bolt of pure magical energy.

ARCANE WARRIOR I

Mage Armor (0/10):

You surround yourself with armor created from hardened magical energies.

The average cost to master of any of the Tier I abilities in this new class was much higher than the cost to master similar abilities in the last class. He briefly wondered why, but figured it was probably because the class was much more powerful and gave him more Ability points per level. The higher cost would actually penalize him in the long run because he had just lost a ton of Ability points.

His options were Arcane Mastery, which would help him with his existing spells, Arcane Missile, which would grant him a new attack spell, and Mage Armor, which would help him defensively. James was so excited at the possibility of using magic again that he immediately dumped all three points into Arcane Missile.

ARCANE WARRIOR I

Arcane Missile (3/5):

Range: 100-feet

Cost: 70 Essence

Cast Time: 1 Second

Shoot 1 missile of Arcane energy at your opponent. The Arcane Missile can adjust its direction to follow enemies within range.

Overall, he was happy with his choice once he saw the spell. He'd be able to fight from much further away and would have less of a chance of getting injured. Currently he was a close-range fighter, but maybe he could transition to more of a long-range fighter if he assigned his points right.

Putting the point into Arcane Missile also revealed more of the Ability tree. Three nodes branched off of the Arcane Missile tree.

ARCANE WARRIOR II

Longer Ranged Arcane Missile (0/20):

*Requires Arcane Missile 1

Increases the range of the Arcane Missile Spell.

ARCANE WARRIOR II

More Powerful Arcane Missile (0/20):

*Requires Arcane Missile 1

Increases the power of each individual missile in the Arcane Missile spell.

ARCANE WARRIOR II

More Missiles (0/15):

Requires Arcane Missile 5

Each point in this Ability adds an extra missile to your Arcane Missile spell.

James really wanted the More Missiles Ability. He could see himself filling the air with missiles, obliterating his enemies. It would be awesome.

Happy with his choices, James closed all his notifications. It was time to head back to the entrance of the dungeon.

He was ready to get out of this place.

Chapter 43

Back at the entrance, the clatter of bones echoed off the walls as the Defiled Skeleton patrolled the perimeter. James waited until the sound faded away before trying the trapdoor, but it wouldn't budge. Cursing, he felt around the edge of the crack, looking for a latch that he could use to crack it open, but he couldn't feel anything.

The rattle of bones grew closer, so James froze, hoping the skeleton hadn't heard anything. He waited for the sound to fade into the distance again and resumed his attempts to open the door.

Clearly, fiddling with the trapdoor wasn't going to get him closer to unlocking it. Instead, he went over his options. He could go back to Ozure and ask for directions out of the dungeon, or he could keep trying to get out through the trapdoor under the chest.

A strange sensation caught him by surprise, and he stared at his sword. It was as if it was speaking to him. Hadn't its prompt said that it could cut anything? He normally wouldn't use a sword to cut into stone for fear of harming the blade, but he was pretty sure that he'd be fine with a Mythic sword.

James unsheathed Tyrfing, shuddering at the rush brought on by the cumulative knowledge of its past owners. He made sure the skeleton was still out of earshot and stabbed directly into the rock, tracing the edges of the trapdoor. Tyrfing cut through the rock like butter and before he knew it, the stone fell, almost hitting James as it smashed into the ground.

Loudly.

James climbed up and tried to run out of the room before the skeleton returned, but by the time he was halfway to the other side, the Defiled Skeleton was back. It let out a blood-curdling shriek and raced towards James, who was suddenly finding it hard to move.

> *YOU BEEN AFFECTED BY THE STATUS EFFECT [FEAR].*

He swung his head around wildly, searching for an exit, but before he could bolt, a warmth spread from his sword hand, winding up his body, washing away the fear. The warmth enveloped him, coating him in calming energy. He sighed in relief as the warmth pushed back the fear that had permeated his body, leaving pure rage in its wake.

> *STATUS EFFECT [FEAR] HAS BEEN DISPELLED.*

He could kill this creature. He *would* kill this creature. It was an insanely high level, but James had a mythical sword that could cut through anything. He just needed an opening. James summoned his Essence and cast Arcane Teleport.

Five.

The world stood still as he dashed towards the Defiled Skeleton and slashed at it with Tyrfing, confident that the blade would cut through the skeleton with ease. The sword hit the skeleton and stopped mid-strike, unable to make a mark on the skeleton's body.

Four.

What was he doing wrong? The sword should have sliced clean through the middle of the motionless skeleton.

Three.

James cursed. If he couldn't kill the skeleton, he'd be dead. There was no way he could compete with a high-level creature in a fair fight, even with a Mythic weapon. He could have tried to escape with Arcane Teleport instead of running in haphazardly without a plan. That didn't seem like him, but he had no time to think about it as the timer continued to count down to his death.

Two.

Wait. The Ability said something about interacting with enemies. James pulled up the Spell prompt and searched for the problem.

One.

There! He couldn't interact with anything while time was frozen. James cursed. His time was almost up, and the skeleton was going to attack him as soon as the timer hit...

Zero.

Time resumed, and the Defiled Skeleton swung at James. The spirits of the sword took over and blocked the blade, shattering it. As the skeleton reeled, James' sword sliced a wide arc through its body, passing through the spine like a hot knife through butter.

The Defiled Skeleton collapsed into a pile of bones.

Immediately, James was inundated by a slew of notifications.

YOU HAVE KILLED A LEVEL 157 DEFILED SKELETON.

+ 3,244 EXPERIENCE POINTS

- 90% reduction due to level difference greater than 100

ACHIEVEMENT UNLOCKED: DAVID AND GOLIATH.

+ 15 Strength

+ 10 Dexterity

Kill an enemy 100 levels greater than your own.

ACHIEVEMENT UNLOCKED: OBLITERATOR.

+ 25% to all damage

- Titan

Kill an enemy 100 levels greater than yours in one strike.

James felt the now-familiar burning sensation as a brand emerged on his bicep.

YOU HAVE BEEN GIVEN A BRAND: TITAN.

Effect:

+ 10 Resilience

You're unstoppable. A force of nature.

An overwhelming rush of power enveloped him, the pressure building around him as his body struggled to accept the energy coalescing around him. He was the center of a storm, where most of the energy evaporating into rainbow smoke before spiraling away. He was only able to absorb a small amount of the experience, but his heart still raced as his body tried to contain the power. He'd just gained more experience from one kill than he had from every other kill to that point combined.

> # LEVEL UP (X4)!
>
> ## YOU ARE NOW LEVEL 19.

James wanted to assign his Stat and Ability points, but he was worried that the noise from his fight with the Defiled Skeleton might have drawn attention, so he raced back through the tunnels. Before he knew it, he was back at the cage bars.

He cast Arcane Teleport to get through the barrier but realized there was a big downside to his new Spell—it wouldn't let him pass through solid objects.

Without hesitation he drew Tyrfing and lashed out at the grate. The blade rang like a bell against the hardened metal bars, but only cut halfway through before it stopped, unable to cut through a core of blue metal. The sudden impact sent a shockwave of force up James' arms, knocking the sword out of his hands. Embarrassed, James retrieved his weapon and tried again with the same result.

Do I really have to use this belt again? It's disgusting.

James tried to cast his Slick Skin spell, but didn't feel any energy circulation in his body. A notification appeared.

> ## YOU DO NOT HAVE ENOUGH MANA TO CAST SLICK SKIN

James felt dread rising in his stomach. *Does this mean I can't gain spells from enchanted items? What about my legendary necklace?* He had the immediate urge to test out the spell, but decided against it. He was still underground.

Even though he couldn't cut through the core of the metal bars with Tyrfing, James could cut the outside metal. It might give him just enough room to squeeze through the bars and into the room. Terrified of touching Tyrfing's blade, James gripped the sword by the handle and proceeded to shave off the softer outer metal of the bars.

Eventually, he stripped two of the bars, exposing the cores. He tried to squeeze through but found that he was still too thick to make it. *I knew I shouldn't have eaten that extra helping.* Sucking in his gut, James tried again, and, with a grunt of effort, he slipped through, stumbling but catching himself before he tripped.

James cheered as he approached the bars on the other side of the trap and started shaving them. But halfway through, the dungeon rumbled, and the bars moved.

James stumbled back from the moving bars, almost dropping Tyrfing, terrified that he'd accidentally cut himself with it. Then the rumbling stopped. The bars had shifted much closer together, removing any possibility of escape.

He was trapped. Again.

James pulled at his hair in frustration. He had to be the unluckiest bastard in this entire world.

He paced around the room, wondering how he was going to escape. But just like every problem in life, it could be fixed with the sword. If he couldn't get out through their exit, he'd make his own.

Tyrfing cut through the stone next to the bars with ease, and James grinned. *I'm a genius.* His first two strikes were perfect. The third one hit something. Something hard. James' smile froze, and he cut the wall to see what had stopped his blade. Another bar.

A few frantic minutes of cutting later, it dawned on him. He wasn't just locked in a room. It was a cage, with bars surrounding him on all four sides.

But I bet they didn't think of this. James stabbed his sword into the ground and swiped in a huge circle. He was getting out of here.

There was another rumble, and the earth opened beneath his feet.

Fragment of Divinity

Chapter 44

He landed on a pile of rubble, bruised but mostly unharmed. The opening he fell through was about twenty feet above him. He took a second to thank his boosted stats. The room was about the same size as the cage above, but this room had no bars and only one exit.

I guess I'm going that way.

James followed the tunnel until he reached a golden door, emblazoned with the head of the skeleton. With trepidation, he pushed, and it swung open easily.

He entered a brightly lit, circular room with a raised platform in the center. The walls of the room were lined with shelves of bones, and an enormous crystal hung from the ceiling above the platform, filled with the shimmering orange light that mimicked the flickering of flame. It cast beautifully dancing shadows across the crypt, giving it an otherworldly look. Behind him, the door slammed shut.

Before he could react, a dark portal opened in the center of the dais. A robed figure glided out, accompanied by the reek of death.

> *CYPRESS, LORD OF SHADOWS (BOSS: LEVEL ???)*

The Lich was clad in midnight robes with blue flames flickering along their edges. Instead of embers, small icicles fell from the fire and hit the ground with a crystalline clatter. His eyes danced with eldritch fire, illuminating his horrifying facial features. His was a combination of four or five faces, poorly stitched together by someone who didn't have a clear grasp on human anatomy. Each part of the Lich's face was in a different stage of decomposition. A maggot crawled from the mouth on his forehead down to the center of his cheek, where it entered one of his noses.

James gagged at the sight, then vomited, almost missing the Lich's words.

"He wants me to leave you alone." Cypress' voice was rasping, as though his throat were filled with chalk. He raised his hands, fingers contorting into arcane gestures. Another mouth, on the side of the Lich's neck, murmured arcane words, and an icy glow built up around him.

As soon as James saw the Lich casting, he started casting too. The world, including the Lich, froze around him and the blue grid appeared.

All thoughts of fighting were cleared from James' mind as a primal part of his brain took over, filling him with a deep terror.

His timer ran out just as he reached the entrance, where he grabbed the ornate handle and pulled. The door cracked open an inch before a burst of energy hit it, expanding into a wall of ice. James pulled his hand free a moment before it would've been enveloped by the creeping freeze.

He yanked Tyrfing out of its sheath and hacked at the ice, frantically cutting off large chunks. If he could cut through it, he could use Arcane Teleport to escape. But with every chunk he cut, another grew back.

Ghastly laughter echoed through the chamber and a bolt of dark energy hit the ground next to him. The shockwave lifted him off his feet and slammed him into the ice with a loud *crack*. James' vision went black as his head hit the ice and he slid to the ground. His essence bar flashed as it dropped from 1100 to 700 from the barest of glancing blows. He could hear the Lich speaking as if through a great distance.

"—keep you as my slave forever."

James saw red. He'd rather die than become a slave again. Throwing caution to the wind, he activated Arcane Teleport again and ran at the Lich, who was frozen with his head tossed back in laughter. The Lich's hood had fallen back completely, revealing a patchwork of hair. Short red stubble bordered long locks of greasy, matted blonde.

When James reached the Lich, he placed Tyrfing directly against Lich's throat and rested all of his body weight against it. When time resumed, he would fall directly into the Lich and cut off its head.

Zero.

Quicker than James had thought possible, Cypress spun and slapped away his blade and grabbed him by the throat. James' legs dangled helplessly as the Lich lifted him off the ground, bony fingers digging into James' neck. Cold leeched off of the Lich's hand and sunk into James' skin. Every shallow, icy breath was agony. James tried to pry at the skeletal fingers, but the Lich's grip was like iron. As the edges of his vision blackened, James' struggling got weaker and his thinking slowed. His essence bar drained precipitously in the corner of his vision.

The hand grasping his throat was barely covered in skin that clung miraculously to the skeleton underneath. He let out a soft chuckle that came out as a wheeze, as a vision of visiting his grandmother in a retirement home when he was a kid popped into his head. Her skin clung tightly to her gaunt form in much the same way. When she'd reached out to pinch his cheek, he'd screamed and run away. The absurdity of the connection sent James into a fit of hysterical giggles that got cut off halfway out of his throat.

The pain from his laugh brought James back to reality and he suddenly realized that he'd been holding his sword the entire time. He swung Tyrfing and severed the Lich's arm at the elbow. He fell to the ground gasping for breath as he pried the lifeless hand from his throat. Before the Lich could retaliate, James activated Arcane Teleport and climbed the dome.

As the timer ran out, James stabbed Tyrfing into the central crystal, leaving him dangling high above the Lich. James grabbed hold of the crystal with one hand and pulled his weight off of the sword. He then levered of the sword up and down, creating a small indent in the crystal. He pulled the sword out and made a series of cuts and twists to widen the indent.

Below him, the Lich was surrounded by a nimbus of black energy. With a gesture, the abomination sent a bolt of darkness toward James. It smashed into the crystal, and James almost lost his grip. He tightened his grasp and increased his speed until he'd formed a cavity, just big enough for him to fit into. James scrambled inside as another spell hit the crystal, causing the entire structure to shake. He breathed a sigh of relief but couldn't rest. Spurred on by the relentless bolts of magic, he cut his way further into the crystal until he was encased deep within it.

Every few seconds, another magical attack sent spasms through the rock. Glowing dust and small crystalline chips littered his tunnel. If he didn't get out of there soon, the entire thing would collapse.

That's pretty stupid of the Lich. If he knocks the crystal down, it will fall on his head.

A light bulb flashed above James' head, or maybe it was just the crystal. Either way, he had an idea. It would be dangerous, but it was his only hope. To improve his chances of survival, James pulled open his stat page to assign the 36 stat points he'd gotten from the skeleton. He was about to dump everything into Constitution, when a new notification popped up.

> Would you like to convert your basic stat points into advanced stat points?
>
> Advanced stat points can be used to upgrade hidden stats.
>
> Points can be traded in a 10:1 ratio.

James winced as the crystal rocked with the force of another blow. He didn't have time for this. He quickly and converted thirty basic stat points into three advanced stat points and dumped them into Resilience. The stat most likely to save his life. He then dumped his last six points into Constitution and took a deep breath. It was time to do something stupid.

Chapter 45

James ignored the part of his brain that told him this making a huge mistake, then swung his sword in the long arcs. Each swing destroyed a large portion of the crystal and weakened its structural integrity.

The crystal shook with the combined efforts of James and the Lich until with a loud *crack*, it dropped.

James hit the ground hard, his essence bar flashing dangerously. As he collapsed to the ground in a cloud of dust, slew of notifications flew across his vision.

> You have killed Cypress Lord of Shadows, Level 271 Lich.
>
> *+3500 experience points (99.97% reduction due to level difference greater than 500)*

> LEVEL UP (X3)! YOU ARE NOW LEVEL 22.

> *ACHIEVEMENT UNLOCKED: DAVID AND GOLIATH II*

> *+ 20 Strength*
>
> *+ 15 Dexterity*
>
> Kill an enemy 250 levels greater than your own.

James' bones cracked as his body rearranged itself to compensate for his increased Strength and dexterity. He let out a soft whimper as he sat up, amazed that he wasn't dead. Everything hurt. Gingerly, he reached for the pouch at his waist to summon his Weak Health Potion. He pulled up its description to see if it had changed to heal Essence, but it hadn't.

> Weak Health Potion (x1):
>
> Rank: Common
>
> Heals 100 Health
>
> A Weak Health Potion crafted by a novice.

James brought the potion to his lips and drank. The potion didn't say anything about Essence in its description, but hopefully his Absorb ability would still work.

> *YOU'VE ABSORBED 50 ESSENCE FROM WEAK HEALTH*
> *POTION.*

It wasn't much, but the potion brought James up to a hundred essence. James poked through his bag in search of something else to help heal him and pulled out a bottle of Unfermented Bleufruit Cider.

> You have drunk Unfermented Bleufruit Cider.

+1 Endurance

You have absorbed 350 Essence from Unfermented Bleufruit Cider.

Once he'd made sure that a stiff breeze wouldn't kill him, he got to his feet. He stood in the center of a pile of destruction. Massive shards of crystal were scattered around the room and there was no sign of the Lich. He searched the room for the Lich's corpse but found nothing. He tried to move one of the fragments of crystal, but even with his newfound Strength, it barely budged.

James unsheathed Tyrfing and cut into the crystal, periodically removing pieces in his search for the Lich. It was tedious work, but the promise of loot spurred him on. A spot of darkness among the glowing crystal caught James' eye—a skeletal hand poking out from beneath a nearby chunk of crystal.

A few minutes of hacking later, James was glaring at what had once been a powerful Lich but was now a flattened tangle of bones and rotting flesh.

Well, shit.

When the crystal crushed the Lich, it had also destroyed all of its gear. The only usable item was a single ring from its undamaged hand.

Cryptkeeper:

Rank: Rare

+ 50% damage with Ice Mana

+ 50% Damage with Death Mana

+ 10% chance to cause [Horrified]

> You can hear the agonized wailing of trapped souls coming from this ring.

James shuddered at the evil he felt emanating from the ring. It was powerful, but wrong. He resolved to find someone who could destroy it and save the souls trapped inside.

> YOU HAVE BEEN GIVEN A QUEST: RELEASING THE DAMNED I.
>
> Releasing the Damned 1: Find a mage powerful enough to destroy Cryptkeeper and release the tortured spirits inside.
>
> Suggested level: 45
>
> Reward: Unknown
>
> Penalty for failure: -5 Charisma

The equivalent of fifty basic stat points was a hefty price to pay for failure, but James accepted the quest. He would free those poor souls no matter what.

James searched the room for any signs of a treasure chest or exit, but came up empty. After almost an hour of searching he gave up and retreated back to the pit he'd fallen down. He scaled the walls and easily climbed back up to the cage trap where he stared at the bars in exasperation. He wasn't any closer to getting out of this dungeon than he had been before.

At least I got an interesting quest from that ring. Ring. Wait a second.

James smacked his forehead and pulled the Cursed Ring of Flowing Thought from his pouch.

> Cursed Ring of Flowing Thought:
>
> Rank: Epic

> + 1,000 Mana
>
> + 100% Casting Speed
>
> -90% Health
>
> -90% Stamina

The ring was incredibly powerful for mages but would turn anyone who used it into a glass cannon. Unless they didn't have health. Hopefully the ring would give him Mana without any downsides, because he didn't have any health to reduce.

When James equipped the ring, he felt its energy swirl around his finger, unable to enter his body. Focusing on the energy present in the ring, James concentrated and cast Slick Skin. The ring vibrated as the energy coalesced and shattered, sending shards of metal into his skin and damaging him slightly.

A slick substance oozed from his pores as the spell activated. Barely. It was enough though, and James slipped through the metal grate and back into the entry room.

Once he was sure he was safe, he assigned his points. He had twenty-seven free points to assign. When he reviewed his stats, he realized that he'd become unbalanced, with his highest stat, Strength at 75 and his lowest stat, Constitution at 40. He was becoming too easy to injure, so James converted twenty points into two advanced stat points and placed them into Resilience, before dumping the rest into Constitution. His total Essence had increased with his level and was at 450/2,200.

James sat down and leaned against the stone. He could use a breather to rest and assign the Ability points he'd been collecting. There were a lot of them.

With his first two ability points, James brought Arcane Missile to Rank five, which brought its cost down to 50 Essence.

James still needed more defense, so he used ten Ability points to purchase and fully upgrade Mage Armor. It wasn't as helpful when he was trapped without a way to recover Essence but would hopefully keep him alive in the future.

ARCANE WARRIOR I

Mage Armor (10/10):

- Use 100 Essence to create a shield that will absorb 150 damage.

You surround yourself with armor created from hardened magical energies.

After James assigned the points into Mage Armor, two new Tier II abilities revealed themselves.

ARCANE WARRIOR II

Self-Repairing Mage Armor (0/25):

*Requires Mage Armor 5

Continually channel Essence to repair damage done to your Mage Armor.

ARCANE WARRIOR II

High Efficiency Mage Armor (0/50):

*Requires Mage Armor 10

> Your mage armor flows as you fight, concentrating its energy where it will be hit. This allows the armor to block more damage for the same Essence cost.

James put his last nineteen points into Arcane Mastery in an attempt to improve his Essence efficiency. Arcane teleport was easily his most powerful spell and he wanted to increase it as much as he could.

ARCANE WARRIOR I

Arcane Mastery (19/30):

- 19% Essence cost for Arcane Spells and Abilities

+ 10% Casting Speed for Arcane Spells and Abilities

Your control of Arcane magic increases granting increased control, damage, and casting speed when using Arcane spells.

When James put the points into Arcane Mastery, he could feel a change in the way essence moved through his body. It almost felt like his Essence was flowing quicker and well, *better*. His Arcane Teleport Spell now cost 162 Essence instead of 200, and a quick check confirmed that his other spells and abilities had also gotten cheaper. He'd also unlocked the next tier of abilities.

ARCANE WARRIOR II

Arcane Vision (0/5):

Requires Arcane Mastery 25

Gives the caster the ability to see ambient magic.

ARCANE WARRIOR II

Imbue Arcana (0/35):

Requires Arcane Mastery 15

Gives the caster the ability to imbue Arcane energy into their normal attacks.

With that, James was ready to leave the dungeon. He approached the stone door that he hadn't been able to open earlier and placed the tip of Tyrfing against it. The sword bit into the stone, easily slicing small sections that James methodically moved to a pile to the side.

When James finally managed to make a hole small enough to look through, he could see the room he woke up in when first brought to the dungeon. He finished destroying the door and entered the small chamber, crouching to avoid the low ceiling, and approached another door at the far side of the room.

James slipped into stealth, watching in fascination as his skin turned translucent. He loved his cloak. With the utmost care, James cracked open the doorway and peered out, ready to pop up if he was discovered. But there was nobody around.

Shouldn't there be at least one person guarding the entrance to a dungeon? Did they have that much confidence that I wouldn't escape?

Unsure whether he should be insulted or not, James decided to be grateful that he wasn't going to have to fight his way through a group of guards.

He silently crept through empty corridors, searching for an exit. Every once in a while, he'd stumble over a crack in the ground or a slightly raised stone—moving while invisible was more difficult than he'd realized

James passed through creepy chambers filled with cobwebs that appeared as though they hadn't been used in years. In one room he found an ivory book sitting on top of a small dais.

The Teachings of Sytar

Rank: Common

Durability: 350/350

A bone-bound copy of The Teachings of Sytar, one of the main religious texts for followers of Sytar.

There was a small coat of dust on the cover, so James blew it away and cracked it opened it to a description of a ritual to honor the dead. He closed the book and put it in his pouch. Based on the book and the fact that he'd been kidnapped by priests of Sytar, he was probably in the Temple of Sytar, in a part that was clearly abandoned.

Or is it?

Chanting voices ahead alerted James that there was a group of priests, presumably, headed his way. He crouched in the corner of the room, relying on his invisibility to keep him hidden..

YOU HAVE GAINED 1 SKILL RANK IN STEALTH.

YOU ARE NOW SKILL RANK 18.

James followed the group, surprised at just how much quieter his movement was. They advanced through the tunnels under the temple, passing by abandoned rooms until they reached a large open area that was gradually filling up with Dwarves, arranging themselves on benches set up around the perimeter of a large circular cavern with a raised dais in the center, where a dwarf read from a thick black book.

This clearly wasn't the way out. But if the priests were all praying, there was a good chance he wouldn't run into anyone else, so James turned around and headed back the way he came. There had to be another way.

Before he got far, James heard noises coming from down the hallway ahead of him as a new group of priests made their way to the room. James had nowhere to go, trapped between an oncoming group of priests and a room full them. Someone was bound to either be able to see through his invisibility or bump into him if he didn't do something quick.

A familiar voice came from behind him "I thought I heard a little mouse."

James tried to turn and see who had spoken but couldn't move. He hadn't noticed the bands of violet energy creeping up his limbs and encasing them. He was stuck fast, unable to even turn his head.

Footsteps approached from behind, and a figure stepped into view.

Chapter 46

Danforth had his hands behind his back and projected a casual air.

"Bastard. Where are my friends?" James growled through gritted teeth.

"Don't you worry about that. You'll be joining them soon enough."

Two priests roughly grabbed James under the armpits and dragged him through the temple. The violet energy encasing him faded away, allow him to wiggle his fingers a little bit. He pushed against his magical bonds, newfound muscles straining to break free.

One of the priests grunted with effort as James squirmed. "Feels like he's gained fifty pounds since the last time."

"Yeah, and why's his skin so slick?" the other priest complained, letting go of James' arm for a second to wipe his hand on his robe. Sensing the opportunity, James twisted like an eel. He was still coated with a thin layer of oil from earlier and quickly slipped from the priests' grasp.

James pulled back his arm and punched one of the priests in the face. His fist smashed into the dwarf with more force than he'd anticipated, hurling the priest into the wall so hard that the stone cracked.

YOU HAVE GAINED THE SKILL: UNARMED COMBAT.

> Unarmed Combat (Skill Rank 1):
>
> *+ 1% to attack damage and attack speed when fighting without a weapon*
>
> Congratulations, you can flail around with your fists. How barbaric.

Oops. Didn't expect that to happen.

The shocked look on the other dwarf's face showed that he hadn't expected it either. But bravely, the dwarf charged towards James, drawing a dagger from his belt. James reached down to grab Tyrfing but realized that he'd been frozen again. This time the bindings were like iron and didn't budge no matter how much he strained against them. His brand, Mark of Sytar, flashed white hot.

"What is the meaning of this?" an angry voice came from behind James, "Who are you and why are you attacking my priests."

I'm getting awfully tired of not being able to see who's talking.

"That won't be necessary, your excellence. This one is with me. I apologize for any inconvenience," Danforth interjected smoothly.

"He's here to receive his last rites?" The new voice changed from angry to quizzical. James slowly spun in the air until he was facing the speaker.

> NAME: KASTER DEATHTOUCHED
>
> RACE: DWARF
>
> LEVEL: ???
>
> CLASS: HIGH PRIEST OF SYTAR

The high priest wore robes of pure midnight, with the faintest of white trimmings around the edges. His hands were adorned with rings on every finger, and a necklace hung around his neck.

"Actually, no," Danforth replied. "The king requested he receive the Champion's Blessing. One of our fighters seems to have retired early. "

Kaster's eyes narrowed. "Surely the king can spare one fighter. Perhaps I could take him instead"

Danforth's voice lowered dangerously "Surely you aren't asking him to."

The two glared at each other for a second before the high priest nodded. "Very well." He looked at James. "Good luck, champion." He turned back to Danforth and nodded. "Please, after you."

"We can escort him ourselves," Danforth replied stiffly

"Of course, of course." Kaster raised his hands defensively. "I just thought I'd offer my services. He did almost escape."

James tried to move while Kaster was distracted, but his bindings were impossible to shift. He couldn't even talk.

The two priests grabbed him again and resumed dragging him, accompanied by Kaster, who kept James magically bound. He was lugged to another room where he was placed on his knees in front of a stone basin with his head tilted upwards. Danforth looked at Kaster. When he saw that the high priest wasn't leaving, he reluctantly approached James and drew a dagger from his belt.

Then he spoke, jaw clenched. "Vither, father to honor, brother to revenge. I ask that you bless this fighter. May he live with honor as his blood stains the sands." Danforth pulled down James' tunic and lightly traced James' right clavicle with the knife. Its razor edge cut into his skin, painlessly drawing a line of blood. "Sytar, father of the damned, mother to the rest. I ask that you bless this fighter. Should he fall, welcome him to your realm with an open heart." Danforth drew his knife against James' left clavicle in the same way. The wo identical lines of blood dripped down his chest and met before falling to the stone basin below.

> YOU HAVE BEEN BLESSED WITH [CHAMPION'S BLESSING]
>
> 24:00:00 duration
>
> +10% experience gained
>
> -20% damage taken
>
> -20% pain

"Happy?" Danforth snapped at Kaster.

The high priest gave him a sardonic smile, but didn't reply. He stalked out of the room, snapping his fingers as he did so.

James fell to the ground, no longer bound by the high priest's magic. Immediately, James cast arcane teleport. He glanced at his essence as he rushed to the edge of the grid. 288 left. One more cast would leave him defenseless.

James rushed down the hallways of the temple, searching for an exit.

Or at least he tried to.

There was a small pinprick of pain at the back of James' neck. A numbing sensation slowly spread up his body and he stumbled forwards, just barely steadying himself with a hand to the wall.

> YOU HAVE BEEN POISONED WITH [POTENT PARALYSIS POISON]
>
> 00:30:00 duration
>
> - unable to move or speak

Man, you really can't catch a break

James slowly lowered himself to the ground, unable to support his own weight anymore. Footsteps sounded behind him as Danforth approached. He gestured for his priest to lift James up and they dragged him through the temple to a waiting carriage.

The sun burned overhead as they exited the temple and James wished he could lift a hand to ward it off. The carriage was decorated brightly, painted a festive green and gold, festooned with matching streamers. It didn't look at all like the type of carriage James would've expected to be kidnapped in. The guards tossed James' limp body inside and closed the door. With a jolt, the carriage started moving.

As the carriage trundled through the streets, James became aware of a distant roar. As they got closer to the source, the carriage rocked back and forth, as if pushed from outside. Voices screamed in unison.

Tribute! Tribute! Tribute!

Above it all he could hear the booming voice of an announcer.

"Welcome to the arena!"

***

The carriage came to a stop with a jolt and James, unable to brace himself, slid across the floor. There was the sound of a key turning in the lock and he was dragged down a hallway and into a cell.

"Your match is tomorrow. Rest until then," one of his captors said before taking James' sword and pouch. "You can have these back before your fight. No weapons allowed in the cells." The guard closed the cell door, locking it behind him.

"James? Oh, my gods, James!" Nidra rushed over to wrap him in a hug. "What happened to you?"

She silently waited for his poison to wear off. When it did, James spoke. "Nidra! You're a sight for sore eyes. Where are the others?"

Her face fell and she gestured at the door. "They're fighting their matches right now. We're up tomorrow."

"But that means…"

Nidra nodded. "We're going to have to fight them."

End of Book I

Thank you for reading

Thank you

This is the first book that I've ever written, and it means the world to me that people are actually reading it, so from the bottom of my heart: Thank you for reading.

- Jamey

<u>Please leave a review on Amazon!</u> As a new independent author, it's the best way to help me promote my books

Interested in supporting me more?

Want free stuff?

Follow me on Facebook for giveaways!

The LitRPG Guildmasters

Who we are: The LitRPG Guildmasters is a group of dedicated LitRPG and Gamelit authors trying to spread the word of our favorite genre. By working together and introducing new people to amazing books we hope to expand the genres that we love. Sign up to our Newsletter to get a **free book** and follow us on Facebook to keep up to date on our latest work. If you love LitRPG check out the LitRPG Guild Website, our Discord server, and the LitRPG Adventurers Guild Facebook Group.

LitRPG Guildmasters Titles:

Altered Realms: Ascension by B.F. Rockriver

Brightblade by Jez Cajiao

Ethria: The Pioneer by Aaron Holloway

Grim Beginnings: The Ashen Plane by Maxwell Farmer

Primeverse by R.K. Billiau

Shattered Sword by TJ Reynolds

Tower of Gates: Hack by Paul Bellow

Cipher's Quest by Tim Kaiver

Watcher's Test by Sean Oswald

Star Divers by Stephen Landry

Fragment of Divinity by Jamey Sultan

Hive Knight by Grayson Sinclair

Jamey Sultan

LitRPG Communities

LitRPG Books

Adventurers Guild

LitRPG Podcast

To learn more about LitRPG, talk to authors including myself, and just have an awesome time, please join the LitRPG Group.